SARAH SPRINZ

Translated by Rachel Ward

ISBN: 9798893311075
Specs: Paperback with flaps and stenciled edges,
5 ½″ × 8 ½″
Price: $18.99 US / $25.99 CAN
Publication Date: 1/6/26

This is an uncorrected proof.
Please do not quote for publication until you check your copy against the finished book.

uncorrected proof

uncorrected proof

Anyone

Also by Sarah Sprinz

Anywhere

Dunbridge Academy: Book 2

Anyone

SARAH SPRINZ

Translated by Rachel Ward

LYX

An imprint of Authors Equity

Authors Equity
1123 Broadway, Suite 1008
New York, New York 10010

Copyright © 2022 by Bastei Lübbe AG and Sarah Sprinz
Translation copyright © 2023 by Rachel Ward
All rights reserved.

Cover design by {to come}
Book design by Scribe Inc.

This is a work of fiction. Names, characters, places and incidents either are products of the author's imagination or are used fictitiously.

Most Authors Equity books are available at a discount when purchased in quantity for sales promotions or corporate use. Special editions, which include personalized covers, excerpts, and corporate imprints, can be created when purchased in large quantities. For more information, please email info@authorsequity.com.

First published in Germany in 2022 by LYX, an imprint of Bastei Lübbe
First published in Great Britain in 2024 by Quercus Editions Ltd., a Hachette UK company

Library of Congress Control Number: 2025943281
Print ISBN 9798893311075
Ebook ISBN 9798893311099

Printed in the United States of America
First printing

www.lyxbooks.com
www.authorsequity.com

This is an uncorrected proof. Please do not quote for publication until you check your copy against the finished book.

Because this book contains elements that could be triggering, you will find a trigger warning on page 439. Additionally, a glossary of terms can be found on page 419. We hope that you will enjoy the book!

Happy reading, from
Sarah & LYX

uncorrected proof

*For everyone who
has lost themselves:
It will never be too late
to find yourself again.*

uncorrected proof

Playlist

two ghosts—harry styles
fuck up the friendship—leah kate
cigarette daydream—cage the elephant
night changes—one direction
partners in crime—finneas
people watching—conan gray
idfc—blackbear
to be so lonely—harry styles
1 step forward, 3 steps back—olivia rodrigo
fool's gold—one direction
always you—louis tomlinson
just fucking let me love you—lowen
moral of the story—ashe feat. niall horan
bored—billie eilish
same mistakes—one direction
entertainer—zayn
favorite crime—olivia rodrigo
all too well (10 minute version)—taylor swift
why won't you love me—5 seconds of summer
the beach—wolf alice
i want to write you a song—one direction
out of my league—fitz and the tantrums
love story—taylor swift
we made it—louis tomlinson

uncorrected proof

uncorrected proof

Anyone

uncorrected proof

SINCLAIR
Second Form

This is my first kiss, with Tori. We're in a dark corridor during a horror-film night at the end of September. Almost the moment Mr. Ringling left the room, Valentine Ward from the third form switched the original DVD for one rated 18. When Ringling's on duty, he generally dozes off in the common room with no idea of what we're actually up to. Tonight I hope the wind whistling around the old walls will wake him.

I wish I could say I'd had to follow Tori out there because she was scared, but the truth is that *she* follows me outside when I get up twenty-three minutes in. It's not like I'm chicken. Or like I'm secretly crying. No way. No way at all.

But I am seriously considering not sleeping at school tonight, calling Dad and asking him to pick me up. On the other hand, then I'd be all on my own at home, in my room. At least here, up in our dorm, I'll be able to hear that the others are around: Henry, who sometimes talks in his sleep, and Gideon, who snores when he's rolled onto his back.

"Hey."

I whirl around to face the Tori-shaped figure suddenly standing in front of me in the semidarkness. She's a world champion at creeping up on people. I should know that by now.

"Hey." I stiffen my shoulders. "You all right?"

"Are you?" she asks, the little glimmer from the light on the stairwell reflecting in her eyes. A gust makes the curtains fly in and ruffles her hair. Tori looks different with it down, tumbling over her back. Girls have to wear their hair up in class, so it's always plaited or in a ponytail. The floorboards creak as she takes a step toward me.

"Yes, I . . . I just realized I forgot to . . ." *What, then?* "Doesn't matter." I gulp. Why the hell can't I think first and speak later?

"I hate horror films too," she says.

I tense. *Too . . .* What does she mean by *too*? Who says I hate them? I love horror films. They don't bother me. But why am I not saying anything? All I can do is keep sitting on this windowsill, holding my breath. Tori's standing there, not moving either. Her eyes, which are actually brown, look almost black. My heart skips as she comes closer. *She's standing-between-my-knees close. I-can-smell-her-peachy-shampoo close. She's leaning-in-and-kissing-me close.*

She's kissing me.

Quick, short, kind of awkward. Just the blink of an eye, a split second. It's over so quickly that I can't even tell if her lips are soft. If they're like I imagined them. I'd seriously doubt whether it even happened, except that my racing pulse seems fairly certain of it.

Tori pulls back as I lift my hand to touch my mouth. My heart is pounding loudly in my ears, and I want her to do it again. I want to grab her wrist and pull her to me. But I don't dare. Because she's my friend. My best friend, who I want to kiss, and . . . Oh, shit. I want to kiss her. I want to. I don't want to be just anyone to her; I want to be everything.

I stand up to reach out to her, but at that exact moment, muffled screams and laughter come from the TV room. We jump. Another gust rattles the windowpane beside me, and somewhere, a door slams.

The next time I glance at Tori, she's looking a bit like a pale ghost. Her eyes are huge and startled. She bites her bottom lip, then starts to speak. "Sorry, I—"

"No," I say hastily, stepping toward her. Does she regret it? Is it because I didn't react, let alone kiss her back? I should . . .

"Hey!" I spin around at the sound of Valentine Ward's voice. He's coming from the direction of the loos. "You two winching out there?"

Tori's eyes flit over me, and it stings like a slap in the face. Then she turns away and gives a bitter, nervous laugh. "Er, no? Sinclair's just scared."

Of course. Charles Sinclair never has the guts, always gets everything wrong.

"I'm not scared," I say, following her.

And how was I to know that that would be the first of so many lies we'd keep telling each other?

1

TORI

"What were you doing in there all that time?"

Smile. He doesn't mean it the way it sounds. And even if he does, it doesn't faze you.

"Just freshening up," I reply, trying to sound as indifferent as possible and stiffening my shoulders. I hear my mother's voice in my head: *If you're going to wear a dress like that, you have to stand up straight. Shoulders back, chin up.*

I know how it works. I've had plenty of chances to practice at events like the Dunbridge Academy New Year Ball. Valentine has too—his family and mine move in the same circles—but although I step closer to him, he doesn't offer me his arm. He doesn't even look at me properly, just turns back to his upper-sixth pals. They're laughing and chatting, cracking jokes that I don't get, and as they stand there smoking, the icy air creeps into my lungs. I can hear the muffled thump of the music in the ballroom. There are little groups of pupils standing around in the cobbled courtyard, which is surrounded by ancient buildings in dark brick. Expensive suits, stunning ball dresses, glittering bangles and earrings worth as much as a small car, watches so exclusive and expensive people only wear them on occasions like this. It's the one evening a year when Dunbridge lives up to its reputation as an elite boarding school. You can practically smell the money. A bit like the dinner parties and other events I sometimes have to go to with my parents.

I look over to the open double doors I came out from. A moment ago, I was boiling, but the cold out here reminds me that it's mid-January. My sand-colored dress may be floor-length and have slim sleeves, but it's in a thin satin that has no warmth in it at all. I shiver and cross my arms as I step closer to Val. The low-cut back is definitely spectacular and was the clincher for buying this dress, but right now, I'm wishing I'd gone for something warmer. I should go back in. I don't smoke, and I could wait for Val in the warm. Or he could offer me his jacket, but the thought clearly hasn't crossed his mind.

My feet hurt, I'm tired, and it's not even midnight. *Pull yourself together, Belhaven-Wynford. Last year you were on the dance floor until past one thirty, and you had the time of your life.* Am I getting old? Is that it? Or has it got more to do with the fact that back then, I was with Sinclair, Henry, Olive, and the others, having way more fun? Where even are they? Val doesn't look like he'd miss me if I joined my friends for a bit. I'm just about to go looking for them when I see more people emerging from the foyer.

Sinclair's dug both hands into the pockets of his dark suit trousers, and he's drunk. I can see it in the way he's standing, even in the dim light of the lanterns and firepits set up out here. Flickering light on the courtyard walls, and the burning expression in my best friend's eyes as he looks at me. I'm familiar with the sight of Sinclair in the dark-blue Dunbridge uniform and the blazer he loathes with such a passion that he slings it over his shoulder if at all possible, but the black suit, leather shoes, and white shirt fit his slim body like a glove. I don't know what he's done to his blond hair, but this evening it's falling extra casually into his face. He should be grateful to me for talking him out of going to the barber just before the ball. When he's had a haircut, he always looks like a freshly clipped poodle. But tonight, he looks good, and he has no clue. Emma and Henry are following him out. She spots me and gives me a wave, unwinds herself from Henry's arm around her shoulders, and walks over to me. I'm pretty sure no one else would rock that skintight, dark-blue dress the way she does. Emma's the sportiest person I know, the most elegant too, and she and Henry—who'll look like a bloody prince whatever he wears—make the ultimate power couple.

"I'll be right back," I mumble, turning away from Val and the cloud of smoke that's wafting in my direction. I feel a bit sick, which isn't just down to the cigarettes. I've been kind of tense all day, so I couldn't swallow a bite of dinner. I'm still waiting for the nerves to calm down so I can finally enjoy the ball.

"Hi, lads and lasses, how's everyone doing?" It's amazing how cheery I can sound when I'm numb inside.

Sinclair's eyes rest heavily on me as I try to suppress my shivers. He takes his hands out of his pockets, and I know they're warm. But I'm not going over to him and letting him put his arm around me just because we always do that and he's the only lad who can touch me without it meaning anything. I stay where I am. Emma says something, but I don't take in what it is. Sinclair's avoiding my gaze. I try to smile, but it's hard because I can't help wondering why things have been so weird between us for a while now. Why being here with Val, spending the evening with him and his friends instead of my own, makes me feel like a traitor. After all, it's not like Sinclair asked me to be his date tonight. The same as every year, I waited, longed for him to, because when it comes to this New Year Ball, every last ounce of feminism leaves my body, and I'm secretly desperate to be asked, like all the heroines in all the books. By *him*. Sinclair. Semi-ironically, of course—as friends, platonic, even though everyone would have read stuff into it. But Sinclair didn't ask me. Of course he didn't. He asked Ellie Inglewood, who bragged about it to her friends. Now Sinclair's danced with her a couple of times and spent the rest of the evening standing around with Henry and the others. Normally, I'd have gone with Gideon or Omar. Someone I like, someone I know well enough to be sure he doesn't want anything else from me. Ha, but this year, nothing's normal because I'm here with Val, who definitely wants something else from me. After all, that's what I like about being with him. Being wanted. Who wouldn't want to be wanted by Valentine Ward, rugby captain and uncrowned king of Dunbridge Academy?

Emma's fanning herself with her hand and giggling, so she's probably a bit tipsy at least. Henry leans down and kisses her. That's the only thing that bothers me about the New Year Ball. The sheer quantity of alcohol that gets smuggled in every year.

I look over to Sinclair, who slips off his jacket. There's a deep frown between his eyebrows as he hands it to me. I hesitate.

"You're freezing," he says curtly. His voice sounds chilly, but there's something in his pale eyes that makes me go weak at the knees.

Before I can even think about taking the jacket, I feel a heavy arm around my shoulders.

"We going back in?"

I can smell the booze on Val's breath, and I want to turn my head away but force myself not to. It'll only piss him off if I embarrass him in front of his pals. He's touchy when it comes to that kind of thing, as everyone knows. And he has his reasons, even if I wish he'd open up to me a bit about them. But I can count on the fingers of one hand how often Val's spoken about his sister since we've been spending more time together. His relationship with her doesn't seem to have improved since she left Dunbridge a few years ago to study at Oxford.

"Sure." I nod as Sinclair slips his jacket back on. His lips are pressed so tightly together that they're just a thin line.

"What've you done with Ellie?" Val asks in the patronizing tone that Sinclair's absolutely allergic to. "Packed her off to bed? Or has she gone to play with her little friends from nursery?"

"Val," I mumble, placating, trying to push him away. It's the only thing that really annoys me. The way he and Sinclair constantly grate on each other, playing all these pointless little power games.

Sinclair clenches his fists. "Shut it, Ward!"

"Enough of your shite, OK?" says Val, taking a step toward him. He's taller than Sinclair, and even if I don't think they're immature enough to start a fight here, I'm getting anxious.

"Yeah? Or what?" Sinclair hisses. "Gonna tell your arsehole uncle? Shame he doesn't teach here anymore."

"Watch it."

"Val . . . let's go." I pull Valentine back by the arm, but he shakes off my hand.

"Does your mummy know you're drinking at her New Year Ball?" he asks.

"No, but I'm sure she'd be glad to know where the booze comes from."

"Get tae fuck, Sinclair," Val growls. I sigh with relief as he finally lets me pull him away. It feels wrong to be heading toward the entrance with him, leaving Sinclair and the others behind. "Sorry," he mumbles once we're out of earshot of everyone else. "I know that was out of order and they're your friends."

I open my mouth, but I'm too surprised to speak. "That's OK." *Is it, really?* I don't like the way he speaks to my friends. But it seems Val's aware of that. And he looks genuinely guilty as he shoves his hands into his trouser pockets.

"This is just as fucked up as my mum's stupid parties," he says, coming to a stop. "Everyone's only here to be seen."

I nod, thinking about Veronica Ward's events, which my family regularly gets invited to. Val's family lives a forty-five-minute drive from my parents' house. Our dads play golf together any time they don't have to partner our mums to some business dinner or other. Val's mum is a big shot in property, while mine runs an art gallery, supplying high society with paintings worth about as much as a nice detached family house. They often work together. You scratch my back and I'll scratch yours, you could say. But the truth is that everyone in our circles likes to stay in their familiar cliques.

So I've known the Wards since I was a wean, and it's the exact same with Val and the Belhaven-Wynfords. Clearly, we were always going to end up at school together too, because Dunbridge Academy is the obvious choice in this neck of the woods for posh kids to get a posh education. We're actually the same age because Dunbridge occasionally offers its pupils the chance to retake a year or to start a year later if you were one of those kids born over the summer or whatever. Basically, for the right kind of money, more or less anything goes, and the school is keen to give as much flexibility as it can to its students, their rich parents, and their often-unusual circumstances. If you were being unkind, you could say such a system saves our parents the bother of bringing us up, but I can't tell—this is all I've ever known. If I were a character in one of my novels, I'd probably hate life in this elite bubble on principle, but I genuinely appreciate the opportunities Mum and Dad are giving William and me here. It would be ungrateful not to, even if I sometimes feel the weight of my family's social standing like a burden on my shoulders. And apart from my brother, Val's the only person I can talk to about it. Most of the time, I'm glad my friends aren't in this world. OK, so they all have rich parents, but their families' lifestyles are so different from mine.

"We could leave," I suggest. My faint hope is extinguished as Val shakes his head. Yeah, it was too much to wish for, a chance to take off these killer heels.

"No, it's fine," he says. "Besides, you're looking too hot to bail out just now. I want everyone else to feel jealous a bit longer."

I flush. Everyone else . . . Sinclair, then. Not that I believe my best pal would actually be jealous of Val. After all, I'm not fussed that Sinclair's into Eleanor in the upper sixth. Not in the least. "If you like," I say.

Val smiles, which isn't a sight I get to see very often. Normally, his face is as hard as the expression in his brown eyes. His bone structure's out of this world. Valentine Ward, cheekbones, cheekbones, cheekbones, and a classical nose that makes him look like one of those proud Greek gods. He's just damn hot, especially when he's wearing a perfectly fitting suit, like he is now, one that emphasizes his broad shoulders. Valentine Ward is tall and athletic.

He puts his hand on the small of my back. "I hear you're coming for dinner next weekend," he says as we walk in.

"Well, that's news to me," I say. "It's the first I've heard of it."

"My mum wants me to be there. I thought you might like to join your parents too. It would make the evening a bit less dire."

I hesitate. It's not like my parents are unaware that Val and I are becoming "good friends," as my mum likes to put it, but it would be the first time we'd seen them as a couple. If we are a couple, that is . . . I really don't know, and I don't want to rush anything. He's my date for the New Year Ball, and that could mean everything or nothing. When Val asked me before the Christmas holidays if I'd go with him, my first thought was of Sinclair. I couldn't be pleased at first. But then Val really put in an effort. He browsed around Ebrington Tales with me, even though he finds reading deathly boring, and then we had a hot chocolate in the Blue Room Café, and he finally asked me. It was absolutely right to say yes, even though I lay awake half the night imagining the look on my best friend's face when he heard.

"I'll ask them," I say hastily. "Is Pippa coming?"

Val's face hardens, and he shakes his head. It's always tricky, mentioning his sister. Philippa Ward left four years ago with straight As throughout her school career, including her A levels, which we do here, like quite a few posh Scottish schools, rather than Highers. Philippa is now reading law at Oxford. She's the epitome of a highflier, the Wards' pride and joy. It's not that Val's parents aren't proud of him too, but they're very focused on their children's academic achievements. And Val isn't exactly a star pupil. Now that he doesn't have his uncle at the school to coach him a bit, he seems to be struggling even more in class.

"No, she's busy," he says briefly, pulling back his hand. Great. Every time he shuts down like that instead of showing his emotions, it's a sharp stab in the chest. I kid myself that it's because he never learned how. Veronica and Augustus Ward aren't cold people precisely, but on the other hand, I can't remember them exactly overflowing with the milk of human kindness.

"Wait here a moment," says Val, glancing rapidly from side to side, then striding firmly toward the cloakroom set up on one side of the foyer. I spot Cillian in a relatively hidden corner, bending over a table. I shiver as I realize what they're up to.

There have always been rumors that the upper sixth are secretly doing coke, but I'd never believed them. Apparently, that was naive of me. I stop as Val walks over. A few third-formers come out of the hall and glance skeptically at us. I hope no teacher spots us. I bite my bottom lip gently as I glance around.

"Tori?" Val's voice is questioning. When I look over, he raises an eyebrow invitingly.

I hastily shake my head. "No, thanks."

Thanks . . . Could you get any dumber?

"Oh, come on." Cillian looks up.

"I don't want to," I say as firmly as I can manage just now.

"Who are you kidding? You're a Belhaven-Wynford! Rude not to, among you toffs, isn't it?"

"Give it a rest." To my surprise, Val springs to my defense. There's a threat in his tone, and Cillian instantly shuts up, but he gives me a scornful look as he turns away.

"Sorry," Val says in my general direction. "I don't normally, but the last couple of weeks have been seriously shit."

I just nod in the weird silence that suddenly prevails as Val leans over the table and puts one finger to his nose. It doesn't exactly look like he's doing this for the first time. And I don't like that. I don't like it at all. It's bad enough the way everybody's drinking, although maybe I'm oversensitive there. I can kind of see where Val's coming from. Things haven't been so easy for him since his uncle had to leave Dunbridge. The upper sixth start their A-level exams in about four months' time, and well, maybe he was counting on his help. I'm not exactly a try-hard, but my grades are reasonably solid. But last time I suggested to Val that we could revise together, he took it the wrong way. It ended up in an argument, and he spent the afternoon in the fitness center alone with the weights and the rowing machine. I decided not to get involved.

Val straightens up. He wipes his nose with his hand and puts his head back for a moment. His nostrils quiver as he breathes in.

"Everything OK?" I ask quietly as he puts his arm around me.

He nods but doesn't look at me. "Want to dance?"

If I'm honest, I'd rather join Sinclair, Emma, and the others. It's the first New Year Ball that I haven't spent with my friends. But it's also the first that I've had a proper date. Which is what I wanted. I force myself to smile.

"Love to."

Val swigs from the gin bottle that Cillian hands him, and my stomach clenches slightly. I shake my head when he holds it out to me.

"Maybe later."

Liar.

Val doesn't say anything, but he rolls his eyes as he lifts the bottle back to his lips. Or maybe I only imagined that.

As we walk through the large double doors toward the ballroom, loud music hits us. I recognize the song from the intro: "Thinking Bout You" by Ariana Grande. The dance floor is full. Sequins and crystal chandeliers glitter in the light. My stomach gives a little hop as Val holds out his arm to me as we walk down the few steps on the broad stone staircase from the entrance. When I glance up at him, he's looking more conciliatory. The light falls onto his face, casts shadows over his sharp features. I'm at the New Year Ball with Valentine Ward. It's really true.

And everyone's staring at us. I feel the eyes on me as we arrive. Val doesn't pull his arm away. He leads me into the center of the hall, past the people standing chatting at little tables around the edge of the dance floor. Younger pupils nudge one another and sneak little glances at us.

It feels a bit like a dream as Val turns to me and puts his hand on my back. I feel his muscles as I take his hand. It's only for a wee while, but I suddenly remember Sinclair and those ceilidh dance classes in the third form. My friend had surprisingly firm biceps, and for some reason, I couldn't touch him without getting butterflies in my stomach. Then Mr. Acevedo nearly had to throw us out because we spent almost every lesson giggling hysterically and getting all the steps wrong. It hits me like lightning as I look over Val's shoulder, up toward the entrance, right into Sinclair's expressionless face. He's leaning on the banisters next to the doors. Emma and Henry have switched to full-on making out; Gideon's standing next to him and his lips are moving, but Sinclair isn't even pretending to listen. He's looking down at Val and me, and his eyes bore directly into my soul.

"Hey, I'm over here."

I turn my head back to Val. His smile doesn't fit his sharp tone. Did he spot Sinclair and the others, or was it meant as a joke? I search his face for any hint that he's pissed off but see none.

"Sorry." I smile.

Val pulls me a little closer. "Having fun?" he asks.

I nod. It's a reflexive action. "Yeah, great."

"Oh, Tori . . ." He sighs as we move in time with the music. "What am I doing wrong?"

"What do you mean?" I reply at once. "It's lovely, honestly."

"Would you rather go back to your wee pals?"

Is it really that obvious? I have to make more of an effort. "No. I'm here with you."

"Yes, you are," says Val. Suddenly, he looks me in the eye. Not just a quick, fleeting glance; it's real and deep, a look that paralyzes me from the inside out. Will we kiss now? In books and films, it would be about the time for it. A tight embrace on the dance floor. Lean in, shut your eyes. Help.

I don't know if Val senses my panic. He moves back slightly, lifts his arm, and I spin. When he pulls me in close again, I feel his hand lower down than it was before. A nervous tingle runs through my body. From the roots of my hair to the tips of my toes. It's almost like I'm hyperaware of each of his movements. The song ends and, of course, it's like all those dire high-school movies. A slow dance starts. Val puts both hands on my bum and presses me up to his body.

"Watch it there, pal."

No idea where she just sprang from, but before I've properly grasped what's happening, Eleanor Attenborough's adjusting Val's hands on my back. And by *adjusting* I mean moving them way up.

"You consider yourself a gentleman, don't you?" She blows him a kiss as he opens his mouth in outrage. Her eyes meet mine and she studies me for a moment. It's not a glare; it's more attentive than intimidating. It's an *Are you OK with what's going on here?* look.

I give her an uncertain smile and it's only then that she turns away and vanishes back into the throng.

"Sheesh, Eleanor," Val mumbles, imitating her. "*Watch it there, pal* . . . Shit, jealous much?"

I don't reply. Val might see things differently, but I don't really get the impression Eleanor's pining for him. How long were the two of them even together? Two months, tops—but clearly long enough for everyone at Dunbridge to have been talking about them. But that's just how it is here.

"If you ask me, she's not all there." I don't have time to react as Val takes my hand and pulls me away. "Whatever. C'mon, let's get out of here."

My gut tells me it would be unwise to contradict him, so I follow. Val does seem kind of jittery. A minute ago, he wanted to dance and not leave yet. Is it the cocaine? In that case, he shouldn't be on his own, should he?

There's no sign of Sinclair, Gideon, Emma, or Henry as we head up the steps to the door. Or Val's friends in the foyer. He doesn't look at me, just pulls his phone from his pocket as we step outside.

"Bet they're behind the gym," he says. "Are you cold?"

My stomach lurches as he actually pulls off his jacket and hands it to me. *Wasn't so hard.* That's my first thought. My second is, *Oh, my God, Valentine Ward's offering me his jacket.* Of course it's too big for me, and I love that.

"Shall we join the others?" he asks.

"Sure."

"Or would you rather find your friends?"

He asks without that tone of reproach, but his eyes are heavy with expectation as he looks at me. There's only one correct answer; I know that.

"No." I shake my head. Besides, I don't even know where they are now. "Let's go."

Val smiles the smile in which only one corner of his mouth twitches. It's so attractive.

"I knew you'd make the right decision," he says. We turn the corner and he presses me up against a wall, in his jacket, in the dark. My heart explodes. "Victoria Belhaven-Wynford, you're way too cool for your lower-sixth pals. Anyone ever tell you that?"

"You're the first."

Val grins. "Am I indeed?"

And then he kisses me.

It's just one single, fluid movement, and I didn't see it coming. I feel the cold wall through his jacket and my heart beating up against Val's lips.

Breathe through your nose. Close your eyes. That's what all the novels say. God, even the women in books who're doing this for the first time can manage it. It's in their blood. And this isn't my first kiss. OK, it is the first proper one, but when I close my eyes, Sinclair's sitting on that windowsill, his blond hair falling into his eyes as we both move back.

Val puts his hands into my hair and pulls me closer. He doesn't ask if this is all right. He just takes ownership of me, as if the only way a woman can survive is to be owned. Books have taught me that this is romantic, but just now, it feels more threatening. Like an invitation to something I might not be ready for.

I don't flinch because I don't get the chance. And because part of me is enjoying what's going on. My stomach is tingling and my knees are weak.

I jump as people come closer. Val pays them no attention. He pushes his leg between my knees, and my body responds. Nervous throbbing. I kiss him.

And my best friend watches.

There's a blank look in Sinclair's eyes, and it shoots directly into my belly, like a jet of ice-cold water. A split second passes. Then he turns away. Val stops as a suppressed sound escapes me.

His lips glisten; his pupils are wide as he pulls back. It scares me in a thrilling kind of way.

"Am I the first?" he repeats.

I don't know what he wants to hear. Would he like it to be true? The kiss with Sinclair in the second form doesn't really count. It was only messing around. I nod. My mouth is dry.

2

SINCLAIR

She's kissing him.

And yeah, what can I say? It feels shit.

Tori's kissing Valentine Ward. Or *he's* kissing *her*. I can't keep thinking about it—it's driving me nuts. There's nothing but hot, paralyzing despair in my belly, which floats up no matter how often I swig this fucking gin.

Tori can do whatever she likes, but do I really have to stand here and watch with my own eyes? I shouldn't have come to this shitey New Year Ball. It's ridiculous. Ellie Inglewood pissed off hours ago to film nasty TikToks with her pals. I bet they're bitching about how boring I am. I didn't even try to kiss her, which I bet she was hoping for. It's the image everyone has of me. Sinclair knows what he wants, goes out, and gets it. He's got condoms in his locker, but he's never actually been within a mile of using them. It's easier to hide behind cheek and double entendres than to admit to who you really are. Never been kissed. Well, almost never, but unfortunately, I've never made it beyond that one kiss with Tori way back when. No wonder she'd rather winch Valentine Ward—unlike me, he seems to know what he's doing.

"Think you should switch to water for a bit?" asks Gideon.

He can shut it. He's steaming, if not as much as me. So what? It's the New Year Ball. Everyone knows we drink; nobody cares. Well, there are some folks like Henry who are stone-cold sober. And he's glued to Emma's lips like she's the only person in the world. I'm happy for my best pal—it's not like that—but lately, I've just been raging.

So I say no, ignore Gideon when he shakes his head, and ask, "Want to go back in?"

"I'm not sure that's a good idea, mate. If the teachers see us like this . . ."

"They're all hammered too."

"Your mum won't be."

I grunt reluctantly. OK, true, my mother—who also happens to be the head teacher here at Dunbridge Academy—definitely shouldn't see me like this. I may be her son, but that doesn't mean the school rules don't apply to me. In fact, sometimes I reckon Mum's extrastrict with me so that no one thinks of accusing her of favoritism. The zero-tolerance policy on alcohol anywhere in the school grounds goes for me too. If we get caught, we're in trouble. Henry's the expert on this—he landed us all with a warning last autumn when he went on an entirely understandable bender after his sister died, but luckily that slate got wiped clean at Christmas. Even so, we don't want a repeat of that right away.

Maybe I've had a skinful already, though—we're suddenly in one of the old greenhouses, and I don't remember how we got here. But I can't forget the way Valentine Ward was pressing Tori up against that wall. I want to boak just thinking about how he was touching her. Why did she let him? That guy's a tool and she's way too smart for him.

I keep drinking. It's not burning my throat anymore. Mind you, the world spins slightly when I shut my eyes, but that's not so bad. I'd like a lie-down. Yeah, good idea.

Someone's trying to hold me up. I can hear voices and smashing glass. OK, I do feel kind of grim, but I don't care. Henry's face swims into focus above me. He says something and looks away again. What's the time anyway? Maybe I'll have a sleep. My eyes are tired. My head is tired, and my heart is kind of tired too. Fucking Valentine. I hate him, seriously. Tori too. Why's she so beautiful? I can see her again. Her face is spinning around, but I want to touch it. I want to tell her that I love her, but you can't do that without wrecking everything. This best-friends shit, it's so frustrating. Must be great kissing that arsehole. So I'll say so.

"What, Sinclair?"

Her voice, it sounds so soft. Soft Tori-voice. That makes no sense, does it?

"Need to boak?"

I hope not. But I hope a lot of things. Not many of them are gonna come true, we know that much. But Tori's fingers are warm in my hair, and my head is heavy—my head is so heavy. I think she's putting an arm around me.

Please, God, don't let her go away.

TORI

Val's pupils are wide, and my stomach's a tiny knot of fear. Maybe I'm paranoid, but it freaks me out when people are on drugs. With good reason, I think.

Even so, I'm out here with him and a bunch of the upper sixth, behind the gym where there's an unofficial second party going on. 'Cause the ball's "lame," and I didn't have the courage to tell him I'd like to go back in. I've got a gut feeling that I need to speak to Sinclair. He looked wrecked when he saw Val kissing me. Wrecked in every sense of the word. And that's not like him. My best friend knows I find drink hard to deal with, unlike Val, but there's no way in hell I'm talking to him about it. My reasons for hating alcohol and drugs are nothing to do with Val, let alone his family.

Someone's got a Bluetooth speaker blaring aggressive rap. Val didn't kiss me again. He's talking to his friends now. I don't get most of their stories. So I smile and decline the booze that's flowing here like rivers.

What even happens if you mix cocaine and alcohol? Can you do both, or should I be worried that Val and the rest of them are about to have heart attacks and pass out? Mind you, they don't look like this is the first time they've tried this combo. And there are some folks around who look vaguely with it. Eleanor Attenborough and her friends, for example. They're a few feet away. I don't dare go and join them, even though I get a feeling they might be more fun. But I don't want to bug them, like a little kid.

Val really could be talking to me. Not exclusively to me—I don't expect that. After all, this is the New Year Ball and he wants to have a good time with his pals. I totally get that. But well, he could include me a bit more, not just leave me out in the cold. But on the other hand, I'm glad he doesn't want to go off to some dark corridor with me to do stuff I'm not ready for yet. If he did, I'd tell him so, straight out. Or at least I think I would.

I'm wearing his jacket around my shoulders, but I'm cold. Hey, it's January. Most of the other girls have changed now, or else they're wearing jackets over their ball dresses.

Maybe I should pop up to my room and put on something warmer. But if I went up there, I doubt I'd have the energy to come back down. It feels like it's getting really late now. I glance at my phone to see the time, but then there are all these messages from Emma.

    E: Where are you?
    E: Tori? Are you OK? Don't want to interrupt anything, but could you come?
    T: I'm with Val and the others behind the gym. Where are you?

To my surprise, Emma's online. She starts typing straightaway.

    E: Heading for the boys' wing. Henry and Gideon are putting Sinclair to bed.

I'm feeling a bit warmer now. Or even hot.

T: Why?
E: He overdid the drink a bit . . .
T: I'm on my way.

When I look up, Val's still with the others; it doesn't seem like he cares what I do. I should say goodbye, but maybe he'd just be happy if I left him in peace now. There was that irritated tone again just now when I was with him and his pals. I don't understand the guy. One moment everything's great, the next the mood swings and I've got no clue what I've done wrong. He's different when it's just the two of us. Sometimes it seems like all he cares about is acting to his friends, especially the rugby lads, like he has no feelings at all.

My feet hurt, and I'm cursing the heels on my Louboutins as I walk down the dark path back to school. I'll give Val his jacket back in a bit. I won't be long, he won't even notice I was gone, and I can grab something warmer from my room before I head back to the gym. It's still hoachin outside the ballroom as I head toward the east wing. My shoes keep getting stuck in the cracks between the uneven cobblestones, and I groan with frustration. I hold on to a pillar under the arcades and slip off first the left shoe and then the right. The ground is freezing, but right now, that's a treat for my throbbing feet. Besides, I can walk quicker this way.

There's no wing time tonight, at least for the older years, but it still feels out of bounds to be heading up the stairs in the boys' wing at this time of night. There's a light on in the lower-sixth corridor. Henry's door is open and so is Sinclair's. As I come closer, Henry's just emerging from his room with a bottle of water and a wet towel. For a moment, he looks guilty, but then he recognizes me.

"Hey, there you are." He nods toward Sinclair's room. "He's pretty out of it."

I bite back the words on the tip of my tongue as I follow Henry through the door. *Why didn't you stop him? I thought we looked out for each other.* But I'm not one to talk—I didn't stay with my friends this evening.

The room's full of people. Emma's leaning against the wall, arms crossed and face worried. Gideon's crouching beside Sinclair, next to his bed, holding him by the shoulder, stopping his upper body from slumping forward. Omar's pulling his shoes off.

I feel numb yet calm. It's not the first time I've seen this, except it's not usually my best pal I have to look after. His face is white, and his eyes are half shut.

I put down my shoes, chuck Val's jacket onto a chair, and take the towel from Henry. It's cold and heavy in my hand.

"Has he whiteyed?" I ask.

"Yes, on the way over," says Emma. "Do you think we should call Dr. Henderson?"

"No, that'll only lead to trouble." And I know what to do.

Omar budges up as I perch next to Sinclair on the bed. He's leaning with his back against the wall now.

"Hey." Great. He's not responding. But at least he groans quietly when I press the wet towel onto his forehead. His head sinks into my hand. "You're a right eejit," I mumble. I mean, what the hell? What's he gone and fucked himself up like this for?

"I think he blacked out for a bit, Tori." Emma's voice is shaking. I get that. It's rough to see something like this for the first time, but so long as you take care of a few things, it'll all turn out all right.

"If he's whiteyed, he should be feeling better soon." I put my fingers under his chin. His head is heavy, but his skin is soft. When Sinclair blinks, I feel kind of jittery. His eyes are blue and drunken. I get goose bumps as he mumbles my name with a heavy tongue.

"So," I say, putting the cold towel on the back of his neck, "what the hell?"

"What?"

"All this. You're steaming, and you're ruining everyone's evening." Sinclair leans his head against the wall as I loosen his tie. *Bet he didn't even hear me.*

"Was a shite evening anyway," he mumbles.

My fingers turn to ice. He looks at me, but his eyelids are heavy. I undo his top buttons and lob the tie at Henry. He hangs it over the back of the chair and puts an arm around Emma.

"You guys can go. I'll stay," I say.

"Are you sure?" Henry asks quietly.

"If I need help, I'll get you," I promise.

"We'll only be next door," Emma says right away.

I grin despite myself. "I know."

Henry studies me. He seems to be torn, because he wants to be a good pal, but then he turns and follows Emma out. Gideon and Omar look more relieved to be able to leave the room. And suddenly it's just Sinclair and me.

"Why was it shite?" I ask, once they've shut the door.

Sinclair's turned away again, and he jumps. "Hm?"

"The evening," I repeat. "Why was it shite?"

"Women," he mumbles. "I'm tired . . ."

"I know, but you have to drink this water before you can go to sleep."

"Tori . . ." He sighs.

"No, not open to negotiation. Sorry, but you should have thought about this before drinking your brains out."

He groans but takes the bottle. Less water ends up on his shirt than I'd been expecting.

"Clothes off!" I order as I notice the vomit on them.

"I'm drunk," he grumbles.

"Exactly." I stand up and walk over to his wardrobe. Sinclair actually raises a hand to catch the T-shirt I throw to him, but he misses. It takes him half a lifetime to unbutton his shirt and pull it off. When he stands up to take off his trousers, I really try not to look, but I can't help seeing the way his shoulder blades move and what that does to his back muscles. At last, he's slipped on the T-shirt, and I take the chance to pull back his duvet. He has to cling to my shoulder. For a moment I'm scared as he stumbles forward, and I'm only too aware of the weight of his body. Sometimes I forget that Sinclair's almost head and shoulders taller than me. That happened kind of overnight. Before the summer holidays at the end of the fourth form, we were almost the same height, but by Hogmanay in the fifth, he could suddenly put his chin on the top of my head when he hugged me at that party in Edinburgh.

I feel Sinclair's forearm, hard beneath my fingers, as I hold on to him. My mouth goes dry. Where the hell did all these muscles come from?

I steer him back onto the mattress by the shoulder and step between his legs. I guess he's feeling dizzy and needs to hold on to something, because I suddenly feel his fingers on the back of my thigh, his hot hands through the thin fabric of the dress he picked out for me, and all at once I wish he'd pull it off me. When he looks up at me, I get butterflies. His blond hair falls into his face. How does he manage it? Even pissed out of his mind, he looks hot. Sinclair's jaw muscles twitch; he gulps. His fingertips stroke my leg very gently for a second. Then he pulls back his hand. My heart thumps nervously. I don't have to tell him to lie down—fortunately, he works that out for himself.

"So what's it like?" he asks as I turn away again to chuck his clothes into the laundry basket.

"What?"

"Being noticed by the person you want to kiss..." He sounds tired, his words are slurred. "Must be a great feeling."

And zap, I'm freezing.

What does he mean? Is he talking about Val?

Who else, Tori?

But why does he sound so reproachful? What's it to him who I kiss or don't kiss? Sinclair's had hundreds of opportunities to do what Val did. Seriously, maybe even more. I can't remember when I stopped counting. Hundreds, thousands, and he didn't take one of them.

Luckily for me, Sinclair doesn't seem to expect an answer. He's too drunk. Probably forgot his words the second he uttered them. I haven't, though. He sinks onto the pillow, eyes closed. How can he just fall asleep?

For a moment, I stand, uncertain, in his room. I'm longing to get out of here, but I stupidly promised Henry and everyone that I'd stay with him.

I suppress a sigh. I'm conscious of standing barefoot in the middle of my drunken best friend's bedroom, wearing a long evening dress. On the night of the New Year Ball. Wow.

And yet I'm kind of glad that I'm now getting undressed in Sinclair's room and not Val's.

Sinclair blinks.

"Shut your eyes," I order as I reach for the zip. Luckily, it's on the side, so I don't need any help.

"I won't look," mumbles Sinclair. His eyes are heavy. They close. "And if I did . . . I know what you look like naked."

"This may come as a surprise to you, but women's bodies change between the ages of twelve and eighteen."

"You were thirteen," he slurs.

Damn it, he's right. But it was dark that night in the second form when we went for a swim in the loch near Ebrington. Skinny-dipping. No one could have seen a thing.

Sinclair's window is open a crack, and a slight breeze catches my shoulders as I slip out of the dress. It falls to the floor around my feet. I'm not wearing a bra—the dress has that low back, and the bust is tight-fitting enough to hold everything in place. I step out of the circle of fabric on the floorboards, turn aside, and pull another of Sinclair's T-shirts from the wardrobe. It's the one from the charity run last summer, and it reaches my thighs.

"OK," I say, turning back to the bed.

Sinclair doesn't respond. He's lying on his back, his head slumped to one side. Toward the wall. His heart-shaped mouth is slightly open, his chest rising and falling evenly.

Well, I guess he really wasn't looking. Well done him.

The weird silence is oppressive as I slip into the tiny bathroom and use his shower gel to clean the makeup off my face. I gargle with his mouthwash, which will have to do for the time being, and drink ice-cold water out of my hands. When I straighten, my eyes look back at me in the mirror, red and tired. Luckily, I find one of my hair elastics in his bathroom cupboard—I leave them all over the place. When Sinclair's hair is as long as it is just now, he sometimes puts his fringe into a wee topknot. I have a bit of a soft spot for that "hairdo," but there's no need for him to know that. I skillfully tie up my long copper-red hair into a bun, because every time I've shared a bed with him, he's managed without fail to roll over and lie on it in the night. It's amazing how painful that is.

Sinclair's still out for the count when I come back into the room. Just to be on the safe side, I put the bathroom bin at the head-end of the bed. You never know. Then I climb over his sleeping body. He twitches as I squeeze between him and the wall.

"Hm?" He blinks.

"Budge up, chicken." I shove him toward the edge of the bed. I'll never stop calling him that. Not since the time in the juniors when we went on a trip to an organic farm in Highbourne and he panicked at the sight of the hens running everywhere.

"I'll fall out," he moans.

"No, you won't. I've got you. But I don't want to be in the way if you boak. There's a bucket next to you."

"Don't need it," mumbles Sinclair. He shifts half a centimeter to the side, and his body is heavy next to mine. I keep my promises, so I roll up next to him and put an arm around him. He immediately grabs my wrist and hugs it to his chest.

"Feel sick?" I ask as he groans quietly.

"Dunno . . . The bed's moving."

I hold him tighter. "You sleep now. I'm here if anything happens."

"Victoria," he mumbles after a while. He's so drunk. He never uses my full name.

"Charles?" And I never call him by his. It feels strange on my lips. Exciting, but not unpleasant. Nobody at this school calls him that. Well, apart from his mum and the teachers. But it sounds kind of soft. Charles. Hmm . . .

He sighs and sinks more heavily into me. "You smell nice."

My belly starts to tingle treacherously. "I'm very sorry, but I'm afraid I can't say the same of you tonight."

"Should I shower?" He tries to pull away but gives up after precisely four seconds. His muscles soften as he falls back into my arms.

"No, I don't need any more drama if you collapse in the bathroom."

"I won't collapse."

"You could hardly sit."

"It's not spinning so badly now."

"Wait till you shut your eyes."

He groans hideously—he must have done just that.

I lift my chin a little. Sinclair's hair doesn't smell of cigarettes. But that's no surprise. Unlike Val, he didn't spend the whole evening smoking with his pals.

Sinclair doesn't speak. I shut my eyes. If I lean forward a little, I could touch his hair with my nose . . .

"Tori?" Sinclair's voice is quiet.

"Yes?"

"You'retoogoodforaguylikehim." Words like chewing gum, heavy tongue. Sinclair swallows the end of it, but I got the gist. Unfortunately.

I'm cold. I don't move and I don't reply. If I just ignore it, it'll be like Sinclair never said that. He didn't. It was just his brain fog. But they say drunks and small children always tell the truth.

Sinclair gives a tired sigh, and the sound of it shoots straight between my legs. It's a deep, relaxed sound. I feel the gentle tremor that runs through his body, as it always does when he falls asleep. His head sinks forward. His hand doesn't let go of mine.

Luckily for me, he can no longer hear my groans of frustration.

3

TORI

My phone is bursting with unread messages as I slip out of Sinclair's room the next morning. He doesn't wake as I climb over him and pull on a pair of his joggers. I avoid looking in his direction as I gather up my dress, Val's jacket, and my shoes. Then I shut the door behind me as quietly as possible.

The whole school is silent as I walk barefoot down the corridors. I reach the west wing unnoticed, open my door, and perch on my bed. Then I read the messages.

- **V:** Have you got my jacket?
- **V:** Where even are you?
- **V:** Eleanor says you left. Seriously?
- **V:** Fine. Goodnight then, sleep well . . .
- **V:** You're not with that loser, are you?

Valentine last texted just after three, by which time I was fast asleep. Next to Sinclair. Maybe I should have let him know instead of just disappearing. Not that it sounds like he was all that worried. He could have asked if everything was OK.

He kissed you, Tori. Yesterday. That part wasn't a dream. It really happened.

I sink backward onto my bed and lift my hand to my mouth. I touch my lips with my fingertips.

I've been kissed. Really, properly kissed. No need to count that time with Sinclair when we were both still children. After all, we never even talked about what that kiss meant. We just ignored it, and the next day, we acted like it had never happened. I can't count how many nights I lay awake imagining us doing it again. But we never did. I never kissed my best friend again. And he never kissed me either.

I stare up at the ceiling. And then there was last night. Sinclair was jealous. I've suspected as much since the start of the school year, when Val suddenly began to take an interest in me and we talked more to each other. Only on Instagram at first, then now and again at break time or when we were on gardening duty together. Sinclair generally acted as if he didn't mind, but yesterday evening, it became clear that he doesn't like Valentine Ward kissing me. Course, he didn't say a word. Apart from his maunderings later on in bed. That was weird. But he was drunk. He didn't know what he was saying.

You're too good for a guy like him.

What does he know? Val's great. He has his quirks, but he gets me. He can understand what it's like to have a family with high expectations of you. I think the Wards would be even more pleased than my parents if there really was something between Valentine and me. And why not? I like him. He's attentive and passionate. Especially when it's only the two of us—it's just that he can't show it in front of his friends. He'd never touch me in front of them the way Sinclair does. So natural and . . . loving. But Sinclair and I have known each other for yonks. It's not the same. He only does it because we both know it doesn't mean a thing. But I hardly had anything to do with Val until a couple of months ago. Things are new and exciting with him. And the fact that a guy like Val Ward is interested in me doesn't do my ego any harm. I've recently turned eighteen. I'm ready to make my own experiences. I've wasted enough time waiting for my friend to take the initiative.

I reach for my avocado cushion and hug it to my chest with both arms.

So what's it like? Being noticed by the person you want to kiss . . .

Why did Sinclair say a thing like that? He's had a thousand opportunities to kiss me. And he didn't take a single one. Even that time in the second form, it was me who kissed him. He didn't exactly brush me off, but he didn't kiss me back either, and he never even mentioned what happened. I'm not going to make a fool of myself by reminding him of it. It was humiliating. And made it very clear that this thing between us is platonic. There's no changing that.

We're the best of friends, and maybe Sinclair *is* the most important person in my life. Maybe I do have more fun with him than I do with anyone else. Maybe he does understand me: He's my soul mate. And possibly he is outrageously good-looking. But none of that necessarily means there has to be anything more between us. It's not like Emma and Henry, who fell head over heels for each other at first sight. The kind of thing where everyone could feel how badly they wanted each other and it was only a matter of time till they finally got together.

It's different with Sinclair and me. We've been joined at the hip since the juniors, everyone knows that. Most of the time, if you find one of us, you've found us both. Sinclair's part of me, like the freckles on my nose, but does that mean I'm in undying love with him? Please . . . I'm not in love with him.

OK, well, not undyingly, only a tiny wee bit, perhaps. But it's hopeless. If he felt the same way, we'd have been an item for ages by now. We've known each other for over six years, and Sinclair's never made one single move in that direction. If we can sleep side by side in bed, then clearly nothing's going to happen. OK, so I'm finding it harder and harder to relax when I'm all too aware of the weight of his warm body, but that's just hormones. If we're together and he puts his arms around me because I've got bellyache from laughing, it does something to me. But Sinclair is a very physical person. In his dad's bakery at night, or at the midnight parties, he's touching me the whole time. Just casually. He strokes my arm, puts a hand on my knee, or massages my shoulders if we're taking a break from kneading, and I could fall asleep. It doesn't mean a thing to him.

Me either. After all, I'm in love with Valentine Ward. It's true. He's the first guy to give me unmissable signals that he finds me attractive. That's what I wanted. Even if I feel a bit overwhelmed by it sometimes, since I'm not as experienced as Val.

Maybe my nerves when I'm with Val are partly to do with the feeling that Sinclair's watching us. That he doesn't like how much time I'm spending with Val. Sinclair doesn't say so out loud, but he doesn't have to. The downside of this soul mate thing is that you feel the other person's emotions even when you'd rather ignore them. But I can't ignore anything that has to do with Sinclair. Things are tense between us, and that's my fault. Even though I can do what I like. Hey, I didn't say a word back in the third form when Sinclair suddenly blushed to his ears every time Eleanor Attenborough walked down the corridor. I just breathed a sigh of relief when she finally got together with Louis in her year and the danger was over. Only for a bit, though—the two of them didn't last long. But luckily, even then, Eleanor didn't go out with Sinclair. Why would she? That would have involved him speaking to her, and *obviously* he's legendary for his skills in that area. I don't think they'd have made a great couple anyway. And I had these irrational possessive feelings for Sinclair back then, so he must be feeling the same way now. Whatever happens with Val, I'll always be Sinclair's best friend, but who likes sharing their soul mate?

I roll slightly onto my side. But what if Sinclair wanted to tell me something last night that he'd never have the guts to say sober? And why does that idea make my belly tingle with excitement? If I shut my eyes and imagine, not Val, but Sinclair kissing me with that unexpected determination, I go weak at the knees—even lying down. The world would implode if our lips ever touched again. So that's probably why it'll never happen. It would be too dangerous for everyone.

It's early morning, and it's the weekend, which means I don't have to do the morning-run shite or get to class either, but I still can't fall back to sleep. My mixed-up thoughts are keeping me awake. They're whirling, not leaving me in peace, even when I reach for my brand-new book. Hope MacKenzie is my absolute favorite author, so I made a special trip to Edinburgh to pick up the signed copy of her latest novel that I preordered from Waterstones months ago. As always, her opening sentence is stunning, but after just a few lines, my mind wanders.

I should reply to Val, say sorry, and take him back his jacket. I should ask my parents about this dinner with the Wards. I should confront my friend with what he said last night. And if I'm honest, I don't really want to do any of those things.

SINCLAIR

Man, was I drinking. No idea what it all was, but my pounding head and furry tongue indicate that it wasn't just a wee bit. I spend the whole crappy Sunday in bed, trying not to whitey. It's grim.

Henry brings me some food from the dining room, but just the idea of eating gives me the boak. I guess the upside of the whole thing is that I can't remember the details as I sit in full uniform for the Monday morning assembly. Mum's standing at the lectern at the front, talking about the ball and what a success it was, and lecturing the third-formers who were stupid enough to get caught with booze. Just like every year.

Tori's sitting a few seats along from me but constantly glancing at Valentine Ward, who looks about as crap as I feel. I haven't seen Tori since the ball, but somehow, I sense a degree of tension between us. It's weird—unless I'm imagining it, she's avoiding catching my eye. Maybe she's just tired. Or maybe I made a dick of myself on Saturday night. After assembly, I have to ask her if everything's OK. Just talking would be nice. We barely see each other. By our standards. Of course, we meet around the school every day, and we're doing some of the same subjects, but at break, Tori's spending more of the time hanging around with Valentine and the upper sixth now. Are they together, or was that just a bit of winching at the ball? No commitment. Totally not Tori's style, but nobody asks me.

Victoria Belhaven-Wynford and Valentine Ward. Shit, why does it sound like something out of a corny novel? They could call their children Valerie and Vincent. Minging little brats. I hate everything, and my head aches.

Victoria Belhaven-Wynford and Charles Sinclair. Nah, doesn't fit. There's no rhythm to our names. Tori and Sinclair. Victoria and Charles. Crap either way. Why am I kidding myself? She's a Belhaven-Wynford, and I'm the baker's son. OK, our families aren't old-fashioned enough that they'd make us think our backgrounds would be an issue. Tori's parents have never made me feel like I'm not good enough for their daughter when I've spent weekends with them or summers at their villa in the South of France. I'd even go so far as to say that Charlotte and George Belhaven-Wynford seem to like me. But I'm not what they'd dream of for their daughter. Not when there's someone like Valentine fucking Ward around, whose family moves in the same circles as theirs and who has something to offer Tori.

I try not to stare so blatantly and turn my attention away from them, toward the rows of pupils in front of me. All in the formal navy-blue uniform, of course, like every Monday. Any other day, we wear our normal school clothes—polo shirts, jumpers, and trousers. I glance back over my shoulder as Ms. Kelleher is having words with Ellie in the fifth form because she and her friends are wearing trousers today, not their pleated skirts. Then she shushes the juniors at the front. The younger years always get restless when there's as much to say as there seems to be this morning. I'm expecting Mum to wrap up the assembly any minute, but she launches into yet another subject.

"Before you leave for breakfast, the upper-sixth drama club has an announcement to make," she says, stepping back from the lectern.

Louis Thompson and Eleanor Attenborough stand up and walk to the front.

"Hi, yes, thank you, Mrs. Sinclair." Eleanor winces as her voice echoes through the hall—she's way too close to the microphone. I can't help smiling. I feel burning eyes on me and glance around. Tori immediately snaps her eyes to the front and crosses her legs. "As you all know, our annual theater production is scheduled for just before the summer holidays," says Eleanor. I force myself to turn my attention back to her. "Normally, all the roles would be filled by lots of the older pupils, but sadly, this year not enough people signed up." Eleanor ignores the quiet laughter that undoubtedly comes from Val and his pals. From what I hear, hardly any lads have joined the drama club this year, for which he's not entirely blameless. Apparently, if you want to play on Val's rugby team, you're not allowed any other hobbies. And almost all the upper sixth want that. "So we talked it over with Mr. Acevedo and decided that the auditions next Wednesday would be open to the fifth form and lower sixth too," Eleanor continues.

A gentle murmur rolls through the hall like a wave. Fifth- and sixth-formers are hanging on Eleanor's every word while the fourth form huff in outrage. I automatically glance over to Tori. I know that she's been thinking about joining the drama club for ages, and I'm worried that the only reason she hasn't done it is to avoid Eleanor. Tori's lips are slightly parted and she looks suddenly excited. Until she spots Val, sitting a bit in front of her, as he laughs scornfully, shakes his head patronizingly, and crosses his arms over his chest. His rugby pals laugh too. They're so transparent—it's blatantly obvious that several of them would actually like to try out for the play if Val wasn't constantly so dismissive of the drama club. Maybe he genuinely hates the theater, but to be honest, it looks more like he'd do anything to score off Eleanor, the queen of drama, because his stupid pride was hurt when she ditched him last summer.

"And so, drumroll please, we'll be performing *Romeo and Juliet*." Louis's taken over. A few of the older year groups giggle. "Yeah, surprise, surprise, same as every year. But I promise that our version will be the best ever. So just speak to one of us or to Mr. Acevedo if you want to audition, and he'll give you your lines." He looks over to Eleanor, who steps back to the mic.

"Previous acting experience would be useful, but it's not essential," she says. "The important thing is that you want to be involved and are prepared to put a lot of work into the rehearsals between now and the summer. So next Wednesday, in the theater at three. Anyone who auditions will be let off from study hour this once. See you then!"

Mr. Acevedo jumps up and gives them a double thumbs-up before starting a round of applause. I join in as I stand. The hall instantly fills with voices, laughter, and scraping chair legs. The younger kids rush for the doors, while a few fifth-formers wait for a chance to speak to Eleanor, Louis, or Mr. Acevedo. The way I'm going to speak to Tori. Or that's the theory. But in practice, she's already in the central aisle while I can't get past everyone else blocking our row. Tori's making her way toward Val. He's raging, but he kisses her and puts his arm around her shoulders. A few fourth-formers have their heads together, whispering. It makes me want to boak.

"Hey, mate, smile," Henry remarks at my side. I glare at him. It's easy for him to say that, with Emma at his side and their irritatingly picture-perfect relationship. OK, that's not true. The two of them went through a lot before they finally got together. And things didn't exactly get any easier when Henry's sister died out of the blue like that. It really knocked him sideways, and even now, almost four months later, there are still days when he looks all at sea. But it's got better. Especially since he's been going to see Ms. Vail, the school psychologist, regularly. I'm glad of that, because it feels like I've got my friend back, but I'm not so naive as to think things are any easier for Henry to deal with just because he seems to be coping these days.

I decide to seize the opportunity.

"Did I say something stupid on Saturday night or something?" I ask.

"Why do you ask?" Henry replies evasively, which can't be a good sign.

"I dunno, I think I had a blackout," I admit. "And Tori . . . she was there, wasn't she?"

"She spent the night with you," says Henry.

My blood runs cold, then hot. Bloody booze. I can't remember a thing.

It's not the first time that Tori and I have shared a bed, but it's been rare lately. And I miss her. Shit, yeah. I don't mind admitting that nobody gives such good hugs as Tori.

But clearly Valentine's the guy getting that pleasure now. If they do hug. Probably they have other things on their minds when she . . . Stop, don't think about it.

"Oh, right." I gulp. "There was nobody there when I woke up."

"She probably left early so you wouldn't get in any trouble."

Or maybe she just didn't want to have to speak to me. Or she headed up a floor at some point. To Valentine. I can't bear the thought of it.

Tori's eyes meet mine as she leaves the hall with Valentine, Neil, and a few others in the upper sixth. She looks away before I can say anything.

TORI

Val hasn't mentioned the other evening, not even once, and that's making me edgy. He laughs and puts his arm around me as we leave the hall. I follow him outside rather than heading for my classroom. I don't smoke, but I want to spend more time with Val, so I guess I'll have to stand out here in the cold with him whether I like it or not. And live with my hair reeking of smoke. Maybe I'd even prefer it to heading upstairs to classes with Henry, Emma, Olive, and Sinclair. It's not like I didn't feel the way my best friend was looking at me during assembly. We haven't spoken since, and it's not very nice. But I can deal with that later. Now I'm with Val. And I should enjoy the fact that he's in a good mood. I'd been expecting us to start fighting the second we met up again.

"How was the rest of your weekend?" I ask as we follow his pals.

Val slows his steps. "You guys go on," he calls as we stop just before the gateway to the courtyard. His tone changes as he continues. "My weekend? Yeah, how was my weekend . . ."

I'm suddenly way too aware of the weight of his arm on my shoulders. Val removes it and faces me. The smile's wiped off his face.

"Yeah, it was great." His voice is dripping with sarcasm. "I waited for an answer from you and didn't get one, but you know that part."

"Sorry, Val." My pulse quickens as I keep talking. "I shouldn't have left without letting you know. But I was tired and . . ."

"Where did you go?"

"Emma messaged me, I wanted—"

"You were with him." Val's face is unreadable. "You were, weren't you?" I hesitate, and he continues. "Don't even try to lie to me."

"OK, yeah," I admit. Anything's better than trying to weasel out now. It'll just end up with Val hearing it on the grapevine, and then he'll be seriously pissed off. "I was with him. Sinclair was drunk. The others needed my help, I—"

"Your help?" Val laughs. "What with? Putting him to bed?"

When I don't say anything, something in his face changes. "Holy shit, Tori. Are you taking the piss?" He doesn't raise his voice. Quite the reverse—he's threateningly quiet.

"I should have let you know," I admit. "I'm sorry, Val."

"Did you get up to anything?"

"What?" I give an anxious laugh.

Val's eyes bore into me. "You know what I mean. Did anything happen between you?"

"No!" It's the moment that my feeling of defenselessness tips over into rage. "Shit, Val, no. You can believe me on that. We're friends. I don't want anything more from Sinclair."

"But he wants something from you," he hisses. "That's blatantly obvious."

My throat constricts as I remember Sinclair's words from Saturday evening.

So how does it feel?

It feels shite. Because suddenly everything's so bloody complicated. But Sinclair's my friend. He doesn't want anything from me, because if he did, I'd know about it.

"Val, I swear there was nothing." I stress each word, but they practically bounce off Val's skin. I shake my head gently and give a quiet laugh. "Sinclair was steaming, and I spent the night in his room because I didn't want to leave him on his own like that. But he fell asleep instantly. And if you don't believe me, I'm afraid I don't know how I can convince you that I'm telling the truth."

For a moment, Val's still giving me that death glare, but then his features soften a little. I breathe out quietly, and he nods.

"OK." He runs a hand over his face and exhales loudly. "Fine, OK, I believe you. You're right. It's no basis for a relationship if we're already fighting over a thing like this."

I can't nod; I'm too numb.

No basis.

For a RELATIONSHIP.

"But do you get where I'm coming from too?" Val reaches for my hand. When he looks at me, I go weak at the knees. "You were suddenly gone, and I had no idea where you were. Half an hour before that, we'd kissed, and then . . . I hate being this jealous, but I couldn't help it. I'm just so fucking unsure of myself around you."

God . . .

Val's never said anything like that to me before. It sounds like he's pretty serious about it. But instead of being glad, I feel panic rising inside me.

"You've known each other so long, and I . . ." He looks down at his toes. "I'm scared that I can't give you what he gives you."

"Val," I hear myself saying. *Think. Say something, Tori. Anything.* "That's crap, Val, and you know it."

He looks back at me. "Do I?"

"I hope you do now," I say, taking a step toward him. What am I doing?

Val looks at me as I stand on tiptoe and give him a quick kiss. I *kiss* him. Just like that, in broad daylight, right there in the courtyard. Because it feels like I have to do it to prove to him that I'm serious about us. About him. Which I am, aren't I?

Val holds me tight when I want to pull away. He smiles, but there's something in his eyes that scares me.

"Have you spoken to your parents?" he asks.

"About the dinner?" I wait for him to nod. "Not yet."

"Let me know. If you don't come, I need an excuse. I'll never get through it without you."

"I will," I promise at the second the bell goes for the first period. I glance over my shoulder, and when I look back to Val, he lifts up my head with two fingers to kiss me.

Butterflies in my stomach. Pins and needles in my skin. He's kissing me like it's the most natural thing in the world. And yeah, it's hot. Valentine Ward is kissing me in the school courtyard, and why can't I just enjoy it?

"Promise me that next time you won't just piss off without telling me first," he insists.

I hesitate, but then I just say it. "I got the impression I was getting on your nerves."

"Getting on my nerves?" Val echoes. He sounds so disbelieving that I feel ridiculous. "You can't be serious."

"Yes, I . . . I'm sorry, maybe I overreacted. But you were only talking to your friends and . . ."

"Tori, I was at that ball with you." He looks so intently at me that my heart skips a beat, and he takes my hand. "I didn't give a fuck about anyone else."

He says it so sincerely that it has to be true. Even if it didn't feel like that on Saturday evening. His eyes rest heavily on me.

"Hell, Tori, I kissed you. Did you really think after that, I wanted to spend time with the guys and not with you?"

I can only shrug my shoulders.

"Didn't you like it?"

"Yes," I assure him hastily. "It was . . . it was nice."

"Nice," Val repeats. A mocking smile twitches at his full lips. "Know what? I found it *nice* too, Victoria Belhaven-Wynford. Next time, I'll show you a step up from nice."

I shiver slightly, but I smile. "Deal."

Liar.

"I was worried, got that?" he says again as he puts his arm back around my shoulders and we walk toward the classrooms. "You suddenly vanished in the middle of the night. What kind of boyfriend would I be if that didn't bother me?"

Boyfriend.

Smile. He's perfect. There's your proof. He can be so affectionate and attentive. He wants the best for you, and how do you thank him?

I walk next to Val in silence. I flinch as Neil walks past and slaps Val on the shoulder. He doesn't let me go, which I guess should please me.

"So, got your lines for the auditions then?" A couple of others in the upper sixth join in the laughter.

"Definitely," says Val. My stomach lurches slightly because

his voice is so derisive. "Doing Shakespeare with those losers? Who'd choose to make a tit of themselves in front of the whole school like that?"

The others laugh some more, and I feel a little cold.

My brave side wants to say that the performances in the last few years have been anything but cringy. Seriously. Each version was intelligent and gripping, and the cast did a great job every time. Every year, I'm amazed yet again at how Mr. Acevedo manages to put on a polished performance in just a few months. And that each year interprets *Romeo and Juliet* in a completely new way. Because it's the one thing Mr. Acevedo insists on: Every upper sixth puts on the same play and makes it their own. Maybe it's not normal that I've spent years imagining that next time around, it could be me standing on that stage as Juliet. That this could be my chance to have a go a year earlier than expected. Even if I didn't get picked for Juliet, I could at least get experience for our form's play next year. I'm not under any illusions that I'd get the main role, because that's definitely Eleanor's.

"We should go along to the auditions." Val removes his arm from my shoulders as we stop outside his classroom. "Sure to be entertaining."

"I'll bring the popcorn," says Neil, although nobody else laughs.

"I was actually considering having a go," I say.

"What?" Val stares at me in disbelief. "You're not serious? You can't mean it. Those plays are lame, everyone knows that. Especially last year's. What even was that?"

"I thought it was pretty cool," I murmur, remembering the

modern staging, which had stuck in my mind all summer long. The performance had really got to me, and I know that my friends felt the same. Sinclair was so impressed that he's been part of the scriptwriting club ever since. It suits him. Storytelling and drama are in his blood. Hardly surprising, the number of films and series he devours. And I know from Sinclair that the rehearsals for this year's performance have been held up because the writers can't agree on the script. Normally, casting starts in late autumn so there's plenty of time to get ready for a performance just before the summer holidays.

"It was freaky," says Val. "When everyone came on wearing those masks and screamed. I mean, what was that?"

The others laugh. I don't join in, but I don't argue back either.

"Besides, you're not into acting," says Val. "Are you?"

If only he knew how much I'd like to change that. But I'm afraid of talking to him about it. Luckily for me, Ms. Ventura comes around the corner at that moment and shoos the lads off to class. I should be heading to English too, which kicks off my week. We've had Mr. Acevedo since Mr. Ward left the school, and he might be less strict, but he won't put up with lateness.

Val leans down. "See you later," he mumbles. The others catcall as he kisses me.

I smile. I turn away and walk to join my friends.

4

SINCLAIR

Monday's going crap, and I've still got a headache. On top of which I was stupid enough to promise Dad I'd do a shift in the bakery tonight. Normally I help him at the weekends, but because someone's sick, Mum's given me permission to be out after wing time so I can have everything ready for tomorrow. Dad gets to the bakery at half past two in the morning so that he can open at six, which means we're rarely working at the same time. When I was a kid, he'd sometimes take me along if I couldn't sleep. It always felt like an adventure being in the bakery so early in the morning, even though it's only a few doors down from our house in the south of Ebrington. These days, to my shame, I spend more time in the shop than I do in my parents' house. That doesn't mean I'm unhappy there, just that my life is focused on Dunbridge Academy, where I see Mum every day at least. I sometimes go home for the weekends, especially if Tori and the others are away.

When I get to the bakery after dinner, the only person there is Margaret, one of the shop assistants. She's emptied the shelves and is cleaning everything down, so soon after that, I'm alone with myself and my thoughts.

I haven't had a chance to speak to Tori. We were in English and French together, and it's not like we aren't talking to each other. That's pretty hard to manage at boarding school, given that you're together at every mealtime and see each other constantly. But when the others are around, it's shockingly easy to just chat about trivial stuff rather than Saturday night. It can wait till tomorrow. Or the day after. Or never. I probably didn't say anything too dumb. And if I did, Tori's sure to have forgotten it by now. Yeah, that'll be better. Don't want to create any unnecessary drama.

I drag a twenty-kilo flour sack from the storeroom and start mixing the dough for bread rolls. Sometimes I help in the shop in the afternoons, but I prefer it here at night, when there's nobody around and the hours just merge into one another as I knead the dough and sweep the floors. I don't need this job, but I love it. And I think my parents are in favor of it too—Dad because the bakery means everything to him, and Mum because it keeps me in touch with honest work. She'd never say so directly, but she stresses often enough that there's more to life than exam results and university applications. I can't really imagine staying here forever and taking over the shop one day, but I like working with my hands. As often happens, I find myself in an almost meditative state. It's quiet, just me and my thoughts as I weigh out ingredients and knead the dough for tomorrow morning. I don't know how long I've been here when I hear a sound.

I pause. What was that? Am I hearing things, given how little I've slept recently? But then I hear the knock again. It's Tori's knock. Four times in a row, and kind of firm.

My stomach leaps as I step through into the shop and see her through the glass door. She's wearing her Dunbridge hoodie under a long coat, and her arms are crossed over her chest. Her cheeks are flushed with cold, and she's stunning.

"Hey." She steps into the bakery without a second's hesitation, as soon as I open the door. For a moment, it's just like old times. Tori creeping out after wing time so that we can be here together. Shut in the shop together for half the night. We used to do this all the time.

"Hey." I turn around.

Tori peels off her coat and hangs it up behind the counter. "I thought maybe you could use a hand," she says.

"Not really," I say, because I'm an eejit. I can't help noticing Tori's confusion.

"Should I . . . ?" She gestures toward the door.

C'mon, pull yourself together! "No." I clear my throat. "You're welcome to stay."

Since when have things been so weird between us? That was a rhetorical question, obviously. I know since when.

Since Tori's been dating Valentine Ward, since she kissed him at the New Year Ball and I got so hammered that my memory skips after that point. Just like my heart when Tori's arm brushes mine as she squeezes past me. I could recognize her just by her touch, just by her smell. Peach, she always smells of peach. And I don't mean the artificial scent of perfumed soap. It's different with Tori. Better. Everything's different and better with her. I pray that that fucker Valentine Ward told her so before he crushed his mouth onto hers. I'm obviously incapable of doing so in his place.

"What shall we listen to?" asks Tori, sitting on one of the work surfaces. I'm opening my mouth to point out the flour, but Tori doesn't seem to care if her leggings get dusty. She pulls out her phone. "True crime or an audiobook?"

Neither, if I'm honest. I want to hear her voice as she tells me stuff from her life that I don't know about anymore. Because we're not talking for some reason.

"Just music?" I suggest, even though I know what that means. Her "Hot Guy Shit" playlist, a.k.a. eleven hours and forty-six minutes of One Direction and the boys' solo albums. It begins with "Kiss You," and I've never been in such agreement with the singer. As is generally the case, I don't even know who's singing just now, but I think it's Zayn. Or Harry. Tori always looks a bit happier when it's him.

This evening, it doesn't seem to be working, though. The music blurs into the background as I turn my attention to the dough. I can feel Tori's eyes on my back. Then I hear her voice.

"How's the head?"

I pause. "Still thumping."

"No surprise there, then." She sounds pretty pissed off. I start to feel guilty. I know Tori doesn't drink. For perfectly understandable reasons. What was I thinking?

"No, I . . . I'm sorry, I think I was pretty drunk."

Tori nods vigorously. "Yeah, pretty drunk." I wish she'd tell me the truth. But she hasn't been doing that for a long time now.

"Did I whitey on you?" I ask.

"Not quite."

Well, at least that's something.

Knead and roll. It's a huge ball of dough, and my arms are burning slightly with the effort, but I don't stop.

"I couldn't help thinking about what you said." Tori speaks fast. Almost like it's a big effort to get the words out. And I scan equally fast through my few scraps of memory of Saturday night. Doesn't take me long, let's put it like that.

"What did we talk about?" My voice sounds rough.

Tori hesitates. "You don't remember?"

"'Fraid not."

"Well, then, I guess it can't be that important."

"Hm." I turn around. "Sounds kind of important to me."

She looks at me, and it must be down to the warm light in here, but her skin looks kind of golden. I want to go to her and touch every one of her freckles. It's not fair.

"Sinclair, I don't know . . ." she says evasively.

"You have to tell me," I persist. "Come on, Tor. Seriously. You can't drop a hint like that and clam up on me."

"You wanted to know what it feels like to be noticed by the person you want to kiss," she blurts. It sounds as though she's spent ages thinking about the exact wording of that question.

There's silence between us. Very awkward silence. And then the memories crawl back into my head.

Shit, she's right. I might actually have said that. Am I that much of an eejit? My body turns to ice as I start to realize what it means. I was pissed out of my mind, and I told her what I want from her.

"And I was just wondering what . . ." She pauses as I still don't say anything. "I was wondering who you meant."

Fuck, fuck, fuck.

Keep calm, man. We know the answer; we both know it. Because obviously I meant her. Because I spend an unhealthy amount of time thinking about how soft her mouth is. About Tori's warm lips, even though I only felt them on mine for a pathetic fraction of a second. Back then, a hundred years ago, I was so overwhelmed that I couldn't hold on to any of the details. It's grim. And now she wants to know who I meant. Tori knows it's her. That it's always been her. All this time. And I should tell her so, but I can't.

"Eleanor."

The lie is out before I have time to think.

And Tori goes pale. Only a shade, but I've spent so many hours of my life watching her. I can't miss the way Tori spends a wee while fighting to keep calm. She gulps, she blinks. It's like someone's slipped a knife between my ribs and is slowly twisting it.

"I don't know, I was steaming," I say hastily. "And then she was there and I, well . . . It didn't exactly help seeing Eleanor."

Shit, what am I saying? I still like Eleanor—she's witty, funny, and intelligent—but she doesn't make me go weak at the knees. I know that, but I'm not sure whether Tori knows it too. I don't like the fact that she's apparently seen Eleanor as a rival since that unfortunate situation in the third form. Maybe I had a wee crush on Ellie back then, but to be honest, everyone knows that that was only as a distraction from my major crush on Tori. Seems to have worked. Better than I intended.

"Oh, I see." Tori's eyebrows twitch as she tries to control her expression. "I thought . . ."

"What did you think?" I ask.

Say it. Come on.

Say you thought I meant you. Because I did. I'm just incapable of admitting it.

"Whatever." She straightens her shoulders. "For a moment, I thought you meant me."

I'm on the point of just nodding, because she's bloody well right, but Tori sounds so sarcastic that I can't move. She laughs, and I'm certain it's the most painful sound I've ever heard. I can hardly bear it, so I join in. What should I do? Maybe I wasn't clear enough, but in this situation, I'm amazed at how impossible it is to find the guts to take the words back. Respect to anyone who can. Evidently I'm a coward, because just the thought of telling Tori the truth has me shitting myself. That I want to kiss her because I've bloody well got feelings for her. That I do care if she kisses Valentine Ward. No, it's not that I care. It's that it drives me insane to stand there and know it's not me holding her like that. And every time I imagine saying so, the same thing happens in my head: Tori looks at me, first surprised, then shocked. Then embarrassed, and then we laugh.

Ha-ha, only joking, ha-ha. Good one. Very funny. Course I don't like you like that. We're friends. Just friends.

I only notice that I've clenched both fists when Tori glances at them. We're not laughing anymore.

"But you really were steaming." She runs her hands awkwardly through her hair. I want to tell her there's a bit of flour on the balls of her thumbs.

"It was boring without you, so I had to drink."

OK, no word of a lie for a change. Even if *boring* doesn't quite hit the mark. *Dire* would be closer.

"So does that mean you and Eleanor . . . ?" She pauses as if she wants to give me the chance to finish her sentence. But I don't, so she continues. "You want to kiss her?"

"Yeah, dunno." I avoid her gaze. "I mean, she's hot. But she doesn't look at me. I'm not kidding myself there."

"Maybe she doesn't know you like her," says Tori slowly.

My mouth is dry. I look at her again. "I think she does."

Neither of us speaks. What's happening here? Tori doesn't move.

"You could ask her out. A date, just the two of you, so you can talk."

"Yeah." I have to clear my throat—my voice sounds so hoarse. I split the dough and slap a lump onto the work surface in front of me. A little flour whirls through the air. I form little round rolls and feel nothing. "It's not that easy, though. Talking to her."

"Maybe you just have to be brave," I hear Tori saying.

I nod silently. This is ridiculous.

"She'll definitely be auditioning on Wednesday, won't she?"

I lift my head. "Yes, I'm sure she will. Eleanor's been in the drama club for years."

Tori pushes her finger over the countertop, leaving a slender trail in the flour. I ignore the shiver that runs down my neck, because I know only too well what that feels like. Her fingers on my skin. Tori drawing patterns on my back or secret messages that I try to decipher as I'm falling asleep.

"You should have a go too," I say. Tori lifts her head. "It must be a sign, the auditions being open to lower forms."

Tori hesitates. "Yeah, I've been thinking about it."

"But?" I ask, although I can guess. And Tori can tell as much, so she lies.

"Dunno. I've never acted before. And Eleanor's bound to get Juliet."

"There are other roles. The Nurse, or Lady Capulet, for example."

"Yeah. I don't know."

"Did Val talk you out of it?"

"No," she snaps back.

He did then. I hate that bastard.

"You shouldn't let him influence you. It's bad enough he's manipulated his rugby pals so that there are barely any lads in the drama club now."

"I don't let him influence me." Tori glares warningly at me.

Why is she sticking up for him? I don't get it.

"OK, I'm just saying," I mumble. "The guy's so cringy."

"You're so childish. That's what's cringy," she retorts. "Val hasn't done you any harm, Sinclair."

Except that he bad-mouths me and all my friends; yelled at Henry in front of everyone after his rugby accident, even when he was lying on the ground; and kept snaking on us to his stupid uncle back when he was teaching me A-level English. Oh, and then he stole my best friend off me. Yeah, he hasn't done me the least bit of harm . . .

I press my lips together. Whatever I say now, we'll end up arguing, and I really don't want that. The fact that Tori reacts so defensively the moment I dare to criticize Valentine tells me everything. And I could live with that if he at least treated her decently. But he's constantly manipulating her and getting in her head. I don't know exactly what he's telling her, but Tori's changed since she's been spending so much time with him. Sometimes it seems like she's a completely different person from the Tori of a year ago. And I know how that sounds. Like I'm the jealous type who wants her all to himself. But it's not like that. It would be OK, I wouldn't interfere, if I had the feeling he was good for her. But Tori's quieter when Valentine's around. She seems less confident, and you're meant to blossom when you're in love, aren't you? She doesn't seem happy, and there are times when I don't recognize my friend, but I can't tell her that without sounding petty.

The only way I can keep my voice calm is not to look at her as I speak. "All I meant was that I think it'd be a shame if you didn't audition."

"Yeah, we'll see." She's silent. Then, "How's the scriptwriting club?"

I sigh. "Don't ask. Lowell and Florence got into a fight over the script. Now Lowell's stormed out. Mr. Acevedo's majorly stressed because we're so late with the script."

"I wouldn't have thought it would be that much work—isn't it only a reinterpretation?"

"Me either," I admit. Naive of me. Because it's not so easy to make something completely new out of old material, especially a classic.

"How far have you got?" asks Tori.

"Tybalt's just killed Mercutio," I say. "So about halfway. But I'm afraid we're going to have to start again. Lowell just took over the whole thing and wouldn't listen to any criticism at all. Nobody's happy with how it is just now."

"Hm." Tori leans on the worktop with both hands. "How long do you have?"

"The text was meant to be ready by January. Mr. Acevedo gave us an extra month, but he needs the script by February so the rehearsals can start."

"Oh." Tori looks at me.

Yes, *oh*. February. The week after next.

"Mr. Acevedo knows we won't make it. He said we could write large chunks of it during rehearsals. That that might even be a good thing, because it'll make the script more authentic and help it fit the cast. He wants to spend the first few weeks focusing on method acting and improvisation anyway to get everyone to relax."

"I see," says Tori. She looks at me and smiles. "You can do it."

"We'll have to."

My hands knead the dough, and "No Control" comes on in the background, a song that I'm embarrassed to like—and it's so true too. I feel like I'm losing control. Tori doesn't have to know that, but that's how I feel.

"What's up with Olive?" I ask eventually.

Bad move. I realize at once when Tori stiffens up a bit.

"Why should anything be up with her?" she asks.

I shrug. I just wondered how she was, same as I always did. "Have you two talked?"

Tori shakes her head. I don't know why, but her face softens as she studies the floor at her feet. She knows she doesn't have to act like she doesn't care if she's fallen out with her best girlfriend. Because she does. Like I would if I had a beef with Henry. Which, luckily, I don't, but since last autumn, things have been weird between Olive and Tori. Between Olive and all of us, to be honest.

"No." Tori tries to sound indifferent, but her eyes remain sad. I want to give her a hug. "She keeps avoiding me, don't know why. I mean, what am I meant to do?"

"It's not your fault," I say. "And Olive knows that."

"But why's she acting like this then?"

I keep quiet. Although I've had an inkling what the problem might be for some time. Olive's jealous, same as me. But not of Valentine Ward—she's jealous of Emma, who Tori's been firm friends with since the start of the school year. Which doesn't mean that Tori has ditched Olive. But maybe it doesn't feel like that to her. And then Emma got together with Henry, who left Olive's friend Grace for her, which definitely won't have helped. But maybe all that is only part of the problem, because I'm worried about how much pressure Olive's putting on herself just now. I happen to know that she's struggling in both politics and maths, and I remember only too well what it's like when you're worried about your grades. But unlike her, I wasn't too proud to let Henry coach me through my maths GCSE last summer.

I'll never be a maths whizz, but at least I scraped through and don't have to retake this year. I wouldn't have the guts to advise her to do the same though. Olive Henderson is the undisputed champion of the world at pushing away anyone who has the nerve to be worried for her.

"You two should talk," I repeat all the same. "I'm sure this situation is upsetting Olive just as much as it is you."

"But maybe she doesn't care."

"*You* care, though," I insist. "And that's why you have to talk to her."

"I've missed this," says Tori, out of the blue.

I look up. My first instinct is to ask her what she means, but I know perfectly well.

This. This kind of conversation, which I can't have with anybody else.

I'm about to answer when her phone buzzes.

That toxic feeling is creeping up on me even as she pulls it out of her pocket. Her eyebrows contract, and she bites her lips softly.

I don't have to ask. I know it's him.

5

TORI

The Wards' house is stunning, set in the countryside across the water from Edinburgh. The tarmacked driveway could belong to a castle, and the curved steps up to the entrance are at least as imposing as the high-ceilinged rooms. It's a listed building, but the kitchen and bathrooms are bang up to date. You can practically smell their money. No wonder, because this property is basically a form of advertising for them.

Val's wearing a dark suit that fits his broad shoulders to perfection. He greets me with a kiss on the cheek after shaking hands with my parents and nodding to Will. It's not until Mum, Dad, and my brother have followed Veronica Ward into the drawing room and the housekeeper has hung up our coats that he kisses me on the lips in the hallway.

"Val," I murmur, pushing him gently away. I wouldn't exactly call my parents prudish, but kissing in front of them feels out of place. "Not here."

He eyes me with an arrogant smile. "Don't want them to know about us? That's kind of sexy—I like it."

"It's not that," I say in a low voice as we follow the others through the high double doors.

My parents, Will, and the Wards are standing in front of a large painting on one of the walls. It's a Jean-René Matignon, which Mum bought at auction at Art Basel last year. She sold it on to Veronica Ward before it even got as far as her gallery.

"You were right. It's like it was made for this room," says Mum, declining graciously as the waitress offers her an aperitif.

"Oh, go on, Charlotte, don't leave me drinking on my own. You too, George." Veronica beckons the caterer to come back and reaches for two champagne glasses. Mum hesitates, and my heart sinks a story lower as she takes one. Dad doesn't comment, but his eyes rest heavily on her.

It's a work dinner, she could hardly refuse. It doesn't mean a thing. Relax.

Val hands Will and me a glass of orange juice each, then takes the last one from the tray. It's almost silly, considering the way he was swigging gin from the bottle and snorting cocaine at the New Year Ball. Maybe he's remembering that too, because there's a hint of challenge twinkling in his eye as he raises his glass to me.

"Nice to see you all," says Veronica Ward. "It's been too long. William, Victoria, I hardly recognized the two of you."

I smile politely and include Will in my thanks for the invitation. Val stands beside me as our parents resume their conversation. There's no way they can see him put his hand on my back, but it still gives me goose bumps. His fingertips stroke the black lace on my fitted dress, which I'm wearing with opaque tights and patent-leather loafers.

"You're looking seriously hot," he whispers in my ear, before turning away and clinking glasses with Will.

It's no secret that my brother can't stand Valentine. But he answers his questions: How's Kit? How's tennis training going? When the caterers usher us through into the dining room, Will rolls his eyes demonstratively at me.

Fortunately, Val doesn't notice. He's sitting opposite me at the long table and next to his mother, who involves me in a conversation about school and my book blog. She's trying to sound interested, but the look in her eyes when I mention Instagram and TikTok tells me what she really thinks of my hobby. Not a lot. Reviewing books and making entertaining videos is a waste of my time. Mum and Dad don't mind me being active on social media, but she plainly thinks it's kind of beneath me. I'd bet my signed Hope MacKenzie that Veronica Ward has no clue about her son's Insta account. Val had the sense not to set it up under his real name. If his mother knew about Val's fondness for topless mirror selfies after training or in the school gym (#shredded #noexcuses), she'd try to get it shut down on the spot. His thousands of followers seem to like them, though, judging by their comments—sometimes seriously weird—beneath Val's photos.

My social battery is almost drained by the time our starter plates are cleared away.

Val's talking to my dad about the rugby season as the main course is served. I glance at Mum's wineglass, and Will looks at me. Our eyes meet. He's clearly about as tense as I feel.

She doesn't stop at one glass. By dessert, Mum's on her third top-up. She's sitting up straight and talking animatedly to Veronica about Val's sister, Philippa. Val plays no part in the conversation. He stares at his plate while his parents discuss Pippa's university career and the various firsts she got last term.

"You must be very proud of her," says Dad. "And of Valentine. Captaining the rugby team is a great honor."

Veronica nods. "Philippa is so ambitious. She never would settle for second best."

"She gets that from you," Val's father remarks.

"Thank you, Augustus." She dabs her mouth with her napkin. "Philippa is focusing on European law. It's a challenging course, but her hard work will pay off."

"What a shame she couldn't be here this evening," says Mum.

"I know, but it is term time after all. I'm always glad if my work takes me anywhere near Oxford so that I can have lunch with her."

"What are your plans for next year, Valentine?" Dad glances over to him.

"Hopefully economics at Cambridge. If I get the results."

"Of course you'll get the results," says his mother. Her voice will tolerate no argument. "So long as you concentrate as much on your A levels as you do on sport, I don't see the problem."

"There's not long to go now, is there?" asks Mum.

"Only a few months," Veronica Ward nods. Then she pauses. "Are you sure you'd like a second helping, darling?" She semi-smiles at the waitress, then looks at Val. For a moment, there's silence around the table. The awkwardness creeps straight under my skin as I see Val freeze. He goes pale, then actually blushes.

"No, of course not." He avoids my gaze as I try to make eye contact with him. I should say something, but it's like my lips won't move.

"Val keeps in very good shape during the season, don't you?" Veronica says. "Even though it's nearly over, that doesn't mean you have to let yourself go as much as you have your grades." She laughs as if she's made a hilarious joke.

Val's ears go a fraction redder still. Then the cool arrogance returns to his face. He reaches for his water glass and doesn't take his eyes off the table. But I can see his fingers shaking. Whether that's with embarrassment or rage, I can't tell. I only know that I don't think it's right of his mother to shame him in front of us all like that. I've seen Val turn down seconds often enough in the dining room or come back late from the fitness center. He's the last person I'd deny an extra helping. Besides, it's generally out of order for his mother to comment on other people's eating habits or figures. Not that it seems like anyone else here cares about that.

Sometimes I'm afraid that the tolerant bubble consisting of my friends and the people I follow on Insta and TikTok isn't necessarily a reflection of reality.

Augustus Ward thanks the caterers, and they vanish. I look up as Val murmurs his excuses and leaves the room too.

Nobody seems concerned by his disappearance. The conversation revolves around the Wards' game stocks, and as I have no desire to hear about Val's dad's hunting exploits in their woodlands, I excuse myself as well.

Instead of heading for the toilet, I make my way upstairs. It's been years since I've been here, but I remember the way to Val's room. His door is ajar. I'm about to knock when I hear quiet sounds from behind it. Cautiously, I push the door open.

The white shirt tenses over Val's shoulders as he does furious press-ups on the floor, one per second. A floorboard creaks under my foot, and his head flies up. Val stares at me. He looks hunted, then unapproachable as he sees that it's me.

"What d'you want?" he barks, straightening.

I stand in the doorway, and he turns to tug his shirtsleeves down.

"Are you OK?" I ask cautiously as he buttons his cuffs.

"Yes." Val won't look at me.

It's only as I step closer that he turns to face me. "Are you looking for the bathroom? Downstairs, second on the left."

I'm surprised by how painful his rejection is. This side of Val gives me stomach aches and sleepless nights, because I can only guess at what I'm doing wrong. Why he can't open up to me. I'm trying everything, I'm attentive and considerate, but apparently, that only gets on his nerves. Just now, right at this moment, that's more than obvious.

"Val," I try quietly, "is it because of what your mum said?"

The spark of pain in his eyes shows me that I'm right. It's only fleeting, though. Val laughs. "You don't really believe that?" He eyes me sharply. "I don't give a fuck what she says, OK?"

I just stare at him, then find my voice again. "Yes, sorry. I thought . . ."

"Don't make an eejit of yourself," Val murmurs before he walks past me out of the room. He's already halfway down the stairs before I realize that he's actually just abandoned me here. A sense of impotence and disappointment rises in my chest. And there's something else: rage at the way Val speaks to me. I was worried about him. I wanted to be there for him. And what thanks do I get?

For a few seconds, I stay standing there, thunderstruck, in the doorway to his room. Then I give myself a shake and follow him down. Or, at least, that's the plan, but Val's stopped on the stairs. His shoulders rise and fall heavily before he turns back. The pain on his face hits me right in the pit of my stomach. I stir and walk toward him. Val holds out his hand. "I'm sorry, I didn't mean to speak to you like that."

His voice is soft, and my knees go weak. "It's in the past," I declare hastily.

"No, Tori, I—"

"What your mum said wasn't OK, Val."

He looks up, and there's something vulnerable in his eyes that I've never seen before. "She didn't mean it like that," he says lamely.

"It doesn't matter how she meant it. What matters is how it affected you," I insist. "And maybe you should speak to her about it."

"About what?" he asks, straight-backed. His voice sounds sharper. I'll have to be careful if I don't want his defenses to come down again.

"The stuff about food?" I suggest.

"What about it?"

"Val, do you think it's healthy to spend hours working out every day and only eat protein and vegetables?"

"If you want to play rugby at this level, then yeah," he answers coolly.

"But do you do that because it's fun or because it stops you feeling anything?" I've hit a sore spot. I'm sure of that when something flickers in Val's eyes. He wants to pull his hand away, but I'm holding it tight.

"I do it because I have to be the fucking best, OK?" he hisses, but there's something resigned in his voice all the same. I'd like to say so many things, but I have the feeling that I'll only hit resistance if I keep on now. Val's never let me see him so vulnerable before. He must feel like he's got his back against the wall, so I shouldn't press him any further. It takes time to admit that something might not actually be the way you pretend, and I'm not the person who should be spelling that out for Val. He knows it himself, I'm sure.

I pull back a little and feel the way the distance allows Val to relax a wee bit.

"You can tell me anything. You know that, don't you?"

His jaw muscles clench, but in the end, he nods. His eyes glide over my face, and he takes a step closer to me. "I don't deserve you, Victoria Belhaven-Wynford," he says, before kissing me.

I feel the banisters at my back and the butterflies in my tummy. We pull apart as we hear footsteps downstairs. It's Will, going to the toilet; I'm sure that's only an excuse, though, because he looks straight up to the gallery. He doesn't say anything when he sees me and Val, but he doesn't disappear into the loo until I nod to him that everything's OK.

Our parents don't seem to have noticed anything when we

sit down with them a while later. Val and I don't talk much, but there's no need. Our stolen glances and feet touching briefly under the table say more than a thousand words.

When my family is ready to leave and Val comes out into the hall with us, he steps to my side. Mum pulls on her coat, and Dad holds out his arm to her. Considering how much she drank this evening, she's looking amazingly sober, and that hurts, because it's not a good sign. Habituation effect, increased tolerance—shit, those are just fancy names for a phenomenon that tells me she's drinking regularly again.

"Hey." I turn around again as Val pulls me back once I've said goodbye to his parents. He glances over to them, but they're talking to Mum and Dad as they walk down the steps.

"Thanks," Val says, looking at me. "For coming and . . . for earlier."

"Anytime, you know that." I look away—I don't know why, but it doesn't feel right to kiss Val goodbye in front of our families. Either he thinks the same or he can read my feelings on my face, because he bends down. His lips brush my cheek.

"See you at school," he murmurs, then repeats the process on the other side. "I'll text you."

"Do that."

"Safe journey home."

He raises his arm in farewell as I'm finally sitting in the car. We left on good terms, but I can't help replaying the moment I stepped into Val's room.

What d'you want?

Don't make an eejit of yourself.

He apologized. We had a good conversation. Val's never shown me such a vulnerable side of himself before, and that's progress, which I should be glad of. I lean my head against the car window, my heart pounding anxiously. It doesn't settle down all the way home.

SINCLAIR

The scriptwriting club meets on Tuesday and Thursday evenings in the old library, and it always used to be fun, but since Lowell walked out, the mood's been deathly. Florence and Quentin seem glad he's gone; Ho-wing and Amara, who usually agreed with him, are just pissed off with Florence for riling him so much that he quit.

"OK, we'll vote on it, or we'll never get anywhere." Florence shuts her eyes and massages the bridge of her nose, then throws back her long curly hair. "Who's in favor of carrying on with our current version?"

Ho-wing and Amara immediately raise their hands. I feel their expectant eyes on me, but I don't move.

"Good." Florence nods. "And who's in favor of starting again from scratch and giving the play a chance?" Quentin and she raise their hands. "No abstentions," she adds, seeing that I haven't voted yet.

I sigh. OK, it's going to be a hell of a lot of work, but my gut tells me that this is the only way the play can live up to our ambitions.

Florence's face brightens as I raise my hand. Ho-wing and Amara huff.

"Guys, seriously?" Ho-wing groans. "We're already halfway done. It's not as bad as all that."

"Yeah, but it isn't good either. And our reputation's at stake," says Quentin. "Last year's play set the bar really high."

"So we won't measure up either way," mumbles Amara.

"What kind of attitude is that?" Florence leans forward. "We're going to rock this. And Mr. Acevedo has agreed that we can push the deadline for the final text back to after the Easter holidays."

"After Easter?" Ho-wing's eyes open wide. "But that's . . ."

"A bit over eight weeks, yes."

"Have you forgotten that we've also got A levels to study for?"

Florence shakes her head. "I have not. But there are five of us. We can do this."

The ensuing silence makes me anxious. Because there's something else I should say. I clear my throat, and the sound is unbearably loud. "Erm, how does it work?" Immediately, I regret having spoken as the others look at me. I see a hint of panic in Florence's eyes as I keep on. "Is it OK to audition if you're working on the script too?"

"You want to audition?" God, she sounds despairing. "Sinclair, please don't do this to me . . ."

"No, it was just a thought." A thought that had taken on very real shape in my mind in the last few days. Not because I'm desperate to get up there on that stage, but because it could be a way to spend time with Tori. Without that bastard Val. Maybe then she'd realize that true friends support you unconditionally in the things you like doing.

Florence sags slightly in her chair. "If you want to audition, you'd better say so right now. Then I can find a replacement."

"No, I . . . I wouldn't go for more than a bit part," I assure her. "But I'd like to have a go. If that's OK."

The others look around and shrug.

"I don't see why it wouldn't be OK," says Quentin. "You'd better ask Mr. Acevedo."

"Yeah." I need to do that anyway to ask him for the lines for the audition. "I think I will. But either way, I'll keep writing with you."

I can see real despair in Florence's eyes. "Or maybe we should keep our current version and just really focus on the beginning?"

Ho-wing's face brightens.

"No." I shake my head. "We can do this. Truly. Amara and I don't have A levels this year, so we can take on a load of the work, can't we?"

To my surprise, Amara nods.

"It'll work out," I insist.

"OK, thank you," Florence says. She's looking a bit more confident now.

"I think it would be better to wait for the cast anyway," says Quentin. "Maybe we can just sketch out the scenes and let the others improvise the exact words. That'll make the play more natural, and we can be certain of creating something totally unique. My sister's lent me her script from the play three years ago. I'm afraid Lowell was very inspired by it. Word for word, sometimes."

Florence gasps. "No way?"

"I can send it to you." Quentin shrugs his shoulders.

"OK, that is totally rubbish," Ho-wing admits.

"It's *Romeo and Juliet*," says Amara. "We're not exactly reinventing the wheel here."

"Of course not, but just doing the same old, same old isn't the point either."

"Right, Quen." Florence looks at each of us. "OK, so are we agreed that we're starting again?"

I nod. Quentin nods. Amara and Ho-wing eventually do too.

"Then let's get going." Florence pulls over her laptop. "Verona, here we come."

6

TORI

I haven't seen Val since the dinner with his family. I didn't go to bed—when we got home, I sat staring at my phone, waiting for him to text, but he didn't. I didn't even hear from him once I got back to school on Sunday evening. It wasn't until Monday, after I'd got a script from Mr. Acevedo for the auditions and was rehearsing in my room, that Val wanted to know if we could see each other. That was the day before yesterday, and this morning I told him I'm going to audition after classes today. I hadn't been expecting him to show up, despite what he'd said. I'd taken his suggestion as a joke.

It wasn't a joke. Val and his pals have made themselves at home along the back rows of the school theater in the north wing. Their laughter is muffled by the dark-red velvet on the old seats. I'm not here often, but the theater has an almost magical fascination for me. The light is dim, and the rows of seats drop down toward the semicircular stage. Memories of previous years' performances before the summer holidays come flooding back. I watched most of them sitting somewhere near Sinclair and Olive, eyes riveted to the stage. Sinclair was generally as entranced as I was, and sometimes, after the shows, we'd reenact our favorite scenes. Nothing serious, just for fun. Now everything's weird between Sinclair and me, and Olive's not speaking to me either.

My palms are sweaty as I step up a few rows from the entrance. Mr. Acevedo's down below, walking to and fro between various groups of pupils.

I stop as I spot him. Sinclair's sitting down there. He's got his back to me but I'm sure it's him. And sitting next to him in the front row is Eleanor. She's saying something, and her long dark hair looks so silky as she tosses it back over her shoulder, laughing. It's not fair. She's the perfect Juliet, everyone knows. But that's not why I can't take my eyes off her.

I didn't know Sinclair would be here. I don't see anyone else from the scriptwriting club, but maybe Florence and the others are backstage somewhere.

The warm light falls from one side onto Sinclair's face as he lifts his head. Like he felt my presence in some magical way, and shit, he's gorgeous. His blond curls flop into his face in the most ridiculously casual way. I don't know what it is, but the look he gives me from down there does something to me. He leans his hands on the armrests, but just before he has a chance to stand up, I hear my name.

"Hey." I jump as Val clicks his fingers. "Over here."

I look to the side. Does he really think I hadn't noticed him and his pals? They're way too loud for that.

"Really, Valentine, if you please." Mr. Acevedo's voice rings up to us as he points toward Val's feet on the back of the seat in front of him. "Furthermore, anybody who is not genuinely intending to audition may now leave the theater."

Val rolls his eyes as he swings his feet down. He beckons me over, and my treacherous body starts to move. "We're just trying to psych ourselves up to it, sir," he declares. "And it'll be good for a laugh," he adds, just quietly enough that Mr. Acevedo can't hear him. I suddenly wonder what I'm doing. Val shoves Neil off the seat beside him so that I can sit down. I guess I should be pleased, but the truth is that my stomach is now grumbling more nervously than ever. I shove the slip of paper with my lines on it into the back pocket of my trousers and squeeze past Val's friends.

"Hi." Val leans over and kisses me, almost before I've sat down. He puts his arm around my shoulders as I sink deeper into the plush upholstery. "You OK?"

He doesn't seem to have any plans to discuss the evening with his family. Not in front of his pals at least. I'm sure we'll talk about it later, in peace.

I nod. Sinclair turns back to face the front. Maybe it's better if I can't see his face.

"Yeah, fine." I gulp. *Relax.*

"He auditioning too?" Val's voice sounds mocking as he points down toward Sinclair.

"I don't know. He's in the scriptwriting club."

"Fancy." Why does Val sound so arsey? And why aren't I saying anything? "Well, then, I guess we'll know who we get to thank for this freak show."

Stop it. He has to stop it.

A few fifth-formers slip through the door and sit in the rows in front of us. Mr. Acevedo glances at his watch. "Good." His voice fills the theater, making the conversations ebb away. "Let's get started. It's nice to see so many of you. As you know, you're here to audition for a brand-new play entitled *Romeo and Juliet*." There are a few nervous giggles, and Val snorts scornfully.

"Freak show," Neil repeats, on the other side of Val, under his breath. Val just nods. His fingers are drumming restlessly on my left shoulder. I'd prefer it if he took his hand away, but I don't want to be difficult. Or to reject him in front of his friends. Either way, it would just cause trouble.

"There are sixteen parts to fill besides the principal roles, and they are no less important than those of Juliet and her Romeo," Mr. Acevedo continues. "I don't want you to be thinking about who you want to play when you get up on this stage in a little while. Show me something of yourselves. In this place, you can be anything you like. This theater is a safe space in which nobody will judge you. That is very important to me."

My face flushes as Mr. Acevedo's eyes wander up to the back rows. Val juts out his chin challengingly as he looks at him. The moment Mr. Acevedo turns away again, he puts his feet back up on the seat. I want to say something, but I don't dare.

"So let's get started. Who would like to go first?"

"Man, she's up herself," Val murmurs as Eleanor Attenborough stands up after a brief hesitation. "Always has to steal the limelight."

I want to say something like "Isn't that the point of an audition? To be in the limelight?" but my throat is too dry. So I just sit there, watching my self-confidence dissolve into thin air as Eleanor takes to the stage. She's a huge talent, not that that's any surprise. She's so good that she was in last year's performance too, even though she was only in the lower sixth. Val just fake-yawns disrespectfully as everyone else applauds after Eleanor's scene. I don't clap, which leaves me feeling like the world's worst feminist. Sinclair's spent the whole time devouring Eleanor with his eyes, and now he's applauding enthusiastically. Mr. Acevedo makes conspicuous notes, as if he didn't know he'd found his Juliet long ago.

The next hour passes me by like a film. One by one, people audition, and everyone's so good it scares me. Val and his pals make their unnecessary remarks, and with every one of them, I lose a wee bit more of the courage to stand up and go down there onto that stage. I go hot and cold just thinking about it. I should have sat with Sinclair. He keeps looking up to us each time Mr. Acevedo asks who'd like to go next.

My heart lurches as Sinclair gets up when Joshua from the fifth form leaves the stage. Does he need the loo? But Sinclair doesn't climb the stairs to the exit; he takes to the stage. What's he doing?

Val seems to be asking the same question. He straightens up a little. "Uh, guys, this is getting interesting," he says as Sinclair approaches center stage. His face is a smooth mask, presumably meant to hide how nervous he is just now. I can see through it, though, even from this distance. His shoulders are tense, and he looks at his feet.

Sinclair pulls a folded slip from his pocket, unfolds it, and . . .

does nothing. He just stands there in silence. Mr. Acevedo watches him and waits. "Start whenever you're ready," he says.

Sinclair nods. I see his Adam's apple jump nervously.

"That guy's such a clown," somebody mumbles.

I've lost all feeling.

I can't say what I'm afraid of. Of Sinclair embarrassing himself? Of Val and the others laughing at him and making him feel awful? God, it's horrible. Did he even prepare for this audition, or was it just a spur-of-the-moment thing to impress Eleanor?

Everyone else in the front row is whispering to each other now. Sinclair shuts his eyes. And then the room falls silent.

When Sinclair starts to act, I forget everything. Because I had no idea he had such a presence, could be so incredibly captivating. It must be the bloody Aquarius in him. I should have known. He's an air sign: He belongs on the stage. Why didn't I think of that before?

The whole auditorium is shocked by how good he is. I can feel it. And Sinclair can feel it too. His voice grows firmer, his gestures grow larger. Mr. Acevedo is holding his pen in one hand, not moving.

Sinclair's still holding the paper with his lines, but after a while, he screws it up and starts improvising. I get goose bumps. Where did he learn to do this? And why is my face glowing as he speaks these lines and looks up into the audience? In my direction. My heart's thumping in my throat. I feel dizzy, and I'm seriously glad I'm sitting down.

A spotlight shines on Sinclair's face, and he puts his hand to his hair, smooths back his curls. Everyone can see him because he's made to be noticed. Help.

Val's not speaking now. He's sitting beside me, and I can feel how edgy he is. I don't care, and when Sinclair's finished, I join everyone else in thunderous applause. It costs me a huge effort not to jump to my feet.

Sinclair's chest is rising more rapidly as he looks out. It almost seems like he's only just coming back to reality now. He looks kind of surprised at himself.

"Thank you, Charles. That was . . . that was very good," says Mr. Acevedo as the applause dies away. He writes something down and clicks his pen. "Very nice. So . . . is there anybody else?"

Sinclair mumbles, "Thank you," and leaves the stage. My stomach ties itself in knots as Eleanor taps happily on the seat beside her. She immediately leans over to Sinclair, almost before he's sitting next to her again, and whispers something to him.

"Nobody else?" I jump as Mr. Acevedo, who's sitting in the front row, glances around over his shoulder. "This is your last chance."

I feel the velvet upholstery under my clammy fingers and Val's heavy arm on my shoulders. I can't get up. I just can't, however much I want to. I'm almost sure my knees would give way if I tried to now.

"Tori." It's Sinclair's voice cutting through the hush. He's stood up again, and everyone turns toward him. "You wanted to, didn't you?"

My blood runs cold, and a second later, I'm flushed hot.

Shit. What's he up to? Does he think he's doing me a favor? If so, he's very much mistaken.

"Victoria?" Mr. Acevedo looks up. "Last chance."

Val gives a mirthless laugh. My face is burning.

Say something. Anything.

"No, I . . . it's OK."

Sinclair's staring at me; Mr. Acevedo hesitates. A few seconds pass, my heart is racing. I don't speak, just shake my head slightly. Then Mr. Acevedo turns away again and claps his hands.

"Good! Well, that's that, then. Thank you all for auditioning, so many of you. I'll be announcing the final cast shortly, so you can wait here until then."

The first people stand up. Voices grow louder. There's nothing but roaring in my head. Sinclair's still looking in my direction.

"Tori?"

"Hm?" I jump.

Val's stood up. "Are you coming or not?" he asks.

"Yeah, sure." My heart is thumping the heavy beat of overwhelm as I follow Val and his friends out of the gloomy theater. The last of the daylight is falling through the foyer windows, but that's not why the last hour and a half feels like a dream that I'm only slowly waking up from.

"Sorry, I . . . I think I'll just wait here a moment," I say and stop still. Val's a little way ahead and turns back toward me. "I wanted to ask Mr. Acevedo something."

He eyes me suspiciously. "OK. I've got training soon. See you later."

"Yeah, have fun." I smile and watch Val follow his friends. I don't know why I said that. I haven't the least intention of asking Mr. Acevedo anything.

"Hey." I whirl around as I feel a touch on my arm and find myself looking straight into my best friend's blue eyes. The urge to shake off Sinclair's hand washes over me, almost irresistibly.

"What?" I snap at him. Sinclair freezes. He looks surprised by my grumpiness. I guess I should say something about his audition. Tell him it was great. Because it was. Amazing, even. But I can't get a word out.

"What was all that about?" he asks slowly.

I force myself to breathe deeply. "I don't know what you mean."

"Tori, you wanted to audition," he says, like I hadn't known that. *Oh, yeah, so I did. Almost forgot. Thanks for reminding me, pal.* It's not like I don't know I wimped out. And it doesn't feel great, but it's too late now. So what can I do?

"Yeah, I changed my mind." I turn away, but Sinclair's holding me tight. My stomach lurches.

"Tori," he growls. "Did he make some dumb remark?"

"No!" I say. "Do you really think I'm that easily influenced? I can make my own bloody decisions."

Sinclair takes his hand away. It feels almost like someone pulled the ground out from beneath my feet. "But . . . why?" he asks quietly.

"I didn't want to in the end. Doesn't matter. I don't have time this year anyway."

Sinclair doesn't reply. He spares me the humiliation of further questions. Because that's a downright lie. I've got classes and garden duty and library work, the book blog, Bookstagram, and TikTok, but I don't play an instrument, and I'm not on any of the sports teams. And Sinclair knows that. He knows my timetable by heart. Like I do his. So he knows I'd have time for the play if it was important enough to me. But it isn't. End of story.

He opens his mouth, and because attack is the best form of defense, I cut him off. "Why did you even audition anyway?"

Sinclair runs a hand awkwardly through his hair. "I, er . . ." His eyes go past me. I wouldn't have to look to know who he's staring at. But I do anyway. Why the hell? Seems like I enjoy torturing myself. Eleanor is standing with her friends, apparently very deep in conversation. Expansive hand movements, bright laughter. A Capulet laugh, there's no doubting that.

"I see." I look back to Sinclair. "You were good. Maybe it'll work out."

"You could ask Mr. Acevedo if he might still let you—"

"Exactly which part of *I changed my mind* didn't you understand?" I interrupt. "It's got nothing to do with Val!"

"Oh, no?" Sinclair glares at me. "So why do you feel under attack the moment I even mention him?"

"I don't feel under attack."

"Yes, you do."

I laugh unhappily. "Who do you think you are anyway?"

"Someone who knows you." There's a pleading tone in Sinclair's voice now. He takes a step toward me. "Shit, Tori, it's obvious. You've changed since you've been hanging around with Val and his gang."

I don't want to have this conversation. Especially not as there's a little voice in my head screaming at me that Sinclair's right. But he has no idea. And what does he even want anyway? He should just be happy that it looks like he's about to be spending heaps of time with Eleanor. Without me. That's what he wants, after all.

"Yeah, surprise, people change," I hiss. "Don't have to explain that to you, do I?"

Sinclair narrows his eyes to slits. "What do you mean by that?"

"That I'm not the one who randomly turns up at auditions when he's never acted in his life before."

Sinclair eyes me sharply. "At least I'm not giving up on my dreams because some wanker laughed at them."

I force myself to keep my voice down. "Are you jealous because I'm spending so much time with him?"

He laughs. "You know what? You can do one. Seriously, Tori, I'm not the one running around after bawbags, yelling at my friends when they're worried about me."

"Oh, no?" I retort, totally overwhelmed. "What's all this with Eleanor, then? And anyway, I'm not running around after Val, because unlike you, I'm at least being noticed, as you recently remarked so correctly."

What the hell? I ask myself the second I've said the words.

Sinclair looks at me. Disbelieving at first, then full of disappointment. He's seen through me, and I hate myself for that, but instead of admitting to it, I had to go and hurt him back just so he'd finally shut up.

Looks like I've succeeded.

He opens his mouth, as though he wants to say something else, but then he just snorts disdainfully and shakes his head.

"Mr. Acevedo's announcing the cast," someone calls.

Sinclair turns away without looking at me again.

I should go. I really should just get out of here, but it's like the theater doorway is magically drawing me in. So I follow everyone else but stop near the door. Sinclair's already gone down. I want to run to him and tell him I didn't mean it. That I said things I wish I could take back, but now it's too late. And let's be honest, if there hadn't been the tiniest scrap of truth in them, I wouldn't have had the desperate urge to say those words.

Does that make it any better? Hardly . . .

SINCLAIR

This is the thing: If I feel unfairly treated and I'm pure raging, I can't keep discussing things; I just want to cry. That's how it is. I lose every last scrap of self-control. It's shit, and I have no choice but to go back down the stairs, working at keeping my cool. Because I can't be certain whether Tori actually left or is coming back into the theater as Mr. Acevedo announces the cast.

I can't stand conflict. No, worse than that: I hate it. Seriously. There's nothing worse. Especially when it's Tori I'm telling things I don't mean. And the problem with knowing someone so well is being perfectly aware that she feels the same. I saw it in Tori's eyes, even while she was hurling insults at me. The instant regret.

All I can do is force myself to stop thinking about it as I come to a stop down near the stage. I don't even hear Mr. Acevedo's first few sentences. My head is full of rage at that fucker Valentine who's making Tori go against her own wishes and principles. I don't get it. If you love someone, you should want the best for her or him. And either Val really is as empty as he seems or he's deliberately putting her down. I don't know which would be worse. The latter, I guess, because he does it in this creepy way where he persuades her it's what she actually wants. But it isn't. I know that. I saw the light in her eyes when she talked about the theater and this opportunity. God, she was the whole reason I came here. But no, Valentine had to go and sit there with her and fuck everything up.

Fifth-former Ismail cheers, which makes me jump, and his friends crowd around him. I'm guessing he got picked for Lord Montague, because Mr. Acevedo goes on to say that Heather in the upper sixth will be the lady. This is followed by Friar Laurence, Tybalt, the Apothecary, Paris . . . I glance up at the door, and Tori is actually there, arms crossed. She looks at me, and I instantly tear my eyes away.

Unlike you, I'm at least being noticed.

She can get tae fuck.

Besides, Eleanor does notice me. Not that I'm reading anything into that. She's cool and pretty sound. She seemed genuinely friendly and pleased for me after my audition just now. But Tori always has to go and make something of the whole shitshow with her—which is entirely my own fault, seeing as I was the one who mentioned Ellie's name last time. Obviously, I wasn't talking about her on the night of the New Year Ball. And obviously she isn't the person I want to kiss. Tori knows that. Doesn't she?

I jump as Mr. Acevedo speaks again. "Juliet's nurse will be played by . . ." He pauses for a moment here because he's a sadist. Then he looks up from his notebook. ". . . Grace Whitmore."

Grace squeals quietly and actually hops up and down with excitement. I have to smile. She deserves it. If it weren't for Eleanor, I'm pretty sure she'd have been Juliet. But we've got next year's play to look forward to, when our form will get to shine in the main roles. This year, the stage belongs to the upper sixth.

To Grace's joy, Mr. Acevedo announces Gideon as Benvolio. Louis Thompson in the upper sixth is Mercutio, causing some obvious confusion. In my mind, it had long been settled that he and Eleanor would be the leads. Mr. Acevedo seems to see things differently though. It's all up to him. And this means that only the two protagonists are yet to be cast. The realization hits me unexpectedly hard.

Damn. I might only have auditioned for Tori's sake, but I was surprised by how much I enjoyed being on stage earlier. I'd never have expected to get such an adrenaline rush standing up there, knowing everyone's listening to me. That it has an effect on them if I drop all my inhibitions and turn myself inside out. And that it does something to *me* too. Because it did. Hey-ho. Maybe at least Mr. Acevedo will let me be one of the servants or some other walk-on role. And I'll try again next year.

"So we come to the two main roles," says Mr. Acevedo. There's a solemn note in his voice. "I can't exactly say that this was a difficult decision. So let's make it quick and painless." Eleanor clenches her fists tightly, but God knows whose name will be called if it isn't hers. "Our Juliet will be played by Eleanor Attenborough. Congratulations, Eleanor. You gave me goose bumps."

The relief escapes Eleanor in a little scream of joy. Two seconds later, she's got herself back under control and is smiling her unapproachable Juliet-smile. I'm smiling too, and the others clap. She'll rock this, no question. "And now, there's only one role remaining," Mr. Acevedo declares. "Romeo Montague: Charles Sinclair."

I'm all set to clap again when I realize that everyone's eyes are suddenly fixed on me. And then Mr. Acevedo's words make it to my brain.

Hold on . . .

HOLD ON.

I can pretty much feel every scrap of color draining from my face.

I misheard. I misheard, didn't I?

"Yes, Charles, really you," says Mr. Acevedo, which must mean that the shock is written on my face. "Your audition was compelling. You were genuine, and you've got an incredible stage presence. And I'm sick of all these neat-and-tidy Romeos. Your interpretation was interesting. You've got personality. It'll be great. We'll let your hair grow a little for a more rakish touch. I'll clear that with your mother." He sounds genuinely thrilled, but I'm not sure if he knows what he's letting himself in for. I've got no idea how to act. I can't do a thing. Not a thing. Seriously. Shit, I wanted to play a bloody tree or something, to be close to Tori, not the fucking lead role. Romeo? Me? This has to be a joke . . .

Mr. Acevedo is now reassuring the people left over and casting them as servants, townspeople, and musicians. I still can't move.

I don't go over to him until he's explained when the rehearsals start, dismissed us, and packed his notebook into his leather satchel.

"Sir, I . . ." My voice is hoarse. He lifts his head. "I don't know if I can do this. Play Romeo, I mean . . . I've got no experience at all."

Mr. Acevedo waves this away. "Nonsense. You have talent, and we'll winkle the rest out of you by the time of the performance, you'll see."

"I'm in the scriptwriting club," I manage to say.

"Yes, that's true." He eyes me, head on one side. "Your fellow scribes won't like this, but you're one of us now. I'm sure they can find someone to stand in for you. They must see that we need the best for this play. And that includes you, make no bones about it. Eleanor and you, you'll make a breathtaking couple." He claps his hands. "And now it's time to celebrate a little. Not many actors get the chance to play a great role like Romeo."

Yeah, I get that. It's pretty much the biggest role I can imagine. And nothing that a total beginner like me should be attempting. Shakespeare would be turning in his grave if he got wind of this.

"Sinclair!" Eleanor hugs me. "Congrats, this is going to be so cool."

Help, she's genuinely pleased. She doesn't look at all fazed that it's me playing Romeo and not Louis in her form. Or Terry, who got stuck with Tybalt.

"Thanks," I mumble. "Congratulations to you too."

She smiles. "We've got this, OK? Don't worry about the fact that you haven't acted before."

I force a confident smile. To my surprise, Louis gives me a friendly clap on the shoulder. "Well done, mate." He sounds unexpectedly cheerful.

"Sorry," I say, on instinct. Louis might hang around with Valentine Ward sometimes, but he's actually all right. I can respect him. Unlike Valentine. "I thought you'd be Romeo. I didn't want—"

"Hey, relax," he says cheerily. "To be honest, so did I, but Mr. Acevedo's the boss. There's some kind of chemistry between you and El, no denying it. And Mercutio's a cooler role, to be fair."

I make an effort to smile, but the corners of my mouth are aching.

"And we get to fight a duel! Awesome, huh?"

I nod, but not very enthusiastically. Louis is in the fencing club. And so's Terry, thinking about it. I have to fight him too, don't I? Fuck, I've forgotten half this stupid play already. All I know is that it doesn't turn out too well for me. How ironic.

I congratulate Grace and Gideon, who are looking really happy and excited. I honestly wish I felt that way too. But all I feel is panic. Which tips slowly over into defiance as I look over the rows of seats straight into Tori's incredulous face as she shakes her head, turns, and leaves.

7

TORI

There are few aspects of boarding-school life I hate as much as the morning run, but table duty definitely comes close. It must be some kind of bad joke that I'm paired with Olive of all people to get to the dining room ahead of everyone else this week and set the tables for our year group. And sadly, at breakfast time, that doesn't mean you're let off the morning run; you just have twenty minutes less for a shower and getting dressed.

Olive simply nods as I mumble hello and proceeds to ignore me. I can't stand it, and the worst part of this whole thing is that I don't understand how things got like this between me and her.

I can positively feel Olive's anger. She's putting the cups and plates down on the long tables with more of a slam than necessary. Normally, we'd be chatting and working so slowly that Joseph would have to yell from the kitchen several times for us to get on with it, but today it's the exact opposite. We set the tables in silence and collect the bread baskets, teapots, and coffee jugs from the kitchen. Olive stares at the floor every time we come close.

I'm not totally certain, but it looks like she's been crying.

"Is everything OK?" I ask quietly, once we've finished, and Olive stops by the table for a moment.

She doesn't answer, just sighs barely audibly. I see her roll her eyes in irritation, and it's a stomach punch.

"Livy," I plead.

"I've got nothing to say to you, Tori."

"Yes, you do. Don't lie to me, Olive. Please. Can we just talk about whatever the problem is?"

"There's no problem."

"Do you really not care?" I can't help raising my voice. "About anything? Your friends, your classes . . . me?"

Olive's face is composed, and the look in her green eyes is ice-cold. "Well, no, if you really want to know, no . . . I guess I don't."

Her words land like a blow to my heart, but I try not to let that show.

"Why would you say a thing like that?" I whisper.

"Because it's the truth," she replies, and her voice breaks on the last word. Because she's lying. Because I've known Olive Henderson for more than six years now, and I know, for reasons that make absolutely no sense to me, she always thinks she has to sort everything out for herself. She's not doing well, anyone can see she's not, but instead of letting anyone help her, she's pushing away everyone who means anything to her.

Or else I'm totally wrong about Olive. About our friendship. I don't know which idea is more painful.

For a moment, we stand there motionless, facing each other. Then Olive turns away as people start to walk into the dining room.

Only a few weeks ago, I'd have had no hesitation about following my friend. This time, it takes a few seconds for my legs to start moving as if of their own accord. I don't know what to say to Olive. She just made it utterly clear that she doesn't want to talk to me, but I can't just stand there and act like nothing happened.

I dodge groups of juniors, but by the time I reach the double doors, it's like Olive's vanished off the face of the earth. Instead, I run slap into Val.

"Hey." He drops back behind his friends and comes over to me. "Forgotten something?"

"What?" I mumble, standing still, as I really can't see Olive anywhere in the old cloisters. "Sorry, no, I . . . Doesn't matter."

"You look good today," Val says, right out of the blue.

I freeze. I'm waiting for him to add something to his compliment like *Joke, ha-ha, you should see your face*, but nothing of the kind happens.

"Thank you," I say, so hesitantly that it almost sounds like a question.

"Wow, I guess accepting compliments isn't your strong point." Val laughs. "We'll have to practice that." He puts an arm around me and pulls me into the dining room. My smile is somewhat forced. "So what's up?"

"Nothing." I get some words out at last. "I was on table duty."

"Pain in the arse." He groans.

"How was training yesterday?" I ask.

"Yeah, good. What are you doing at the weekend? We'll be down in the Dungeon on Friday night. Want to come?"

He looks so expectantly at me that I nod, even though the upper sixth's party cellar is just about the last place on earth I'd voluntarily spend time. "Sure," I say anyway, because I don't want to disappoint Val. I guess I can manage an hour or so with him in the school's old undercroft before crawling back to bed.

"Perfect. I'll message you." He lets me go. "How did the auditions turn out, by the way? Louis and Eleanor?"

Val doesn't know? How is that even possible, given the way gossip runs through this school like wildfire? But sure, he was at rugby training yesterday evening. Maybe he really hasn't heard. I didn't see him anywhere at dinner last night.

He turns to face me. "Someone else get it? I'd laugh if it was someone from the lower sixth instead of Eleanor."

"No, she got the part," I say colorlessly.

"And Romeo?"

I wish I could just shut my eyes and be somewhere else. "Sinclair."

This is ridiculous.

"Sinclair?" Val repeats incredulously. Then he bursts into unkind laughter. "Shit, they're two of a kind. Isn't he into her?"

Val's question feels like someone's slipped a very sharp blade between my ribs and is slowly twisting it. I shrug brusquely. "No idea."

"Ha. Well, maybe he'll leave you alone now," Val says.

I feel kind of sick. If only he knew that that's exactly what I'm worried about. My best pal and the woman he's secretly smitten with, playing the most famous lovers in history. They'll get to spend heaps of time together in the next few months.

Get to know each other, rehearse together . . . Shit, they're going to kiss. My blood runs cold. Sinclair's going to kiss Eleanor Attenborough, after which I'll have to applaud with the rest of the school.

"So, are you glad you didn't embarrass yourself by auditioning?"

I try not to flinch. Like I hadn't spent half the night lying awake and imagining how the afternoon would have turned out if I'd just found the guts to get up on the stage. I might not have got Juliet, but I would have had a chance at the Nurse at least, or Lady Capulet. But no, now I'm nothing at all, except frustrated and pissed off with Eleanor and Sinclair. And myself. And—if I'm honest—maybe a bit with Val too. If it had been me, I'm pretty sure I'd have encouraged him to do what he wanted to, not convinced him that he wasn't good enough anyway.

"Don't you think I'd have had a chance?" I ask.

Val looks at me. "Well, you've got no acting experience, have you?"

I shrug. "Neither has Sinclair."

"Exactly. He's going to make such a tit of himself. No way you could want the same thing."

I gulp. What makes him think he knows what I want and don't want?

"You'll thank me one day," he declares, giving me a friendly slap on the shoulder as he turns away. "At least by the summer holidays, by the time the whole school's laughing at that play."

SINCLAIR

There actually are a few people at this school who are less happy than I am that I've got this stupid leading role. Hard to imagine, but it's true. Next time the scriptwriting club meets, the air is so thick you could cut it with one of the blunt butter knives from the dining room. Florence looks jittery, while Amara, Quentin, and Ho-wing are more despairing.

"Romeo, for fuck's sake . . . I don't know how you think this is going to work," Ho-wing repeats. "By the end, there'll be a rehearsal every day."

"Yeah, by the end," I say. "But the script will be finished by then, and we won't have as much to do."

"Sinclair, I think you're underestimating this," Florence suggests. "There are only five of us, and we're so late with the script. Any other year, the whole thing would have been finished for ages by now."

"We can write in parallel to the rehearsals," I suggest. "That could actually work out really well—if I'm one of the actors while we're working on the text, it'll make everything way more natural."

"It'll be total chaos," says Amara.

"I've been thinking, and I reckon we have to split the roles." Florence looks at me.

"Split them?" I echo. "What do you mean?"

"There's a reason for having the drama club and the scriptwriting team separate. I don't think it's a good idea to mix the two."

"Meaning?"

"I think you have to decide which you want to do."

She's serious. I open my mouth but I can't speak.

"Unless you disagree?" Florence turns to Amara, Quentin, and Ho-wing—who, obviously, stab me in the back. They shake their heads.

"That's not fair," I blurt. "You said it wouldn't be a problem if I—"

"If you got a *bit part*, yeah," Quentin interrupts. "But we had no idea that Mr. Acevedo would go and make you Romeo."

I drop both elbows to my knees, shut my eyes, and massage the bridge of my nose. I'd love to say something like *You'll never manage this without me*, but sadly, I'm not that self-deluded. I know that Florence is probably right. That there are presumably reasons why the main cast don't work on the script and vice versa.

"Anyway, you're in the lower sixth." Florence is sounding a bit more conciliatory now. "You can be involved in scriptwriting again next year."

Or I could have a part next year instead. Maybe that would be more sensible anyway. Eleanor, Louis, and the others in the upper sixth didn't make me feel like I was robbing them of anything, but I still feel guilty. Besides, it would probably be less problematic because then I wouldn't be playing opposite Eleanor. It would be Tori—because if there's one thing I'm certain of, it's that I'm not going to stand by and watch her put herself down like that and not audition. Even I managed to do it, and I was totally unprepared.

So objectively, it would be better for all concerned if I went to Mr. Acevedo and gave up the role. But part of me is already addicted to the kick I got on the stage on Wednesday afternoon. I'd never experienced anything like it. It was madness, and I want to feel it again. I want to forget everything around me, and I want to feel that light. I'm desperate for it.

The closest comparison I can find to it is when I ride out on Jubilee or another of the school horses and gallop along that straight section of the path through the little clearing in the woods. Reins loose, slightly out of the saddle to reduce the weight. Speed, tunnel vision, going with the flow, and then the adrenaline. We're flying. I had no idea you could feel anything like that on a ratty old school theater stage.

"Sinclair, it's OK." I jump and look up. Right into Florence's face. "You have to do what feels best to you."

I sigh. "And how will the four of you manage?"

She shrugs her shoulders. "We'll find someone else who wants to join in."

"You could ask Tori," I say, without thinking.

Florence frowns in confusion. "Does she write?"

"No, but she reads a lot."

"Yeah, mainly trash if her videos are anything to go by," murmurs Quentin. He looks away hastily as I glare sharply at him.

"Young adult romance novels are not trash," I say, because Tori's answer to that kind of provocation is deeply ingrained in me now.

"You mean dirty books for horny teenage girls to get off on," Quentin laughs quietly. "Not that she needs them now that Ward's looking after that for her."

He freezes as I leap up off my chair and instinctively clench both fists. "Take that back." I step threateningly toward him, which does the trick. Quentin raises his hands in self-defense.

"Whoa, easy, it was just a joke."

"Hey," Florence's voice cuts through the silence that follows. Amara tugs me down by the sleeve while Ho-wing just rolls his eyes. "Pull yourselves together."

"Just shut it, OK?" I growl in Quentin's direction, avoiding Amara's warning expression.

Quentin exhales, barely audibly, shaking his head as if to say *What's the fuss about? True, isn't it?* My blood is boiling as I reluctantly sit down. I still want to deck him, even though I know my reaction is way over the top—and that Quentin might even be right. About Tori and Val, that is. The rest was total bullshit. But maybe Tori is actually reading less now because she's with Val and doing . . . Fuck, I don't want to think about it.

"Can we all just calm down now, please?" Florence looks from Quentin to me. I stare at the old floorboards of the school library in silence.

"And let's face it, *Romeo and Juliet* is kind of trashy too, if you look at it like that," Amara murmurs. "Except there's no happy ending."

"*Romeo and Juliet*'s a classic," Quentin immediately contradicts Amara, and she rolls her eyes at him.

"So will Colleen Hoover's books be in a few years' time."

"Guys, seriously," Florence cuts in. "If you," she looks at Quentin, "can't ditch your medieval ideas of literature, then you might as well have walked out with Lowell. And I'm begging you from the bottom of my heart to ditch them, because we can't lose another team member now."

Quentin crosses his arms and leans back, but he's looking mildly guilty. Florence turns to me. I can see in her eyes that she would actually prefer it if I stayed and wouldn't be doing this if it wasn't necessary. "Do you think Tori would be interested?" There's a hint of hope in her voice. "If she reads a lot, she'll have a good sense of storytelling and an ear for language."

"You should ask her at any rate," I say. "I'm sure she'd do a good job."

I might be pissed off with Tori, but I'm not a bad friend. I know she might enjoy this. And enjoy doing something just for herself. Without that jerk Val making her give up her dreams.

"I'll ask her," Florence says, looking at me. "Does this mean we'll have to make do without you from now on?"

I feel four pairs of eyes on me. And then I remember the addictive sensation on the stage. The certainty that I have a talent I'd had no idea about.

I nod slowly.

I guess it does.

TORI

Plot twist: I didn't party with Val and his pals in the Dungeon on Friday night. Around lunchtime, it suddenly hit me that Arthur would be there any moment to pick me and Will up, by which point I didn't have time to tell Val. I hastily packed my weekend bag, and half an hour later, my brother and I were getting into the big dark car. This trip home had been planned for ages, long before

I knew I'd be spending last weekend with my family too, for the dinner at Val's. If I'd remembered sooner, I might have made my excuses and stayed at school, but our driver was on his way over by then, and I don't want to be a bad daughter. Or a bad girlfriend. So as I chat to Arthur, I make a mental note to text Val in a bit.

Arthur is more than just a chauffeur—he's been part of the family for twenty-two years and helps to look after the estate too. I can't imagine life without him—or without Martha, our cook and housekeeper, or Deborah, our old nanny. For as long as Will and I can remember, they've been there, living in estate cottages on the other side of the grounds.

My family home looks like a scaled-down version of Dunbridge Academy, about sixty miles northeast of Ebrington and right on the coast. As always, a warm feeling spreads through me as Arthur turns the car through the wrought-iron gate and up the gravel drive to the front door. It's not late, but it's properly dark now. Golden-yellow light shines out of the windows, and lanterns line the drive.

Will is sitting on the back seat beside me and now looks up from his phone for the first time since we left.

"Is everything OK?" I ask as we pull up and Arthur gets out.

Will freezes. "Yeah. Why shouldn't it be?"

"I just wondered . . ." I begin. "Who were you texting?"

"Nobody," he snaps, undoing his seat belt.

Kit, then. I can only speculate about whether something's up between my brother and his boyfriend—last time I asked, Will didn't want to talk about it. But I haven't seen Kit around at school for a few days.

I don't say anything now, though, because Will's opening his door and getting out. Dad appears to greet us, so I follow his lead.

Arthur opens the boot. "Let me get that, Victoria," he says before I can take my bag from it.

"It's not heavy," I lie, heaving it over my shoulder. The wide strap digs in a bit, reminding me very clearly of the seven books I packed because I couldn't decide what to read this weekend. Even though my room here bears a strong resemblance to the Dunbridge library.

"Hi, Dad," I say as he comes down the last few steps toward me, having greeted Will.

"How was the journey, love?" he asks, taking my bag and giving me a hug. "Let me see you. Is everything OK?"

I hate it when he does that, because it means I'm going to have to work at keeping my face under control. Smile then. Glow. Everything's fine. "Missed you," I mumble, pressing my face into the smooth cotton of his shirt.

"Missed you too, kid," he says, dropping a kiss on the top of my head. Then he lets go. "Come on, inside with you now or you'll freeze."

I turn back. "Thanks for the lift, Arthur."

He smiles. "Nice to have you home."

I glance at Dad in mild confusion—Arthur isn't putting the car away in the garage as he usually does.

"Your mother's still out," Dad says. "Theresa Tomlinson's birthday. She must have lost track of time—she was planning to be back before you arrived."

"Oh, right." I don't say anything else. I'd rather not think about what that means.

"Have you two eaten?" Dad asks as we walk into the house.

"No, not yet," I say. "Aren't we waiting for Mum?"

"I was with a client until just now, but I tried to call her." Dad shrugs. "Martha's getting dinner for seven o'clock."

"I'm not hungry," Will mumbles, slipping off his shoes and coat. He pockets his phone. "And I'm tired. Is it OK if I go straight up to my room?"

Dad hesitates, and I see the disappointment in his eyes. It's rare for us all to sit around the table together as a family, especially since Will and I have been at boarding school, and the evenings when we do mean the world to our parents. I know that as well as my brother does. But then Dad smiles. "Of course. Get some rest. Martha can put something aside for you in case you get hungry later."

"Thanks, Dad," he mumbles, grabbing his bag and vanishing upstairs as fast as he can.

"Is he all right?" Dad asks under his breath as Will's footsteps fade away. "Trouble with Kit?"

I shrug. "I hope not. I couldn't get anything out of him."

"Hm . . ." Dad's silent for a moment. Then he puts my bag at the foot of the wide staircase. "OK. Do you want to freshen up and then we can have dinner on the sofa instead?"

I have to smile. "Only if we can watch *Spider-Man*."

"The Tom Holland version, of course." Dad nods. "Sounds like a plan."

"See you in a bit, then."

Will's door is shut as I cross the upstairs landing. It's only a week since I was last here, but as always, stepping into my childhood bedroom feels like entering a whole new world. It's at least three times the size of my room at Dunbridge, but it feels less like home. I've rarely slept here for more than a few days at a time since the juniors. We spend most of the holidays away. It's ages since I stayed in this room for more than a week. And every time I'm back here, I think what a shame that is. It's dark outside, so I can't see the sea, but when the tall lattice windows are open, I can hear the waves breaking against the cliffs.

I turn away and feel an overwhelming urge just to drop onto my bed. But I resist. Instead, I open my wardrobe, swap my school clothes for leggings and a fluffy jumper, and head back downstairs. Dad's just carrying two plates of lasagna into the sitting room.

"Good?" he asks. My stomach rumbles in approval. "Lord, don't they feed you at that school?" he jokes. "What are we paying all that money for?"

"For the nonfunctioning smart boards," I reply, taking my plate.

Dad grins. "I thought they were working now?"

"They are. I just couldn't think of a better line."

"OK, fine. Eat up, pet."

I can't wait for Dad to start too—it smells way too tasty.

"Charles would be so jealous," Dad says as the film starts. He leans back with his plate on his lap and looks at me. "How is he?"

I almost choke. "Sinclair? Yeah, he's fine, I think."

"He hasn't been here for a long time now."

"He's a busy man." I shove a forkful into my mouth. "He's an actor now too."

"Charles?" Dad sounds astonished. But then he says, "That doesn't actually surprise me. There's something about him."

I nod because that's true.

Dad looks seriously at me. "But are the two of you OK?"

"Dad, don't ask like that. It sounds like we're a couple."

"And you're just friends, I know." He gazes at me with an expression that makes it clear he doesn't believe me, but he's too cool a dad to keep on about it. But past experience has shown me that nobody sees through me as well as Dad does. I don't like that, but I'm eighteen now, and a Leo. I've got a mind of my own.

Considering all that, I don't know why I don't tell him about Valentine and the New Year Ball instead. Probably because I can guess what Dad would think of it. Unlike Mum, he doesn't see Val as the perfect son-in-law. At any rate, he was less pleased than she was that I went to the ball with him and not Sinclair. I imagine that if it weren't for Mum, he wouldn't have quite as much to do with the Wards. But that's just how it is. There are people you can't avoid and can't afford to offend. Keep your friends close and your enemies closer, or something like that.

We eat in silence and watch the film. Will doesn't put in an appearance, and by about halfway through, I can hardly keep my eyes open.

"Go to bed, love." I jump. Dad's smiling at me. "Had another midnight party?"

"No, I just couldn't sleep," I say.

"What were you thinking about?"

"Dunno. Everything, kind of. Sinclair, Val, the play . . ."

It's only when Dad pauses that I realize what I just said. "Valentine Ward? So he's more than just your date to the ball?"

Oops. "Maybe."

"So I did see right at that dinner last weekend?"

Damn it. He saw, of course he did. He's my dad: He sees everything.

"What did you see?" I ask hesitantly.

"That you seemed very friendly," he replies diplomatically.

"Yes, I . . . We've got close lately."

Dad eyes me in silence. "Is he kind to you, pet?" he asks in the end.

"Yes," I say hastily. "Val's great." *Most of the time.* "We can talk." *Sometimes. At least when his pals aren't around.*

"I see," Dad says, not taking his eyes off me.

"I need some sleep," I mumble, standing up. I say goodnight and go upstairs. It's not late, but even so, I drop into bed like a stone once I've done my teeth.

My eyes are burning as I scroll through my phone. My latest BookTok recommendation has gone surprisingly viral. I roll onto my side to read the comments. I've been experimenting with using short dialogues between the characters as a way of sketching out the plot, and it seems to be going down well. I scroll through my For You page for a bit, then switch to WhatsApp. Sinclair's online, but our chat's been dead for days now. And so's mine with Val—and I never did tell him I was coming home for the weekend. He's probably in the Dungeon right now, waiting for me to turn up. I'm about to message him when a text pops in from Florence. I'm frowning as I open it. She's never messaged me outside our year's group chat before.

> **F:** Hi Tori, missed you after class today, and Emma said you'd gone home. Sinclair suggested asking you about the scriptwriting club because we really need new people. Especially now he's dropped out. So yeah, I thought I'd ask if you feel like joining. We'd love to have you.

I read the message three times, but surprisingly, the words don't change. Does that mean Sinclair's not in the scriptwriting club now? So that he and Eleanor Attenborough can rehearse together in peace? And now they want me behind the scenes, tinkering about with their love story? What could possibly be nicer?

I toss my phone aside and bury my face in my hands.

Am I jealous? Is that it? And if I am, of what? I'm dating Valentine. There's no reason for me to feel crap just because my friend might have a chance with the person he fancies. I should be supportive and give him advice on winning Eleanor over. But I can't. All I feel is this grim helplessness when I remember the way everyone clapped for them both. Because Sinclair made such an unusual Romeo and Eleanor's so perfect and self-assured.

Eleanor and Sinclair. My thoughts are toxic, and I want this to stop. Why did he even audition? What even was that? He was dying to work on the script, but suddenly he wants to be on stage himself? Was it just for her sake?

God, it's all so stupid.

I don't know when I nodded off, but at some point, I wake with a start and a head that weighs a ton. The mattress sags with a creak as a body lies down next to me.

"There you are, lovey."

What the . . . ? My tongue feels furry from too little sleep. "Mum?"

"How are you? Is everything OK? I wanted to be back earlier, but it got rather late, so . . ."

I smell the alcohol on her breath, and my stomach ties in knots. My bedside lamp comes on now that I've finally found the switch. I screw up my eyes. "Mum, what's the time?" My voice is husky.

"I've missed you so much, Tori. You and your brother, you're hardly ever here."

"It's only been a week, Mum," I point out. "But we're here now."

"Thank God." She sinks down beside me. "It's horrible without you, the house is too big . . ."

"Charlotte, let her sleep."

I raise my head. Dad's standing in the doorway in his pajamas, and memories wash over me. Dad putting my drunken mother to bed. Quiet, discreet. My younger self standing in the bedroom door, not daring to breathe so that Dad won't notice I can see them.

"I just wanted to say hello," Mum slurs.

I force myself to smile, but my heart is numb.

"Well, you've done that now," says Dad. Mum does actually get up as he comes closer. She's swaying slightly. "And we'll say hello to William in the morning. He was very tired earlier." Dad's eyes meet mine as he leads her out.

I sit on my bed, listening to their fading footsteps. So it wasn't just a one-off last week with the Wards. It's a long time since she's been as drunk as she was just now. At least while Will and I have been here. I hear Dad's muffled voice from their bedroom and don't move.

I wait, the way I've always waited, for Dad to come back to me. With every minute that goes past, the irrational fear grows inside me that this time he might not.

I hold my breath as I hear the floorboards creak. Dad leaves my door ajar as he comes in.

"Are you OK, pet?" His soft voice is heavy with disillusionment. But he still tries to smile, just to reassure me, which finishes me off.

"Yeah," I whisper. And then I ask, even though it's obvious, "She's drinking again?"

"It was Theresa's birthday," says Dad, and it's awful. Codependency. Finding excuses that make it more bearable somehow. The last therapist explained that to us, just before Dad threatened her with divorce and getting custody of us, to make Mum finally go to that clinic. Back then, I hadn't understood it can't work that way. That she has to want it for herself. To dry out. Far away in my idyllic boarding school, it was all too easy to forget that my mother isn't some invincible heroine in shining armor.

I nod in silence. It was naive to think she'd recovered. That things could never get this bad again. There were signs, but I ignored them because otherwise it's unbearable. Dad's evasive answers on the phone, the times he said Mum was still "out." The way she acted at the Wards, the moment I saw her with a glass in hand again.

"Don't you worry, OK?" Dad says. "Sleep well, love."

"You too, Dad," I whisper.

I don't allow myself to cry until he's shut the door behind him.

8

TORI

At breakfast on Saturday morning, we act like nothing happened and I can't stand it. Mum doesn't look as hungover as I'd have expected given her condition last night, which can mean one of two things: Either she's used to it, or she's started the day with the hair of the dog. I don't want to know, because whichever way, it's making me crazy. Because I don't understand. How can she do this to Dad? To him, to Will, to me? And above all, to herself . . .

Of course we don't talk about it. Mum and Dad ask about school, ask after Kit, ask if we want to come to Davos for February half-term, and the thought of a skiing holiday and Mum in all the Swiss après-ski bars gives me stomach cramps. Talking about Val seems like the lesser of two evils, so I let Mum bring the conversation around to him. She's thrilled when I tell her again about him and the ball.

"So are things official between you two now?" she asks, reaching for her coffee cup.

"I think we're in the process of working that out."

Mum smiles. "You make a lovely couple; Veronica says so too."

She shakes her head. "I always thought Charles would be the one, but it's so lovely that you've found someone like Valentine, who's on an equal footing with you."

Will lifts his head.

"On an equal footing?" I repeat slowly. "Because Sinclair's dad's a baker?"

"Of course that's not what I meant."

"What did you mean, then? That he's beneath me, or what?"

"Tori, you're twisting my words. I meant it positively," Mum exclaims. "Charles's a lovely friend, but Valentine is someone who can provide for you, if you see what I mean. I'm thinking about your future."

"I'm sure our daughter will be perfectly capable of providing for herself, Charlotte," Dad says calmly.

"Of course she will, George. But life throws all kinds of things at you that are easier to deal with as a pair. And for families like ours, it's important to have someone you can truly rely on."

Sinclair. Her words bring Sinclair to mind, not Valentine. I suppose that should make me think. Anyway, Dad took her surname—his background wasn't nearly as posh, which didn't stop Mum falling in love with him. Why should it? His career in marketing might not be as fancy as her art gallery, but that doesn't make it any less important. Besides working for his own clients, Dad also does the marketing for Mum's business and Veronica Ward's. Mum would love it if Val took over Veronica's firm one day and I stepped into her or Dad's shoes too, no question. Not that I even know what I want to do at uni just now. If I had to choose between their two fields, I'd be more likely to go for something like online marketing, but really my heart is set on English lit. Still, I'll worry about that later. Not yet.

I can hardly swallow the scrambled egg that Martha's made me. Dad's just asking about our plans for the day when Will's phone rings.

"Sorry," he mumbles and reaches for it. He goes pale as he glances at the display. "Can I leave the table? This is important."

"Of course," Dad says, but he sounds puzzled.

Will doesn't even look at us, just hurries out of the dining room. "Where are you?" I hear him ask, and his voice fades away.

"Kit?" Mum guesses.

"Probably." I shrug my shoulders.

Will doesn't reappear, and once breakfast is over, I go to look for him, feeling uneasy. The drawing room with its huge fireplace, where we welcome guests, is as deserted as our private sitting room. I finally find my brother in the conservatory next to Mum's office and our small library. He's curled up on the sofa under the Ólafsdóttir that Mum bought at auction a while back, with his elbows on his knees. He's holding the phone to his ear with one hand, and he's wiping his face with the other.

"No, I gave Henry the key," I hear him say. I stop in the doorway. "He knows about it. No, he won't say anything, you can trust him. You can just ask him for the key and sleep in my room. Kit, please. It's January. Listen, I'm serious. I'm worried about you. Or shall I send our driver over?"

Will goes quiet. When he speaks again, he's keeping his voice down. "Stop it. I love you, OK? We'll work something out, Boo."

This conversation is clearly not meant for my ears. As I move away, one of the old floorboards creaks. Will's eyes shoot up, but he relaxes a bit when he sees me.

"Sorry," I whisper, but he just gestures for me to wait.

"Call me when it's sorted," he says. "Yeah, really, now. Bye. Love you too."

The silence is unbearably loud as Will lowers the hand that was holding the phone.

"I'm sorry. I didn't mean to listen in."

"No, it's OK."

"Kit?" I ask, unnecessarily. Will nods. "What's happened?"

He gives a long, quiet sigh. I come closer and sit beside him.

"Will . . ."

"His dad," he says, not looking at me. And I understand. The other day, Kit showed up to school after the last rugby match of the season with a black eye. When he's not even on the rugby team.

"Shit," I say quietly.

"Yeah." He gulps. "It is."

"What did his dad do?"

"It's always the same. Things get tense, they argue, and every time he drinks, it escalates." Will's hands are clenched into fists, but he doesn't move. "Then when he's sober again, he's really sorry, apologizes a thousand times, but it doesn't last. Kit's trying to spend as little time at home as possible."

"Where was he last night?" I ask.

"He slept in the old greenhouse." Will laughs mirthlessly. "It must have been freezing. Shit . . . It's so stupid—why didn't he tell me?"

"He probably didn't want you to worry."

"Yeah, that'd be like him."

"So Henry's got the key to your room for him?" I guess.

Will nods. "I had a kind of feeling it would be a good idea for Kit to have somewhere to go in an emergency. Henry was chatting to him the other day, asked if he was OK, and he told him then."

"But they didn't go to Mrs. Sinclair?" I blurt. Will shrugs. "Why not?"

"Kit didn't want to. I dunno . . . What could she do anyway?"

"Call the police?" I wish I could just snatch Will's phone and call them myself.

"No, Tori. It's his decision. I'll talk to him again as soon as I get back. Maybe by then he'll be ready to speak to Mrs. Sinclair."

"Want to head back early?" I ask. "I could tell Mum and Dad I've forgotten an important bit of homework."

"Tori, that's . . ."

"No, seriously."

"I know, but there's no need." He looks at me. "Or do *you* want to go back today?"

My throat tightens a wee bit as I feel Will's eyes rest heavily on me.

I don't want to, because it's nice to spend time at home. But at the same time, it's way easier to ignore certain things there than here.

"D'you think it was just a slipup?" I ask quietly instead of answering Will's question. I don't have to be more specific. He knows what I mean.

"Stop. I can't think about it." Will buries his face in his hands.

When he lifts his head again, he asks quietly, "She came in to you last night, didn't she?"

I nod. "But not to you?"

"No, but I heard your voices."

"It was someone's birthday," I say slowly. Will doesn't nod.

"Last week at the Wards' . . ." he begins, and I shut my eyes.

"Yes," I say, blinking. "But at least she doesn't get like Kit's dad when she drinks."

"That's true."

For a moment, there's silence between us.

"Did Dad say anything?" he asks. "Is she back in therapy?"

"No. I mean . . . I don't know."

"OK." Will glances at me, then he puts his arms around me and hugs me. "Growing up is realizing that your parents are just human beings with problems, I reckon."

"Growing up is shit," I whisper.

"Yeah, definitely."

I rest my head on Will's shoulder.

"Let's go back this afternoon, OK?" he suggests. "I'll talk to Mum and Dad and tell them about Kit."

"Are you sure?"

"Yes. Then they hopefully won't be so disappointed."

"You're right."

"Of course I'm right."

I shut my eyes. There's only just over a year between us, but sometimes it feels like Will's older than me. But maybe that's just the Libra in him, always keeping him so sensible and balanced.

"And in other news?" he asks after a while.

Oh, great. He wants to talk about Sinclair. "What do you mean, other news?"

"Is it true that Charles's going to play Romeo?"

"Yes." I try to pull away a little, but Will holds me close. "Why do you ask?"

"Well, you know, I think I'd be jealous if it were Kit who'd got one of the lead roles with somebody else."

"Yeah, but you and Kit are endgame."

"You and Charles could totally be too."

"Don't keep calling him that."

"Why not? It's his name."

"It feels wrong . . . He's Sinclair, not Charles."

"I saw this TikTok the other day about two best friends who fall in love," Will goes on. "It made me think about you two. Hold on, I'll send it to you."

I pull away from him. "Will, please."

"You just have to tell me once that you genuinely want Valentine and not Charles, and I won't say another word about it."

When I don't answer, Will raises an eyebrow. "Thought as much."

"You've got no idea how complicated it is. Sinclair's into Eleanor."

"Everyone's kind of into Eleanor."

"Very funny."

"No, seriously. She's class. But Charles doesn't look at her the way he looks at you."

"We're best friends." I'm so sick of those words. Because, if I'm truly honest with myself, Will's right. And my brother's the only person I feel I can be completely open with about this stuff. So I close my eyes and just say it. "If I take the first step and he doesn't feel the same way, things will be awkward between us forever."

"So would you say it's not awkward between you just now?"

I hate my brother. I really do hate him.

He smiles knowingly. "Come on, Tori. Be brave. You don't have to wait for him to take the initiative."

I wrap my arms around my knees and sink my head onto them. "But I'm scared."

"What of?"

Same game as just now. *Shut your eyes. Tell the truth.*

"Of being rejected."

"Which is a perfectly understandable fear."

"Fantastic, thanks, Will."

"But fear is good. Fear means that you care. And that means you're in love with Charles Sinclair."

"But he's not in love with me."

"You can't know that if you don't ask him."

"No way am I asking him. You don't understand, I'd make a right eejit of myself. I'm meant to be joining the theater group too, to help write this play. Fab, huh?"

"Really?" Will raises his eyebrows. "Cool, Tori."

"Yeah, so cool."

"You can't change Juliet kissing the poison off his lips, I guess, but you'll have a say in how it happens, if you see what I mean." Will leaves a significant pause. Typical Gemini ascendant . . . They don't usually come across strongly, but when they do, it's in this downright manipulative way.

"Are you encouraging me to be a bad feminist?"

"No, of course not. But this play is pretty problematic anyway, isn't it? I mean, with all due respect to Shakespeare, it really is time for a bit less toxic masculinity. If you work on the script, I'm seriously hoping it can be modern yet romantic at the same time. And I bet our good friend Charles would notice that too."

As if Sinclair would ever notice anything . . .

But OK, what my brother's saying is indeed a possibility I hadn't considered before. If I was in the scriptwriting club, I'd be right there at the source. Maybe I wouldn't have such a feeling of powerlessness, watching as Eleanor and Sinclair get it together. Hey, I could help them along . . . Great. But anything feels better than sitting around uselessly in my room while they're rehearsing behind closed doors and all I can do is guess at what's happening on the stage.

"So if you were me, would you do it?" I ask slowly.

"Tori, I can't tell you what to do or it'll be all my fault if it goes wrong."

"Yeah, what else are brothers for?"

Will laughs quietly.

I put my head back and stare up at the fancy wrought-iron ceiling. Everything within me balks at the idea of having to write the love story for which Eleanor and Sinclair will be cheered by the entire school in a few months' time. But here's the thing: They'll be cheered either way. It's my bloody job to make sure that at least the play isn't sending out too many problematic messages. And if that means I get a wee bit of control back over this whole thing, it's no more than a pleasant side effect.

Will looks at me in silence.
I shut my eyes.
"I hate that you're always right."

Red Flags
Relationships Edition

The ones you ignore because you're so, so in love:

- Out of nowhere, they're bored by you.
- They focus on your mistakes and not their own.
- They expect you to be able to read their mind.
- They get pissed off when you can't.
- They continually comment on your appearance.
- They blame you for the emotions that they stirred up in you.
- They judge you or laugh at you, your hobbies or your interests.
- They don't apologize when they've made a mistake.
- You're scared that every argument could mean the end.

9

SINCLAIR

"I can't believe it, Charlie," Dad says for the umpteenth time. "The lead role, that's amazing." He looks up as Margaret comes through from the shop into the bakery. "Have you heard, Margaret? My son's going to be an actor."

"The whole village has heard, Peter," she says, nodding her thanks as I hand her a tray of fresh scones. "You realize we're all coming to see the play, of course?"

"Please don't!" I laugh, but I'm deadly serious. If only I could ban even my parents from being in the audience in the summer, but I'd never have the heart. They were thrilled when I told them yesterday that I'd got the role of Romeo, since when Dad's been telling everyone he meets.

"I never expected to have a chance," I say, popping a tray of rolls into the oven.

"Don't talk like that," Dad immediately reproves me. "You have no reason to put yourself down."

"Well, no, but I've got no acting experience," I say, with a shrug.

"That's as may be, but it clearly didn't bother anybody." Dad looks up from his dough. "You're really enjoying yourself, aren't you?"

"We'll see—we haven't started rehearsing yet. Maybe then they'll throw me back out."

"Charles," Dad tells me off, "a little more self-belief, if you please. Did Tori get a part too, by the way?"

It's an effort not to flinch. "No, she didn't audition."

"Didn't she? Doesn't she have any ambitions in that direction?"

She does. But these days, she's got a toxic boyfriend too. I keep that to myself, though. "She didn't want to."

"Pity," says Dad. "Is she well? I haven't seen her for such a long time."

"Yes, she's fine," I say lamely.

"Would Tori like to come for dinner with us again soon?"

"I can ask her." Which, of course, I won't. "She's been hanging around with a different crowd lately. Valentine Ward and all those arrogant rugby boys . . ."

"Oh." Dad looks at me but doesn't inquire further. Being married to Mum, he obviously gets to know a fair bit about the hierarchies among Dunbridge pupils, and Valentine's mother likes to queen it on the school council at any opportunity, so he's well aware of the Wards. "Charlie, I've been meaning to say—you don't have to help me here all the time," he says to my surprise. "I know your old man running the bakery isn't exactly glamorous."

I pause in midmovement. "What are you talking about?"

"I only mean—"

"You think I'm ashamed of my family? Come on, Dad, do me a favor."

"I know what people your age can be like."

"Anyone who feels like looking down on me can take a running jump."

There's a hint of a smile on Dad's lips. "I'm proud of you, son."

"I'm proud of you too, Father."

"God, that makes me sound so old . . . Don't call me that." He laughs.

"Well, it's the truth, isn't it?" I grin.

"Just call me *Dad*, OK, not *Father*."

"Duly noted." I hesitate, then just say what's on my mind. "And you'll still be proud of me if I'm wasting my time on this drama malarkey now?"

Dad eyes me. "You don't waste your time."

"I probably won't be able to help in the shop so often."

"Like I said, you don't have to."

I nod.

"Why would you think I wouldn't be proud of you?" Dad asks.

I shrug. "Because it's kind of nonsense, isn't it? Acting, rehearsals . . . It's not honest work, it's not real."

"Charlie, you're too smart to think that," he says dryly. "We're not sending you to that school so that you can end up as a baker one day."

"What if I wanted to?"

"You want to go to university," Dad says, because he knows me. "And that's a good thing."

I swallow.

"So what are your plans there? Still interested in scriptwriting?"

"I think so."

"That's great," Dad declares. "I can't wait to see where you end up."

"Me either," I say. Or who with. Until a couple of weeks ago, I'd been sure I'd do creative writing at St. Andrews. And that Henry, Emma, and Tori would be there too. But who knows? Maybe Valentine Ward's put her off since then and talked her into applying to Cambridge, where he's bound to get in to do economics. Not because he's got what it takes, but because his folks have the money to grease the wheels.

I can't believe Dad would really think I'd be ashamed of him and what he does. No way. I'd be ashamed if I only got anywhere in life thanks to influential parents. I'd be ashamed if I were Valentine Ward, who puts other people down so that he can feel better about himself, and always gets whatever he wants. Rugby captain, coaching through his A levels despite being thick as, and Tori—especially Tori. My friend who isn't talking to me these days. It wasn't until the assembly this morning that I even knew she and Will had been home at the weekend. In the old days, I would have done. I might even have gone with them, but I can't remember the last time we went to her family home in Holloway together. Perhaps Val was there with her . . .

I slap a lump of dough onto the counter. Dad glances up but doesn't say anything.

And neither do I.

Not saying things is what I do best.

TORI

Since the auditions, things have been even weirder between Sinclair and me. We see each other in class and in the dining room for meals. On the morning runs, I toy with the idea of going the official route with Emma and Henry instead of taking the shortcut with Sinclair, but then I remember who I am. And there's no way I'm a person who'd run any further than they had to just because they've had a pointless row with their best friend.

"What are we doing for Sinclair's birthday?" Henry asks me in a low voice a while later, once Ms. Kelleher's sent us off to break.

A good question, because he's turning eighteen. Entering adulthood. So it's time to swallow my hurt pride. I glance over to Sinclair who's a few yards ahead of us, walking down the corridor with Emma and Gideon. Before I get a chance to answer, I spot Val standing with his friends a slight distance away. We've barely seen each other for the last few days. Outside class, he's practically glued to either the rugby field or the gym equipment. Similarly, Olive is spending so much time in the school pool that I'm surprised she hasn't grown webbed feet. I don't know when I last saw her with dry hair. Even now, her dark head is still wet as she comes around the corner. She looks up as Henry beckons her over.

"Have you got a second? It's about Sinclair's birthday," he says.

Olive seems reluctant to slow her steps. When her eyes meet mine, I don't see the rejection I've got used to lately. She looks uncertain.

"Yeah?"

"If we throw him a party, are you in?"

Olive looks surprised. "You mean you want me there?"

Henry's taken aback. "Of course we do." I don't feel able to say the same, so I just nod when Olive glances at me. "He's turning eighteen, we're his friends . . ."

"OK, I . . . Just text me, let me know what I can do to help," Olive says, looking past Henry. "I need to speak to Dad quickly, sorry." She hurries toward the sick bay to find Dr. Henderson, who's working there this morning.

"Are you two still not getting on?" Henry muses.

I shrug my shoulders. "Looks that way." Although Olive was less standoffish than normal just now . . . But maybe that was down to Henry being there.

"She'll come round," he says.

I sigh. "Got any top tips on conflict resolution?"

"I might be school captain, but I'm not on the peer mediation team," he says.

"Yeah, but they're kind of similar . . ."

Henry smiles and shakes his head. "I think the whole business is as upsetting for Olive as it is for you."

How does he always manage to hit the bull's-eye? I exhale quietly. "Maybe it's me. It seems like I'm fighting with all my friends just now. Hey, perhaps you'll be next."

Henry ignores my pathetic attempt at humor. "Sinclair too?" I don't reply.

"You mean because of Eleanor and the play?"

"I know it makes me a rubbish friend that I can't be happy for him."

"Hey, I wouldn't be thrilled if Emma was up on stage with some other Romeo either."

"Yeah, but you and Emma are a couple."

"Exactly," Henry says. He seems fully aware of the effect of his words, because he just keeps talking while my thoughts start to whirl. "But the point was, midnight party for Sinclair in the old greenhouse so that we can all see his birthday in together—what do you think?"

I try to pull myself together. "Sounds good."

"Or is that too boring?" Henry wonders.

"What else were you thinking? Want to hire the Mahiki?"

He laughs. "Yeah, along with a private jet to take us to London."

"I'll ask my mum," I say dryly.

"Sinclair would hate that," Henry remarks.

"He would."

"You too." Henry goes quiet. "We should arrange something he'll really enjoy."

"How about a film night? We can get hold of a screen and a projector, and then we'll watch all his deathly arty films in the greenhouse."

Henry's eyes light up. "That sounds good! I'll take care of it."

"What sounds good?" asks Emma, who's suddenly popped up. Sinclair has stopped too, and he looks from Henry to me.

I bite my bottom lip and pray that he didn't hear.

"Tori was suggesting having another games night," Henry declares, without batting an eyelid. "This evening, my room?"

"I'm doing a shift in the bakery," Sinclair says. "Sorry."

"Before that?" Henry asks.

"Riding lesson," Sinclair murmurs.

"OK, another time then." Henry takes Emma's hand. They're so in love, so perfect together. And they walk away, leaving me with my best friend and nothing to say to him. We're standing in the corridor of our school, avoiding each other's eyes, feeling guilty, but neither of us can admit that, because it would be weak.

Sinclair looks at me for a wee while, straight in the eye. He nods, he turns away, he leaves, and I don't do a thing about it. Instead, I wait as Val intercepts me—after a minor staring contest between him and Sinclair.

"Hey," he says, and my heart sinks even further as I realize how frosty he sounds. "Still in the land of the living, then?"

I'm confused for a moment, and then I'm boiling up as I remember I never did text him at the weekend. "Oh, God, I'm so sorry," I say at once. "I meant to message you. I went home for the weekend and then—"

"Went home?" Val interrupts. "Funny that Neil saw you in Ebrington yesterday morning with that Emma."

I fight back the urge to shut my eyes. "Will and I got back on Saturday evening," I explain.

"Uh-huh."

"Uh-huh, what?" Hot rage boils up in me, but I try to keep my voice down. There are people everywhere at break time, and the walls have ears. And I can very much do without being the number-one topic of conversation at Dunbridge right now. "Val, please," I beg quietly, as my irritation seems to bounce off his stony face. "I would have told you, but I totally forgot we were going home until right at the last minute. I'm sorry for not texting, but I wasn't on my phone very much while I was with my family."

"But you still had time to upload two TikToks?"

I gulp. "They were prescheduled."

He actually rolls his eyes. "I can bust my own balls, Tori."

"Val." I reach for his arm and feel his hard muscles under my fingers. "I really am sorry, but—"

"No, come on, drop it. I can't be arsed to fight with you."

I open my mouth, but lose the nerve to say anything. Because I know perfectly well that, whatever I say, Val will turn it against me.

"Did you have a nice weekend?" I ask in the end.

Val groans, then shrugs. "I dunno. I kept wondering if you were with him . . ."

"With Sinclair?" I ask, in disbelief. "Why would I be with him?"

"I don't know. Why was his name the first thing that occurred to you?"

Shit. So that was a trap. "Val, I was with my parents," I repeat. "I didn't see Sinclair all weekend."

He stares at me so long that I'm about to start explaining myself again, but then he sighs. "Fine, I mean . . . you're the only person who knows if you're telling the truth. I can't check up on you. But forget it." He pushes me aside into one of the alcoves in the corridor. "Friday evening, in the Dungeon?" he asks out of nowhere.

I feel the mood plummet again. "I've got plans."

"Then cancel them." I don't answer, and he huffs with irritation. "OK, what about Saturday?"

I nod hastily. "That would be better."

"What plans, anyway?" he asks.

Oh, please, no. You really don't want to know . . .

I sigh and seriously consider lying, but there's too much gossip at this school—Val's going to hear about it sooner or later either way. And I don't want to think about what would happen then.

"I'm going to the scriptwriting club."

Val laughs. He actually laughs. My hot rage returns. "Wow, OK, you seriously mean that?" He goes silent as I pull away from him a bit. "Why? Does Sinclair need help with his script for Eleanor? Don't worry, she doesn't usually take too much persuading."

Enough is enough.

"Are you kidding me?" I snap.

Val laughs like he cracked a real funny.

"You can't say things like that, Val."

"Why not? It's true."

"Sorry, but do you actually listen to yourself?" I mutter, and I want to pull away, but Val gets hold of my wrist.

"Hey, it was a joke, OK?"

"Not a very funny one."

"God, come on . . . What are you allowed to say then?"

"Not stuff like that."

"Tori, she's my ex."

"Yes, and it says more about you than it does about her if you talk about her like that."

All I get for that is a glare.

"Don't you think it might give me something to think about?" I ask.

"Why should it give *you* something to think about?"

"Because there's a possibility you'll be saying stuff like that about me one day."

He laughs. "Tori, please. You're not like the others." He presses me softly against the wall.

"Val, it's no compliment to tell a woman something like that."

He groans. "Jeez, do you know how hard it is to pay you a compliment? *That's problematic, you can't say that* . . . So maybe I'd better just never say anything, but you don't like that either."

I open my mouth, but I'm too confused to reply.

"Sometimes I wonder if you're actually trying to take everything I say the wrong way."

"When you slag off your ex-girlfriend and I ask you not to?"

"God, you took that the wrong way too." He leans down.

"Val, stop it," I say as he tries to kiss me.

"You're in a mood, got it." He pulls away. "The scriptwriting club is sure to help. Nice chatting to you." The mockery in his voice is like a stab to the chest as he gives me a sarcastic salute and vanishes into the throng.

I have to force myself to take three deep breaths before I head to my own classroom. I've got Mr. Acevedo for English. He took over the A-level course when Mr. Ward left.

The class just crawls by. My thoughts are circling around my argument with Val, and with every passing minute, my aggravation gives way to a guilty conscience. What if Val's right and I'm oversensitive? But the stuff he said really isn't OK.

Mr. Acevedo's teaching is way more interactive than Mr. Ward's was, but I'm still finding it hard to concentrate. When he keeps me back after class, I'm sure he noticed and wants to talk to me about it.

"I have no desire to keep you from your well-deserved lunch break, Victoria, and I am aware that this is something of an ambush," Mr. Acevedo begins as soon as the others have vanished into the corridor. He emerges from behind his desk. "I was surprised that you didn't audition for any of the parts."

Oh, no . . .

"I didn't really feel up to it," I prevaricate.

"That's a shame," he says. "But it's your decision. Now what I wanted to ask you was this: Could you see yourself as my assistant director? I need someone reliable to help me out."

Assistant director? *Me?*

My lips are frozen, but Mr. Acevedo goes on: "You'd be at all the rehearsals and the performance, and you and I would be responsible for making sure everything runs to plan. It's a lot of work, of course, and you'd get merits for taking part, just like the cast. It wouldn't do your university application any harm either."

Mr. Acevedo smiles, and I'm sure he knows how much I'd

like to agree. Because I threw away my chance of being on stage myself, and this way I can at least get a sniff of the theatrical air. And it would be experience, which would definitely come in handy for our play next year.

But: "Florence Swindells asked me to join the scriptwriting club, now that Sin—ah, Charles is playing Romeo."

"Oh, that's excellent news! You'd be the go-between between the script and the cast." Mr. Acevedo looks delighted. "But it would be a great deal of work, of course . . . So it's entirely up to you to decide."

"You don't think it would be a problem for me to do both, sir?"

He shakes his head. "Quite the contrary. You'd know what was going on, and you'd be able to tackle problems directly. This year, I'm seriously considering encouraging closer cooperation between the writers and the main cast anyway. A lot of the script usually gets cut during rehearsals, and we're so short of time this year that we really can't afford any other delays if we're going to be ready by the summer."

"That makes sense."

"Think it over," Mr. Acevedo says. "I'm calling a joint meeting of the script group and the actors for tomorrow evening. You'd be very welcome to come along."

"I will," I say firmly. I might not have thought this through entirely, but I don't care. I only know that it's a chance to get closer to Sinclair again, so I have to take it. "I'll happily take the job. If you really think I can do it."

Mr. Acevedo looks at me with that smile. "I certainly do, Victoria."

SINCLAIR

I knew what to expect the moment Henry turned up in my room the evening before my eighteenth birthday and said I should hurry up and get dressed. Soon after wing time, we reached the old greenhouse, which was completely dark—at least it was until we'd walked in and I could see what the others had organized. The greenhouse had been transformed into a miniature cinema, with a screen on which we watched a Sherlock Holmes film before the party started.

They're all here: Henry; Gideon; Grace; Omar; Emma; Olive; Tori's brother, Will; Kit, who he's been dating for a while now; a few others from our form; and some fifth-formers too. And yes, Tori. And the only thing I can think of, as we sit on blankets and watch the film, is that horror night back in the second form. I don't know if she's thinking about it too. If she even remembers. Or if she knows that that was my first and last kiss. Even now that I'm eighteen; somehow that fact bothers me more than it should. I wish I could convince myself that age is just a number and that I shouldn't measure my experiences against other people's, but everywhere I look, I see my friends who've managed to do something I can't. Henry, with an arm around Emma, unable to stop looking at her. Gideon, who keeps absentmindedly staring at Grace. Will and Kit, who seem so comfortable together. And then there's me. Eighteen, a virgin, pretty much never been kissed, in love with my best friend, who's with the biggest arsehole in the school and isn't talking to me now because I always have to go and screw everything up.

Tori's copper-red hair is really wavy today, falling over her shoulders like a gleaming waterfall. I want to touch her. Her hair, her shoulders, her lips, which she bites nervously anytime she looks in my direction. When she finally comes over to me and pulls out a rectangular parcel from behind her back, I know what's coming. I know, but until a moment ago, I wasn't sure if this birthday would be the one where—thanks to everything that's come between us—Tori would break with her tradition. Every year, she gives me a book that made her think of me when she read it. They're not just novels. They're novels filled with her handwritten notes, Post-its, and markings. It would be easy to underestimate how long it must take her to reproduce all her scribbles from her own tattered copy in a fresh one for me. Slipped between the pages are notes with Spotify codes and song lyrics that fit the text, printed out Pinterest photos that suit the mood, and other things that matter to her. The end result is a work of art. A reading diary from her, made only for me. Being inside Tori's head for a few hundred pages and reading her snappy comments, interpretations, and dry jokes, which aren't always easy to decipher, especially when she has a lot to say. Flicking through those books makes me feel as close to her as if she were lying there beside me. It might be the nicest thing anyone's ever done for me. Because it's personal, and Tori always hits the mark.

I eye the book. This is the first in a new series by her favorite author, Hope MacKenzie. Tori idolizes her, so I know how significant this gift is. I flick through the first few pages and stop at one of the Post-its.

Happy Birthday, my very grown-up best friend—and I'm sorry for what I said.

I look up.

"Genuinely sorry," Tori whispers, chewing gently on her bottom lip. "I'd take it back if I could."

Me too, Tori, me too.

"Say something," she whispers pleadingly.

I clap the book shut. "Thank you." I have to clear my throat. "And I'm sorry too."

"I'm so happy for you," she adds, "that you got the part. You deserve it."

"You would have deserved one too," I say, but stop when Tori shuts her eyes. I don't want another argument. So I hastily step toward her.

She looks a bit startled as I hug her, but after a few seconds, she wraps her arms around me too.

She still smells of peach and, for a moment, everything's like we've gone back in time a couple of years. If I shut my eyes, she's not seeing Valentine Ward. And I can be the one to kiss her and fall asleep beside her.

Tori's cheek brushes mine as we move apart. She pauses in front of me. Her gaze darts from my eyes to my lips and back again; her fingers run down my chest, slowly—she doesn't pull them away. And God, does she know what she's doing? It's more than just a casual touch; it's soft and deliberate, and it does something inside me. A shiver runs through my body, Tori looks at me, and her lips part slightly. I want to kiss her. Fuck, I really do. Every sound fades into the background—at least until I hear Gideon calling to me.

Tori pulls back and shoves her hands into her hoodie pockets. She steps past me; I follow her to the others. They seem to be talking about the uniform, and Tori immediately plunges into the debate, as always when the conversation comes around to how sexist it is that girls have to wear skirts, not trousers, on Mondays. Henry's sister, Maeve, started it, and since then, the issue keeps bubbling up. There seem to be two camps—people who don't really care because *it's always been that way* and people who can't wait to get it changed.

"Yes, I know it's only one day a week, but it's the principle of the thing," says Tori.

"What principle?" someone asks. I'm not quite sure who, because it really is hard not to keep looking at her the whole time.

"For everyone to be able to wear what they like," she snaps.

"So boys should be able to wear skirts, or what?"

"You may find this hard to believe, but yeah, they really should." Tori and I turn simultaneously to Olive, who's been sitting in an armchair in silence until now, not getting involved in the discussion. She and Tori look at each other until Olive breaks the eye contact.

"Well, I wouldn't mind wearing the school skirt now and then," Will says. His boyfriend Kit glances at him with a smile.

"Has anyone ever asked Mrs. Sinclair what she thinks about it?" Emma inquires.

"It's tricky," Henry says, then he, Olive, and Tori take turns to fill her in on all the conversations we've already had about the issue in the last few years. When Maeve was still at school here and kicked off the debate, it was amazing how many pupils were in favor of changing the uniform policy. It never came to anything, but I get a feeling it's about time we raised the subject again.

10

SINCLAIR

We sat in the old greenhouse together for ages, talking into the wee hours of the morning. The hard core, which consists of Tori, Emma, and Henry—and normally Olive too, but she went back to her wing early with the others. I came close to asking Tori if she'd like to sleep over at mine, the way Emma followed Henry into his room as if it was the most natural thing in the world, but that would have been pushing my luck. So I just hugged my best friend in the hallway that leads to the west wing, wished her goodnight, and went back to my cold, empty bed, where I lay for ages, flicking through her notes in the book, until I must eventually have fallen asleep.

The next day, I get a cake for breakfast in the dining room, and everyone comes to wish me a happy birthday. Even Mum gives me a hug when we bump into each other in the corridor. This evening, she and Dad are taking me out for dinner, and on Sunday, my grandparents are coming around for tea. I'm really looking forward to it, but I could have done with a bit more sleep as I head to the riding school for stable duty. I don't have an official lesson scheduled for today, but I'm hoping to exercise Jubilee. The Trakehner mare isn't one of the school horses—she belongs to Kendra in the fourth form—but recently her owner has been less interested in her horse than in going out with her friends, so her parents and Mrs. Smith, our riding teacher, agreed that I'll care for Jubilee too. It's amazing how easily I forget she isn't actually mine, since I've been working with her so often.

I've often known horses and their owners not to get along very well with each other, but there's absolutely no connection between Kendra and Jubilee. They seem equally scared of each other, which sometimes causes trouble. But Jubilee's an amazing horse when you know how to handle her.

The moment I step into the stables, people crowd around to wish me a happy birthday. I chat to them briefly, and then everyone gets back to work. I can see my breath hanging in the air in little clouds as I walk down the cold stable lane to Jubilee's paddock. I'd been intending to do a bit of schooling with her, then pop a few jumps. That was my plan, but as I approach her box, I see Kendra trying to lead the mare out—without much success. I force myself not to speed up, because Jubilee's looking tense enough as it is. Her ears are back, and she's deeply suspicious: she's got whale eyes, and she's not budging an inch.

"Hey," I say, drawing attention to myself calmly but clearly as I come closer. Even so, Kendra jumps and whirls around. "Are you two OK?"

"She never wants to go out!" Kendra exclaims. She looks so frustrated that I feel sorry for her. "Could you just . . . ?"

She holds out the halter to me, and because Jubilee's already looking seriously stressed, I take it. Kendra immediately retreats to the edge of the box as I murmur a few soothing words to Jubilee, then lead her out onto the path. She calms down almost immediately in my presence, which in turn seems enough to tip Kendra over the edge.

"She hates me," she whispers when I glance over.

"She does not hate you," I reply at once.

Kendra laughs. "Just look at her. She's a completely different horse any time you come near. I just can't handle this whole thing with her anymore."

I reach for Jubilee's grooming box, which Kendra's already brought out, and throw her a currycomb.

"No offense," I say as I join in with brushing Jubilee's pale-brown coat, "but do you actually enjoy all this? Working with horses, riding lessons?"

Kendra is silent. Then she shrugs her shoulders. "I wish I did, but . . . no, I'm sorry, it's just not fun anymore."

"So why do you do it?"

"Because my parents want me to," Kendra says. "They bought Jubilee because I begged them. But maybe I only liked the idea of having my own horse. Going in for events with her, I wanted all that . . . but it's actually not really my thing."

"Have you ever told them that?" I ask.

Kendra nods. "Yes, but they said I wanted her, so now I have to look after her properly."

"Hm." I give a slight nod.

"They can't just give her back."

"No, that's true," I say slowly, looking out to where the horses Mrs. Smith doesn't need for today's riding lesson are grazing in the paddock. "Maybe it would be possible for the school to take her on."

Kendra looks up. "Do you think so?"

"You could suggest it to your parents."

"Would you ask your mum?" Kendra asks. "I mean, you get on so well with Jubilee. Then at least I'd know she's got someone she really means something to."

I nod, because that's way better than the idea of Kendra's parents selling her on altogether. I've been riding her for over eighteen months now, and we've really bonded. She still wouldn't be mine if the school bought her, but at least I'd know she wouldn't suddenly be gone. I definitely need to talk to Mum about it.

"We'll sort something out," I promise Kendra as I send her off to the tack room. My hands are dirty, and my head is calmer when I'm here. I don't have to, but once she's saddled up, I follow Kendra and Jubilee into the arena. There aren't many others here today, so I come down to give Kendra a few tips, set up jumps for her, and take them down again. She's really trying, but after a half hour battle that brings Kendra to the verge of tears, I let her dismount and promise to look after Jubilee. Kendra looks guilty and relieved in equal measure as she leaves the hall. My feet are like ice, but after that short session with Kendra, Jubilee's stressed out and dripping with sweat, so I don't want to go without having ridden her dry for a minute or two.

I'm wearing thin gloves, but my fingers are still freezing as I mount and take the reins. I'd love to jump with her a bit, but

Jubilee seems worn out, even though she didn't take a single fence with Kendra. It's clear that there's no trust between them, because Juby's a brilliant jumper. If Mum really did buy her for the school, maybe I could enter a few events with her in the summer . . .

I let my mind wander for a bit, but then I look over to the arena fence.

Tori's leaning both arms on it, watching us. How long has she been here? It's turned into kind of a thing between us that Tori comes to see me at the stables once she's finished gardening duty with Mr. Carpenter and Mr. Ringling. They often finish way earlier than I do.

The spectators' area is slightly raised, so we're about eye to eye as I ride toward her.

"Hi," she murmurs. Tori looks freezing, and her cheeks are flushed with cold. I jerk my thumb to the door that leads to the manège. As Tori moves to take up my invitation, I swing a leg over the saddle. As always when my feet are this cold, a stabbing pain shoots down my legs as I hit the ground. Tori comes closer and lifts her hand to greet Jubilee.

"Hi, Queenie," she murmurs as I take off my helmet and hand it to her. I can't even remember when this ritual began. It must have been back when Tori and I were hanging around together twenty-four seven and I was teaching her to ride. She doesn't really seem to have the horsewoman gene, but we got into a habit where she gets into the saddle for a few cooldown rides after the lesson. Jubilee seems relaxed enough now for me to risk it today.

I glance at what Tori's wearing and consider her leggings and trainers good enough. Jubilee is considerably taller than Tori, so

I give her a leg up. I might just be a wee bit proud of the smooth way Tori swings herself into the saddle.

I take Jubilee by the bit ring and start moving, aching feet and all.

"Why are you still here?" Tori asks, and I glance over my shoulder to her in surprise. "It's your birthday."

"Stable duty," I answer, as if she couldn't tell. "But I'll head home later."

"Doing anything nice?"

"Mum and Dad are taking me out to dinner."

"You're tense," Tori says out of the blue.

Yes, I really am. And it doesn't exactly make it any better to think about last night and her hands on my chest. Her eyes wander over me, from my jacket to my tight-fitting jodhpurs, and her looking at me like that does something to me.

"I'm just tired," I say. Which is true. "I started your book last night."

"Really?" Tori's expression brightens, almost like she's genuinely surprised that I've even looked at it.

"Of course," I reply, sounding a little offended. *I'm not Val*, I add in my mind, but I bite the words back, along with the irritation that's trying to rise up inside me. Juby's a sensitive horse, and I don't want to risk anything with Tori on her back. She's not as safe in the saddle as I am.

"I'm glad you like it," Tori says.

I like everything you do.

"About the other day," I say instead. "I didn't mean to have a go at you like that after the auditions."

"I know, Sinclair. And you might have had a point. If Val hadn't been there, maybe I'd have been braver."

"You could always ask Mr. Acevedo," I begin, but Tori shakes her head.

"He's already spoken to me and asked me if I'd like to be assistant director."

"Oh." I gulp. "And . . . would you?"

"I think so. He said I can just come along to the next rehearsal and then we'll work everything out."

"That would be so cool," I say. "We'd get to spend more time together again."

I'd forgotten how Tori's smile warms me. "We would."

"And about Eleanor . . . I really don't want anything more than friendship from her, OK?"

"Sinclair, it's fine. Best friends support each other in everything."

And yeah, what can I do but nod?

TORI

Things have been better between Sinclair and me since I apologized to him on his birthday. You'd never believe it, but apparently just talking to one another really does solve problems. Even so, there's still a bit of tension when I turn up to the joint drama and scriptwriting club meeting on Friday evening.

Florence sent me the script as it stands at the moment, and I was up until the wee hours reading it. And now I understand why the others are unhappy. The language is old-fashioned and the dialogue feels unnatural. Perhaps it really isn't a bad idea of Mr. Acevedo's to get the cast and the writers working on the text together.

Florence, Amara, Ho-wing, and Quentin don't look exactly thrilled when he tells them about it, but they don't dare complain, because Mr. Acevedo's arguments make sense, and time's running out. He introduces me to everyone as this year's assistant director and then lets us get on with reading through the current script.

Sinclair, Eleanor, and the other actors have it up on their iPads. Sinclair's settled down cross-legged on the stage, and it seems to me that he looks in my direction fairly often. Since his birthday, I somehow haven't been able to think straight. There was something between us, even if I don't know how to describe it. But there's no way I'm imagining it.

I scroll forward a page as Florence jumps to the next section and force myself to turn my concentration back to the text.

Romeo: She's unlike anybody else I ever met. I never saw true beauty till this night.

Val's voice in my head and that uneasy feeling in my stomach. It's not a compliment if they're putting other people down in the same breath. Is that really so hard to understand? And why is being different even so desirable?

"All agreed?" Florence asks as she moves on. The others nod, heads down. They only look up when I start to speak.

"Don't you guys think that's kind of a stupid way of putting it?"

Florence stops. "What do you mean, Tori?"

"Well, this bit here from Romeo. 'She's unlike anybody else.'"

"What about it?" Quentin asks.

"It's complicated. Why can't Romeo compliment her without disrespecting other women? Quite apart from the fact that he has to comment on her appearance . . ."

Quentin looks at me. "It's Shakespeare. What did you expect?"

"For us to write a modern version," I say curtly. I don't care that he and the others are irritated. I'm more than ready to debate this point. Especially when it would be so easy to change.

"What do you think?" Florence looks around.

Amara, Sinclair, Eleanor, and a few others nod, but Quentin and Terry just shrug their shoulders.

Florence turns to Mr. Acevedo. "What do you think, sir?"

He raises his hands deprecatingly. "It's your play." But the look he gives me later makes it clear that he shares my opinion.

"I'd like to change it." Suddenly everyone's looking at Sinclair. "It's my line, and I wouldn't feel happy saying a thing like that. And you're right, Quen, they were different times back then. But we should have the ambition to write a feminist play."

"It's *Romeo and Juliet*," says Ho-wing. "There's nothing feminist about it."

"So that's why we're sitting here making sure that changes." Eleanor straightens up a touch. "Don't you think?"

"Exactly," Florence agrees. "So make a suggestion." She pulls over her laptop and raises her eyebrows expectantly when nobody speaks.

"'She is the sun, temptation,'" says Sinclair. He blushes to his ears as everyone looks at him again. He clears his throat. "Or something like that . . . Then the compliment wouldn't be about her appearance but her aura, you know."

Florence nods enthusiastically and makes a note. I can't move because Sinclair's looking at me still.

"Everyone happy?"

Florence's voice makes me jump, and I nod hurriedly. "Yes, much better. Thank you."

"So can we continue? Or is there anything else?"

I throw caution to the wind. "To be honest, yes. While we're on the subject . . . on the next page, Juliet's talking to herself about why Romeo has picked her over everyone else. 'He could have anyone he liked. If he were just to snap his fingers, every virgin in Verona would stand in line . . .'"

"What about it?"

"Seriously, Quentin? He just has to snap his fingers?"

"That's how Romeo is. It's what makes him attractive. He's a player, and Juliet is drawn to him even though she's uncertain and inexperienced."

"So do we want to tell the audience that a woman needs a man's approval before she can become aware of her own beauty?"

"It's a current trope," says Florence.

"Yeah, and it's bullshit," puts in Eleanor. "Tori's right. There'll be so many young girls watching us, and we should give them a different message. I wouldn't be very happy if that stays in."

"I'm in favor of cutting it too." Florence turns back to her laptop, and Quentin sighs in annoyance.

Eleanor glances at me. She smiles, and it feels like a small victory that unites us for a while. But something else in her eyes scares me. A quiet warning, as if she knew who I was thinking about earlier. She's Val's ex: She must know what he's like. And now he's bad-mouthing her, which is one of the biggest red flags, if all the mental-health accounts I follow on Insta are to be believed. But nobody tells you how much harder it is to spot things in real life that sound so obvious in theory. And then to pluck up the courage to do something about it.

Yes, Val says problematic things, and his behavior is dire. But he has his own demons to fight.

And I'm looking for excuses for his behavior. Another of those dangerous things.

"OK, shall we go on?" Florence asks.

I raise my head. I look into Sinclair's face, and my thoughts stop whirling.

I nod slowly.

11

SINCLAIR

Looks like I underestimated this whole drama club thing. We have group rehearsals three times a week—one of them is with Mr. Acevedo for just Eleanor and me. Oh, and Tori, because she's assistant director, and Fate apparently finds it amusing to stick me in a theater with the woman I'm secretly in love with *and* the one I'm pretending to be into to disguise that fact. Do I need to point out how awkward that is?

"I hope you three realize that you'll be spending a lot of time together over the next few months," says Mr. Acevedo as he walks up and down next to the stage. Tori's sitting in the front row, one leg crossed over the other. We've been doing method-acting exercises, and the rest of the group has already left. Today, that meant getting rid of everybody's inhibitions by spending an hour wandering aimlessly around on the stage and all yelling as loudly as possible at the imaginary audience.

I hadn't thought that things could get any worse, but now Eleanor and I are meant to be acting a scene for just the two of us. It's the first time Romeo and Juliet meet, and even before we get close to the kiss that's still ahead of us, Mr. Acevedo interrupts us.

"OK, that will do." He raises his hand, and I immediately take a few steps back from Eleanor. "I've seen enough. You're playing probably history's greatest lovers, and I'd like us to be able to feel that from down here. Victoria," he looks at Tori, "are we feeling it yet?"

Tori's eyes wander over me, then back to Mr. Acevedo. "I think there's room for improvement."

"Well, then, we're in agreement." He turns his attention back to us. "I'm not demanding that you two fall madly in love with each other, just that you take your jobs on this stage seriously. Because it will only be then that the audience can take you seriously."

Eleanor looks focused, but I'm mainly just sweating. I once heard that fear-sweat smells stronger than normal sweat. Please don't let that be true. If, on top of everything else, I'm stinking the place out, I'll never be able to look Ellie in the eyes again.

"I want you two to get to know each other, and you're not going to do that on this stage but by spending time together. How you do that is up to you. Go for coffee, party together, I don't mind, so long as you study each other and find out what makes the other person tick. Understood?"

Tori stares at her notes.

"Got that, Charles?"

"Yes." I clear my throat. Eleanor gives me an uncertain smile.

"Wonderful. Do you enjoy giving presentations?"

"Sorry?" Eleanor frowns.

"Presentations," Mr. Acevedo repeats. "Speaking in front of others. Do you find it easy?"

Eleanor pauses, then answers, "It depends on the topic."

"On the topic, uh-huh." Mr. Acevedo is strolling back and forth again. "Is it the same for you, Charles?"

"Erm, I generally find it stressful."

"What's stressful about it for you?"

The exact thing that's raising my heart rate right now. Attentive eyes on me. Silence, expectation, having to say something. "This," I say. "Attention. Being looked at."

"Being at the center of things?" Mr. Acevedo continues. "Why is that unpleasant?"

"I don't know."

"Charles, please. You can be honest—we all know what it feels like."

Tori is watching me, chewing her bottom lip.

"It's probably the fear of making mistakes. Embarrassing yourself, being laughed at."

"And where would be the problem with that?"

"Well, like I said, it would be embarrassing." All these questions are starting to get on my nerves, but he seems to be in the mood to keep poking.

"And *well, like I said*, where would be the problem with that?" he asks.

I sigh with frustration but don't speak.

"Making yourself vulnerable, perhaps," he suggests. "Showing a side of yourself that you don't want anyone to see? Especially not a room full of people you know?"

I nod. Mind you, I don't know whether it would be easier if they were all total strangers.

"Perfectly understandable," says Mr. Acevedo. "According to one study, nine in ten people would rather run into a burning building than make a speech in public. Yet you're standing here on that stage, and soon you'll be facing a huge audience who have paid money to watch you. So what do we do about that?"

"Put it to the back of your mind," Eleanor mumbles.

Mr. Acevedo raises his eyebrows. "Really, my dear Eleanor. We do not suppress it, we *use* it. We let our fear become Romeo's or Juliet's fear. Contrary to popular opinion, it is not an actor's job to inspire emotions in the audience. We have to bring them out within *ourselves* and let the audience share in that. And to do so, we have to show all the aspects of ourselves that we normally keep hidden from others." Mr. Acevedo looks at Eleanor. "That will be easier for you, Eleanor, because you're a woman. Society hasn't taught you to be embarrassed to show your emotions and vulnerabilities in the way that it has for men." He turns to me. "Charles, I know that some of your schoolmates in the audience will think they've got it sussed, that they know what matters in life, but I fear they still have a lot to learn. There are no rules on how to be a man or what one ought to feel. What I'm asking you to do on this stage might be the total opposite of what counts as cool among your friends. I'd like your acting to be unconditional, and to do that, you'll embarrass yourself, make a fool of yourself, laugh, scream, cry, the whole works. But this is a safe space where there's no room for judgment. I want you to know that. Especially you, Charles. Please stop always wanting to be liked, and show me who you really are."

Those might be the truest words anyone's ever spoken to me. And I might not yet be ready to accept them. I feel the resistance within me to what Mr. Acevedo just said, because I feel under attack and don't want him to be right.

But I force myself to nod. Not to look in Tori's direction. Why am I even thinking about her at this point? Maybe because she's the only person who knows me like that. Who's been with me when I've embarrassed myself, made a fool of myself, screamed, cried. And despite that, there are those times when I'm so incredibly shy around her.

"Good." Mr. Acevedo claps his hands. "Very well, then. Let's try it once more and see what happens."

TORI

I don't know how often I've asked myself during this rehearsal what I'm even doing here. Earlier, with the whole cast, I could understand it because keeping the group in order seemed an impossible task for one person. But now, when there's only Eleanor and Sinclair on stage, I wish I could just leave.

Mr. Acevedo sees things differently though. He thinks I should stay so that I'd know which scenes they were rehearsing. I spend as long as possible fiddling with my clipboard and reading through the notes I made earlier, but eventually I have to turn my attention back to the two of them.

Eleanor and Sinclair retake their positions once Mr. Acevedo's given them a little lecture. Not that they were bad earlier. There's chemistry between them, unfortunately, I have to give them that, but Sinclair in particular seems kind of restrained. Maybe it's because I'm here. Or because it's Eleanor he has to look at in that intense way.

She shuts her eyes and seems to be pulling herself together. Sinclair doesn't move. Is he looking at me? What's he doing? He should be looking at his Juliet, not into the audience.

When I frown, he seems to remember that too and turns away. He shakes his shoulders slightly and takes a deep breath.

The two of them are a good five meters apart. Eleanor opens her eyes, and she's so beautiful. She's standing there, erect and proud; she knows how gorgeous she is. Sinclair looks her over slowly and self-confidently. Entirely unrushed, as if he were suddenly no longer himself. He starts at her feet and raises his eyes to her knees.

I get goose bumps, because it's so quiet, and I can feel every bloody drop of desire as he studies Eleanor's mouth. The emotions are tangible when she opens her lips slightly and casts down her eyes. Shit, it's absolutely magical, and I don't like it. Well, I do like it, of course, because what the two of them are doing just now is art. But I'm afraid Sinclair at least isn't acting. He's just allowing himself to show the things he normally hides. All his fucking feelings and fascination for Eleanor. *The sun, temptation* . . . I could cry.

They move toward each other, and to me, it feels like a dance in total silence. Sinclair's steps are soundless, impatient, and proud. All at once, he's Romeo; I can see it clearly. All that cool arrogance and passion. I see that he wants Juliet and makes no secret of it. And it's attractive. It's so damn attractive because he seems surprisingly self-assured. I see him through Juliet's eyes, and he's the handsomest man in Verona. I want him to look at me like that and tell me without words that he wants me. I want it so desperately, so much that it hurts.

When he stops in front of Eleanor, I catch my breath. Eleanor's upper body is turned away from him slightly, because she's a mysterious woman, playing with Romeo and throwing him these fervent glances over her shoulder. I want to be her. And Romeo wants to have her.

There's a timeless elegance to Sinclair's movements. He takes her hand. "'I don't believe we've met.'"

Eleanor gives this astonished and flattered laugh—it's so charming that it's just not fair. "'No, I would have noticed you if we had.'"

"'May I take that as flirtation?'" Sinclair asks.

"'Take it however you like.'"

"'Good to know. Are you having fun?'"

"'The party's kind of lame.'" She studies him and sips her drink. "'I hope you haven't ditched your friends on my account?'"

"'Which friends?'"

Eleanor smiles knowingly. "'So you're alone here?'"

"'Not anymore.'" Sinclair's not taking his eyes off Eleanor as he reaches for her drink. "'If I drank from your glass, it would be like a kiss, don't you think?'"

"'Would it?'" Eleanor asks, putting her hand on his as he lifts her glass to his lips.

"'Or so I've heard,'" he says huskily.

Their eyes are liquid heat. "'Then it must be true,'" Eleanor breathes. "'Let lips do what hands do when they pray.'" She presses the palm of her hand to his and follows his strong arm up to his shoulder. Sinclair bites his bottom lip, and my mouth goes dry.

I flinch as Mr. Acevedo applauds.

"There, you see! That's exactly what I was talking about. That's exactly the vulnerability and passion we need. Fantastic work, you two." Sinclair blushes visibly and immediately shrinks two steps back from Eleanor, because he's such a bloody gentleman. She gives him a quick smile. I want to boak. "Victoria, what do you say?"

I freeze, but I smile. All the same, my voice is revealingly croaky as I say, "Yeah, it was amazing."

12

TORI

I think I'm jealous. There's no point in denying it any longer. I feel more and more toxic with each rehearsal as I'm forced to look on while Eleanor and Sinclair's stupid chemistry deepens even further. It's horrible. I don't want to be like this, but my emotions aren't giving me any choice. It gets on my nerves the way Sinclair's eyes keep straying in my direction every time they've played a particularly intense scene. It's almost like he has to keep checking I'm OK. I'm the assistant director: It doesn't matter to me. All I should care about is the play being a success, which is why I'm giving them tips I've got from books on ways they can build up even more tension. I let them have their starring-role moments and make an effort to grin and bear it. It's easier when I'm there and can watch. The afternoons that Eleanor and Sinclair are spending alone together *to get to know each other better* are a different kind of dire because they leave everything to my imagination. It's only too easy to picture them falling in love with each other, having deep and meaningful conversations on long walks through the wintry countryside around the school. I usually try to arrange to meet Val at the same time because that feels a bit like revenge and taking back control. If I'm honest, though, it's also incredibly childish.

I haven't seen Val this evening. He's probably in the gym, doing another round of weights, like he always does after rugby training. It doesn't seem particularly healthy to me, the importance he sets on his appearance and the existence of unnecessarily ripped muscles, but last time I tried to talk to him about that, he said it might do me a bit of good to come as well, sometimes. Obviously I took that as an insult, so now the only thing that helps me not keep thinking about Val, Sinclair, Eleanor, and this whole complicated mess is to read. It works for precisely five minutes, then Sinclair messages me.

S: What are you doing?
T: Nothing. You?
S: I'm at the bakery.
S: Want to come?

It's ages since he asked me, and I haven't dared just turn up unannounced. Who knows? Maybe he's been inviting Eleanor around there so that the two of them can shape bread rolls together, or do other things. Which would be OK—they're meant to be getting closer. I don't have a problem with that, even if that place and our nights together there were always just for us. Besides, I'm sure he comes up with more exciting plans for Eleanor. So I'm left with the bakery.

T: Give me five minutes.

Of course I need longer than that just to choose a jumper and put my hair up in a bun that looks flattering yet messy enough to make Sinclair think I didn't do it just for him. The usual thing.

The February night is clear and frosty as I leave the school grounds and walk to the village in the dark. If I hadn't lived here for seven years, I might find it creepy, but Ebrington is deserted at this time of night. Sinclair's Bakery is the only shop with a light on. It feels like déjà vu when I knock on the glass door and, a moment later, Sinclair opens it. He's wearing his dark-red apron and a beanie hat to keep his hair out of the way. His hands are dusty with flour, his forearms strong and muscular as he kneads the dough and I listen to his lines. When he suggested it, I jumped at the idea because it's a handy way of avoiding other conversations.

"'It's easy to laugh at this pain if you've never been hurt,'" he says, practicing a speech about Rosaline, who broke Romeo's heart. He's very convincing. "'I used to think it was pathetic too, but she caught me off guard. Lucky for me that I've stopped spending every waking second thinking about her since I met Juliet. Hold on . . . That's her house, isn't it? Why is there a light on this late? It's . . .'" He pauses, and his hands stop kneading.

I give him a moment, but when he looks to me for help, I prompt him. "'The east.'"

Sinclair looks even more confused now.

"'It is the east and Juliet is the sun,'" I repeat.

His face brightens. "Oh, yes." He looks away again and clears his throat softly. The way Sinclair slips in and out of this role is the most attractive thing I've seen in ages. His expression is almost transfigured when he's Romeo. I wish he could be like that all the time. "'She is the east and . . .' Wait, no."

I have to laugh. "Maybe that way works too."

He looks at me with those Romeo eyes that cut me to the quick. "'It is the east and Juliet is the sun. She is the sun, temptation, and the daughter of my accursed enemy. A Capulet, what a bad joke . . . But does that mean I want her any less? Of course not.'" His eyes flit over me. "'I shouldn't be here. If anyone sees me, there'll be trouble. But I can't leave; I must hear her voice. Just look at the way she's leaning her head on her hands.'"

I flush as I realize I'm actually resting my chin on my palm. I hastily straighten up.

Sinclair clears his throat. "'She's so far away, but I can't forget how soft her skin looked. Oh, God, I can't put her out of my head just because she's a Capulet.'"

I feel kind of dizzy as I speak Juliet's line. "'Woe is me . . .'"

Sinclair keeps looking at me. "'She speaks,'" he whispers. "'Oh, speak again, bright angel, speak and let me hear your voice.'"

"'Oh, Romeo,'" my voice is shaking, and I'm praying he won't notice, "'Romeo, this is all a bad joke. Why are you my enemy, a Montague, a man I may not love? As though, once I'd seen you, my heart had any choice . . .'"

Sinclair says nothing, so I look at him. His eyes are on me; he's stopped kneading the dough.

"Now you."

He twitches. His voice sounds rough as he continues: "'OK, she's talking to herself here, and eavesdropping is seriously uncool. But who knows when we'll ever meet again? We can't be seen out in the town. If our families knew . . . I can't leave now. I must speak to her.'"

I glance down at the script before continuing with Juliet's monologue. "'Refuse your name and give it to me. I mean what I say. Let me be yours and I will no longer be a Capulet.'"

"'Let me be by your side'?" Sinclair suggests as I frown. "Otherwise it makes her sound like an object."

I have to smile. "Yes, better."

"'Your name is the only thing that makes it impossible for us to be together,'" I continue. "'Love found me, yet I must push it away for the sake of a name. But what's in a name? Put your name aside and take me in its place, I beg you; o sweet heaven, give me this man.'"

Sinclair turns to me. "'I'll take you at your word.'" His voice trembles, his yearning is making me dizzy. "'Tell me that you want me, and I'll forget who I am. Listen to me, Juliet, the Capulets can't stand in my way. Your eyes are more perilous than their swords.'"

He looks me right in the eyes. His lips are flushed.

I have to stay as Juliet. "'Wait, who's there? What kind of a creep are you, listening in when I'm talking to myself by night?'"

"'It's me, my love. And I will take your name, don't doubt it. My own is hateful to me because it is an enemy to you.'"

"'Is that you, Romeo?'"

"'It is, my love.'"

"'Wow, we only spoke a few words to each other at that ball, yet I know your voice. Romeo. A Montague . . .'"

"'Not for a day longer if you dislike it.'" How can he sound so sincere about this unreal thing? I don't get it. How did he get to be this stupidly talented?

"'What are you doing here? It's madness! My parents will have a fit if they find out that you're in our grounds. Come on, Romeo, you know that.'"

"'I have night's cloak to hide me from their sight.'" He truly believes it; he sounds so proud—and I'm finding it endlessly attractive. The dash of arrogance that he usually lacks. "'It couldn't interest me less, Juliet. I will not allow the pointless feud between our families to stand in the way of our happiness.'"

"'I fear we do not really have a choice.'"

"'Why not? You said it yourself. I'll cast my name aside. It's all the same to me. All that matters is that we can be together.'"

"'Oh, Romeo, those were just glib words.'"

"'Is that so? It sounded very much like the truth to me.'"

I hesitate. "'OK, you're right. Let's stop beating around the bush. I'm sick of acting like I don't want you. But don't you go thinking I'm a pushover, that I was only playing hard to get so you'd put some effort in. Nothing could be further from the truth.'" I stop and jerk up my head abruptly.

"We'll change that," says Sinclair, before I can open my mouth. "It's bullshit, isn't it?"

I nod slowly. "It's a bit unnecessary."

"Of course Juliet's not easy. Besides, even if she was, why

would that be a problem?" he says, and I can hear real annoyance in his voice. "Because it's unladylike?"

"They were different times," I say lamely.

"Yes, but in *these* times, a woman should have the self-confidence to say that she wants a man, just the same way he can."

My mouth is suddenly dry.

"Or don't you think so?"

"Yes." We look at each other. It's quiet. All I can hear is my heart thumping.

Does that mean he wants me to say it?

No, come on, get over yourself. This is about Romeo and Juliet, not the two of us. Why wouldn't it be? For pity's sake . . .

"You should ask Eleanor what she thinks about it," I say hurriedly.

"I don't care about Eleanor," he blurts. "I mean . . . I do care, but you're the scriptwriter here. It's your call."

"You two have to act it."

Sinclair gulps.

When he doesn't reply, I continue, "But maybe Juliet should actually say that, and then he can point out that it's wrong. Like you just did."

"You mean to give the audience a chance to question the statement?"

"Exactly." I force a tiny smile, but it doesn't really work. I'm about to ask if we should carry on when Sinclair opens his mouth.

"Has Val said stuff like that?" he asks.

I feel cold. "Why do you ask?"

"I've heard the way he talks about Eleanor."

I don't ask what he's heard, and to be honest, I don't want to know. I shrug. "He doesn't mean it."

"So why would he say it?"

"Sinclair, that's how he is. He doesn't think about stuff. He's never really got his head around feminism and all that."

"Is he planning to?"

"How would I know? Doesn't matter to you, does it?"

"Yes, it does."

I sigh. "Oh, my God. He doesn't always think before he speaks. But he doesn't mean anything bad by it."

"So he means it nicely? Oh, well, that's all right then. And anyway, I get the impression he knows exactly what he's saying. And exactly how he needs to act to get what he wants."

"What do you mean by that?" I ask quietly.

Sinclair says nothing. His gaze weighs a ton. We both know the answer to my question.

"He manipulates you," he says, in the end. "He tries to make you believe stupid stuff."

"You can't know that."

"Tori, I've got eyes in my head. And I know you. You're different when he's around."

"And what makes you think that's a bad thing? Maybe I'm different because he treats me differently." *Differently from the way you do . . .* Like I'm desirable. Because he shows me he wants me, and I don't have to keep guessing at what he feels for me. "Anyway, you're different when Eleanor's around too."

"Tori, leave Eleanor out of this."

"Why? It was you who brought her up."

He clenches his fists and shuts his eyes for a moment. "Why can't we talk about this stuff without fighting?"

"I'm not fighting," I say coolly.

"No, of course not."

"I'm just asking myself what you expect. What do you want to hear from me, Sinclair? That Val treats me like shit and you were right? Is that it?"

"I'm just bloody well worried about you, OK?"

"In that case, everything's fine. Just as well we spoke about it."

"Tori," he growls.

"What? *What*, Sinclair? If you want to tell me something, then do it. Right now. I'm all ears."

We look at each other. His blue eyes spark, but I can see uncertainty in them. His jaw muscles stand out, and he swallows. He doesn't say anything. Same as ever.

I exhale loudly. "Good, that's what I thought." I look at the clock behind him. "It's late. I should head back. Or do you still need me here?"

"Tori . . ."

"Do you still need me here?" I repeat.

He looks at me. I'm praying he'll shake his head.

"No."

Great.

I reach for my script and turn away.

All the way back to school, I'm wondering why it always goes like this. Why we keep hurting each other and lying to each other. But maybe they're not lies. Maybe it'll just never happen. Maybe

I've spent six years reading too much into this thing between Sinclair and me. But in that case, how is it possible that I want to burn up whenever he looks at me? Can you really be that wrong about something?

The night is cold. My heart is too.

I'm afraid you can.

SINCLAIR

You shouldn't decide anything when you're angry. Mum's said that so often it ought to be engraved on my heart. Normally, I try to listen to her words, but right now, I don't want to be sensible. I want to pound the shit out of this sourdough, and because there's nobody here to see, I do so. Frustratingly, it doesn't even make a satisfying sound when my fist connects with the soft mass. I repeat the process twice more, but it doesn't relieve my feelings the way I'd hoped, so I pull out my phone and use my floury fingers to bring up my contacts list.

I've never messaged Eleanor, and I wouldn't normally dare. But there isn't normally rage boiling in my belly because I have—yet again—picked a fight with my best friend. Eleanor Attenborough wouldn't normally have given me her number after our last rehearsal, and we wouldn't normally be acting together in the main fucking roles in our school play. So I just type.

S: Hi, it's Sinclair

Fuck, she's online. OK. I didn't think this far ahead, but there's no going back now.

 E: Hi? What's up?

I shut my eyes for a moment, then keep typing.

 S: I hope you don't mind me just messaging you
 E: That's why I gave you my number
 S: What are you doing tomorrow? Want to go for a walk or something?
 E: Yeah, sure. After study hour?

I answer hastily, before I lose my nerve.

 S: Perfect. Looking forward to it!

I slowly lower my phone, feeling like a traitor. And then I focus on my work again.

13

TORI

"This looks a bit like a hand, doesn't it?" We've got an art session in enrichment, and Emma's spent hours working on this lump of clay, but despite all her efforts, it's more reminiscent of some kind of accident. "What do you think?"

I just nod because I haven't the heart to tell her the truth. Emma might wipe the floor with the rest of us when it comes to sport, but her artistic talents leave a little to be desired. It's kind of hilarious how similar she and Henry are in this respect. His clay sculpture is just as shapeless, but I'm trying not to look in his direction—he's sitting next to Sinclair.

"Tori?"

"Hm?" I look up.

Emma's leaning down to take a closer look at my work. "Why does yours look so much more realistic?" She sounds so disillusioned that I start to feel sorry for her.

"You have to pay attention to the proportions. You haven't made the fingers long enough, I'm afraid."

Emma sighs in frustration. "I'm sick of this."

"It's still pretty good, Emma."

She glances past me to where Henry and Sinclair are sitting. "I'm going to join the boys' table and make myself feel better by laughing at Henry's model," she announces cheerily. I make no move to follow her, so she pauses. "Aren't you coming?"

I shake my head. "I'm in the zone just now."

Liar . . . I've been staring at my work for at least ten minutes without lifting a finger.

"Hm." Emma sits back down. "What's wrong?"

"What do you mean?"

"What's the problem?" she says, not taking her eyes off me. "Something's wrong, isn't it?"

"Why do you say that?" I ask feebly, but Emma's too good a judge of character—we've barely known each other six months, but she can see right through me.

"You're upset," she says.

I want to cry. My stupid eyes are welling up, so I blink a few times. "I'm just tired," I say, forcing myself to smile.

Emma looks over at Ms. Barnett, who's marking tests at the front.

"Come on," she murmurs, nodding at the door. In these enrichment classes, we're allowed to chat, and we don't have to ask permission to leave the room to use the loo.

I follow Emma to the sinks, where we wash the clay off our hands. Sinclair glances across and immediately looks away again. As we pass Olive and Grace, Olive keeps her head firmly down. A room full of people who used to be my friends and now hate me. Great.

Emma shuts the door behind us. I don't know why, but being out in the corridors during lessons still feels kind of out of bounds.

"So," Emma says as we walk side by side, "is this about Sinclair and Eleanor?"

I laugh. "What—because they got the main roles? Rubbish. I'm happy for them."

Emma eyes me skeptically. "OK . . . Val, then? Or Olive?" she adds, and I don't know why, but her name is like a stab in the chest. For a moment at Sinclair's party, I felt a bit hopeful, but since then, Olive's been just as off with me as she has for weeks. We haven't even discussed the uniform thing, and I'd hoped the subject might bring us closer together again. But it looks like we just don't have anything to say to each other anymore.

"Maybe a bit of everything," I admit.

"I don't want to interfere in your friendship, but would it help if you and Olive just talked? Just quietly?"

I can clearly hear how carefully Emma's picking her words. But they still make me angry. I'd love to do that—talk to Olive—but if she doesn't want to, what can I do? I can't make her open up to me.

"Sorry, but no. It's like we don't have anything to say to each other."

"Do you really mean that?" Emma asks.

"OK, not exactly. It's Olive who doesn't have anything to say to me. I'd love to talk to her, but we hardly ever do. We haven't even had an actual argument. Suddenly, things were permanently tense, and she's got more and more withdrawn ever since." I feel my throat tighten.

"Is it possible that Olive's dealing with some big load of baggage and thinks she can't tell anyone about it?"

I'm silent for a while. "Maybe, but that doesn't make it any better. We always used to be able to talk about anything."

"Sometimes people forget that."

"Emma, why are you even sticking up for her? Olive wasn't exactly nice to you last term."

Emma stares at her shoes. Then she shrugs her shoulders. "I can see myself in her. And I got so much wrong."

"You didn't do anything wrong."

"I could understand why she was angry, and it's much better now."

"Did she ever apologize to you?" I ask.

"Not directly. But in her way, she did." Emma looks at me again. "When Henry was in the sick bay, she got them to let me in to see him. It felt like her way of making peace."

"It really was."

"Maybe something like that could work for you two."

I sigh quietly. Maybe. But maybe not. The only thing I'm certain of is that, if things carry on like this, I'm going to lose Olive. And that would kill me. She, Sinclair, and Henry are my oldest friends at Dunbridge. But she's more than that. She's the sister I never had. We've never had secrets from each other, and it hurts that that's changed. "I hope so," I say.

"Oh." Emma looks guiltily over her shoulder as we hear footsteps behind us. It's Mrs. Sinclair coming around the corner with Mr. Harper.

Emma glances at me, but they've already seen us.

"Good morning," I say as they walk past. I avoid addressing Mrs. Sinclair by name if at all possible. Outside school, I'm allowed to call her Nora, the same way that Sinclair's on first-name terms with my parents, but here she's Mrs. Sinclair to me, the same as for everyone else.

"Tori, Emma." She gives us a nod. "Shouldn't you two be in class?"

"We were just heading back," Emma says. She's pretty much the worst liar I know.

I'm sure Mrs. Sinclair thinks the same. She studies us briefly. "Well, be quick about it, please."

She continues her conversation with Mr. Harper as we walk on.

"Loos," I say the moment they're out of earshot.

Emma nods at once.

"How's things with your dad?" I ask.

Emma doesn't answer right away. It's a tricky subject, I know. But Emma's become too good a friend for me to leave it at that. I want to know how she is and what's up in her life.

"He's making an effort," she says. "Seriously. He messages regularly and asks how I'm doing. We might be meeting up next week. He wants to get to know Henry."

"That's nice," I say. Emma's not looking thrilled. "Isn't it?"

"Yeah, it is. I think it's going to take time. I have to see first if he really means it this time. Otherwise, I'm only gonna get hurt again."

"That sounds wise." And I know what I'm talking about. Getting hurt by someone who doesn't really mean something is my specialist subject.

"So everything's OK with Sinclair?"

Great. She's not going to drop it till I tell her the truth. I sigh, which is meant to sound irritated, but all at once, I'm on the point of bursting into tears.

"Oh, Tori," Emma murmurs as it's getting harder and harder for me to blink away the tears.

"I don't think anything's OK, really." I eventually get some words out. "Not me and Sinclair either."

"Henry says you're working on the script now too." She doesn't have to say anything else. I'm sure Emma knows exactly how shite that feels.

"Yeah, I dunno." I wipe my eyes with my sleeve. "It's all gone so wrong, Emma. But I shouldn't care. I can't expect Sinclair not to like anyone else when I'm dating Val."

"Are you happy with Val?" she asks.

"Yeah, course. But well . . . Why isn't it enough for me? Why aren't I happy, Emma?"

"Maybe your heart's trying to tell you something," she suggests quietly.

I gulp, because I can't think about that. "But it doesn't matter either way. Sinclair's into Eleanor. He said so himself."

"Come on, Tori, let's face it—even he doesn't actually believe that."

"Yes, he does. He told me so the night after the New Year Ball, when he was so wrecked."

Emma looks thoughtfully at me. "What are you afraid of?" she asks in the end.

My chest constricts slightly.

Yeah, OK, what? Everything, to be honest. Of being rejected, of making a fool of myself. Of mistaking friendship for feelings, and of losing Sinclair. "I don't want to break what we have," I say. "And then there's Val."

"So are you two together?" Emma is clearly making an effort to sound neutral.

I shrug. "Don't know. Kind of." Even though we've barely seen each other lately.

"And is that what you want?"

Not. A. Clue.

Honestly, I don't know. I don't know anything anymore, haven't done for way too long.

Something about Valentine Ward fascinates me. Maybe just that it's *me* he's paying attention to. But is that enough to be with someone for?

I want to be with Sinclair, but that's not an option.

"Did you ever try not to like him?"

Emma looks at me thoughtfully. "Henry?"

I nod.

"Of course I tried. The whole time. But I knew it was hopeless. It was destiny, him and me."

Destiny. It really was. Made for each other, no arguments.

But if that was true for Sinclair and me too, some higher power would have brought us together ages ago by now.

Maybe it really is just time for me to get over Charles Sinclair.

SINCLAIR

I don't know why, but strolling down to Ebrington with Eleanor after study hour so that we can "get to know each other better" feels like cheating. The two of us haven't spent much time out and about alone together before, but this never gets awkward. Eleanor is just so easy to talk to. She asks me questions and tells me things about her life as if we'd done this forever. I really do like her, I realize—if I hadn't before—when we're sitting opposite each other in the Blue Room Café and she pulls out her phone to make a note of the films I've been recommending.

"They all sound really cool," she says, putting her phone away again. As she looks up and smiles at me, I sense we're through the small-talk part of this conversation now. The waiter brings tea for me and a caramel latte for Eleanor and sets them down. I wrap my fingers around the dark-blue china cup.

"Honestly, I don't know the best way to say this," she says, suddenly sounding nervous. My stomach grumbles as Eleanor glances down. "So I'd better just get started and spit it out. Well, we're supposed to be getting to know each other, and I want to be completely honest with you, to avoid any silly misunderstandings." She looks at me again.

My blood runs cold.

She knows. She knows I'm pretending to have a crush on her. Doesn't she? Stuff like that gets around a school like ours, and Eleanor has plenty of friends.

Should I deny it? Not that she'd think I really . . .

Eleanor takes a deep breath. "Me and my girlfriend are OK

with kissing scenes in rehearsals and the performance. We've talked about how far I'll go."

She speaks so fast that I just nod. It's only then that I take in the meaning of her words.

Hold the bus.

Girlfriend?

Does that mean . . . ?

I only realize I'm staring at Eleanor when she lowers her head again.

"OK, yeah," I say hurriedly. "Cool. Uh . . . not cool, good." *Shit. Stop talking.* "But it is cool too. Fuck . . . Sorry, I'd better just shut up now."

Eleanor looks at me, and I trail off. She bites her bottom lip, and a second later, the tension between us breaks as she laughs loudly. It's so infectious that I join in too and feel myself relaxing.

"Oh, wow. I was worried it would be weird to tell you, but I didn't know it would be *that* weird!"

"Sorry, sorry," I repeat. "That's a hundred percent just me."

"I wanted you to know," she says, sounding more serious again now. Her eyes flit around the café, and although there's only us and a group of older women here, she lowers her voice. "And it would mean the world to me if you didn't tell anyone." She gulps. "It's . . . all still megaconfusing, and nobody at school knows except my best friends. I . . . I don't know, maybe it's silly, but I don't feel ready yet."

"It's not silly," I say. "Not at all. It's your decision, and if that's what you feel happiest with, I totally respect it."

A slight smile creeps over Eleanor's face. "Thank you, Sinclair."

"Thank you for trusting me," I say, and I really mean it. "Do I know her?" I ask.

"We got together online," Eleanor says, burying her face in her hands. "On TikTok."

I can't help laughing. "No way?"

"Yeah, it's a bit cringy, but what can I say? Sophia's a student in London, so we've only met in person a couple of times." A fine red blush spreads over Eleanor's cheeks. She looks like Juliet. At that moment, I understand who she's thinking of when she slips into her role.

"That's so lovely," I say. "Seriously, Eleanor. And I promise not to tell anyone."

Not even Tori . . . Even though it would probably make things instantly way less complicated if I let her know that Eleanor's got a girlfriend. But she told me in confidence, and if there's one thing I'm good at, it's keeping stuff to myself.

"How about you?" Eleanor asks. I lift my head. "Are you OK with kissing me on stage?"

"Sure," I say at once. Should I have hesitated a bit longer? I don't want her to think I want more from her.

"I just wondered. Because of Tori."

I freeze. "Why because of Tori?"

"Uh, well, I thought you two—"

"We're just friends," I interrupt.

Eleanor's left eyebrow climbs in slow motion.

"And she's with Valentine," I add, more bitterly.

"True." Eleanor sounds just as somber. "But I guess that doesn't change how much you like her."

My ears go hot. "She's my best friend," I say.

"The chemistry between you two is out of this world," Eleanor says, as if she hadn't even been listening to me. "And I'm sure Val can see that too. He can be very difficult if he doesn't get what he wants." Eleanor glances at me, then continues without waiting for me to reply. "I regret having been with him. God knows what that was all about. He's got charisma, and he can really turn on the charm when he wants to. But if you wind him up, things get nasty. Which they did when I realized I didn't feel the same way about him as about Sophia. Sometimes I feel like I should warn Tori about him, but I know it's none of my business."

"Me too," I say, not quite knowing which I mean—the warning-her part or the none-of-my-business part. A bit of both, probably. "But sadly, I can't talk to her about it without it turning into a fight."

"So you do like her?"

I shut my eyes, and then, for the first time, I nod. Slowly, but it feels good. To finally admit to the truth.

Eleanor's silent. Then, "Does she know how you feel about her?"

"Of course not." I laugh. "She thinks . . ." I hesitate. ". . . She thinks I'm into you."

"That shows," Eleanor says, to my surprise.

"Great." I sigh.

"And are you planning to tell her how things really are?" Eleanor sips her coffee.

"I don't know," I say.

"What's stopping you?"

I raise an eyebrow. "Valentine Ward?"

"Oh, please." Eleanor laughs. "I get the impression it's more about your feelings."

"We've known each other so long," I say slowly. "If it was meant to be, it would have happened a long time ago."

"How can it, if you're both waiting for the other one to take the first step?"

OK, face the facts. Eleanor can see through the whole business between Tori and me from a mile off.

"But anyway, it's none of my business," she adds. "I just wanted to be open with you about it. We can discuss stage-kissing technique instead if you'd rather."

"You mean . . . fake kisses?"

"Yeah, wait." Eleanor glances around, then leans forward and puts both hands on my cheeks. Her fingers are warm from her glass, and all I can think about is Tori's lips on mine. Eleanor puts her thumbs on my lips. I hold my breath. She comes closer to my face until there's only a hand's breadth between our mouths. "And if we turn away from the audience slightly, nobody can tell the difference." She lets go of me. "Would that be better?"

I nod. I'm boiling.

"Sorry, I didn't mean to jump on you like that."

"No, it's OK." I clear my throat. "But . . . yeah, maybe it would be better if we did it like that."

"All right." Eleanor smiles. "Then we will."

14

TORI

Getting over someone means acting like an adult around them. No more ignoring them or looking away. I notice I'm confusing Sinclair by being *perfectly ordinary* instead of huffy. And lo and behold, after French, he asks if everything's OK. In a slightly guilty-sounding way that's probably meant kind of as an apology. Normally I'd tell him to piss off, but as I'm over him now, I pull myself together and offer to listen to him practicing his lines again if he likes.

We agree to meet up in the theater at the end of the school day and head off to our own classes. I'm early for history and can't see Emma anywhere, but the door to the English classroom is ajar. I pause as I hear voices from inside.

"What's wrong, Olive?" Mr. Acevedo. I hold my breath. "I thought your last test result was just you having a bad day, but the latest one was worse, I'm afraid."

There's a long silence. Part of me wants to creep away as quietly as possible, to wait somewhere else.

"I don't know." Olive's voice sounds thin. "I didn't do enough revision."

"I'd be happy to believe you, Olive, but all your teachers are concerned about you. It's not just in my subject where you're struggling. I know A levels are a big step up, and we all want you to do as well as you possibly can in your exams next year."

My throat clenches. I'd noticed that Olive's grades haven't been amazing lately, but I hadn't known quite how bad they'd got.

"I'll do better." I hear her quiet voice. In the ensuing silence, I can practically see Mr. Acevedo's serious, worried face. "It's just that everything's kind of difficult just now."

"I'd like to help you, Olive, but you have to tell me what you need."

"Nothing," she says at once.

"Let me make a suggestion. As you know, we've started rehearsals for our end-of-year play now. We could always use some help behind the scenes, with costumes and makeup and so on. Would you like to get involved in that? I'd be very happy to have you and it always looks good to have taken part in this kind of activity—I can mention it when I write your reference."

"I'm not sure if it's really my thing," I hear Olive say.

"Having something to take your mind off your troubles, whatever they are, might be beneficial, Olive. I can't emphasize enough that we want to help you get the grades you deserve."

"I'll think about it."

"Please do. And you can always come to me for personal concerns as well as schoolwork. And if you'd rather speak to a woman, Ms. Vail's door is always open, as you know. So is Mrs. Sinclair's.

But I don't have to tell you that, Olive. You've been at this school long enough, hm?"

"Yes, thank you, I do know."

"Good. Well, be off with you."

I step back hurriedly as I hear approaching footsteps. The door opens, and Olive sees me on the other side of the hallway. She hesitates as Mr. Acevedo follows her out of the room and hurries away.

"Hi," I say before Olive can vanish too. She eyes me doubtfully. "It would be fab if you were in the drama club too."

Her face instantly hardens. "You were listening in?"

Shit . . . My cheeks start burning. "No, sorry, I . . . OK, yes. I was early for history, and I couldn't help overhearing, but I . . ."

"Why do you always have to stick your nose into other people's business?" Olive snaps. There's no hint of brokenness in her voice now. "We're not friends anymore. What part of that is so hard to understand?"

I flinch. "I thought—"

"Stop it. Just stop it, OK?"

There's so much I want to say, but Olive doesn't let me. She turns away. I watch as she shakes her head, and I feel grim. Because she's right; it really wasn't OK to listen to her conversation with Mr. Acevedo. And my stomach churns when I think about what he said. It's out of character for Olive not to give a shit about anything. Something must have happened, and I can only hope she's got someone to talk to about it. It never even occurred to me that Olive might be finding the work so hard.

She's always done well at school—no more of a straight-As kind of person than I am, but always good enough.

I find it hard to concentrate on my next classes. I'm not with Olive for anything today, and I don't bump into her in the corridors anywhere. After lessons finish, I'm about to go up to our wing to look for her when I run into Sinclair, who reminds me that we agreed to practice his lines. He asks if I'm all right, and I just nod, forcing myself not to think about Olive. Maybe I'll get a chance to speak to her in the next couple of days and apologize. Maybe I could use the uniform thing as an excuse to talk to her. It got kind of forgotten about after Sinclair's party, unfortunately, and I've got my hands full with the scriptwriting club and the assistant-director business. But it's too important to me to just drop it again, especially after last Monday, when another group of fourth-formers staged a protest by wearing trousers to the morning assembly and were sent back to their rooms to change.

We've got an hour before the rehearsal, and we have the theater to ourselves until then. I'd been expecting the doors to be locked, but they open when Sinclair gives them a tug. He steps to the side and lets me go ahead of him. The carpeted stairs swallow the sound of our footsteps. It's almost unnaturally quiet once the doors have shut out the buzz of voices from outside.

"Which scene do you want to go through?" Sinclair asks, throwing his bag onto a seat in the bottom row.

"Hold on." I reach for my iPad and open the cover. "We're in the middle of writing the farewell scene when Romeo gets banished from Verona."

"After he's killed Tybalt?"

"Yes, that's the one." I scroll down my document. "Romeo's sent into exile and Juliet's just heard about it from her nurse."

"OK." Sinclair walks to the edge of the stage and presses both hands onto it. He pushes up, and in one smooth movement, he's sitting on the stage. "Shall we carry on with that scene and you can write as we go?"

"Yeah, sounds good." I put my stuff on the stage and I'm about to walk around to the little flight of steps to one side when Sinclair crouches down and holds his hand out to me. I hesitate for a moment, then let him pull me up.

He sits facing me, one leg bent, his eyes on the original text we're adapting for our version. His blond hair flops into his face.

"Good." I clear my throat quietly. "So Juliet's shocked at Mercutio and Tybalt dying, but she's standing by Romeo. And she's in despair because her father has just promised her to Paris and wants them to get married this same week. There's no way you want to leave her here, but you know you won't survive the night in Verona if you bump into the Capulets. You'd rather flee under cover of darkness, but you can't psych yourself up to it, so you stay until daybreak. OK?"

Sinclair looks one hundred percent focused as he glances up from the text. I'm still as fascinated as ever by watching him slip into the part, shedding his own identity as he does so.

"OK, let's get started. We haven't settled on the words for this bit yet, so just improvise and we'll see what happens."

I try to gather myself, then speak Juliet's first lines.

"'Is it true what they're saying in the streets, Romeo? Tell me it isn't so.'"

Sinclair's expression is blank, and I can see the shock and despair in his face. And feel him pulling himself together for Juliet.

"'What are they saying?'" he asks tonelessly.

"'That Tybalt's dead. That you killed him. Is it true, Romeo?'"

His jaw muscles stand out as he lowers his head. "'I'm not proud of what I've done.'"

"'My God, Romeo! Do you know what that means? My father is raging! He wants you dead, he wants—'"

"'I know, my love,'" he interrupts harshly. "'It wasn't my intention, but Tybalt left me no choice. He would have killed me, he was so angry. And as for your father . . . I can't stay in Verona. I've come to bid you farewell.'"

My throat constricts. I'm amazed—we're only acting, and yet, somehow, we're not. "'So it's true?'" I whisper. "'You're banished?'"

"'It's the only way, my love.'" Sinclair's eyes are on me, his expression so insistent that I can't move. "'I can go and live, or stay and die.'"

"'Then I'm coming with you.'"

"'Don't be silly.'"

"'I'm not being silly, Romeo, I'm desperate! Don't do this to me.'"

"'Do you think this is fun for me? I'm going out of my mind at the thought of having to be apart from you.'"

"'Then stay here,'" I beg. "'Please, at least for a few hours more. It's not morning yet; you can stay.'"

"'Can't you hear? The birds are singing; the sky is growing lighter. I have no more time.'"

"'Let me go with you,'" I whisper. "'Take me with you, I mean it.'"

"'You know I can't,'" says Sinclair, looking me right in the eyes. "'It's too dangerous.'"

"'I don't care.'"

"'But I do. I must always care when it comes to you, don't you see?'"

I gulp. "'So is this goodbye? For how long? Forever? I can't bear a single day without you.'" I put down my script. "'But I'd never forgive myself if you stayed for my sake and they found you. Perhaps it is better if you get away for a while. Just until things have calmed down again here.'"

"'Yes, perhaps.'"

"'Look at me. You're deathly pale.'"

Sinclair doesn't move. He looks at me and, for a moment, I'm sure he doesn't know what comes next. "'It's just the light, my love.'" My stomach drops; he leans forward a little. "'You know what? I don't care. Let them catch me and put me to death. What would life be without you? Come, then, death, and take me! If I cannot be at your side, I have nothing to lose.'"

"'What are you saying?'" I slide a little closer. I feel the fear in my belly. I'm Juliet, and the love of my life is going to leave me because our story is star-crossed. There's no way out. "'You can't mean that. Don't you believe in our love? That it's stronger than hate? Than our families' senseless feud? Run away and come back once the dust has settled. I must believe that, and so you will too.'"

"'Juliet, it's no good,'" he whispers. "'It's getting light outside. I have to go.'"

"'Promise me that we'll meet again.'"

Sinclair nods without a second's hesitation. "'This is not farewell forever, I give you my word.'"

His eyes are full of pain and longing. I feel like I'm drowning in them.

"And then you have to kiss her," I say as I remember the script and hastily look away. "OK, fine. So where shall we pick it up again?"

"Right here." His voice is hoarse. He looks at me as I raise my head.

"What do you mean?" I ask, and before I can blink, he's beside me. His mouth is on mine, and everything goes up in flames.

Years of my life in which I've tried not to want him, gone in a split second.

Sinclair's lips are just the way I remember them. Warm and soft. Gentle and skillful, but demanding too this time. Just like his hands, holding me. He puts a hand on the back of my neck; I lean in. Heat burns through me as he pulls me between his legs, and I'm suddenly half lying on him. I feel the hard stage beneath my knees and his erection against my thigh. I'm dizzy because it's all so greedy, and at the same time, it feels like the last piece of the puzzle in the whole universe is slipping into place.

I don't know who I'm kissing. Romeo or Sinclair. Sinclair or Charles. The boy I fell in love with in the juniors, or the man who's been driving me insane for weeks. Either way, it's better than anything. Better than I ever imagined.

He smells the same. Of milk and honey and something tangy that's making me lose my mind. His hands run over my trembling body, and every single reason why this shouldn't be happening disappears into thin air. It's as though we'd kissed a thousand times before, yet everything is intense in a way that only a first kiss can be. Our lips, which open for each other, his hot tongue in my mouth. His face under my fingers, that warm, soft skin and his firm body. Muscles he developed while I was busy trying to kid myself that I wasn't in love with him.

He stops and looks at me. "God . . . Tori."

His gruff voice sends the heat between my legs. I kiss him again. He runs his fingers through my hair. I forget my own name. And where we are. On the stage in our school theater. It's only when the door opens at the back of the auditorium that I remember. Voices, laughter, Sinclair freezing as I startle and pull back, push away from him.

SINCLAIR

The love story of Romeo and Juliet is totally divorced from reality. For so many reasons.

One: Getting married as soon as possible for reasons of social respectability is anything but a desirable life goal (let alone the road to happiness).

Two: Romeo and Juliet set eyes on one another, want each other, and have not the least doubt that they're meant for each other. (So simplistic!)

Three: You can't just kiss somebody once and expect that to solve all your problems at a stroke.

Tori and I are living proof of that. I spend the whole rehearsal looking uncertainly in her direction and away again the moment she notices. We're doing method-acting group work, and by now, I almost doubt that it actually happened.

I feel dizzy at the thought of the hard stage under my shoulder blades and Tori's soft body on top of mine. Her lips—they fit mine as if they were made for each other.

"Charles! Wake up!" Mr. Acevedo is waving his script in the air. I jump. Apparently, I missed his instructions for the next exercise. The others have already paired up.

"Shall we?" Eleanor asks, suddenly appearing at my side.

"Yeah, sure." I watch the others. "What are we meant to be doing again?"

Eleanor frowns. "Eye contact, and we're not allowed to break it."

"Oh." I look at her. "OK."

Just as well I don't have to do this with Tori. I wouldn't last more than three seconds before I'd want to take her face in my hands again.

Eleanor's eyes are brown. Not as pale as Tori's. They're more like molten chocolate.

"Are you OK?" she asks.

Damn.

"Don't look away, Sinclair." She smiles, but her eyes remain serious. Why is this so bloody hard?

"Sorry." I tense my shoulders. Can you tell what Tori and I were doing just by looking at me? My lips are still throbbing when I remember our kiss. And so's my crotch, by the way. "And yeah, sure, are we meant to be discussing anything in particular?"

"Just talking about our week," says Eleanor, head aslant. I want to seek out Tori. I want to look at her. Until I find answers in her eyes as to what just happened between us. And what it means. "So how was your week?"

"Great," I lie. "How was yours?"

"Stressful. Didn't get anything done and I'm exhausted."

"You don't look it."

Tiny lines shape Eleanor's face as she smiles. "Whoa, you're such a liar."

"It was the truth, I promise." That might be the first true thing I've said today. Eleanor's glowing—she's positively radiant. Is that because she's in love? I want Tori to look at me like that. For my sake. And she won't. Which is my fault. And because Valentine Ward is a tool and I don't even want to think about what would happen if he heard that we kissed. Which he's bound to do eventually. Isn't he? Or is Tori planning to act like it never happened? I start to sweat.

"Spit it out," Eleanor says. "What's wrong? I can see something's wrong, Sinclair. Don't look away."

"Tori and I . . ." I lower my voice so that nobody around can hear. "We were going through my lines just now. A kiss scene. We rehearsed it very thoroughly."

"I see." Eleanor's eyes sparkle. "Very thoroughly, uh-huh."

"And now I'm freaking out."

"Why are you freaking out?"

"Because we didn't get to talk about it. People walked in."

"Who kissed who?" Eleanor blinks innocently.

"I think that was me."

She smiles. "Wow. I'm proud of you, Sinclair."

"But maybe she wasn't OK with it."

"Did you ask her?"

"No." I shiver. "Not really."

"Did she pull away?"

"Not really."

"Interesting, in-ter-est-ing."

"Very good, well done!" Mr. Acevedo calls. "That will do."

I immediately look to the side. Tori's watching Eleanor and me. Her face is expressionless. She looks away before I can read anything in her face.

"How did it feel? Louis?"

I can't listen. It's torture, not being able to speak to Tori. I can barely keep my mind on the stage the whole rest of the time. We're rehearsing an early scene, one with Mercutio, Benvolio, and Romeo. I'm rubbish. I can feel it.

"Stop." Mr. Acevedo interrupts the scene. My heart sinks to my boots. Louis and Gideon look inquiringly at me. Mr. Acevedo studies us. "May I ask where the problem is?"

"Which problem?" asks Louis.

"Yes, which problem . . . which problem? Let's ask our Romeo."

All eyes are on me, and I want to die.

"Charles, please. What's wrong?"

"Nothing, I . . ." My voice fails, and someone laughs. I kissed Tori, and now she won't look at me. That's what's wrong. "Wasn't it any good?"

"Wasn't it any good?" Mr. Acevedo repeats. "Did it feel like it was good?"

I don't reply right away. "No," I say in the end.

"Well, there's a thing." Mr. Acevedo looks around the group. "So make a note of that. If something doesn't feel good, it's very probable that it isn't good."

The others start talking. Mr. Acevedo keeps looking at me.

"I'm sorry. Shall I start again?"

He doesn't react. What does he want? Am I meant to read his mind? I notice that I'm getting angry. Helpless, angry, and overwhelmed. The others are whispering, heads together.

Mr. Acevedo waves at the stage. "Please."

What, then? Why's he being so weird?

I exchange glances with Louis and Gideon, who are looking about as confused as I feel. I step a few paces to one side and take up my starting position. The others begin their dialogue, which is lively and engaging. The role of Benvolio seems tailor-made for Gideon. I make the mistake of looking to the side. Down to where Grace and the others are watching the scene intently. It's only Tori who isn't focused on Gideon and Louis. She's watching me.

She chews her bottom lip gently, and she has no idea how wild that drives me. Her lips are as red as her cheeks. I can feel her warm skin under my fingers and her soft mouth.

"Charles!"

It makes me jump.

Fuck.

Louis and Gideon are looking expectantly at me, not speaking, which must mean that I've missed my cue.

"OK, good." Mr. Acevedo turns around. "We're done for the day. You can pack up." There's silence, followed by a murmur of voices. "Not you, though, Charles."

Louis and Gideon are looking sympathetic as they leave the stage. Mr. Acevedo beckons me down. Tori's left.

"I can make you replay the scene three times to try to get you up to your normal standards, or you can just tell me what's wrong," says Mr. Acevedo as soon as we're alone. "So what's wrong?"

"It's nothing." I clear my throat. "It's been a long day. I'm sorry. I didn't get much sleep."

Mr. Acevedo eyes me intently. "Well, do you honestly want me to advise you to go to bed in better time, or would you prefer to stop making this like getting blood out of a stone?"

Silence.

"Does it have to do with anyone in this theater?"

Stubborn silence.

"If so, I would advise you to take a leaf out of Romeo's book."

"From what I heard, things didn't work out too well for him," I mumble.

Mr. Acevedo smiles. "Well, at least you've still got a sense of humor. And the option to do better than he did."

"If only it was that easy." I look over to the door. Maybe Tori's waiting for me.

"I believe in you, Charles. Truly. Off with you, now. I get the impression you need to talk to somebody."

I beat it.

I walk up the steps, open the door.

The corridor outside the theater is deserted. Or so I think. Then I see them, at the end of the hallway, just turning a corner. Tori and Valentine. Hand in hand.

I stop. My body goes numb, and I get the hell out of there.

15

TORI

I don't know when my life turned into this soap opera where I've been kissed within the space of a few weeks by my crush and my best friend.

I feel like I'm having an out-of-body experience as I step out of the dark theater. Rays of sunlight are falling through the windows of the north wing, and the others are chatting. They walk away. I stop. Their voices grow quieter as the last of them disappears around the corner, and I'm left there on my own.

What now? Should I wait for Sinclair? What did Mr. Acevedo want to talk to him about anyway? It was obvious that Sinclair's mind wasn't on the job. And we both know why. Even though it's starting to feel like what happened back there on the stage was nothing but a crazy fever dream.

But it was a kiss. No, that's not true. A *kiss* sounds so harmless. It was way more. They were *kisses*, plural. It was passion, out of control. It was the thing I've been fantasizing about in so many fake scenarios that I'd forgotten how intense reality can be. Real touches, catching breath. I didn't want it to stop.

That moment when he just kissed me felt like the first day of my life.

"Tori."

No.

Not now...

I turn to face him, forgetting to slap on a smile.

Val frowns as he comes closer. Judging by his clothing and sports bag, he's come straight from either rugby or the gym.

"What's up?"

A guilty conscience expressed in the form of stomach cramps, that's what's up, my dear Valentine.

If he knew, oh, God, if he had even the faintest inkling of what I was doing just now. Did I cheat on him? I did, right? So am I now no better than all the women in all the books who made me so angry because they went against my principles? Why did nobody ever tell me how easily a thing like that can happen? Especially when it's the person you've wanted to kiss for so long. And are Val and I an official couple now or not? Is this a relationship? Is it a game? Who knows? Because every time I think I've worked it out, it slips away from me like a bar of wet soap.

"Not much." My voice sounds an octave too high, but Val doesn't seem to have noticed. His eyes scan the theater doors as he approaches. "We just finished. Mr. Acevedo wanted to discuss something with me."

Val makes an incomprehensible grunt and leans down to me. And then this day goes down in history as the one when I let two different guys kiss me maybe an hour apart.

"What's up with you?" I ask as he lets me go again. "Rugby?"

"Been to the gym to let off a bit of steam," he says curtly, taking my hand. Normally I'd ask why, but I don't dare just now. Val's skin is warm, but not as soft as Sinclair's. I follow him unresistingly, and I have no idea where we're headed. "So what've you been up to?"

I stiffen slightly. "What do you mean?"

Val's eyes rest on me. "Your day? How's it been, what've you been up to?"

"Good, I . . . Why do you ask?"

"We haven't seen each other for ages. And I'm trying to take an interest. To be attentive. Or is that wrong too now?"

"No." I breathe deeply. "It's great." Smile. "Really."

"What are you doing later?"

"Don't know yet. I should make more content for Insta and TikTok, and I haven't done any reading since the start of the week either."

"You can read when you're old and ugly."

"Hey."

"It's true. You should get out and live a little. Have fun, party. We'll be down in the Dungeon after wing time. You'll come, won't you?"

I don't answer. Val stops, and because he's holding my hand, I have to as well. "Oh, I . . . The others were talking about maybe having a midnight party in the old greenhouse," I say, remembering that Emma and Henry had been messaging our Midnight Memories group chat earlier.

Val laughs. "Come to us then, save yourself from that

nursery-school stuff. I mean, a midnight party . . . How old are you? Twelve?"

I bite back the remark that Val and his friends had had their parties in the old greenhouse until less than a year ago. Like everyone in the fifth and lower sixth. School tradition. The old greenhouse is ours, and the upper sixth have the undercroft beneath the school for their territory.

"I'll have to see," I say evasively. "I've been kind of short on sleep in the last few weeks."

"Tori, you do realize I've only got a few weeks left here?" Val drops my hand. "A levels start soon, and then I'll leave. And you'd seriously rather hide in your room, reading, instead of having a good time with me and the others?"

"Of course I want to have a good time with you."

But I'd rather spend time with my friends. And my *best* friend, so that I can find out if that kiss just now was more of an accident or something genuine. Either way, it means that I can't do this with Val anymore. Maybe it was the sign I needed to tell me that being with him will never be enough. But how do you tell someone that?

I'm just so fucking unsure of myself around you. Val's voice, his penetrating stare every time I've reassured him, yet again, that there's nothing between me and Sinclair. He didn't believe me, and in the end, he was right. I thought he was pathologically jealous, but maybe he wasn't. It was all me, because I'm evidently a bad person.

Val's looking so expectantly at me that I feel kind of ill. This matters to him. I matter to him. I have to tell him. And better sooner than later. I could try to speak to him alone this evening, and then his friends would be around if he took it badly. God, I can't... But what choice do I have?

"After wing time?" I begin.

Val's eyes gleam with hope. He nods. "Half ten, eleven, thereabouts. You in? I'll pick you up."

"I'll find my own way down," I say. Val frowns. "Don't want anyone to catch you. Ms. Barnett hears everything."

"Yeah, OK." He nods.

And I don't want Emma or anyone to find out that I'm meeting Val instead of going to our midnight party. I could come later. Once I've done what needs doing. It'll be better if I'm not on my own in my room then, because my gut tells me that Val might react kind of unpleasantly. With reason. What I've done is kind of unpleasant too. Unforgivable even.

"Perfect." Val smiles and stops at the corner of the cloister before heading to his wing. "I need a shower."

He eyes me, slowly. My breasts, my belly, down to my legs. Have I overlooked something? When Val looks back to my face, there's something in his eyes that's making me nervous. Something dark and impenetrable and unsettling. It makes me want to run. Now, right now, far away. To some place where I can hide from this whole stupid mess. With Sinclair. So he can pick up where we got interrupted.

"See you later." My lips feel numb as I turn away. My steps are hasty. I'm not thinking, just walking to the west wing. It's not until I get to my room that I dare breathe properly again.

I shut the door, listen to the silence. And then I lift a hand slowly to my lips and touch them. Sinclair touched them earlier.

With *his* lips. For the second time in my life. But this time it was him who started it. It wasn't in a dark school corridor. It was on a stage. OK, so we were our own entire audience, but that doesn't matter. He kissed me. He leaned in without a second's hesitation.

I shut my eyes.

But was it really Sinclair kissing Tori, or Romeo seducing Juliet? Was he still in character? Was he thinking about Eleanor?

He said your name...

Yes, he really did. I didn't imagine that. No way.

My phone lights up, but it's only Gideon asking a question in Midnight Memories.

Should I text Sinclair or wait for him to text me? It would probably be better to talk face-to-face. About whatever. Then I'll be able to tell him I've broken up with Val. And then I need to know what that kiss meant. If it was serious. The very thought sets my entire body tingling.

I walk around the room. My bed looks tempting, but I can't sit or lie down now. I have to do something to take my mind off the conversations I've got to have later on. I could rearrange my bookshelves. They started out with the spines in rainbow order, but that's got so messed up there's not much of it left. Every time I've finished with my photos or videos in the last few weeks, I've just shoved piles of them in wherever they'd fit. The mess has been kind of bugging me, but I've never got around to doing anything about it. Until now.

My thoughts are still whirling as I stack books on my bed and my desk. I'm antsy enough that I even dust the empty shelf with a damp cloth. My phone's within sight, but Sinclair doesn't text, and with every passing minute, I get angrier. There's no way he's been held back this long by Mr. Acevedo. And it really would be a good idea to talk about that kiss. Or was it really only a Romeo-kissing-Juliet kiss, and he's not wasting another thought on it? God, I'm losing my mind.

I've finished about half the shelf when there's a knock at the door. My heart skips a beat, but before I can start to panic, I hear Emma's voice outside: "Coming to dinner?"

I shove the pile of books in my hand into their new place, turn down the volume on the speaker, and go to the door.

Emma eyes me expectantly as I open it.

I nod and turn away again. "Yeah, hang on."

Emma follows me into my room without waiting to be asked. "Hey, 'Hot Guy Shit.' That can only mean one thing."

"Which is?"

"You're reorganizing again."

"Only the books." I stop the music and slip my shoes on as Emma picks up a book. "You should so read that," I say.

"She's your favorite, right?" she asks, turning it over to skim the blurb.

"Yeah, I love everything she writes. Apparently, they're making a film of one of her books, with Scott Plymouth doing the soundtrack."

"Who's he?" Emma asks.

"PLY," I say, waiting for light to dawn, but Emma's still looking like she hasn't a clue what I'm on about. "The Canadian singer? 'Skin Deep,' 'More' . . . You'll definitely have heard them."

"Oh, is he the one who used to wear that mask?"

"That's him."

"You've got a playlist for him, haven't you?"

I nod. Obviously. After all, I needed the right soundtrack to read fan fiction to. And there's loads of Scott Plymouth fan fiction. And now he's with the author who wrote probably the most famous story about him, which in itself could be the basis for her next book, but let's not go there.

"Can I borrow it?" Emma asks, waving the book. It's my signed copy of the new Hope MacKenzie. I nod hesitantly. "I won't break the spine, neighbor's honor."

"Was it so obvious I was going to say that?"

"A bit." Emma takes the book and follows me to the door.

"Are you really bringing it down to the dining room?"

She nods. "I'm going straight over to Henry's after dinner."

"And I'm sure you'll be reading . . ."

"He's got a biology presentation to write."

I laugh softly.

"What?"

"Nothing. Biology presentation . . . Bennington's such a teacher's pet."

Emma shrugs her shoulders. "I'm mainly going to stop him falling asleep before midnight, as we all know that's his specialty."

"And we all know how well that worked out last time," I remark, remembering that Sinclair had found the two of them sleeping like babies in Henry's room.

"Cut it out," Emma says, but with a smile she can't completely hide.

It's a small, sharp stab in my chest. It's not that I'm not happy for her and Henry. I am, really happy, because they deserve to be happy. But lately, everything that any other couple has has been reminding me of everything that Sinclair and I don't have. Apart from that kiss, but unfortunately, we still don't even know what that meant.

Henry's waiting for us outside the dining room, and I can't bear how cute it is as he kisses Emma, then takes the book because he's Henry Bennington and genuinely interested in what his girlfriend is reading and thinking and what she's been doing today. There's no sign of Sinclair. I wait a full ten minutes for him to appear before Henry mentions in passing that he's gone home for dinner today. Which has nothing to do with me. Or I hope not, anyway. But today of all days, I could have done with a chance to intercept him after the meal.

OK, fine. I'll have to speak to him later. He'll definitely be back for the midnight party even if he's got a shift in the bakery after that. And it's half a lifetime since Sinclair last slept at his parents' house in Ebrington in term time.

I feel Eleanor's eyes on me as the upper sixth line up at the serving hatch. For more than just a moment. My blood runs cold. Does she know? Is that why Sinclair isn't here? Did he go to Eleanor to tell her everything? Or did he do it earlier when they were paired up for that drama exercise? It was unbearable, the two of them staring deep into each other's eyes for so long, but I couldn't look away either. I couldn't hear what they were talking about. But I know the answer. He'll have told her, the way I've got to tell Val later.

I catch sight of him next, but Val doesn't glance my way even for a second. He's chatting to Cillian and roaring with laughter as they walk to the front. At that moment, I wonder for the first time if it wouldn't be more sensible not to tell Val anything. It's only a tiny thought, but I know it would be wrong. I can't keep on like this. It's killing me.

Finally, it's our turn, but I've got no appetite. I feel detached from myself. Olive's ahead of me in the queue, and she's ignoring me. My best friend kissed me. Everything's coming apart at the seams, which is exactly what I was trying to prevent. Outstanding work.

SINCLAIR

Sitting calmly at dinner with Mum and Dad and not constantly glancing anxiously at my phone was harder than I'd expected. But that would have tipped them off that something's wrong, and if there's one thing I don't have the nerve for today, it's explaining to my parents what happened. It's not that I can't talk about things to them, but whatever it is between Tori and me is kind of a running joke at home. She'd never say a word at school, but here, Mum doesn't disguise the fact that she sees Tori as her future daughter-in-law. I can tell her as often as I like that we're just friends, but she secretly believes that as little as Dad, who keeps asking when Tori will come around for dinner again. Hey, a few hours ago, I'd have had the self-confidence and naivety to say that they'd quite likely be seeing a lot of her soon, but the more time passes, the less sure I am of that. I kissed her. I didn't even wonder, let alone ask her if she'd be OK with that. And instead of talking to her about it, I watched her wander off with Valentine Ward. It's all so fucked up that I could scream. So I invited myself home to eat with my parents at short notice, just so I wouldn't have to see her.

I push all thoughts of Tori aside, tell them about Jubilee and the rehearsals. I don't mention my conversation with Mr. Acevedo. I hope he won't talk to Mum about me. It would be awkward, but then again, it might mean her and Dad dampening down their expectations a bit. Since they heard that I'll be playing Romeo, they've been talking nonstop about how much they're looking forward to the play in the summer. If it wouldn't be totally daft, I'd try to ban them from coming. It'll be bad enough if I embarrass myself in front of the whole school. And if things carry on like this, I will. Through and through.

Luckily, I've got other worries just now. They start with *k* and end with *issed Tori*. I don't know how long I've been dithering, staring at my phone, now that I'm back at school, in plenty of time for wing time. Emma's next door with Henry, and I remember that we're partying in the old greenhouse later. I wish I could skip it, but it occurs to me that Tori might not even be there. I bet she'd rather hang around with the upper sixth in their dingy Dungeon. Not too long ago, I'd have texted her without a second thought. I don't know when that changed. I only know that I hate it. Seriously. I loathe the fact that Tori's no longer the person I can tell everything. But more than that, I hate that *she* doesn't tell *me* things anymore.

Opening our chat is like a punch in the guts. The last message was over a week ago. Trivial stuff. It's not like we even used to communicate all that much by text message. Why would we when we were together practically twenty-four seven? But the last *What are you doing? Can I come over?* message was yonks ago. And I know that won't change unless I do something about it. But I can't text her. We kissed; she went off with Valentine Ward. You can't get clearer than that. No way will she have told him what happened. So what do I even want to talk to her about? That was answer enough, wasn't it?

Henry messages later, saying, *Shall we go?*, and I'd prefer to pretend to be asleep. But then he'd know for sure that something's wrong, and I can definitely do without explaining everything to him.

But Henry wouldn't be Henry if he didn't notice anyway. I sense him looking at me when I can't stop watching the door, as if Tori might stroll in at any moment.

"Isn't Tori coming?" Henry asks, his face is a picture of innocence as he wanders over.

"Why would I know?"

He studies me, then says, "I was just wondering."

"I suppose she's with Val and his friends."

Henry raises his eyebrows in surprise. "Interesting." He keeps watching me, and now I'm raging.

"What?"

"Nothing . . ."

"Not that I care. She can chill with whoever she wants."

If I don't care, why am I so defensive?

"I get that it's annoying," Henry says.

"Why would it be annoying?"

He shrugs ever so slightly. "I'd be annoyed if Emma preferred hanging around with the upper sixth to being with me."

"Emma's your girlfriend."

Henry says nothing. Sometimes, silence speaks louder than words. He looks away, and I follow his gaze. Emma's sitting at the other end of the greenhouse with Omar, Salome, and Inés, and they burst into loud laughter.

"Looks like she's really at home here now."

Henry smiles his proud-boyfriend smile as I glance back at him.

"I think so," he says with shining eyes—it's almost unbearable, but he really deserves his dumb luck. I don't switch my smile back on in time as he eyes me again.

He gestures to the door. "Want some fresh air?" By which he means, *Want to talk privately?*

No, not really, but every other time I've poured out my stupid problems to him, it's been a major relief. I nod hesitantly and follow him out.

The night is fresh, but it's not as bitterly cold as the evening of the New Year Ball. It's early March now, and the days are mild enough that the afternoons are starting to feel like spring.

Henry pulls up the hood on his Dunbridge hoodie all the same and shivers as he wraps his arms around his chest.

"Want to tell me about it?"

"Tell you about what?" I ask.

Henry shrugs. "You tell me."

I sigh.

"Tori?" he asks. I shut my eyes. "Tori," he says as if to himself. "Thought as much."

"Answer me one question," I demand. "How did you and Emma get it together?"

"What do you mean?"

"Things were seriously complicated between you. You were still with Grace. Emma wasn't planning to spend more than a year here. And yet you managed it."

"Do you want the romantic answer or the realistic one?" Henry asks.

"Neither."

"Then you shouldn't have asked. So . . . there were more reasons to be with her than not to be with her. Stop rolling your eyes, you know what I'm talking about."

"Was that the romantic version or the realistic one?"

"Whichever you prefer," says Henry dryly.

"Not helping, man . . ."

"Communication," Henry says, more seriously now. "Communication's the key."

I groan with frustration.

"What did you think I was going to suggest? Staying passive and waiting for a miracle isn't the most promising approach. I know it's crap, but there you are. Some problems just disappear the moment you talk about them. Crazy, but true."

"Bennington, don't fuck with me, I can do that for myself."

"OK, no. Sorry, you're in despair, I get it."

"No, I don't think you do." I straighten up. "We kissed."

"Back in the second form, I know."
"No, I . . . Hold the bus." I stop. "How do you know that?"
"I saw you when I was going to the bogs."
"Now you tell me!"
He shrugs his shoulders. "Your business, not mine."
"God, you're impossible, Bennington."
"I thought you knew that I knew."
"No, why would I?"
"I don't know. Anyway, now you do."
"OK, wow." I look up to the sky. "But I meant something else just now."
"Huh?"
"We kissed again."
"You kissed again? Man, Sinclair, why didn't you tell me?"
"Because it was only today. This afternoon."
"Oh, my God," Henry murmurs. He sounds way too excited. Happy and excited. Like there's hope when there isn't. "Tell me everything."
"There's not much to tell. We were going through my lines before the rehearsal. It was a kiss scene; she was playing Juliet. And somehow . . . yeah."
"Oh, God," Henry repeats. "So then what?"
"Then the others walked in and we didn't see each other again because she walked off hand in hand with Valentine Ward." However hard I try, I can't keep the bitterness out of my voice.
Henry hesitates. "I see," he says in the end. "That's clearly suboptimal."
"It's fucking shit, Henry."

"You could put it like that. Why don't you ask her if you can talk?"

"I can't talk to her."

"Why not?"

"Because she's definitely with Valentine just now. Which tells me everything."

"Do you think she didn't like it?" Henry contracts his eyebrows as if that would be seriously weird. But I think he's wrong there.

"She . . . kissed me back. Well, as long as we were alone together. But I have no idea. Shit, Henry. Why is it all so difficult?"

"It always is, I'm afraid. Because you two really need to talk."

"Why is she with him and not here?" It's surprisingly painful to ask that aloud. "What does she even want with that fucker? It makes no sense. She's way too good for him, you know? He treats her like shit, but she keeps going back to him. I don't get it."

"She probably doesn't get it herself," Henry suggests. I don't reply, so he goes on: "I only know that you're the person here she trusts most of all. Anyone can see that."

"Maybe she used to. We're hardly talking. I hate it, because it feels like I've lost my best friend."

"You have to talk," Henry repeats. "Seriously, Sinclair. What if she's thinking the same as you? She sees you with Eleanor the whole time. Maybe that's making her insecure."

For a millisecond, I'm tempted to tell him about Eleanor and Sophia, but I don't. It's Eleanor's secret. She told me in confidence, and she asked me not to tell anyone else.

"She knows we're only acting partners," I say instead.

Henry's expression speaks volumes. "Are you sure of that?"

I don't reply because at that moment, my phone buzzes. My heart skips a beat, but it's Eleanor's name on the screen, not Tori's.

E: Are you still up?

"Is that her?" Henry asks, but I ignore him.
What's going on, and why do I feel nervous butterflies in my stomach when I see that Eleanor's staying online?

S: Yeah, why?
E: We're in the Dungeon, and Val just walked out with Tori. I think they're fighting.

My blood runs cold.

E: Can you come?
S: I'm on my way

"Sinclair?" Henry grabs my shoulder. "What's wrong?"
"I have to go," I say.
"Is everything OK?"
"I'm afraid not."
I start to run.

16

TORI

I've never understood why the upper sixth make such a big deal of their party cellar in the tunnels beneath the school. The old greenhouse isn't just bigger, it's more comfortable than the Dungeon. Because that really lives up to its name. Dark and kind of grim. It smells of beer and stale cigarette smoke, despite them being banned anywhere on school property. There are threadbare sofas and armchairs, which are saggy and covered with stains—God knows what, and I'd rather not think about it.

I'm sitting next to Val, trying to touch the seats as little as possible. When I arrived earlier, he was almost OTT in his enthusiasm and introduced me—quite unnecessarily—to the whole room in a slurring voice. I'm uneasy with how drunk he is already. And I could really have done without feeling the whole upper sixth staring at me, either amused or dismissive, as I gave an awkward wave before he pulled me away so he could get himself a top-up. There are times when I find it hard enough to watch how much the others drink at our midnight parties in the old greenhouse, but here it's worse. Not even Eleanor and her friends are sober.

Nobody tried to force me, but I can tell that Val's irritated by me sticking to cola and water. My friends are so open-minded about it that I'd forgotten not everyone feels the same way.

Sinclair's the only one who knows why I don't drink. I can't. How can I enjoy something that's slowly but surely taking my mum away from me? It's not really about the fear of losing control myself. I just don't see any sense in voluntarily dosing myself with the drug that almost destroyed my family. And still might. I've barely been in touch with Mum and Dad lately, so I don't have a clue how things are going. And seeing that Sinclair and I aren't talking, there's nobody but my brother that I could discuss it with. Val absolutely mustn't hear about it. Veronica Ward might stop doing business with my mum if she knew about her alcohol problem. I wouldn't put anything past her, even though I don't believe Mum's anywhere near the only one who has a problem with particular substances. It's no secret that some of her friends will take any opportunity to do a line of coke with as big a banknote as possible.

At least Val's not doing that tonight. Or not that I've seen, anyway. Maybe he did before I got here. I'm not sure. His pupils are probably wide because it's dark down here. I can't think about it if I want to stay calm. Is he even sober enough to have the conversation? There's no point if he's not in a fit state to remember it tomorrow. But I have to do it. There's no way around it; I just have to wait for the right moment.

I can't join in much of the conversation because there are too many in-jokes, but Val at least tries to explain as many of them as he can to me. At first, anyway. By this point, his hand's on my thigh and wandering ever higher. I cross my legs, but he doesn't take it away. Instead, I feel his other hand on the back of my neck.

My pulse quickens as he looks at me. He's attractive, no question. And when he kisses me like he's doing now, my body responds. Because Val knows what he's doing. His hand on the back of my head, his mouth only just grazing my lips.

"You're looking hot tonight," he whispers by my side.

I get goose bumps, because this is all wrong. His hand strokes my hip. I pull away and clear my throat.

"Want to head out for a bit?"

Astonishment crosses Val's eyes. He doesn't answer, just kisses me again and takes my hand.

The music grows quieter as we step out into the dark corridor and the door shuts behind us. I open my mouth, but before I can say a word, Val's lips are on mine.

Looks like he got the wrong idea.

For a few seconds, I'm too out of my depth to do anything about him drawing my head up to his and pressing me against the wall with his body. I feel the cold stone through my jumper, Val's hard crotch, and a slight hint of panic because I'm suddenly all too aware of his strength.

"Val," I say, between kisses. He doesn't respond. I push him away a little, and at the same moment, the door to the Dungeon opens. I shouldn't be surprised that it's Eleanor of all people, stepping out with her friends. Her eyes immediately scan the corridor and stick fast to us. My pulse calms a little once I realize we're on her radar.

"What?" Val asks, glancing aside.

"I wanted to talk to you," I start.

"Talk," he repeats sarcastically.

"Yes, there's something I have to tell you."

"It doesn't bother me that you've never done it before," he declares.

And I don't say anything.

I just don't say anything.

It takes me a good three seconds to twig what he means. And another three for the disbelief and rage to rise inside me.

"Oh, how nice that it doesn't bother *you*."

Val seems surprised by my mood swing. He opens his mouth and frowns. "Wasn't that what you wanted to hear?"

I laugh mirthlessly. "No, Val. Shit . . . Do you only say things because you think they're what I want to hear?" When he doesn't answer, I run both hands over my face and take a deep breath. It's no good: I can't duck the nasty part of this conversation. "OK, whatever. That wasn't what I wanted to say."

"So you've done it? With him?" I hear the threatening slur in his voice and start to feel afraid. "Come on, tell me. It was with him, wasn't it?" Val laughs. "Of course it was him."

"I don't know what business it is of yours, but no, I haven't, if you really want to know," I snap. OK, well, I haven't done *that* . . . I've done other things, though, and that's what I need to tell him.

Val eyes me, and I can see he doesn't believe me. And I don't care because, to be honest, there's no reason why I should convince him. I made a mistake today, but I don't have to tell him whether or not I've ever slept with anyone else.

"What's the problem, then?" His voice is cool and his eyes are drunken. Alcohol affects your self-control. Everyone knows that. And Val's not the greatest at self-control even when he's sober. It feels like chickening out, but I'm suddenly not sure if I should go through with this. I'm always in favor of telling the truth, but not at all costs. Not when I'm worried for my safety.

"Tori," he says, more insistently.

"Doesn't matter."

Wow. I should at least have come up with a better lie. Val's eyes narrow as he looks at me.

"What?" he persists.

"Val . . ."

"You've got a guilty conscience," he says. "Is that it? You were so weird earlier. Have been for ages, to be honest. Since you've been seeing him the whole time at the rehearsals." Val steps toward me. "Are you cheating on me?"

"No," I retort at once, but my voice sounds rather squeakier than normal.

"Stop taking the piss."

"Val, I think it would be better to talk about this calmly." I glance around.

"Tell me right now what's going on," Val growls.

I can smell the booze on his breath. "I'd rather discuss it when you're sober."

"And I want to know right fucking now."

"Val," I say quietly.

"Tori, stop the bullshit!"

"Everything OK over there?" Eleanor's still standing with her friends, but she's looking in our direction.

"Yeah, is everything OK?" Val repeats. "Good question, El. I've got one for you. Is your costar fucking you too, or is that just something between him and Tori?" I feel all my blood rush to my legs. Eleanor opens her mouth, but Val won't let her speak. "I'm sure it's all just staying in character, right?"

"Val, go and sleep it off." How can she stay so calm? Maybe she's wiser than me and knows that things can only go downhill if you respond to his provocations. "You're steaming."

"So how do you justify it to yourself?" Val turns back to me. "Is it for the role you wanted but weren't good enough for? Inspiration for the script? Is he good, at least? Come on, tell me about it, or are you too frigid even for that?"

"Val . . ." My voice is trembling. "It was a kiss, all right? One kiss, and nothing else. It happened this afternoon, and that's why I wanted to talk to you. Because I'm afraid I can't do this anymore."

"Wow." Val's voice is dangerously quiet and way scarier than when he was yelling just now. I can't breathe. He laughs quietly. "So it's true. You were lying to me."

"I didn't mean—"

"And I asked you so often, but you denied it. So what are we going to do now, Tori?" His eyes bore through me.

"I'm sorry, Val." My voice is shaking with suppressed panic. I really wish he'd get mad, scream, swear at me, but he's doing the exact opposite, and it's terrifying. "I didn't intend it to happen, you have to believe me."

"Do I? Do I have to believe anything you say? Maybe I should have believed my gut. What do you reckon?"

"Val, stop it," I beg quietly.

"Stop what? Stop what, huh?" He takes a rapid step toward me. As I instinctively step back and feel the wall at my back, my heart starts racing. He's so close to me that I can't move. I can feel his breath on my lips and his hand on my shoulder. "Look me in the fucking eye!"

I do so, and I'm afraid of this man. It's the worst feeling in the entire world, but I don't dare disobey him. He's taller than me, stronger, he's pressing me into the cold stone, and my mind stands still.

He leans down until his lips are by my right ear.

"Get tae fuck, Victoria Belhaven-Wynford!" he hisses. I shut my eyes; I can't breathe. "And take your shitey wee pal with you."

He lets go of me. I turn away at once, even though I feel like I might collapse in front of him. My legs start to move. *Please don't let him follow me.* I want to shut my ears as I walk away from him. He's hurling insults after me, words I'll never forget. I walk. I want rid of the feeling of his hands on my body. But it clings. I can feel him, smell him, taste him the whole way down the dark corridor to the stairs. I feel so sick that I want to stop and curl up, but I have to get out of here. I need to get somewhere safe. I need to get to Sinclair. He's all I can think of. Nothing else helps.

"Tori?"

I freeze as I take in the figure coming downstairs toward me. And then I go weak at the knees as I recognize him. I only realize I'm crying as Sinclair comes closer. I see the pain in his anxious face.

I can't move as he gently strokes my face with the back of his hand. "Fuck," he mutters, balling his hand into a fist; a deep frown engraves itself between his eyebrows as I flinch. "Hey," he says, instantly much calmer. "Look at me. Look at me, Tori." He takes my face in both hands as I don't pull away. "Breathe," he whispers. My heart is pounding in my throat. It just won't settle. But I force myself to do as he says. Breathe. Shut my eyes as Sinclair rests his forehead against mine. Anything to forget we're still here in this dark passageway. *He's here, you're safe. Nothing happened. Nothing happened at all.* So why is my whole body shaking, and why won't it stop?

Sinclair sounds like he's deliberately keeping his voice calm as he now pulls away slightly. "What did he do?"

"Nothing." I shake my head. Because Val didn't actually do anything. It was only words. Words I deserved. I'm the one who messed up. OK, he held on to me and wouldn't let go, even though I asked him to. It's like I can still feel the weight of his hand on my shoulder.

"What did he do, Tori?" Sinclair repeats, more emphatically this time. It's no longer my best friend facing me now. I've never heard him like this. His voice is quiet, but it's shaking with suppressed emotion. If I didn't know him so well, I'd most probably be scared of him. He looks past me, and his body tenses again. "Is he still down there?"

"Sinclair, no, come on . . ." I try to grab his wrist, but he pulls away. I want to boak as he runs down the rest of the stairs.

Everything seems to happen in slow motion yet incredibly fast. I follow him, I call his name. I run faster. I try to pull him

back. Val's still in the passage. Cillian and a few others are with him.
They nod slightly toward us. Val turns around. At the exact moment that Sinclair's fist connects with his face.

SINCLAIR

I've never been a fighter. I remember that the second Valentine Ward hits the deck in front of me and the rest of the upper sixth stare at me like I've lost my mind. They're probably not far wrong.
I couldn't care less. All I feel is the seething rage in my belly and the painful throbbing of my right hand. Shit, why did nobody ever tell me how much it hurts to punch someone in the chin?
There's silence for about three seconds, and then all hell breaks loose. Tori grabs my arm and tries to pull me away. Valentine sits up. His nose is bleeding. I might have broken it, but he's the fucking rugby captain; I don't think he's that fussed. But there's a spark of something in his eyes that's bordering on madness. Fuck, is he drunk? Looks like it.
For a moment, we face each other, breathing heavily, then Val's fist shoots out. Somebody screams—Tori, I think. The others roar. I duck in time. The blood is pounding in my ears. Eleanor pulls Tori back as she tries to step between us.
"Fucking wanker," I mutter through gritted teeth. I don't know exactly what happened between him and Tori, but just the sight of her made it clear that it's time for him to get what's coming to him. A split second later, Val's fist lands in my belly. The

pain paralyzes me, and the nausea makes me groan as I crumple. Tori screams my name. Val's knee comes out of the blue, hitting me hard under the chin. The sound as my teeth clash together is so grim, I want to boak.

Shit, I didn't think this through. I have no idea how to fight. In films, it always looks so easy, but it really isn't. I'm on the floor before I've even got started. Once I've stopped feeling like I might lose consciousness any second, I see that Louis has pulled Val back. He's steaming drunk and mad as hell, and this was a fucking mistake. But all I can think of is Tori's tearstained face and the panic in her eyes. A metallic taste spreads through my mouth. I gag as I pull myself together. The adrenaline makes me raise my arm again as Val tears himself away. I hit him somewhere; something in my hand cracks. I'm on the floor again before I can blink. What did I expect? I never had a chance against Valentine Ward. Not in a fight, not with Tori. Not in this life. Neil and Cillian, his teammates, are trying to hold him back, but there's no telling what he'll do next.

I flinch as I hear my name. My first name. It cuts me to the quick, because it's Tori yelling it. She's white as a sheet; Eleanor's holding her up. I only glance her way for a second. Her face is a picture of fear.

Charles . . .

Her eyes widen; she screams. I whirl around. I don't see Val's fist coming.

17

TORI

Fuck.

Fuck.

What the hell have I done? I only realized it was my voice calling his name when he stopped. He heard me and looked my way, confusion, surprise, and shock in his eyes. His body is tense; my breath catches. He's only distracted for a split second, but it's enough for Val to raise his fist.

There's a suppressed scream as Charles hits the floor. It comes from me. A punch, Val's fist in Charles's face, and I feel all the blood drain down to my toes. Val wipes his bleeding nose with his forearm.

"Stop it, stop it!" My voice is shaking; Eleanor lets go of me. Neil grabs Val's arm and pulls him aside. There's a ringing in my ears as I kneel next to Charles.

He's propped himself on his elbows and is feeling his nose with one hand. The blood runs down his fingers and pools in the sleeve of his jumper. But his eyes are fixed on me.

"Shit, I'm so sorry," I whisper as I see his face. Charles just shakes his head. He looks from me to Val, who's spitting a little blood onto the floor as the others pull him further away. "Can you stand?"

My heart is thumping as Charles gathers himself up. He suppresses a groan. I reach for his arm, because he's swaying. I'm not thinking. I just want to get out of here. It feels like I can't breathe again until everyone's voices have faded behind us and we've made it up the stairs. Charles clings to the banister and stops. It's only for a moment, but I see it.

"Here." I dig a tissue out of my pocket and try to pull myself together.

Breathe, Tori. Don't freak out now. Go through your options, and work out what to do next.

Charles wipes the blood from his face. He's pale, but I can see the adrenaline still in his eyes—it'll drop off any moment, though.

"Look at me," I insist. "How bad is it?"

"Not bad," he mutters. His voice sounds choked, but he's trying to get himself together.

"Want to go to the sick bay?"

He's shaking his head before I even finish the question. "No."

"Are you sure?"

He hesitates, and I can tell he's not sure. I hold my breath as a motion sensor comes on further down the hallway.

"Damn." I pull him aside and shove him into a wee niche. How much noise were we making just then? Did anyone hear? The school walls are thick, but the teachers' flats are in the building opposite.

Charles groans quietly as I press him against the wall and footsteps come closer. I put my finger to my lips and hold my breath. If anyone catches us like this, and his mum hears that he and Val were fighting, we're doomed. It'll be pretty obvious in the daylight tomorrow, judging by Charles's face now, but it would still be better not to be caught out here together after wing time.

It's Ms. Cox, the first-form girls' houseparent, and I breathe again once she's walked past. Her footsteps fade away, and then I feel Charles's warm body pressed against mine. I immediately move away.

Distance. Now. Right now.

"C'mon." I take his hand and pull him with me. His nose is no longer bleeding quite so badly by the time we reach his wing. All the same, I finally take in the full extent of the disaster when I turn the light on in his room. He looks dreadful, and his jumper is covered with blood.

I shove him into the bathroom where he leans both hands against the washbasin and glances in the mirror.

"Ah, fuck . . ." he mumbles, pinching his eyes shut.

"Take that off," I order him, pointing to his hoodie. If that blood's ever going to come out, I need to soak it in cold water right away. Well, once he's stopped bleeding. I need to get some ice. *OK, Tori, calm down. One thing at a time.*

He actually does what I say. His T-shirt rides up a little as he pulls the jumper over his head and reveals a strip of bare skin. I flush hot. I might like to joke that riding isn't a real sport, but his six-pack begs to differ. Which is entirely irrelevant just now. He's not doing well. He suppresses a groan as he pulls off the hoodie. I take it from him and make him sit down on the closed loo seat, then wet a towel and run ice-cold water into the sink to soak it. There's a bit on his T-shirt collar too, but like hell am I asking him to take that off right now. In the worst case, he'll have to throw it away.

When I turn back to him, he's leaning his head against the wall. Memories catch up with me. The New Year Ball. Charles drunk, me with him in this room. This time everything's different, yet nothing's different at all.

He blinks as I step between his legs and take his chin. His skin is warm, and I feel his jaw tense beneath my fingertips. The area around his left eye is already starting to swell.

"Don't move," I order him as I dab away the blood. I'm being as careful as I can, and I'm sure he's trying not to show anything, but he flinches when I accidentally get too close to his nose.

"Sorry," I murmur.

"'S OK."

"It doesn't look very OK to me."

He groans again and lets his head droop.

"Is there any ice in your kitchen?" I ask.

"No idea. I can go and have a look."

"Don't even think about it," I warn him. "You stay right where you are. Here, for your nose." He reaches for the wet towel I hold out to him. I get goose bumps as his fingers brush mine.

This is nuts. My best friend's been in a fight. For my sake. Because we kissed. All in one day. I'm seriously doubting my state of mind as I flit down the corridor to the boys' kitchen.

The layout's similar to ours in the west wing, so I have no

problem finding my way in the dark. To my surprise, amid the mountain of frozen pizzas and ready-made lasagnas, I find a bag of peas.

Charles is standing in front of the mirror again when I get back to his room. He's pulled off his T-shirt. Does he have a death wish? I can't deal with his ripped upper body right now. His jeans are pretty low-slung.

I stop in the bathroom doorway, and my throat is suddenly dry as dust.

"Here." I cough and hold up the bag of frozen peas. "Best I could do."

He looks at me, and he's gorgeous, even now with half his face swollen and a split lip. I want to kiss him. I want to say his name until I forget who I am. I want all of that, and I sense that tonight, I don't have the strength to stop myself. And that's not good because I'm alone with him in his room.

"Did he hurt you?"

His voice is quiet, but it cuts me to the quick. Maybe it's better to act like I didn't hear him.

"Tori?" he asks, more insistently. I can't say a word when he turns to me. He doesn't move. He doesn't come toward me, because he knows that then I'd have to step back. I feel an overwhelming urge to burst into tears. He gulps and keeps watching me. "Please . . ."

"No . . ." I manage to say. Val didn't do anything. Apart from kissing me and holding me when I didn't want him to, and if I'm perfectly honest, that wasn't OK. And if I'm brutally honest, a lot of things haven't been OK. And everyone knew it. Everyone was warning me, the whole time. Emma, Henry, Will, Charles. And I didn't want to listen because I thought I knew better. Because I thought I'd read enough novels that nothing like that could happen to me. And I'm not strong enough to face that just now. Let alone to allow myself to feel the emotions. I don't have a clue what it means. I need to think it all over and work out where we go from here. And until then, I can't show any emotions. Let alone weakness. Not in front of Charles. Not in front of myself. Not in front of anybody.

"Are you sure?"

"For fuck's sake, yes." My voice cracks, but I don't cry. I gulp, because I can't help it.

You're all right. You're doing fine.

Cold water runs down my forearm, and I remember the peas.

"Here." I hand them to him. "You need an ice pack."

"Tori, if he did anything you didn't want, we have to tell Mum..."

"We don't have to do anything," I reply, too loudly. "Any more than you had to go and start that fight."

Charles stands there like he's been rooted to the spot.

"I was just about to leave, everything was perfectly fine. I had it all under control, got that?"

"Yeah, that's just what it looked like." He takes the peas.

"What were you even doing down there?" I ask as I remember that he was meant to be at the midnight party with the others.

"Eleanor messaged me."

I freeze. He was there for her. Because Eleanor messaged him. I stop feeling anything.

"She saw you with Valentine, and she was worried about you."

I turn away. "You shouldn't have come."

"Fuck it, Tori. Stop all this crap!"

I flinch. "No, don't you get it? I don't need you; I didn't need rescuing. I had everything under control until you turned up and started throwing punches, like a Neanderthal. God, what were you thinking?"

"What was I thinking?" he repeats. "That that wanker would finally get what's coming to him! He walks around this school thinking he can treat everyone like shit without ever taking the consequences. He did the exact same thing to Eleanor!"

Eleanor. Of course Eleanor. Always, always Eleanor. I can't stand it anymore. And I'm furious. With Valentine, with Charles, and most of all, with myself. Why can't I even come close to living out my values in real life? Why is it so much easier to roll my eyes when the protagonist of one of my books makes stupid decisions and doesn't speak up? Why are things so much more complicated in reality? Why didn't I tell Val what I wanted to say? *No.* Clear and concise. *Let me go; never touch me again.* Why? And why do I now feel guilty about that? Why did I let things get to the point where my best friend was fighting for me only hours after kissing me, and why haven't we spoken about it again the way we should do?

I know that I'm not being fair, I'm very well aware of that, but when Charles takes a hesitant step toward me, I can't help myself. When he raises his hand and the tears threaten to choke me again, the rage comes, along with the desperate urge to push him away. Because he is the only person in the world I can't pretend to.

"No," I snap at him. "It wasn't OK, do you get that? I didn't ask you to fight for me and pull all that toxic shit!"

He freezes. "Tori . . ."

"A punch-up? Seriously, Charles?"

"I was trying to help!"

"And I didn't need your help!"

Charles stares at me. I don't know if anything has ever hurt as much as the sight of the emotions playing across his face. Disbelief, confusion, followed by disappointment, and finally, he shuts down. It hurts, but it's the only way I can bear it. I can't tell him that a too-large, weak part of me wanted to cry with relief when I saw him. That I just want to cry now. That I want to throw myself into his arms and hide there from the whole bloody world. That I might be endangering our friendship, but I don't care. But I don't do that, because I have no strength left. Because my heart's been broken so often and in so many different ways. And his has too. I saw to that myself.

His eyes grow cold, and his face hardens. "So it's all my fault," he says slowly.

I bite my tongue and nod.

"I see." Two syllables, sharp. It works. "Honestly, Tori, fuck you."

He doesn't mean it; he doesn't mean it.

He really does mean it, and I deserve it.

I bite my back teeth together as hard as I can. *Do anything, just don't cry.*

"Fuck *you*, Charles."

SINCLAIR

No idea how it happens so fast, but the very next day, the entire school seems to know about my fight with Valentine. I keep my head down as I walk to class behind Henry and Gideon, but the whispers aren't far behind. I haven't seen Val yet, but I hope with all my heart that his face looks at least as crap as mine. At the morning run, I had succeeded in keeping out of Tori's way.

Fate is against me again, because in the south wing, I run right into Mum. Her eyes fall on me as I walk toward her. Briefly, I regret not having told her. Then I could have explained things and wouldn't have to risk her saying anything here, in front of everybody. She doesn't, but I see the disapproval in her face. There's little she tolerates less than violence. All the same, after an unbearably long moment, she walks on without comment.

I lower my head so that my curls fall down into my face as I follow Henry. It's not until Val comes toward us that I raise it again. He gives me a total death glare, which I return only too happily. It's daft. But there's so much rage inside me, and it's at least doubled since last night.

Tori, who's already approaching our classroom, doesn't even look at me. And I don't care. I don't give a shit. Seriously. She can do one. And Henry too, if he gives me even one more of those knowing glances. He eventually accepted that I'm not going to tell him what happened, but he's well enough plugged into the school grapevine that he'll have heard it all hours ago. Besides, he's got eyes in his head. The left side of Val's face is slightly swollen, and there's a bruise adorning his nose, but sadly, he looks fairly normal apart from that. If you didn't already know what had happened, you might think it had just been an extrabrutal rugby session. Even so, Henry gives a smile of satisfaction at the sight of him, just for a second, then he's the serious school captain again, shoulders back. But I know why he's my best pal, unlike Tori, because the main thing I feel when I look in her direction is despair. And rage at myself. Because I know she's right. It was pointless to act like that, to sock Val one. I'm not like that. I'd have bet, with almost total certainty, that I'd never be the one to pick a fight. It seems I was wrong, but what can I say? I didn't go looking for trouble. And Val practically left me no choice. I couldn't help myself. Great, I sound like Romeo justifying having killed someone.

Anyway, it's not true. You always have a choice, and last night I made the wrong one. But I'm too much of an eejit to admit that. Not even to myself, let alone to Tori.

I spend the rest of the day being as chilly to Tori as possible, and I hate it. But it's probably just as well. I'd love to know if she's spoken to Valentine again, but I'm trying to act like I'm not interested. It works reasonably well, and I sigh with relief when I see later that Mr. Acevedo's not around today. He seems to be ill, because there's a notification on the school app that the rehearsal this afternoon has been canceled too. It's been rescheduled for Sunday evening, which causes some disgruntled muttering. I don't care, so long as I can avoid Tori. I divide the weekend between the stables, the bakery, and my room, until Sunday, when I have to stop hiding. Mr. Acevedo is still a bit under the weather as he greets us in the theater. Tori hasn't arrived yet. But

Eleanor comes over. I might have been ignoring her messages all weekend.

"Hey," she says, eyeing my face. I can't blame her. It still looks rough.

"Hey," I say feebly.

"You OK?"

"Yeah, fine. I'm fine."

"Seriously, Sinclair." Eleanor looks worried. "It looked really bad."

I shrug.

"Is Tori OK?"

"How would I know?"

I don't have to say anything else. Eleanor understands that I didn't manage to speak to her. About any of the stuff that matters. Kisses that tasted of longing. The truth, for fuck's sake.

She looks past me, up toward the doors. I don't need to follow her gaze to know that Tori's walked in. I turn my back on her even though everything within me is yearning to look at her. To go over to her, to make sure she's all right.

"Is everyone here?" Mr. Acevedo pops up from somewhere and looks around. His eyes rest on me. His eyebrows shoot up. I bite my bottom lip and stare at the floor. "Wonderful," he says. "Then let's get started."

We begin, as always, with a few warm-ups, and I'm able to avoid any contact with Tori. It's ridiculous. We both know it, and we're both doing it all the same.

We practice a scene with the Nurse and Lady Capulet. Then it's just Eleanor and me. To my own surprise, never mind anyone else's, I'm good. I can use my anger and channel it into Romeo's passion. This might even be a chance to escape reality and no longer have to be the useless Charles Sinclair. Romeo is the opposite of him. Romeo knows what he wants and has no difficulty conveying that to Juliet. Because he's not such a bloody coward. And because he is—God knows why—entirely confident that Juliet wants him as much as he does her. It's easy. It really is that bloody easy.

I act, and I forget reality. At least for a few minutes. Until I look into the auditorium. At Tori and her icy glare. It's fucking her up how good we are. I can feel it, and I try to be better still. I'm an arsehole, but I can't help it.

I look at Eleanor and raise my intensity so high that I see amazement in her eyes. Because it's genuine. Because she's no longer either Eleanor or Juliet, but Tori, and this is a version of reality in which I finally get to tell her what I've wanted to say for years. There's no risk. She will reciprocate. We're doomed, but at least we'll be side by side.

We fly through our scene, and the kiss is looming. This is going to be the first time we do it in front of the whole cast. At first, Mr. Acevedo only let us rehearse the intimate scenes in front of him and Tori, but at the end of the year, it'll be the whole cast plus the whole of Dunbridge Academy. Including Valentine Ward.

My pulse picks up as Eleanor looks at me and softly bites her bottom lip. I have to do this; I have to start. Hands on her cheeks, thumbs on her lips. Turn away from the audience slightly, so that it looks real.

Tori's sitting in her seat like a block of ice. And I want to hurt her the way she hurt me.

"'Your mouth has cleansed my lips from sin.'" I touch Eleanor's face, but I do so the way I touched Tori's. Soft, firm, everything at once.

"'Then give it back to me,'" Eleanor replies.

And then I kiss her.

I kiss her properly. Eleanor hesitates for a fraction of a second, and then she kisses me back. I can tell that it looks real because it feels real. It's not acting; they *are* Romeo's and Juliet's mouths claiming each other and wanting more.

I wait for Eleanor to pull away, but she doesn't. I kiss her longer than necessary. I do it on purpose. I kiss her with all my rage and pain, and hope that Tori can feel it.

"Eleanor, Charles, please. I really must insist." I jump, the way I've done every time since Thursday night when someone's said my first name and it hasn't been Tori. Did she even realize what she'd said? I did, at any rate, and I still get goose bumps at the mere thought of it. She stressed it differently, she said it softly, as if it were a promise I'd break. And now she's got the proof.

Mr. Acevedo is waving his hands in the air as I pull away from Eleanor.

"Wasn't it good?" I ask, without taking off Romeo's arrogance.

"It was very good, but ninety percent of your audience is underage. We'll have to send the juniors out if you're going to repeat that on the big stage."

The others laugh, Eleanor strokes her hair back from her face. Tori doesn't move. And I don't move either. I feel no triumph. No satisfaction. I feel her disappointment, her pain, and all at once, I feel regret.

I don't hear what Mr. Acevedo says next. I think he's happy otherwise. Gideon and Louis come up onto the stage, Tori stands up and says something to Mr. Acevedo. He looks at her, then nods with understanding.

Her eyes meet mine as she turns away. I succeeded in hurting her the way she hurt me, and I want to make it unhappen. Right now. I want to apologize, and to cry. She's pale. I feel sick. She leaves the room without even looking at me.

18

TORI

The tears sting my eyes as I walk down the hallway. Rapid steps, head down, don't look at the few people who come toward me. I wish I wasn't so weak. I really wish I didn't need to cry after Charles kissed Eleanor on that stage, the way he's meant to. But it wasn't like before. Stage kisses that look amazingly genuine but aren't. It was different today. Today he kissed her on the lips, kissed her furiously and for ages. To go with my favorite bit of dialogue in the whole script.

Your mouth has cleansed my lips from sin.
Then give it back to me.
Hell.

He did it on purpose. He wanted to make me feel it, and I hate him, because it worked.

Fate seems to have it in for me, because just before I turn off toward the girls' wing, I run right into Val and his pals. His eyes look me over for a split second. Then he blanks me. What do I care? Even so, I can't help studying his face.

Val doesn't look as bad as Charles, but there's no denying that he's been fighting.

I only realize I'd been holding my breath as I turn the corner and slowly exhale again.

To my own surprise, the relief I've been feeling since Thursday night is beyond words. I'm not proud of what I did, but it seems to have drawn a line under the thing with Val. A thing I still can't classify. Were we a couple? Have we split up? Did I cheat on him? Or did we go on a few dates and have a nasty breakup before it got serious?

I haven't the faintest idea. My head's splitting as I climb toward my floor. The stairs seem never-ending today. I've only got to the second floor, but I want to sit down already.

By the time I reach our corridor, I'm feeling dizzy, but I force myself to keep going. I want to cry in my room. And break something.

I drop onto my bed and shut my eyes, but I can't get rid of the images of Eleanor and Charles. His hands on her face, his mouth on hers. My lips are tingling. I can feel his breath on her skin. I can taste him. I'm a hundred percent certain he meant it. I felt it; you can't imagine a thing like that. Or so I thought.

Being kissed by Charles felt like the first day of my life. Like all my wishes had come true at once, and I should have known that that feeling was too good to be true. Because nothing's gone right since then.

It's the exact opposite of going to plan. I didn't tell my best friend how I feel about him, but I've lost him anyway. All I wanted was to protect our friendship. And now we can't even look each other in the eye. We've smashed it up. Us. The years we've known each other. All gone. And I don't know if anything has ever hurt as much as the knowledge that things will never be the same between us ever again. I'm not just brokenhearted over the boy I'm secretly in love with. No. I've also lost my best friend. There's nobody I can talk to about the way I feel. OK, so that might not be true, but neither Emma, nor Henry, nor Will nor anybody else will be able to understand that. Olive might, but unfortunately, that friendship's fucked too. I'd hoped she'd take up Mr. Acevedo's offer and join in with the rehearsals, but she hasn't shown her face. Of course she hasn't—she knows I'll be there.

Maybe it's me. Maybe I'm just incapable of maintaining any ordinary friendship. There's no other explanation. Instead of going with my feelings, I get caught up in dubious relationships with guys who give me bellyache and push my friends away when they try to talk some sense into me.

There's no point in denying it. Emma, Henry, Charles, Will . . . they were all right. Valentine Ward made me feel things I didn't want to feel. He might not have done it on purpose, but there again, he might have. He's the only person who can answer that. All I know is that I never felt that way around my best friend. So insignificant and demanding. Like I was being unreasonable, and then I'd get compliments that felt fake. Being close to Val was like riding a roller coaster, because I never knew which version of him I was going to get. The cheerful, euphoric one; the sensitive one he always tried to hide; the suspicious one who could tip over into unpredictable rage if I didn't say what he wanted to hear. It was stressful. It was anything but safe. I got caught up in something

I can't explain. Because it went against my principles. My values are important to me, but Val said and did so many things that trashed them. I'd always been sure that I'd speak up when it mattered. But I didn't, and I'm ashamed. I'm ashamed of having kept defending him to my friends, and above all, I'm ashamed of myself. I feel like I don't even know who I am anymore. What I stand for, my identity. Like I lost myself in trying to do the right thing. But it never was the right thing. It was stubbornness and my own fucking stupidity. And this is my reward.

I roll onto my back and press the balls of my thumbs against my eyes, but they don't stop burning. My body feels like a lead weight, and my legs ache. Everything aches. My stomach, my heart. I don't even have the energy to distract myself.

When Emma asks if I want to come down to dinner, I say I'm not hungry. It's not even a lie. I feel sick; my head is pounding and dizzy at the same time.

I don't know when I fell asleep; I only know that I wake up at some time in the middle of the night because I'm so cold that I can't stop shivering. My window's open a crack and I didn't pull my bedding over me, but things are no better even once I've shut it, peeled off my clothes, and cuddled up under the duvet in my thickest pajamas. Ms. Barnett has hot-water bottles we can use, but I haven't the strength to get up. I just want to sleep; the headache is driving me crazy. However still I lie, every heartbeat throbs directly under my scalp. I should get up and look for some paracetamol . . .

It feels like only a second later when my alarm goes off, and I wake up, dripping with sweat. It's a quarter of an hour before

I'm even able to sit up. I feel a bit better once I've had a shower, but I'm still considering telling Ms. Barnett I'm ill. The only reason I don't is Charles and my stupid ego. If I don't turn up to class, he's sure to think it's because of him. I don't want him believing he has that much power over me. Because he doesn't. I don't care what happens to us. If he wants to kiss Eleanor, let him. And if he thinks that bothers me, he's got another thing coming. I'm not in the mood for that primary-school stuff.

Emma's running late, and I'm waiting for her—it's almost time for the morning assembly and she and Henry have been out voluntarily for a run because they're both nuts. I'll never understand how they can do that to themselves every day. On top of the official morning run and even on Mondays—such as today—when we have assembly instead.

"Are you OK?" Emma asks when she eventually emerges from her room. Her hair's still wet.

I feel sick, but I nod. "Didn't sleep very well," I mumble as we walk downstairs. If she hadn't sounded so concerned just now, I'd have asked her to slow down a bit. But she did, so I don't. Not even when we're among the last people to slip through the doors before they're shut. Everything within me rebels when I reach the row for our form and see that Charles and Henry have kept two seats between them. Like always. Charles joins everyone in standing up as his mother walks into the room.

Emma straightens her uniform, and I wish I could sit down. No, I don't wish it, I've got to. My pulse is racing, it won't stop, and with every passing second, when I can feel my heart pounding right in my throat, I get a wee bit more scared.

Charles glances at me and away again. I'm hot and cold all at once, and then this buzzing starts in my ears. Slowly at first, but it gets louder, and there's a white mist coming over my eyes so that I feel like nothing's getting through to me anymore. Not even Charles, who's looking at me again.

He says something; I don't hear it. I break into a cold sweat. My knees go weak, and I lose all feeling in my fingers. Something's not right. It feels like I'm disappearing inside myself, and there's nothing I can do about it.

I have to sit down. I have to . . .

I grab Charles's arm because I'm scared of falling. I hear his voice; I don't know what he's saying. I feel sick, sicker than ever in my whole life. He reaches for me, the buzzing in my head swells to a roar, and then it's finally, finally quiet.

SINCLAIR

I didn't sleep. I spent the whole bloody night thinking about Tori's blank gaze and the disappointment on her face and regretting what I'd done. Not just for her sake—to be perfectly honest, it was anything but fair to Eleanor too. OK, so she'd said she wouldn't have a problem with real kisses on stage, but I crossed the line. I used her to get revenge on Tori. I'm so mortified, I want the ground to swallow me. I spent the rest of the night composing apologies. I even reached for my phone to make a note of them all. There were a lot, but then there are a lot of things I need to apologize to Tori for.

Sorry for being such an arsehole.
Sorry for intentionally kissing Eleanor in front of you.
Sorry for yelling at you.
Sorry for not just saying the stuff I want to say.
Sorry for acting like a fucking prick and starting a fight with Valentine.
Sorry for denying your feelings and interfering in your relationship with him.
Sorry for being a coward.
Sorry for being an *angry* coward.
Sorry for taking everything out on you.
Sorry for kissing you.
OK, no, not sorry, because I wanted it so much.
But sorry for kissing you without asking permission first.
Sorry for acting like it never happened, ever since.
Sorry for the first time turning out like that.
Sorry for being unable to talk about my feelings.
Sorry for pretending to like Eleanor.
Sorry for being so scared.

It's a list I could continue forever. I'm genuinely praying I'll be able to remember all those things tomorrow, but knowing my luck, I'll end up standing face-to-face with Tori, still not knowing what to say.

No. That's not going to happen. If necessary, I'll have to pull out my phone like a loser and read out all the words I'll never otherwise get over my lips. Even though she deserves better. I bet

Valentine Ward could manage it. Stand there and tell her what's what. God, I can't bear it.

In the morning, by the time I go down to assembly, I'm more nervous than I was before my audition. I barely slept, but the adrenaline is keeping me wide awake. I got here extra early this morning, but even after ten minutes' hanging around by the doors, Tori hasn't turned up. I'm just about to check whether I've missed her and she's actually in the hall with the others when Mum arrives.

I don't know how she does it, but I always get the feeling she can see right through me with a single glance. The day after the fight, she called me in to inquire whether I had anything to tell her. I said no, and Mum accepted that. Did she ask Valentine too? If so, he must have kept his mouth shut, or we'd have been back on the mat in her office together.

I cough slightly and mumble, "Morning."

"Did you sleep well?" she asks, though I'm pretty sure she can see that I didn't. Either way, it seems to have been a rhetorical question, because Mum's still talking. "Are you waiting for someone?"

I hastily shake my head and turn to follow her down the central aisle. I join Henry in our row. It's traditional to leave the two seats between us free. For Emma and Tori, although I bet she'd rather sit anywhere but next to me today.

"Where's Emma?" I ask as Henry straightens his tie.

He nods toward the aisle as, at that second, Emma and Tori reach our row.

Great. So much for my intention to catch Tori at the first good opportunity and ask if we can talk. In my experience, there's just as little time between assembly and breakfast as there is between breakfast and first period. And I want to get this conversation right. Not in front of the others, just Tori and me. Like she deserves.

She hesitates at the sight of me. I see the disappointment on her face, and it's like a punch in the guts. I want the old Tori back, the one who'd come up to me without a second's pause to whisper something to me like I was the most important person in her life. I want *us* back. I hate being the one who screwed it up. And I'm the only person who can fix it.

She doesn't say a word as she stands beside me. Mum steps up to the lectern.

"Tori?" I gulp, and then I force myself just to say it. "I'm sorry. Can we talk later, maybe?"

She doesn't reply; she just keeps staring motionless, dead ahead. The room is buzzing with voices, but she must have heard me. Or are we ignoring each other now?

"After breakfast? Or this afternoon? Please, Tor."

Her arm touches mine; I turn to face her and realize she's swaying. My blood runs cold as she grabs me.

"Tori?" Her fingers are freezing. "Are you OK?"

I look at her; Mum's starting to speak.

"Do you need to sit down?" I suggest, but I'm not sure if Tori can hear me.

My stomach cramps as her fingers dig deeper into my forearm. "I think I should . . ." she murmurs weakly.

Her chair scrapes as she stumbles back. I grab her and pull her toward me, but it's too late. Her body grows heavy; her head falls against my chest. Henry reaches out to us, but everything happens so quickly that I stumble to the floor with Tori. The next moment, I'm kneeling beside her. A gasp runs through the room as the others turn to look.

"Hey, Tori. Tor, look at me." I grab her head, but her eyes stay shut. My heart is thumping; my hands are shaking. Her cheeks are burning when I touch her face.

"What's happened?" Mum's voice is on the sound system, cutting over the swelling chatter. "Will someone please fetch Dr. Henderson?"

Henry leans over; he and Emma push the chairs away a little. Mr. Acevedo and Ms. Buchanan are coming over, and the others are making room, but Tori's still not moving.

"She's fainted," says Mr. Acevedo. "She needs some fresh air."

I nod on autopilot. Everyone's eyes are on us as I lift Tori and carry her down the aisle. She's heavy, but what does that matter? Valentine Ward appears out of nowhere; Ms. Buchanan stops him getting in our way. Henry goes ahead of us and opens the double doors. Dr. Henderson is already heading our way.

I walk, I hear people saying things, and I can't take anything in. Everyone's calm; nobody's freaking out the way I am on the inside. Tori just keeled over, and I've got so bloody much to say to her. My arms are burning by the time we reach the sick bay. Dr. Henderson tries to send us out again almost as soon as I've laid Tori on a bed. I don't move as he and Nurse Petra bend over her.

Henry tugs on my shoulder.

He's saying something, but I can't hear him. I can't breathe. I've never seen my best friend in this state. I can't stand it.

"Hey." I jump as Henry speaks to me again. "Look at me."

He's staring at me insistently, as only Henry can, and somehow it works. I calm down. "They'll look after her," he says, leading me out. "Everything will be all right."

I resist the urge to shake my head, because how the fuck does he know that? Could he stay this calm if it had been Emma just fainting in his arms? I doubt it, but then he doesn't know what it's like. Emma was the one who was standing on the rugby pitch in a panic, barely able to move, when he had that accident at the end of last year. I get it now. It makes perfect sense. Because if Tori's not well, I can't breathe.

"Charlie?"

I turn as I hear Mum's voice and the click of her heels on the stone floor. Seems like assembly ended early today, for obvious reasons. Henry lets go of my shoulder and steps back.

"How is she?" Mum sounds anxious, and something about that makes me want to cry.

"I don't know," I begin. "They sent us out."

"I see." Mum nods, walking past us. "I'll make inquiries so that I can let her parents know." She stops as I try to follow her. "You two wait out here, please."

"Mum," I beg, but she shakes her head ever so slightly.

"I'll be right back."

She doesn't see. I'm losing my mind. She walks into the sick bay, and I stare up at the ceiling. All I can think of is Tori's body burning up, the way she crumpled in my arms. Like she was a puppet and someone had cut her strings.

Henry doesn't even ask if we should go to the dining room. He just waits with me until Mum walks down the corridor toward us. She's looking serious.

"And?" I walk up to her, try to read her face, gauge how serious it really is.

"There's flu going around the juniors, and Dr. Henderson thinks that's what Tori's caught. She'll soon be back on her feet."

How can she sound so calm? Didn't she see the way Tori fainted?

"Is she awake?" I ask. "Mum?"

The look in her eyes makes me feel like my knees might give way. "Not just now—she's got a high temperature, but Dr. Henderson is looking after her."

I feel sick. "But . . . shouldn't she be in hospital?"

"Charles, I'm quite certain that Dr. Henderson is best placed to judge how serious the situation is," Mum says. "They're giving her fluids and something to get the fever down. She'll be better soon."

"Can I see her?" I say, without much hope.

"She needs rest."

"I'll be quiet," I say at once. "Seriously, I just need to . . ."

"Charlie, we don't want anyone else to catch it. The sick bay is almost full as it is. It would be irresponsible of us."

My eyes are welling with tears of rage and helplessness. Because Mum doesn't understand how urgently I need to see her. It's truly important to me, OK? I have to see that Tori's all right. I kissed Eleanor for real, on purpose. Because I wanted to hurt my best friend. Was she already feeling ill? Yesterday evening? And I didn't notice because I was too busy raging and getting revenge? I'm the world's biggest arsehole.

"Hey." Henry puts a hand on my shoulder. I can't bear it.

"Mum, please," I whisper, but she shakes her head. I hate how much she has to be the head teacher as soon as we're at school.

She takes a step toward me, and I want to flinch. But I don't. I feel the hot tears in my eyes as she puts her arms around me. Normally I'd be embarrassed to cry in front of her and Henry, but right now I have other worries.

"I'm sure it looked worse than it was, pet," she says quietly.

"She just fell over, Mum," I whisper.

"Lucky you were there, huh?" She looks at me, and I wonder where she's getting all the horrible sympathy. Am I blowing this out of proportion? Maybe . . . But I can't help it. "I'm sure that Tori will be doing much better in a day or two. Then she'll be able to have visitors." She lets me go. Henry is discreetly studying some kind of invisible message in the flooring, and he only looks up again when Mum continues, "I'll tell Tori's parents. You two, please get to class." She gives Henry a look that presumably means something like *Take care of him for me.* He nods at once. "And if either of you starts feeling ill in the course of the day, please tell your houseparent immediately. Got that?"

I want to argue, but I have to face the facts—making a scene wouldn't do any good. Then they wouldn't let me see Tori at all. I gulp, but the stupid lump in my throat won't disappear as I glance at the door between me and Tori. Everything within me wants to go back to her, just to convince myself she's OK.

"Coming?" Henry's voice makes me jump.

I nod absentmindedly.

"Sinclair, she'll get better," he says as we walk down the corridor. He has no idea.

"I kissed Eleanor," I say.

Henry stops.

"Yesterday," I continue.

"What?" He's looking at me like he didn't hear properly. But he knows he did. I can see it in his face. "Just like that?"

"For the play. Not just like that. But . . . I went too far—I kissed her an extralong time because I knew Tori was watching. Because I was raging and wanted her to feel like I felt."

Henry eyes me. "Have you talked since?"

"No." Of course not. "I wanted to apologize before assembly. But . . ." My stomach clenches.

"You'll apologize as soon as she's better." Henry sounds firm. As if that meant it was done. "Why did I do it?" I stutter.

"Because you two are in love." He says it like it's the most natural thing in the world. And it kind of is. "Because you have feelings for her, and you were hurt. But Sinclair, you have to find the guts to tell her the truth if you don't want things to be like this between you forever."

It sounds so simple when he puts it like that.

"It's not that hard," he adds as if he'd read my mind. "And it's worth it, I promise."

Maybe Henry's right. But maybe I've fucked up. Maybe Tori won't listen, which would be perfectly understandable.

Emma's waiting for us at the corner on the way to the classrooms. She's pale and her eyes are wide with worry. "How is she?" she asks at once.

I let Henry answer. I don't listen as we walk to class. I can't concentrate on anything. I do try, but all morning, my thoughts are anywhere except the classroom. I stare out of the window, so that I'll see if an ambulance arrives. By lunch, I feel so grim it would be a good enough excuse to go to the sick bay myself.

I barely manage to choke down a mouthful. I feel Henry's eyes on me and try not to let it show, but Tori hasn't replied to the texts I've sent her, which must mean she's too ill even to have picked up her phone. Or that she hates me. Neither option is exactly soothing.

I fight my way through two more lessons, then head to the stables. It's the only answer when I can't think straight. There isn't time for a ride before study time, but that means the stables will be empty right now.

"I've fucked up," I whisper once I've cleaned Jubilee's hoofs and straightened up again. She snorts quietly and twitches her ears toward me. There are few things I believe as firmly as that she can sense my emotions. "With Tori. I've fucked the whole thing up. And d'you know what? The worst thing is that it started when I got the part in the play. It went so wrong. I only auditioned so that we could spend more time together again. It was meant to be the answer. But it turned out to be the opposite. This stupid play has just made everything even more complicated."

Jubilee turns her head toward me as I knock out the hoof-pick and throw it back in my grooming kit. Then I reach down to pick up the currycomb and body brush. Brushing her soft coat has an almost meditative quality.

"I mean, what was I expecting?" I ask, as if Jubilee could

actually answer me. "I'd hate it too if she was playing the lead. With Val. That fucker, wow . . ." The mare immediately tenses, and I make an effort to calm my voice. "I would really have hated it. Even if they were only costars, only stage-kissing. What on earth was I thinking?" I duck beneath Jubilee's lead rope to get to her other flank. For a while, I brush her in silence, but the thoughts are getting louder and louder in my mind. "I guess there's only one solution, unless you have any ideas?" Jubilee stays quiet. "Shit, OK. I'm afraid you're right. But at least that way, I'll have more time for you."

She snorts smugly, almost as if she'd really understood me. Maybe she had. Although I'd be surprised. Lately, even *I* don't understand me.

"I was really enjoying it, you know?" I shut my eyes. "But I've got no choice, have I?"

She snorts again.

"Thought not."

19

SINCLAIR

I could stay here forever, brushing Jubilee and pouring my heart out to her, but study hour is looming and I really need to speak to Mr. Acevedo first. I'm dreading the conversation, but I still feel kind of calmer as I walk back to the school.

The sky is gray on gray, and I want to know how Tori's doing. Is she feeling better? What if she wakes up and she's scared because she doesn't know what happened? Everything within me yearns just to take the corridor to the sick bay and ask after her, but I know they won't let me see her. Especially not in my dirty stable clothes. I'm just crossing the courtyard when a dark car drives through the gate.

I stop as I recognize the driver. Tori's dad doesn't even wait for Arthur to stop the car—he's already opening the door. He's wearing a black suit and looks like he's come straight from a business meeting. His gaze roams over the school walls, then comes to rest on me.

"Charles." He's looking worried, but his smile seems genuine as he walks over. "Nice to see you."

I just about manage a hello. He hugs me before I get a chance to warn him that I'm all dusty and reek of the stables. It starts to drizzle.

"How are you?" he asks. Doesn't he know what I did? Tori gets on well with her dad. She tells him everything. Or almost everything . . .

"Fine, thanks, George." I gulp. "Are you here to see Tori?" I've spent plenty of weekends and holidays with the Belhaven-Wynfords, but it will always feel weird to be on first-name terms with Tori's parents, however much they insist. Especially here at school, where Tori calls my mum "Mrs. Sinclair" like everyone else.

"I was in Edinburgh for work when your mother called me," he explains. "Apparently, there's a flu bug going around here."

It sounds so harmless, the way he says it. But maybe it really is, if you didn't happen to have been standing right there when Tori just keeled over. I nod.

"Aye, well, I hope she hasn't passed it on to you," he says, and I shiver. Does that mean he knows we kissed? Or is he just assuming that Tori and I still spend every free second together?

"Me too," I say lamely.

He nods. "Anyway, I just wanted to pop in while I was in the area. It's this way to the sick bay, isn't it? It's ages since I was last here."

"I'll show you the way," I offer.

"That would be grand, thank you."

I have no idea what we talked about as we walked, but it's never seemed so far to the sick bay in the far corner of the north wing.

Mum had said that nearly all the beds were full, but it's quiet as I follow Tori's dad into the room. They can't do more than just send me packing, so it's worth a try. Maybe I can see her for a moment.

No such luck—I realize that when Dr. Henderson spots me. He's sitting with Nurse Petra at a desk in the lobby area. He's normally only here in the mornings on Mondays and spends the afternoon seeing patients at his surgery in Edinburgh. But apparently, he's got his hands full here today.

"Mr. Belhaven-Wynford," he says when he sees us. "How nice that you could come." He glances in my direction. "Petra will take you to see your daughter, and I'll join you shortly."

Tori's dad nods and follows Nurse Petra. As I try to take a step in their direction, Dr. Henderson stands up and blocks my path. "Charles," he says, and my hope vanishes. "Am I mistaken, or did study hour begin two minutes ago?"

"Please," I beg. "Just for a moment."

He shakes his head. "We don't need any more patients just now."

"I'll sanitize my hands."

"I'm very sorry, Charles, but you'll have to wait a few days."

I hate doctors and their whole bloody professionalism. That fact dawns on me yet again.

"Is she any better?" I ask quietly.

I still can't read his face. "Her temperature has gone back up, but you mustn't worry. I'm sure Tori will be up and about very soon."

"OK. Could you please tell her that I was here? And that I'm sorry? It's important."

It's the first time I've seen a hint of sympathy in Dr. Henderson's eyes. "Of course I can."

"Good." I glance past him, but can't see a thing. "Er . . . thank you, then."

"Off to study hour with you, Charles." He waits until I'm back in the corridor before he turns. Walking away feels so wrong.

Her temperature has gone back up. What does that mean? Given that Tori was burning up enough that she fainted, it can't be good. Didn't Mum say they were trying to get the fever down? Isn't it working? And isn't that dangerous?

My thoughts follow me all the way back to my wing. Everything's quiet on the stairs and up on our corridor; all the doors are shut, as always at study hour. Only Mr. Acevedo's is open, so he'll notice if anyone tries to make a break for it.

He's sitting at his desk and immediately looks up as I stand in his doorway.

"Well, here's a surprise," he says. "You're in luck—I was just about to mark you down as absent."

"I'm sorry—I was at the stables, and on the way back, I bumped into Tori's dad." I might be imagining it, but Mr. Acevedo's eyes seem a little more understanding now. He must have seen how much I was losing it this morning. "I just had to show him the way to the sick bay—you can ask Dr. Henderson."

"I see." He turns back to his computer. "Off you go, then." I don't move, and after a while, he looks up again. "Or is there something else?"

For once, I force myself to do the sensible thing and listen to my gut. "There is, actually. Have you got a minute?"

Mr. Acevedo beckons me in. I sit down on the chair that's normally reserved for getting a bollocking. He rolls over on his office chair and crosses his legs.

"I can't play Romeo any longer." One simple sentence. Effective. Like ripping off a plaster. Doesn't make it painless, though. Mr. Acevedo doesn't bat an eyelid. He doesn't say a word for five endless seconds. He just eyes me as if he wants to give me the chance to take back my words. Or to explain. But I'm not doing either of those things.

"You can't play Romeo any longer," he repeats slowly. I nod. "Why?"

"I don't know—it doesn't feel right. I should never have auditioned. It was a spur-of-the-moment thing."

"A spur-of-the-moment thing?"

God, would he ever stop that? It's not like I don't know perfectly well how ridiculous this all sounds. We've been rehearsing for weeks; the performance is getting closer. And there's no understudy for Romeo.

"I know it's out of the blue. And it'll probably cause chaos, but I can't carry on. I'm really sorry."

"Charles, I don't expect you to explain your decision to me. I only want you to know that I'm surprised. And somewhat disappointed. Have you really thought this through?"

I nod, although everything within me is shaking its head. *Thought it through* . . . I can count the things I've thought through properly lately on the fingers of one hand.

"You're letting down the rest of the cast. And letting yourself down. Maybe you did audition on the spur of the moment, but in my eyes, it was the best decision you could have made. You've got talent, Charles. I haven't seen such a refreshing Romeo as you in a long time."

I lower my head and fight the urge to shut my eyes.

He has to stop this. Right now. I can't listen to it. Any more than I can think about Eleanor and the rest when they hear I've quit. Or how I'm going to miss it. But I can't do it. This role has caused nothing but trouble, and I can't risk it driving me and Tori apart forever. It's only a stupid play. I can try again next year. It's not so important. Not as important as Tori's feelings, which I keep hurting, again and again, even if she'd never admit that to me.

"I know, and I'm really sorry," I say. "I should have known from the start that I couldn't do it. And I wouldn't let you and the others down if I had any choice. But I don't."

"Is this to do with a certain person in the upper sixth?"

I hadn't expected Mr. Acevedo to ask so directly. I slowly shake my head, even though I'm not quite sure whether he means Eleanor or Val. Whatever. Either way, it's got nothing to do with either of them. "No."

"Good, because I would find that very depressing. It's undoubtedly true that not everyone at this school is mature enough to understand that theater is an art form which requires you to face up to your emotions. It demands more courage to make yourself so vulnerable to an audience than to sit up in the crowd, mocking others."

"I know." I'd been aware that Mr. Acevedo wasn't too impressed by Valentine Ward and his hangers-on, but I'm surprised he thinks that little of them—and that he'd tell me so. "But it's for personal reasons."

"Does that mean I'll soon be having to do without my assistant director too?"

My blood runs cold. "I hope not." Because that's the whole point. If Tori doesn't have to watch me standing on that stage with Eleanor, then hopefully she'll be able to get back to enjoying the rehearsals and working on the script.

"So do I." Mr. Acevedo leans back. "It would be just as painful as losing you. But I'm afraid there's no changing your mind."

"No, I'm afraid not too." I gulp. "Louis would make a good Romeo. He and Eleanor get on. Ephraim or Tom could be Mercutio."

"We'll see," says Mr. Acevedo. "Is that all?"

I just nod.

"Good. Or not good, whichever you prefer. I hope you know what you're doing, my dear Charles."

I definitely don't, but with a bit of luck, this will be the first decision in ages that I don't end up regretting.

Or maybe not. I'm uncertain again as I leave his office and head to my room for study hour.

TORI

Headache. Tired. Dizzy.

My throat hurts, everything hurts. Why is it so freezing cold?

"Hey, kiddo."

I blink. There's an unbearable throbbing behind my forehead. The light is harsh. Wince, headache's getting worse. My whole body is shivering, my teeth are chattering, I can't do a thing about it.

"Dad?" At least, that's what I try to say, but all that comes out is an unintelligible croak. What's he doing here? And where even am I? At home?

He says something, but I forget what in the same second. My head's still really buzzing. And I'm tired, so very tired . . . I hear his voice, words like *sleep* and *rest*. His hand on my burning brow. Cool fingers, darkness.

I don't know if I'm dreaming, but Charles's saying my name. Repeatedly, urgently. Kind of distraught. What's wrong, what's he afraid of? I'm sure it can't be that bad. He's holding me and I'm falling, but then he's kissing Eleanor, with all the rage that's in his eyes as he looks at me. Valentine's fist connects with his face. I scream. He needs stopped, but I can't move. My feet are stuck fast to the cellar floor. Valentine's spitting on Charles, who's down. And it's my fault. It's all my fault. *You've changed, Tori.* Charles's voice. Disappointed, reproachful. I know, and I'm sorry. I didn't want this. I just wanted something that worked. I didn't want to smash us up. I'm so hot, I think I'll catch fire.

It's all right, Tori. There's a hand on my brow and something cool, wet. *It'll be better soon.*

I'm not sure about that.

I'm really not sure about that.

20

TORI

It does get better, but not for five days. Almost a week during which I mainly slept and about which I can remember scarily little. Thursday is the first day when I can keep down a little tea and a mouthful of soup. By Friday, my temperature is finally normal. On Saturday, I have a shower, followed by a lie-down because it's so exhausting.

Nobody is allowed to visit apart from Mum and Dad, who ask if they should take me home with them. I smile and say no, thank you, and once my parents have left, I have a secret cry. It's not like I wouldn't rather be with them. But Mum was sober and so bloody jittery and nervous I couldn't bear it.

Emma's sent me loads of entertaining TikToks and film recommendations, but I spend most of my time asleep anyway. I get a bouquet of flowers and a "get well soon" card from the theater club, which everyone except Sinclair has signed. It's a slap in the face, and however much I try to kid myself that he might just have forgotten, I can't help imagining him at a rehearsal just sitting there and passing the card on without a word. It's so painful that I have to ignore the WhatsApp he sends me asking how I am, because my pride is hurt. It's probably just his guilty conscience forcing him to ask after me—he doesn't really care. But I have nothing to say to the guy anyway. I can only dimly remember the last week, and nothing at all about the day on which—according to Dr. Henderson—I fainted in morning assembly. But the images of the evening before that won't disappear. Annoyingly. I wish they weren't so seared on my mind. Charles kissing Eleanor and making sure I can see. I still don't know how I feel. Angry, helpless, disappointed. A bit of everything. I really wish I didn't care. Indifference. That's one thing I'll never feel toward Charles, and it's driving me mad. If only I could never see him again. But at the same time, I spend every waking moment talking silently to myself about everything I have to say to him. What on earth was he thinking? Is he proud of himself? Do I really mean so little to him? Why the hell?

I know I'll never ask any of those things. Maybe everything's over between us. Just now, I don't feel like I could ever look him in the eye and not see everything that's happened in the last few weeks. The way he kissed me and then pushed me away. Or I pushed him away. We pushed each other away. I don't know. Everything's too confusing, and it's making my head ache, but I can't stop thinking about it. The stupid card's there on the bedside table, mocking me.

Eleanor signed it and added a tiny heart after her name. If it wasn't so important to me to be a good feminist, I'd hate her. For her guilty heart and her lips on Charles's. But she didn't do anything, I tell myself, it was him who kissed her, so I force myself to keep hating him. It doesn't make the whole thing any easier, but Eleanor's acted perfectly to me from the very start. She helped me when I felt uncomfortable around Val. Almost like she could sense it. It would be so much easier if I could just hate her, but unfortunately, I can't. All the same, I don't know how I'm ever going to face her and Charles, and put a brave face on things in rehearsals. It would probably be better if I gave up my job as assistant director. My work on the scriptwriting team is done, the script's pretty much settled, and to be honest, I really don't give a damn what does or doesn't happen on that stage in the summer. I'm past caring. I can't just keep on getting hurt and kidding myself it doesn't matter. Because it does matter. It matters a lot. Because I'm in love with Charles. Have been for way too long, and it hurts. I don't want to lose him, but if there's no other way, then I'll have to suck it up because I can't and won't go on the way the last few weeks have been.

I'm sure of that the next Monday afternoon, when I'm allowed back to my room because they need my bed in the sick bay for boaking second-formers. I've spoken to Ms. Barnett, and I'm going back to class tomorrow, but I can leave anytime if I don't feel up to it. Considering the mountains of missed schoolwork I've got to catch up on, I have to give it a try. At least I missed the French and history tests last week.

Emma doesn't leave my side on Monday evening; she makes us tea and settles down on the edge of my bed to bring me up to date with everything. I was only out of it for a week, but it feels like there's a whole month of classes and gossip I've missed. But when Emma sips awkwardly at her tea, not meeting my eye, I realize there has to be something she's not telling me.

"Did Sinclair ever get in touch?" she asks casually.

I tense. I'd like to say no, but that wouldn't be true. He did get in touch. "Yeah, he texted." Emma looks at me. "What?"

"Nothing. I . . . He was pretty worried."

Oh, was he indeed? Don't make me laugh. "Good to know. He didn't even sign the drama club card."

"Oh." Emma hesitates. "That's probably because he's not in the drama club anymore."

"What?" I laugh, because I'm sure she's pulling my leg. But Emma's expression is serious. I fall silent. "What do you mean?"

"He quit."

"He *what*?"

"Last Monday. Then he cried his eyes out at Henry's."

"Hold on, hold the bus!" I raise a hand. "You're kidding me, right?"

"Tori, no." Emma gulps. "I didn't tell you because I didn't know if he wanted to tell you himself. But well, I thought you ought to know."

"But why?" I blurt. My mind is racing. Charles quit the role. "So who's playing Romeo now? There wasn't an understudy, he can't just . . ."

Emma shrugs. "Gideon reckons Louis will probably step in, but it's apparently been total mayhem ever since."

I can imagine. God, he's dumb. What did he do that for?

For your sake? whispers a naive, hopeful voice in my head. No.

No, no, no. I can't think that. The whole world doesn't revolve around me. Charles made a decision, and it's nothing to do with me. Jeez, it's all so confusing.

"He's at the bakery, I think," Emma says just as I'm wondering where he is. It's almost creepy how well she knows me. "But please wrap up warm."

SINCLAIR

Dad didn't ask any questions when I offered to do a few extra shifts at the bakery even though I'd already worked the weekend. I think he understands that the bake room is the only place I can find peace just now. Quiet—just me and the dough, which doesn't look reproachfully at me or start whispering the moment my back's turned. Like the rest of the drama club, or indeed the whole school, now that the news is out that I chucked everything away.

I'd hoped to feel more relief. I'm rid of the role and all my problems with it, aren't I?

Of course not, because—sadly—I care way more about what happens to the play than I'd like. Besides, I'm scared of how Tori will react when she hears about it. Mum says she's doing better and she'll be able to leave the sick bay soon, which, on the one hand, is a relief and, on the other, sends me into a blind panic. Because it means I'll have to talk to her. Have a conversation I've run through so often in my head in the last few weeks that there's no way I can screw it up now. Unless, of course, Tori departs from my imaginary script.

I've just put the dishwasher on and I'm wiping down the work surfaces when I hear the knock. Four quick taps in succession. But even so, God knows why, it never occurs to me that it might be Tori. Maybe because she's ill and the rainy streets of Ebrington are the last place she should be.

My heart skips a beat as I see her out there. I hurry to open the door.

"What the . . ." I start as she comes in. "Hi," she says.

We're standing face-to-face, and I'd forgotten how beautiful she is. It's only a week since we saw each other, but it feels like a lifetime.

"What are you doing here?" I ask slowly.

Tori shrugs her shoulders. Her pale skin looks almost like porcelain. Even her freckles seem faded. The rings under her eyes make her look tired, and her cheekbones are more prominent. She looks knackered. Like someone who should be in bed with tea and a hot-water bottle, not standing here with me.

"Are you out of your mind?" I step toward her. "You're meant to be in the sick bay, not—"

"Dr. Henderson let me out," she says. Her voice sounds scratchy. I want to take her in my arms and never let her go.

"When?"

"This afternoon."

"And does he know you're here?"

"I don't see what business that is of his," she retorts.

"Because you should be resting," I snap at her. *Because the last time you stood next to me, you just keeled over, and since then, I've been feeling like I can't breathe. Is that really so hard to understand?*

"I can take perfectly good care of myself, thank you very much." She sounds irritable, which is probably a good sign. But I don't want to argue.

"How are you?" I ask quietly.

The antagonism vanishes from her eyes, making way for something soft, vulnerable. God, I've missed her. Not just because I haven't seen her for a week. It's felt like we've been drifting ever further apart for months now. I had a brief moment of hope after we kissed, but that just made everything even more complicated.

"Better." Tori swallows. "I'm OK."

"Are you sure?"

"Yes, I'm sure."

"You should be in bed, Tori," I insist, but she shakes her head.

"And you should be on the stage."

I freeze. And then I understand. She's heard. Great. Of course she has. What did I expect? That she'd hear none of the school gossip from the sick bay? I should have known better.

"Is that why you didn't sign the card?" she asks. "Or did you just not care?"

I open my mouth, but her question is so absurd I can't even speak.

Not care?

Tori stares at me, and then she nods. "I see."

That's the moment I explode. "Are you seriously asking me that?" She flinches, but I can't stop. "Are you seriously asking me if I care about you, after I've just been through the worst week of my life because nobody would tell me how you were?"

The silence after my outburst is unbearably loud. My heart is pounding in my throat, and Tori's staring at me with her huge brown eyes.

"Shit, sorry." I run both hands over my face, and then I swear again because I'd forgotten how floury they are.

"Charles," she says quietly, but I shake my head.

"OK. Surprise: I care about you. I care more than anything, got that? I think about you all the time. Every day, half the night. Not just when you're ill and I'm freaking out with worry. The whole time. And I wouldn't change that even if I could. Because I'm in love with you, for God's sake. So if you'd be so kind as to go back to school and get yourself back to bed—" I don't get any further.

"What?" Tori looks at me like she's seen a ghost. "What did you just say?"

"You heard me."

"Charles, what did you just say?"

"That I'm in love with you, for God's sake."

"Is that why you kissed me?" she asks quietly. "Or was that Romeo kissing . . ."

I laugh out loud. "Seriously? Of course that wasn't Romeo. That was Charles, who always gets everything wrong, in case you hadn't noticed."

"Meaning you regret it?"

I shake my head.

"Would you do it again?" she asks.

I want to look away, but I owe it to her to look her in the eye. My voice is rough. "Only if you asked me to."

There's a dark flash in her eyes. Tori's lips are pale, but she's still the most beautiful woman in the world.

"'Your mouth has cleansed my lips from sin,'" she whispers. I get goose bumps and shut my eyes, just for a second. "'Then give it back to me.'"

And I take a step toward her.

21

TORI

The caution with which he takes my face in his hands is overwhelming. And so are the softness of his lips and the heat of his breath, which caresses my mouth for a fraction of a second before he kisses me. Firmly, yet gently.

At last.

If I'm allowed only one kiss in my whole life, let it be this one. My eyelids shut of their own accord; my hands seek him out and find his firm shoulders. I have to tip my head back because he's so tall. And I forget to breathe. I only realize that when I start feeling a wee bit dizzy.

Charles pulls away ever so slightly, but his face is still so close that I can't quite get him into focus, and then he abruptly flings both arms around me.

I can't remember the last time he hugged me like this. But it must have been ages ago. And I've missed it. I press my face into his jumper and want to cry, but I don't.

"I'm in love with you too," I whisper instead, feeling the way he tenses. "I've been in love with you as long as I can remember, Charles."

He smells of security, flour, and tea. And his eyes are so endlessly blue when he looks back at me. I recognize the question in them.

"And I was scared that I was the only one to feel that way," I add.

"I was scared too," he admits. "Tori, you're my best friend. That matters more than anything. I couldn't live with it if I lost you."

I dig my fingers harder into his arms. "You won't."

"But maybe I will."

"Why do you think that?" I ask, although I know only too well.

"Because I'm not Val."

OK, apparently, I'm wrong. I let out my breath. "I don't care about Val."

Charles hesitates.

"OK, that's not true, but . . . he never came anywhere close to being what you are to me." My heart is pounding; Charles's looking at me. "Because you're everything. You're my home. You're the person I could always tell everything."

"Yes, but then you stopped," he says. His voice cracks, and I can hear the pain that we share.

I blink as the tears come after all. "I know. And I'm sorry."

"Why, Tori?" His fingers are on my chin. When I look up, his eyes are glinting. "Why did we stop? We were perfect."

"Because we were scared," I whisper. "Or I was scared, anyway. So scared, the whole time."

When Charles gulps, then nods, I know he felt the same. "I was scared too. And I didn't want all this. All the stuff I said to you. Fuck, I'm so sorry, Tori. I'm ashamed of what I did. But I was raging. About the way you let Val treat you. He kept pulling you further away from us all, and I couldn't do a thing about it. And then I treated you just as shit as he did. No, worse. Kissing Eleanor like that, I shouldn't have done it."

I swallow, and although they are words I've longed to hear, I force myself to shake my head. "It was your role."

"No, it wasn't. It was unnecessary. It was Charles, wanting to hurt Tori. Because I'm a fucking arsehole."

"I hurt you too," I whisper. "So I guess I deserved it."

"No, you didn't." His thumbs stroke over my cheeks. "You didn't deserve any of it. You deserve someone who treats you with respect."

My throat is tight. "I think I know someone."

His eyes wander over my face. From my eyes to my nose to my mouth. My knees go weak. "I think I do too."

My stomach tingles as he puts his index finger under my chin and raises it gently up to him again. This time it's not him kissing me, it's *us* kissing each other. Slowly, carefully. I've never felt so safe. Safe enough to press my tongue gently against his lips and to keep going as he opens his mouth for me. When it hits his, waves of heat flood through my body.

I've touched my best friend thousands of times, but never like this. And I've never felt as beautiful as I do in his arms. And that's absurd, because I look awful, I know that, even after I showered earlier. There's no denying that I've spent the last seven days sick in bed.

And Charles knows that. I feel his warm body directly on mine, but he stops when he notices I'm getting out of breath.

He strokes his thumb over my bottom lip, and my heart skips a beat. He looks at me and smiles.

"You're so gorgeous," he whispers. "And you have to get to bed and rest."

"But I want to be with you."

"Tori . . ."

"Please."

He sighs gently. "I'm nearly done here. Give me five minutes and we'll go back together, OK?"

I nod. He studies me for a moment with the same disbelief in his eyes that I feel. How can it suddenly be this easy? Where's the catch?

There isn't one. I really want to believe that as Charles kisses me again before disappearing back into the bake room.

He hurries. I've been sitting on one of the stools by the sales counter for less than five minutes when he comes back. He's taken off the dark-red apron and reaches for his jacket, which is hanging on a hook on the wall. He pulls a woolly hat out of his pocket, but doesn't put it on; instead, he holds it out to me.

"Take this," he demands sternly. My stomach feels warm. I do as he says and slip down from the stool as he reaches for my hand. He doesn't let go of it all the way back to the school. Not even when we're through the gate and a few third- and fourth-formers are coming toward us.

It's almost wing time, but Charles doesn't stop to say goodbye when we get to the point where he should go right and I should turn left. I pause in the west-wing stairwell. He immediately looks at me.

"Everything OK?" His eyes wander over me.

"Ms. Barnett is sure to look in on me." I pull my key out of my pocket and hand it to him. "You go ahead. I'll tell her I'm back and that I'm going straight to bed."

"OK." He leans down and kisses me, slips the key into his pocket, and hurries away.

Ms. Barnett asks three times how I feel and won't let me go until I've taken my temperature. It's normal. She's satisfied and nods understandingly when I say I'm going to get an early night.

My heart is pounding as I walk down the corridor to my room. Charles's left the door ajar, and he's sitting on the bed as I come in. He raises his head, his blond hair falling into his eyes, and my stomach leaps. He's already taken off his jacket and shoes, and he stands up as I follow suit.

Then he pulls me to him and presses me into the mattress. The last time we shared a bed was after the New Year Ball. And I've missed it. His warm body, the fact of how perfectly my head fits his chest.

"Your parents were here?" he asks.

I feel suddenly cold. "Yes, I . . . Did you see them?" I make an effort to sound as unfazed as possible. Did he see Mum too? And if so, did he notice anything?

"Only your dad, last Monday. But Mum said they were here together a couple of days ago, to see you. Didn't you want to go home with them?"

"I was feeling loads better, and it would have been kind of tricky. Dad's got so much work on right now, and Mum . . ." *Shit.* "She's away a lot."

Charles says nothing at first. Eventually, he asks, "Is everything OK at home?"

He knows. Or maybe he doesn't, but he can guess. Of course he can. He knows me. Last time I got ill at school, Mum and Dad picked me up and looked after me at home. But I was thirteen then, and Mum hadn't started drinking like that. Or not that obviously. I was younger. Maybe I just didn't notice.

"Yeah, sure," I say hastily, but my voice sounds a bit high. And the tears spring to my eyes. It's just so hard to keep pushing everything down, not to permanently worry about it all. Has Mum really got it under control? Will Dad manage to persuade her to try another clinic? Would that even do any good if it's not her own decision?

"Hey," Charles whispers, laying his fingers on my cheek. I blink and blink and blink, but I'm tired and thin-skinned, and then I start to cry. "Tori, what's wrong?"

My shoulders twitch, and I get the feeling that, here in his arms, everything that's been holding me together for the last few weeks is just falling away.

"Has something happened?"

I want to shake my head and nod at the same time, because I don't know. Something's happened, but nothing specific. It's more something brewing slowly and scaring me. Because I can only guess at what will happen next.

"It's so stupid," I blurt out. "Sorry."

"It's not stupid," he says at once. "Is she drinking again?"

How could I ever have thought he wouldn't have twigged? I just nod and wipe away my tears.

"A lot?" he asks.

"I don't know." Sobs. Soothing. "Will and I haven't been home since that weekend at the end of January."

"Is that why you came back early?"

I nod again, feeling ashamed. But it's the truth. "And because of Kit," I add. "It was the weekend the situation with his dad escalated."

Charles hesitates. "Was she . . . you know, when they were here?"

"She was sober," I say. "I think. But I don't know. Charles, I'm scared."

He tightens his arm around me. "I know," he whispers into my hair. "Why didn't you say anything, instead of dragging all this around with you the whole time?"

I shrug in silence.

"Or were you able to talk to Val about it?"

The brief laugh that escapes me is a bitter one. "Yeah, course."

"So that's a no, then?"

I wriggle away from him so I can look at him. "Charles, I couldn't talk to Valentine about a thing. Not a single thing, you know? Maybe what it's like growing up in a wealthy family, but that's it."

The pain in his eyes takes my breath away. "So why did you go along with it for so long?"

"I dunno, because I was weak, no idea. I didn't want to believe it. Right from the start, everyone around me knew better. It made me angry, so I started kidding myself. Because I was so bloody stubborn and didn't want to admit that you were right."

"It made me angry too." His voice trembles. "I felt totally powerless. Whatever I said, I knew it wouldn't change anything. It did the opposite. It made everything worse. And I want you to know that I didn't want to interfere in your life. It was just so hard to deal with seeing you unhappy."

"I know, Charles."

He looks at me, and I forget what I was about to say.

"I love it when you say that."

"What?"

"My name."

"Or should I go back to calling you Sinclair?"

"No," he protests.

Phew. It's almost uncanny how weird that already feels, even though he's been Sinclair to me for years. But now he's Charles. And I hope he'll stay Charles forever.

"And I'm sorry, by the way," I mumble.

"What for?"

"For calling your name when you and Val were fighting. I don't think it would have been so bad for you if I hadn't distracted you."

"Maybe not," he says at once. "But I reckon it was worth it."

My stomach flutters. I raise my hand and lay my fingers on his left cheek. There's not much of the black eye left, but if you knew it was there, you can see that the skin around his eye is still slightly dark. "I really am sorry," I repeat.

"And so am I." He sighs. "And I get that you were angry. I was out of line, but I couldn't help it. I wanted Val to get what was coming to him."

"From you?"

Charles raises his eyebrows at my sarcastic tone. "'Cause I wanted to mix it with the rugby captain? Is that really so unrealistic?"

"I'd better not answer that."

Charles laughs softly and hugs me closer again. "Yeah, it was pretty unrealistic, I'll give you that."

"You're always so insightful. It really could have gone to shite."

"Hey, I'm not that much of a weakling."

My best friend is way stronger than I'd thought. "I know, but he was drunk."

Charles understands. I'm sure of that as the smile fades from his face. "I'm sorry for getting so hammered at the New Year Ball too," he adds.

I swallow hard. "Just never do that again."

"I don't think I'll have any reason to in future."

"What do you mean?"

"I was drinking because I couldn't stand seeing you with him."

"Charles . . ."

"I know, that was really pointless."

"Pretty much."

He looks at me, I want to ask what he's thinking, but I can't speak because he's stroking my cheek.

"You're pale," he says quietly.

"'It's just the light, my darling.'" It's my first thought, and Charles remembers. I can see it in his face. His line. Romeo to Juliet, the scene we rehearsed together.

"Maybe I haven't made the smartest decisions lately."

I nod. "I can think of another example."

He immediately understands what I mean, I'm sure of that, even before he heaves this big sigh. "Tori..."

"No, listen to me. You can't give up the part. Eleanor and you were amazing together." It hurts a bit to admit that, but it's the truth. I want to get this right. And if it starts with Charles giving up something he loves for my sake, then we're pretty star-crossed too.

I realize this is in danger of turning into an argument as he sits up slightly. "Tori, I can't do it anymore. I saw how much I was hurting you."

"And I saw how much you were enjoying being on stage."

"I didn't even want to," he retorts. "Don't you get it? I only did it for you. I thought you'd audition, so I made myself try. I hoped we'd be able to spend more time together if we were both in the drama club. I didn't want the lead role. I thought Mr. Acevedo would let me be a tree or have some walk-on part or something, but not Romeo."

"That was before we all knew that you could do it," I say sharply. "Or are you really not enjoying it? Look at me and tell me you're not absolutely in your element when you're standing on that stage, and I'll never breathe another word about it."

He hesitates.

"You see?"

"No, stop it. It's done. Mr. Acevedo will have recast Romeo ages ago. I can't just go to him and ask him to take me back."

"But you'd like to?"

"No, Tori..."

"I'm sure it wouldn't be a problem."

"Tori," he repeats, more insistently. "I've made my decision. It's better this way. For everyone."

"I don't want you to stop doing things you enjoy for my sake."

"And I don't want the things I enjoy to make you unhappy." I open my mouth, but he won't let me speak. "And I don't want to talk any more about it."

I don't like it, but I sense that we won't get anywhere like this. So I let it rest. Maybe I can have a chat with Eleanor and ask her to talk some sense into him. Part of me goes on the defensive at that thought, but I force myself not to listen to it.

Charles is here. Here with me. Of his own free will. Because he wants to be. I have no reason to be jealous. I have to tell myself that again and again.

"Are you tired?" Charles asks at the exact second I imagine how nice it would be just to shut my eyes now. "Did you eat anything? You weren't at dinner."

"Ms. Barnett brought some soup up to me," I say.

"Should I get you something else? When we were at the bakery, we could have . . ."

"Charles," I say quietly. He goes silent. "Everything's perfect."

"Are you sure?"

"I'm sure."

"Want some sleep?" he asks, meaning should he go.

I wrap my arm more tightly around him. "Can you stay?"

"If you want me to."

"Yes," I whisper as he puts his fingers on the back of my neck. I can't remember the last time I fell asleep in his arms. I only know I've missed it. His warm body, his chest, slowly rising and falling beneath my cheek.

We kissed. Today. It was the third time. And this time, everything was right. No secrets, no regrets. No crazy fever dream that I wake from with a start, wanting to cry. Just reality.

SINCLAIR

I didn't know you could be dizzy with happiness. That you could feel this light and content, despite having slept barely a wink. I was tired, but I couldn't sleep. I had to listen to Tori's breathing and take in her smell, feel her warmth and wonder if I was bloody dreaming.

I'm not dreaming. I'm sure of that as I budge over as cautiously as I can and get up just before six. I wish I didn't have to, but in a few minutes, Ms. Barnett will be waking the others for the morning run. I'm sure Tori's been let off for the next wee while, but she might still peek in. By which time I need to be gone.

I actually don't mind the run, but at times like this, I curse being at this school and having to follow rules that make it impossible to just stay here, lying beside her.

Tori stirs as I stand up and slip on my hoodie. She blinks, and I bite my bottom lip.

"Sorry," I whisper, leaning down to her. "I have to get out of here. Go back to sleep."

She groans, which makes me laugh—I'm not sure that she's quite awake. Then she pulls me closer by the fabric of my jumper.

My heart lurches, but I just lean down to her face and press my lips gently onto hers. I don't know why I'm so nervous. Maybe because part of my overtired brain is afraid it just imagined last night. And that today we won't be Victoria and Charles anymore, we'll be Tori and Sinclair again, who kiss in secret and never speak of it.

But then I feel her smile in the kiss and shut my eyes.

"Are you OK?" I ask quietly.

She nods, and I kiss her forehead. Tori's trying not to shut her eyes again as I straighten up. I hope Ms. Barnett will force her to stay in bed today and not come down to class.

It's still quiet in the girls' wing, but the moment I reach our corridor in the east wing, I run straight into Mr. Acevedo. He eyes me without a word, and for a moment, my heart stops.

"I suppose you were wide awake and went downstairs to get a bit of fresh air?" he suggests slowly.

"Yes," I say. "Yes, exactly."

"That's just as well. Otherwise, I'd have to inform your mother."

"I know." Shit. I'll have to be more careful in future. I'd already twigged that Mr. Acevedo isn't as ignorant as we'd like to think. I'm sure he knows that Henry spends more nights in Emma's bed than his own. But even so, I wouldn't want him to catch me red-handed.

I feel his eyes on my back as I head to my room. I wish I could turn around and apologize. Not just for breaking the rules but also about the drama club. No matter that I really didn't have a choice, it wasn't cool to quit right in the middle of rehearsals. I'm only too aware of how hard it must be to recast Romeo without causing trouble with a different role. I'd like to know how they've solved the problem, but it doesn't feel right to ask Mr. Acevedo. I'd rather bug Gideon about it.

Louis and Eleanor get on well, but I'm afraid they wouldn't really work as lovers. Besides, he's such a good Mercutio that it would be a shame if he didn't play him. And the same for Gideon—he's the perfect Benvolio. Besides, he only has eyes for Grace. Even I've noticed that. Lately, Grace has often looked kind of out of it. I'm afraid she hasn't really got over breaking up with Henry, and I can understand that.

Maybe she and Gideon should take the two lead roles, but Mr. Acevedo would never do that to Eleanor. It wouldn't be fair. She deserves to play Juliet. And I wish it wasn't like this, but it feels like I've left her in the lurch. I know that Eleanor and I would have worked on stage. Acting with her was so much fun. But the price is too high. It's Tori's peace of mind, and I can't risk that. Not for a bit of personal fulfillment on stage. Not if I imagine the way I'd feel seeing her up there with somebody else. I know she wants to try not to be jealous and to be happy for me. But I can't demand that of her. So no Romeo for me. We can try again next year. Our real-life love story is more important than the theatrical version.

22

TORI

Ms. Barnett left it to me to decide if I wanted to go to classes today, and under normal circumstances, I'd probably have stayed in my room. I slept amazingly well, but this morning I still feel like I was hit by a truck. The only thing that got me out of bed was the thought of seeing Charles. I want to see him. I really want to see him. It's bad enough that I have to wait until history in period four because I was too late for breakfast.

Almost the moment I enter the classroom, Charles looks at me in a way that makes me weak at the knees, and he takes my hand under the desk. "Are you all right?" he asks.

There's something lovely about how important that is to him. I nod. "Are you?"

"Couldn't be better," he declares.

"Hello, who are you?" Omar comes cheerily toward us, and Charles lets go of my hand. "Hey, guys, I think there's a new girl here."

"Are you feeling better?" Grace asks, popping up behind Gideon. Olive, who is standing beside her, turns away and sits down without interest. Or so I think—she does look over when I answer Grace's question.

"Yeah, much better," I reply.

"Isn't that lucky?" Olive says, almost under her breath.

I try to keep smiling. Charles is pressing his knee gently against mine. Ms. Kelleher enters the room. As we stand up to greet her, Charles puts his hand on my back.

When I turn to him, he keeps his eyes to the front, but he's smiling.

It's hard to focus, and I don't know whether that's down to the slight headache and tiredness or to Charles's hand, which is always on my leg or arm.

"Want to go back upstairs?" he asks as we're packing away our stuff after class. It would be naive to think he wouldn't notice how tired I am.

I shake my head. Before I can say anything, he's swept up into a conversation with Gideon and Omar.

"By the way, we have to do a group project for English," says Henry, appearing out of nowhere at my elbow. "Emma, Sinclair, and I took you into our group. Want to sit down and get started?"

I nod. "Yes, sure."

"How about tomorrow afternoon?"

"Yeah, I've only got classes till half past two," I say, turning to one side. "Charles?" I ask.

He immediately turns to me. Before I can ask him, I realize I've never called him by his first name in front of the others before. Or if I have, it was only to be annoying. That occurs to me as Henry's eyes dart in surprise between us, then take on a knowing expression.

"Tomorrow, just after half past two, library, English presentation?" he asks. Charles nods. Henry smiles.

"Perfect. See you then, Tori." He bites his bottom lip. "See you then, Charles."

"Shut it," Charles says, but the red in his cheeks takes the sharpness from his words.

"Sorry," I murmur once Henry's gone.

Charles shakes his head. "Just takes some getting used to."

"Would you prefer me to call you Sinclair in front of the others?"

"No," he says without a second's hesitation.

"OK."

We leave the classroom. It's not until the others have gone a few steps ahead of us down the corridor that Charles pulls me aside.

"About just now . . . I wasn't sure. Do you want them to know?"

"Do you?" I ask.

Charles studies me. "Yes, I think I do."

"Then I do too."

"Sure?"

"They'll notice soon enough anyway."

"God knows how Henry knew just now."

I shrug. "Henry always knows everything."

Charles kisses me. Because I've got geography, and he's heading in the opposite direction. Or that's the plan, but we haven't got far when I suddenly realize we're being watched. Valentine and some of his friends are coming around the corner, and his eyes are like daggers. I go ice-cold as I hear his scornful laugh. Charles's stopped, and as Val walks right past us, there's a moment when I'm scared they'll pick up their pointless punch-up again. But Charles just takes my hand.

I knew it would come: The moment Valentine Ward found out what's happened between me and Charles. And it feels every bit as dire as I'd been expecting.

"Hey, you were right, man," I hear Neil say. "She's straight on to the next one."

I feel Charles tense. I cling to his hand as he tries to tear himself away.

"And I thought no one could beat Eleanor," Cillian adds. "You always go for the wrong chicks, Val."

"Don't," I whisper as Charles glances at me. There's a threat sparkling in his blue eyes, but in the end, he nods. As I turn away, Val's eyes are on me, and briefly, I make out something close to pain on his face. In that instant, I understand that while he's manipulative, toxic, and mean, underneath that, he's broken. I remember Val doing push-ups in his childhood bedroom after his mother reminded him that sport's the only thing he's good at. It doesn't justify the way he treated me, but it makes everything a tiny bit more bearable. Because I'm sure he's secretly yearning for something genuine but can't learn from anybody how to open up. And more importantly still, I know it's not my job to teach him. It isn't now, and it wasn't then.

Val looks at me, his face hardening again. "Hey, it was never serious with her, lads," he says, and I know it's meant to hurt me, but it doesn't. I'm too far away from him.

I'm with Charles.

I'm where I belong.

SINCLAIR

My rage at that fucker Valentine still hasn't completely died down when I see Tori again in class after lunch. I'd longed to deck him in the dining room, but we all know what would have happened then. So I try to follow Tori's example and ignore him. It's probably the most effective weapon against people like Valentine Ward, and I can feel it working. He must be so angry that Tori ditched him and is with me now.

I'd feel happier if Tori would take it a bit easier, but she seems to think she has to be back in lessons at all costs. I can kind of understand her not wanting to get any further behind, but I wish she'd take the teachers' advice and go back to bed.

Tori still doesn't have much appetite, and as a result, she doesn't have much energy either, so I'm not surprised that she's fighting to keep herself awake in PSHE after lunch.

"Come on," I say quietly as she lays her head on the desk instead of getting up after class.

"My legs are like jelly," she mumbles.

"Want me to carry you?" I tease.

"Don't you dare." She straightens and sighs. "Why am I so tired?"

"I think it might be because you were ill," I reply dryly.

"I have to get to rehearsal, Charles."

I frown. "First you have to get up to your room for study hour."

"Oh, yeah, right."

I don't say anything, just pick up Tori's bag. By the look of her, it'll be more like nap hour.

"Does Mr. Acevedo still check if you're in your rooms?" she asks with a hopeful undertone.

"Not usually. Does Ms. Barnett?"

I can't help smiling as she shakes her head.

"So I could come to yours."

"You could."

"You have to test me on my French."

I just nod rather than arguing. Even if she wasn't dead on her feet, there would be so many other things I'd rather spend this hour on than French vocab. My sneaky brain keeps reminding me, way too often, of how it felt to lie beneath her on that hard stage. Almost as often as it does of the fact that I'm eighteen and still a virgin. Sooner or later, I'm going to have to tell Tori. Or should I just act like I know what I'm doing and hope she doesn't notice?

Today isn't the day to have that conversation, though; I can see that even before Tori drops onto the bed in my room.

"Tea?" I ask, putting our bags down on the desk and turning back to her. She nods, eyes shut, and wraps both arms around my pillow. The boiling kettle and her breathing are the only sounds as I return to my room after rinsing out the two mugs. A quick glance in her direction confirms that Tori's fallen asleep. She jumps as I set the tea down on the shelf next to the bed a few minutes later and sit beside her.

"Hi."

"I wasn't asleep," she mumbles.

"I know." I lean down and kiss her nose.

"Again," she whispers, blinking. "Please."

I have to smile. "You're such a sleepy chicken."

"Don't do that."

"What? Call you that?"

"Yeah, that's your nickname."

"You were scared of the hens too."

"No, I wasn't." She opens her eyes to twinkle at me. "So kiss me, you chicken."

"I thought you wanted me to test you on your French?"

"*S'il vous plaît*," she sighs.

"*S'il te plaît*," I correct her. I can't help it. Maybe I've been spending too much time with Henry.

"D'you know how hot that is?" she murmurs.

"What, me correcting you?"

"No. You speaking French."

"You're so easy to impress."

"Say your favorite sentence," she requests. "Please."

I have to laugh, then I clear my throat. "*Je suis allé au cinéma avec ma famille et mes copains*," I say. It's got me through a surprising number of French lessons with Ms. Barnett. I always get a good mark from her for speaking, even though I've answered the question of what we did at the weekend with the same story for years.

Tori gives a contented sigh and shuts her eyes again.

"I'd go on, but it's the only thing I know how to say."

"Don't lie," she murmurs as I prop myself up on my elbow beside her.

"OK" is all I say as I start to stroke her back. It's unfair of me, but she really needs some sleep. Tori's eyes stay shut, and her face softens. I smile as her lips part slightly. She hates it if I point this out, but when she's really deeply asleep, she drools a bit. I actually find it kind of cute, but that part doesn't seem to get through to her. And today *cute* isn't the word for my feelings as she lies beside me. Her body is heavy and relaxed, and the quiet sigh that escapes her sets my blood boiling.

Jeez, I'm pathetic. And however hard I try to think about maths exams, Valentine Ward, and any other turnoffs, my trousers are feeling tighter. Tori's hip is on my thigh. I can feel it through my clothes, and it's driving me crazy.

It's not like it's the first time she's lain beside me, doing my head in. It's just the first time I haven't been trying to suppress it at all costs. Because we were *just friends*. The biggest lie in the history of the world. We are friends, but we're more than that. She's hot, she's the most beautiful person in the entire world. And she's lying in my bed. Oh God.

I shut my eyes, but that doesn't help. Quite the reverse. She's asleep; I have to stop being this turned on, but it's hard when you're eighteen and are feeling so much. Her warm back under my hand, her soft lips on mine. Everything about Tori is soft. Her hair is so silky, her skin, her voice. And me... nothing about me is soft. Not just now, anyway.

Maybe I should get up and actually pick up a book. Carry on

with our reading for English, learn Latin verbs. Something dull, dry... But I'm only human, and anyway, I wouldn't want Tori to wake up. She really needs this hour of peace because, knowing her, she'll go straight on to rehearsals and not get any rest. She's incorrigible. And I love her. I love her like Romeo loves Juliet. In this totally clichéd, unconditional way. Boak-worthy, I know. But anything else would be a lie. And I've done enough lying in the last few years.

I don't know how I managed to fall asleep, but when my door flies open after one of Henry's short, hard knocks, I barely know what day it is or even my own name.

"Hey, have you . . . ? Oh." Henry stops in the middle of the room as I start to sit up. "Sorry." He has the sense to turn and shut the door. Apparently, study hour is over, because the corridor isn't nearly as quiet as it was earlier. Tori unwraps herself from my arms. Henry keeps his back to us.

"Are you naked? Please tell me you're not naked."

"You're such a dick, Bennington," I say, wishing my voice wasn't so hoarse.

"Oh, really? Well, I'll be off, then."

"No." Tori clears her throat and slides over. "We were just lying around."

"Oh, right." Henry glances over his shoulder. "That's nice. Em and I do that a lot too."

"Jeez, man, too much information."

"OK, *Charles*." He looks way too pleased. "Did I ever tell you how happy I am for you two? So's Emma, by the way. She can't talk about anything else but what a cute couple you make."

"Henry," I say, but not as menacingly as I'd like.

"No, fine, sorry. But we should agree on a sign. A sock on the door handle when you don't want to be disturbed, or something."

"A sock," Tori repeats slowly.

"Yeah, or something at the window so Mr. Acevedo doesn't see. How do you manage it in the west wing?"

"God, what's your problem?" I snap.

"I was just thinking," says Henry, downcast.

"What did you even want, anyway?"

Henry eyes me, then shrugs his shoulders. "Can't remember."

"You're kidding me."

"Sorry. I got a shock. But a good shock. You know. Anyway. I'm going to find Emma." He turns back to the door but looks around again. "A flag at the window would be an option too."

"Henry!"

"Bye . . ."

Tori squats on the bed, as speechless as I am, while Henry disappears as quickly as he arrived. Then she lets herself sink back onto the mattress. Her head lands in my lap.

"Your friend is impossible."

"He's your friend too."

"Yeah, but you're my best friend." She gives me an innocent smile, and I lean down to her. We kiss, laughing at the same time. At least until Tori freezes.

"Wait, what's the time?"

I just about manage to get out of the way as she straightens again and grabs my phone. I know we've slept longer than an hour when she breathes a quiet "Fuck."

Looks like that's that for rehearsals today, then. When I take my phone, I see that it's long past five.

"Why didn't you wake me?" There's a hint of panic in her eyes as she looks at me.

"I didn't set an alarm."

"Hold it, so you fell asleep too?"

I give an apologetic shrug. "It was so peaceful . . ."

"Great."

"I'm sure Mr. Acevedo won't be expecting you back this week."

Tori sighs deeply. "Even so. And we didn't do any French either."

"Such a shame," I murmur.

"Watch it, Charles."

"I always do, Victoria."

"Don't you have to see to Jubilee?" she asks.

I shrug. "No. I'll go to her tomorrow."

"Can I come too?" she asks, to my surprise.

"Sure. If you feel up to it."

"I'm perfectly fine, Charles."

"Yeah, 'cause just falling asleep in the middle of the afternoon is absolutely perfectly fine, isn't it?"

She gives me a gentle punch on the forearm, which means I have to catch her hands and pull them to my chest. Her quiet laugh as I hold her tight and sink back down to the mattress with her is everything.

"Let me go, Mr. Falls Asleep Himself." She puts her head on my chest—the best feeling in the world. "Can we go out for a ride again?"

"If you like," I say. It must be a good six months since we last rode out together.

"I do like," she says, lifting her hand. I immediately get goose bumps as she draws mysterious patterns on my chest with her index finger. Oh, Tori. She hasn't the least idea what she does to me. Or that it can be just a matter of seconds before the tension in my trousers builds up again, and this time she's lying half on top of me . . .

"I'd like something else too." She falls silent, then lifts her head. Puppy dog eyes. Great.

"Tori," I say quietly.

"Please."

"No."

"You don't even know what I'm going to say."

"I know I won't like it."

"You know nothing."

I sigh.

"I've seen how much fun it is for you."

I shut my eyes.

"Stop acting like you can't hear me."

"Well, then, stop wanting to have this conversation," I plead.

"Ha, bad luck, we're already having it."

"Tori, I've made up my mind."

So has she, and she's determined not to let it lie. She sits up slightly.

"Out of everything that happened between Val and me, there's one thing I particularly regret," she says.

"Which is?" I ask when she doesn't continue.

"That I gave up something I enjoyed. For his sake."

I gulp. "You can't compare the two things."

"No, but all the same, I know how it feels. You're talented, you and Eleanor. You carry this play. Nobody can say otherwise. You belong on the stage . . . with her."

For a while, I just look at her and don't speak. I should contradict her. Assure her that I don't mind. But that would be a lie. I really do miss acting. "But I'm hurting you," I say quietly.

"No, Charles. It only hurt while I didn't know what it was between us."

"And what is it?"

"You tell me."

I avoid her eyes. "It's everything. *You're* everything. In every stage kiss, I was thinking of you."

There's no more beautiful sight in the world than Tori's slight blush.

"If it's everything, I can deal with that, do you understand? I want you to be happy. And I don't want to be at the rehearsals without you."

"Meaning you'd stay on as assistant director, despite everything?" My voice is rough.

"Why wouldn't I?"

"I don't know . . . because you wouldn't want to see it. I'd understand."

"Charles, I want to see you. I always want to see you."

I get goose bumps, and I understand this is it. Love. I know because it would be the same the other way around. Because I'd want to see Tori on the stage. Even if I didn't like it because it raised negative emotions within me. Jealousy, the feeling of not being enough. Those would be nothing compared to the desire to see her happy.

I nod slowly.

"Promise me," she insists.

"I'll speak to Mr. Acevedo tomorrow."

Tori smiles.

Green Flags
Friendship Edition

- They celebrate your successes, and they love it when you achieve something.
- You can always talk about whatever's on your mind.
- There's no criticism if one of you changes or develops.
- They show understanding for the boundaries you set.
- They understand that friendship has closer and less close phases.
- They ask how they can help if something's wrong.
- They want the best for you, regardless of whether it's also the best for them.
- They are able to apologize and admit it when they've made a mistake.

23

SINCLAIR

Mr. Acevedo's taken me back. I'd imagined my conversation with him being more dramatic than it was. I didn't have to argue; he just gave me this knowing look and said the stage was all mine.

Somehow, it annoys me that he must have secretly known I'd be back. But I'm just too happy that he's given me another chance, because after I admitted to Tori and myself that I do actually want to be in the play, I was more than a wee bit scared that Mr. Acevedo would turn me down. Then I learn from Eleanor that he continued rehearsals with the cast unchanged for the last week and a half, which means I feel mildly taken for a ride.

But fine, that's just how it is. The main thing is that I get to act. And the other main thing is that Tori's there too. I think she's feeling better, even if she's still often pale and tired. If her voice isn't loud enough at rehearsals, I call for quiet on her behalf so that she can say her bit. It's teamwork; it's amazingly successful. But all the same, I can feel that she doesn't find it easy to see me on stage with Eleanor.

I toyed with the idea of telling Tori about Eleanor and her

girlfriend, but a promise is a promise. Eleanor gave me a contented glance when I set everyone else whispering by kissing Tori hello. Sooner or later, the news about us would have got around anyway. At least most people in our form seem to know already. And I guess the same goes for the upper sixth. And it bugs me that I'm even thinking about this, but I hope Valentine won't cause any more problems when he bumps into Tori. And at the same time, I hope he's still fucked off about it, because that would mean she actually mattered to him in some way.

I'd like to speak more to her about how she feels after everything, but I get the sense that she's not ready yet. And maybe I'm not the person she wants to talk it all over with. Normally, I'd hope she'd confide in Olive, but those two still aren't talking. And I can tell that bothers Tori. Whenever she sees Olive, this worried expression comes over her face. Sometimes, it seems like the rehearsals are the only time in the day when she can forget all that for a while. That's how it is for me, anyway, and I spend whole days longing for the next rehearsal. It's almost ridiculous that not so long ago, I was sure I never wanted to act again. I do, I really do, and best of all, it's working. Tori seems chilled and happy while she's walking from one to another of us on the stage. My dream isn't her nightmare, even if I'd been afraid it might be.

TORI

It takes me almost another week to feel properly back in the swing of school life, and to have caught up with what I missed.

I really don't recommend being ill for so long, and just as I think I'm finally up to date, I realize before maths that I've forgotten an important piece of homework.

"Shit, Henry, can I copy yours?" I whisper as I follow him into the classroom. He eyes me a moment, not reproachful, just slightly amused, as he pulls his iPad mini from his back pocket and opens a document.

"But put a few mistakes into it," he says, handing it to me.

"Thanks." I sit down at my place and pull out my own tablet. "I'll look at it properly later. Study hour or something . . ."

"Never, then," remarks Emma cheerfully, turning up beside us. "We all know that one."

I laugh. "Yeah, OK, let's not kid ourselves."

I manage to slip the iPad back to Henry unnoticed before Ms. Ventura comes in and walks around the class to see everyone's homework.

Later on, Charles has Latin and I've got enrichment with Ms. Barnett. At the start of the class, she tells us to get into pairs and fetch some paints from the cupboards at the back of the classroom. I soon see I'm going to have to work with Olive. Everyone else has already found a partner.

"Shall we?" I ask hesitantly. Olive nods silently but doesn't look quite as frosty as I'd feared as she walks to the back to fetch the paint. Meanwhile, I head over to Ms. Barnett's desk, where she's prepared an array of items for us to collect to create still lifes.

For a while, Olive and I work in silence. In the old days, we chatted so much during pair work that teachers were always having to tell us off. Now we can hardly look at each other.

I'm just getting set up, and I budge closer to the table when I catch something with my elbow. It's the water jar, and it lands in Olive's lap.

"Crap, I'm sorry," I exclaim as Olive grabs it and I see the stains on her pale trousers. Like me, she hadn't put an apron on.

"Ms. Barnett's going to love that," Olive murmurs dryly, once she's eyed the mess. When she looks up, I hold my breath. Then we burst out laughing.

"Shit, you'd better go and change," I say. "I'm sure she'll let you pop up to your room."

"All my other trousers are in the wash already," says Olive.

"Even the blue ones?"

She nods. "I could put my skirt on," she adds, her voice dripping with irony. It's an open secret that Olive loathes skirts and dresses of all kinds. And she hates the uniform with a passion.

"That wouldn't show the mark either," I muse.

Olive sighs and starts trying to dry the water with a tissue, which doesn't exactly improve things.

"I'm so sorry," I repeat.

"Doesn't matter," she says curtly. Then she looks up briefly. "On the subject of skirts . . . did anything ever come of that uniform business?"

"Not really," I admit. I've had way too many other things on my mind lately. But now, when everything's starting to fall into place, we could actually call a meeting and talk about what we want to do.

"Would you be up for it if we—" I begin, but I'm interrupted by Ms. Barnett.

"Victoria, Olive, what's going on over here?" She comes to see. "Oh, Olive, that's why you should always wear an apron. Go and change, quickly. And Tori, you can be cleaning up in the meantime."

Olive glances at me as Ms. Barnett walks away with a sigh. The uncertainty has crept back into her face, almost as though she'd forgotten for a minute or two that she's not talking to me. She looks like she wants to say something, but then she bites her lip, stands up, and walks out of the room.

When she returns a bit later, Ms. Barnett makes a point of looking at our desk, so we feel we'd better focus on painting for a while. All the same, it's like a tiny success when Olive gives me a small smile as we leave the room. I wish I could ask her if we can talk, but I run into Charles. Olive's already heading toward Grace, so I decide to try another time.

Charles's delighted when I tell him over lunch that Olive and I had patched things up for a while. The subject of uniform comes up again in the dining room as the others ask Olive why she's wearing a skirt when she doesn't have to. It doesn't take long for a heated debate about the dress code to break out at our table, but it produces more frustration than inspiration.

I sigh with annoyance as we break up after lunch for our afternoon classes without having made the least progress, and Charles shrugs apologetically. He can't help this being such an exasperating topic, but he still feels bad because it's his mother who sets the rules about what we wear at Dunbridge. Maybe I ought to invite myself around to dinner with the Sinclairs soon so that I can talk it over a bit with her, because I'm not prepared to let it drop again.

Charles and I don't see each other until the rehearsal. I'm a bit early, so I'm the first there. When I step into the empty theater, the silence almost swallows me. It's kind of magical being here all on my own, walking down the carpeted steps. My pulse slows, my body feels lighter the closer I come to the stage.

It's hard to admit it to myself, but even though everything is finally cleared up between Charles and me, I simply can't get rid of the sorrowful feeling of not being on stage myself. The more distance I get from Val, and from whatever we had between us, the less I understand how I let him hold me back from fulfilling my dream. It feels like I haven't been myself and I'm only slowly finding my way back. It's surprisingly painful to grasp that my friends could see that all along. I always thought I knew myself, but apparently, I was wrong. I've avoided Val as far as possible lately. I have absolutely no desire for further confrontation or snarky remarks.

I put my cloth bag down on one of the front-row seats and stand uncertainly for a moment. It's amazing how soulless and empty the stage seems when it's not filled by Charles, Eleanor, and the others. I walk forward and run my forefinger over its edge. A light shiver runs through me as I remember Charles beneath me as we kissed. That seems like a lifetime ago, yet it's barely two weeks.

I glance over to the auditorium doors, then shut my eyes.

"'Woe is me,'" I whisper, making myself jump because my voice sounds so loud in the total silence. Not like half an eternity ago, when I practiced the balcony scene with Charles in the bakery. "'Oh, Romeo. Why are you my enemy, a Montague, a man I may not love? As though, once I'd seen you, my heart had any choice . . .'" I lean on the edge and push myself up onto the stage. Just to stand there for once and pretend I'd had the guts . . . "'Romeo, refuse your name and then give it to me. I mean what I say. Let me be yours and I will no longer be a Capulet, let me be by your side.'" I stand up. When I shut my eyes, I'm Juliet, walking back and forth on her balcony. Restless, desperate, because the man she loves is out of her reach. "'Your name is the only thing that makes it impossible for us to be together,'" I continue. "'Love found me, yet I must push it away for the sake of a name. But what's in a name? Put your name aside and take me in its place, I beg you; o sweet heaven, give me this man.'"

I'll take you at your word. In my head, I'm answered by Charles, but in actual fact, there's a round of applause that really startles me. My eyes fly open.

"Such a shame, my dear Victoria."

I see Mr. Acevedo stepping out of the darkness near the doors and coming down the steps. I freeze. My blood runs cold, then burning shame creeps across my cheeks.

"I'm sorry, I—I thought I was alone." I hurry toward the steps at the edge of the stage, but Mr. Acevedo is continuing.

"I realized that. It's probably why it was so good." He doesn't take his eyes off me. "All the same, I think you'd have won over an audience at the auditions."

I say nothing as I walk back to where I left my stuff.

"Or do you really want to tell me you wouldn't have enjoyed acting?"

I slowly shake my head. "No, you're right, sir. I don't know why I didn't dare."

"That makes two of us."

"It was hard," I admit. "I'm afraid I've kind of lost myself over the last few months. Or that's what it feels like. And the auditions . . . Maybe next year."

"That sounds like a plan." Mr. Acevedo smiles at me. "I get the impression you're rediscovering yourself. Am I right?"

I remember why he's one of my favorite teachers. He takes a genuine interest in our concerns and picks up on way more than some of his colleagues.

"Yes, I . . . It really does feel that way," I admit. "A few things have happened recently, and fallen into place."

"I'm very glad to hear that, Victoria." Mr. Acevedo smiles conspiratorially. We turn simultaneously as the door opens above us. To my surprise, it's Olive.

"Am I early?" she asks uncertainly, ducking back, but Mr. Acevedo shakes his head.

"No, not at all. I'm sure the others will start to trickle in soon. Come down, please."

Olive does what he says, but only reluctantly. My nerves increase as she approaches. Luckily, the door flies open again. The tense silence is broken by voices as the rest of the cast arrives.

Charles looks surprised to see Olive, who's standing a little apart from the group, arms crossed. She joins Grace, who's just walked in with Gideon.

"Olive?" Charles murmurs in amazement as he comes to my side.

Before I can reply, Mr. Acevedo claps his hands. "Good, let's get started. First of all, I'd like to introduce our new team members.

From now on, we will have the help of Olive, Marian, and Nathan when it comes to costumes and makeup. I'll be sending groups of you to join them in the storeroom while the others rehearse. Victoria will go with you to make a note of the costumes. OK?" He looks from me to the others, and I nod, although my stomach knots slightly. With Olive, in the costume storeroom . . . She looks like she can think of better ways to spend her time too.

I force myself to put my negative thoughts to the side as Mr. Acevedo sends Olive, Marian, Nathan, and me to the dressing rooms. We're joined by Gideon, Grace, and Terry, who aren't needed on stage just yet.

I've never set foot in the backstage area before, where there are mountains of costumes and props. It smells of mothballs and magic as we dig through the clothes. Half an hour later, Benvolio, the Nurse, and Tybalt are dressed to our satisfaction, and I snap photos of their outfits on my phone. I've barely said two words to Olive, and she's still trying not to meet my eyes, but I know she's struggling. She keeps staring into space, seeming out of focus and closed off. I don't get a chance to speak to her, though, because now it's Charles and Eleanor's turn.

Olive's eyes flit over to us as Charles takes my hand and ducks behind the clothes rails to kiss me. I see a smile on her face.

"Missed you," he murmurs into my ear, letting go of me again.

"It was thirty minutes, Charles . . ."

"Exactly, and they were incredibly long minutes," he says, looking around. "OK, let's go."

24

SINCLAIR

"I don't know," says Eleanor, studying herself in the mirror. She's wearing a pastel-colored, floor-length dress. "Don't you think it's a bit much?"

"It's perfect for Juliet," says Nathan, twitching at Eleanor's corset slightly.

"You look amazing," Marian assures her, and she's right, but I can see that Eleanor doesn't feel comfortable.

"You don't like it," Olive says shortly. She's sitting on a stool next to the dressing room, and until now, she's been watching in silence. She's changed out of the pleated skirt she had on earlier and is now wearing her hoodie with black gym leggings. Olive's always one of the first to get out of her school clothes at the end of classes and into her own things—usually sportswear, which she lives in when she's not down at the pool.

Eleanor turns to her. "No, I do. It's really elegant."

"But you don't feel right," Tori adds quietly.

Eleanor nods slowly. "It doesn't feel like me. It feels like a costume."

"It is a costume," Nathan points out.

Eleanor shrugs. "But it shouldn't feel like one."

"It doesn't fit with Sinclair's outfit either," Marian admits. "If you wore that, he'd have to put the ruffled shirt back on."

I groan. "Please, no. That was so itchy."

"It looked like a costume too," Tori murmurs. "This is way better," she adds, pointing to the loose-fitting shirt I'm now wearing with beige trousers. It's white linen, slightly see-through, and shows an awful lot of chest, but it works for Romeo.

Olive has stood up. "How about this?"

We all look over to her.

"For Romeo?" Marian asks dubiously, eyeing the dark-red trousers—they're in a flowing fabric and so wide legged that at first I thought they were a skirt.

"No, for Juliet."

Eleanor immediately reaches for the trousers and holds them up experimentally. "Potentially quite cool," she says.

"Don't you think it would be more suitable to stick to a dress?" asks Marian.

"Why?" Olive snaps back. The mood is still pretty tetchy after the argument over lunch. "Because she's a woman?"

"No, because it's classic," Nathan comes to Marian's assistance. "Like the play."

"They might as well wear their school uniform in that case," says Olive dryly.

Nathan doesn't reply.

"Well, I think the trousers are great," Tori says, into the silence that follows.

"So do I," I add.

"We've made my role so modern that I think it would fit to wear something bolder too," Eleanor says, raising her head. "Let me try it at least."

The others nod, and Olive hands her a white blouse that's just as baggy as my shirt. Before she vanishes into the dressing room with Eleanor, to help her out of the dress, she exchanges glances with Tori. It seems to me that she looks a bit more conciliatory than she did earlier.

"Ta-da!" Eleanor steps through the curtains with a flourish and does a twirl. The pleated trousers swing out around her long legs. When she stands still, the way the fabric hangs means they actually look like a long skirt. The white blouse has loose, long sleeves, and Eleanor's tucked it into her waistband. She looks stunning.

"I love it," Tori says at once.

"Yes, isn't it great?" Eleanor beams.

"Sinclair, come and stand beside her."

I do as Nathan says, looking into the others' delighted faces.

"Yes, that's it," says Tori. "Do you both feel good?"

Eleanor nods right away and looks at me, and I follow suit.

"I think we need a Juliet in trousers," Tori declares, which wins her nods of agreement. "Thanks, Livy."

It's ages since I've heard that nickname, and it makes Olive flinch slightly too. She mumbles something that sounds like "'S OK, no problem" and lowers her head.

"Do you guys find the whole uniform thing really old-fashioned too?" Eleanor asks, out of the blue. "I heard a couple of girls talking about it in the hall the other day."

"Yeah," says Tori. "We were only just saying so at lunch. I've been thinking for ages that we need to take a stand again."

Eleanor looks down at herself. "Well, the performance will do it in a way, but we can start before that."

"What do you mean?" asks Olive.

"We don't have to make things unnecessarily complicated. We could all just wear trousers to assembly next Monday instead of skirts."

"And get sent back to your rooms to change?" asks Nathan.

"That's the whole point," says Olive. "Why are you allowed to wear trousers when we're not?"

"And why aren't you allowed to wear a skirt?" I add. "Which you might want to do, Nathan."

"Exactly," Tori says.

"Why would I want to do that?" he asks.

"It's the principle of the thing," Olive insists.

"Totally. You're welcome to keep wearing your trousers like always, but I'm not going to let them stop me doing the same anymore." Eleanor shrugs.

"Me either." Tori and Olive speak at the same time. It's quiet for a moment, they look at each other, then Olive breaks eye contact again. I reach unobtrusively for Tori's hand as I see the disappointment on her face. There's still something weird between them, there's no denying it, but even if Olive's the world champion at pretending she has no emotions, I get the impression they're slowly edging closer to each other again.

"We need our Romeo!"

I jump slightly as Mr. Acevedo walks into the costume store. He stops in the doorway.

"Oh, wonderful!" He studies me first, then Eleanor. "An empowered Juliet and an easygoing Romeo. I knew I could rely on you all." He nods toward Olive, Marian, and Nathan. "Could I borrow the two of you for a moment now? We're rehearsing the next scene."

TORI

Just about two hours later, the whole cast has their costumes and today's rehearsal is over. Olive and I didn't get another chance to speak, but that brief moment during our uniform discussion felt like more progress. Charles asks if he should go on ahead as everyone leaves the theater, and I'm sure he knows what I'm thinking. This is my opportunity to talk to Olive.

I nod gratefully, giving him a quick kiss, then pack up my things extra slowly. Then I see that Olive isn't even here. She must have left in the throng, without me noticing. Maybe I can catch her on the way up to our wing. Or has she got swimming training? What's the time?

I go to take my phone from my back pocket and find it isn't there. It's not in my bag either, and then I remember I put it down on a shelf in the costume storeroom earlier. The last few people are heading for the door as I slip backstage. There's still a light on in the storeroom, and I can see my phone. I reach for it, and I'm moving to turn off the light when I hear a sound.

"Hello?" I say.

There's no reply, but I take a few more steps. And then I see her. Olive's still crouching on the stool by the dressing room. Even if I hadn't spotted the crumpled tissue in her hand, I'd know she's been crying. Her eyes are red and glassy.

She throws the tissue away and jumps up when she sees me. I come closer. "Is everything OK?"

"Fine," she says, wiping her hands on her leggings. "I just wanted to . . . uh . . . you know . . ." There's a look of concentration on her face, and her head is bowed. I know that look. The little ridge Olive always gets between her dark eyebrows when she's putting all her effort into not bursting into tears.

I say nothing. I just wait. It's quiet. Olive doesn't move.

"I miss you," I say in the silence. Her eyes meet mine in the mirror, and then everything happens very fast. Olive's green eyes fill with tears. She lowers her head and buries her face in her hands as a quiet sob escapes her. She just stands there by the dressing room as I walk toward her. And then I give her a hug.

Her shoulders shake, her whole body trembles. I only let Olive go so that I can dig a fresh tissue out of my bag. She bites her bottom lip as I hand it to her.

I wait until she's blown her nose, but the tears keep running down her cheeks. It seems to me almost like everything she's been carrying around for the last few weeks has burst out of her. It scares me, because I've never seen my friend like this. Unlike me, Olive practically never cries. She doesn't cry at films, however sad or emotional they are, and she doesn't cry when she feels unfairly treated. The only time I've ever seen her cry was in the second form, when she fell in PE and everyone thought she'd broken her ankle. It was only sprained, but it looked bloody painful.

"What's wrong, Livy?" I whisper.

She shakes her head.

"Please, talk to me."

"I can't."

"Has something happened?"

Olive swallows hard and shrugs her shoulders.

"Olive." I choose my next words with care. "Has someone hurt you?"

She shakes her head in silence, so I dare to believe her.

"I saw something a while ago," she says in the end. Her voice sounds choked. I can hear the way she's pulling herself together so as not to cry again. "In the autumn. I'd been round to Grace's after study hour, and I was walking back for dinner. It was dark, but a few streets along, I saw . . ." Olive shuts her eyes, and her voice breaks ". . . I saw Mum's car outside one of the houses. I didn't think anything of it at first because she sometimes does home visits in Ebrington." Olive's mum is a midwife. "Normally she tells me, in case we get a chance to meet up. But she hadn't said anything. And then I knew why. Because she wasn't there for work." The hardness creeps back into her face as her eyes fill with more tears. She wipes her cheek with the back of her hand. I pray silently that this isn't what I think it is. "She was coming out of the house. With a man. She kissed him goodbye."

Silence. For a couple of seconds. Then I whisper, "Shit."

Olive presses her lips together, then nods.

"It might have just looked like a kiss?"

"Unfortunately, it was very clear."

"Does your dad . . . ?" I begin.

She shakes her head. "She saw me and came after me. She promised me it was a one-off and told me not to say anything to him."

"But that's . . ." I stop, because there are so many possible words for it. Wrong, dishonest, manipulative.

"Yeah." Olive gives a bitter laugh. "That's what I said."

"Have you told him?"

I can see how much the question is tormenting Olive. "No. I was going to, but then . . . I saw him in the sick bay the next day, and I couldn't. He loves her—he'd do anything for us. He doesn't have the faintest idea and . . . I just couldn't. I wish I'd never seen it. I wish I was as clueless as him. Then I wouldn't feel like a fucking traitor."

"You're not a traitor, Olive," I say, although I know perfectly well that I'd feel the exact same in her shoes.

All she does is shrug.

"I'm really bloody sorry," I say.

"I don't know what to do, Tori."

"There's nothing you can do."

"What if they get divorced?"

I daren't promise her that won't happen. I know only too well how quickly that fear can become a reality. "If they do, you'll survive," I say. "And you know why? Because you're not alone, Livy. Even if it feels like you are."

Olive takes a deep breath and tips her head way back. Then

she looks at me. "I'm sorry." Her voice is quiet, but I hear what she says. "I'm really sorry, Tori."

"Why didn't you tell me before?"

"I couldn't. I just couldn't. I didn't want anyone to know. News always gets out here, and Dad would have heard rumors."

"I won't tell a soul," I promise.

"OK," Olive says. "Thank you."

"And I'm here for you, Livy. Always."

"I know," she whispers. "Even though I don't deserve it. I've been a crap friend. What I said to you that time in the corridor, and in the dining room . . ."

"Long forgotten."

"No, it was out of order. It wasn't fair on you. And I wasn't fair on Emma either." Olive is visibly wrestling with herself as she continues, "I couldn't bear it. I was desperate, and so angry with Mum. I didn't want to be in league with her, just standing by while she cheated on Dad. And then Emma came along, and I thought, now it's happening all over again with her, Grace, and Henry."

At that moment, I understand. It's like all the puzzle pieces are coming together in my head, forming answers to the questions I've been asking since last autumn.

"Emma didn't do anything wrong, Livy," I say quietly.

"I know. It was unfair of me to judge her. But I was raging. And nobody understood."

"I do."

"I didn't want this," Olive whispers. "For things to get like this between us."

I swallow. Part of me wants to be hurt and upset. Insult her, make her feel the way I felt. All the rejection and despair. But a bigger part of me is just relieved that Olive is speaking to me again. That there were reasons for the way she acted. Reasons that aren't to do with me.

"It's not too late to change that."

25

TORI

I'm surprised by how nervous I feel as, for the first time in my six and a half years as a boarder here, I come down to the morning assembly on Monday wearing my beige chinos and navy-blue blazer. It seems like news of our plan has got around, because Eleanor and Olive aren't the only others to have opted not to wear their skirts and tights. Emma, Inés, Amara, Salome, and a few of Eleanor's friends in the upper sixth have too.

And it doesn't take long for the first teachers to point out the breach of the dress code. My heart pounds anxiously as I shake my head when Ms. Kelleher asks us to go back upstairs and change. A short time later, when I'm standing in Mrs. Sinclair's office with the others, my doubts about the wisdom of our action are increasing.

"You know that this is against the rules," Charles's mum says, walking to and fro by her desk.

Eleanor nods. "Yes, we do, Mrs. Sinclair."

"And yet you chose to do it anyway?"

"Yes, to make a point," I say. "We want there to be equality at this school."

She's startled. "Meaning that you don't think this is the case at the moment?"

"I'm afraid not," I say nervously. "We consider it sexist and unfair that girls are forced to wear skirts."

Mrs. Sinclair is silent for a moment. "So you'd prefer to wear trousers too?"

"We would prefer it if everybody could choose to wear whichever they feel more comfortable in," Eleanor explains.

"I see," Mrs. Sinclair says slowly. "And I'll see what can be done. I'm sure you understand that I can't make a unilateral decision here."

"Why not?" I blurt. "You're the head teacher."

"That's true, but I very much value the opinions of those who support our school. I will raise the subject at the next governors' meeting." Mrs. Sinclair looks at us. "Until then, I must ask you to stick to the official rules." Olive opens her mouth in outrage, but doesn't get a chance to speak. "I'm sorry—I know that's not what you were hoping to hear. But I appreciate your taking a stand, and I will treat it as a matter of urgency."

As she moves back to stand behind her desk, I realize that, as far as she's concerned, this conversation is over. It feels like a defeat as we leave her office.

"She wasn't totally opposed," Eleanor says, not very enthusiastically.

I just shrug. That may be true, but we've achieved precisely nothing. It's pure humiliation to go up to our rooms and change for breakfast and classes. On the way back down again, Valentine's eyes rake over me. He and his pals start to crack jokes as Emma, Olive, and I walk past them.

Charles immediately looks up expectantly as we join him and Henry.

"And?" he asks, apparently before he's clocked what we're wearing.

I sigh quietly, then fill them in on what we've managed.

SINCLAIR

There's no negotiating with Mum. Not even when I go to see her in her office later on and raise the dress-code issue again. Part of me understands that her hands are kind of tied, but another part shares Tori's frustration at the school's outdated rules. On the other hand, Mum did tell me she's spoken to Kendra's parents about what will happen with Jubilee. If it all works out, the school will soon be buying her. I've been hoping for that very thing for weeks, but given the uniform argument, I can't be as glad as I guess I should be.

After study hour, I head over to the stables. I work with Jubilee for a while in the arena, then walk back to my room to shower before dinner. As I stand beneath the jets of hot water, I'm going through my lines for later. This evening, we'll be rehearsing one of the key scenes in front of the whole cast for the first time.

We do a few group exercises first. The others have spent the last couple of weeks, while I wasn't there, working on Juliet's visit to the friar, when he gives her the potion that will send her to sleep for three days so that she can fake her own death. Luckily, Romeo doesn't feature. To make up for it, though, my first scene with Eleanor today is one of the most intense.

Despite going over my lines earlier, now, while I roam the gloomy Verona churchyard and discover Juliet's lifeless body in one of the tombs, I feel like I've forgotten everything.

My head is blank, my thoughts are silent, and I've missed this. The effect that acting has on me. It still works. Even though I know that dozens of pairs of eyes are fixed on me. Including those of the person I wouldn't hurt for anything in the world.

I kneel on the floor beside Eleanor and touch her. My heart beats faster and my breath quickens, because I've been running and I'm in a panic. Because Romeo is hoping that what they're saying in Verona—that Juliet's dead, poisoned, buried—isn't true. How can she be simply not here, despite her promises? Oh, man, it feels like shit, and all at once, I could weep because I'm no longer acting the emotions, I'm *feeling* them. They're suddenly there.

"'Juliet?'" I whisper. Then I repeat her name, more loudly. "'Look at me, my love, come on.'" Eleanor's body is heavy, her head falls back as I lift her slightly, and my despair is genuine. Because when I remember how Tori just keeled over in my arms, the sheer terror makes me sick. I force myself not to repress it any longer, but to feel it. The panic that drives hot tears to my eyes and makes my chest clench. "'My God, Juliet . . . Don't do this, OK? Look at me, for heaven's sake, look at me. Say it's not true. Tell me so.'"

But she says nothing, and her eyes stay shut. My fingers shake, my voice is choked. I lower my head.

"'You're already cold.'" You could have heard a pin drop. I force myself not to look into the auditorium, but then I do. Just for a split second. Tori is tense in her seat, leaning forward. She's gripping her pen, and her lips are parted a touch. I think about her as I look away. "'Simply open your eyes once more and I'll be the happiest man in all Verona. Damn it, if only I could feel your lips on mine, just once more.'" My voice breaks as I lean over Eleanor. She doesn't move as I raise her face to mine. "'One last kiss, my love. With my lips I seal a bargain with deceitful death.'"

I lay my thumbs on her lips and turn her head away slightly before I kiss her. I know that it looks more real than it feels. Eleanor doesn't move. The way Tori didn't move.

"'Here, here will I remain, among the dead, if this is the only place that I can be close to you. Juliet, I'm coming to you—without you, everything is senseless. I will be with you soon. Do not be afraid, my love.'"

My hands shake as I let go of Eleanor's head.

A moment later, there's a thump. I freeze, and Eleanor groans, blinking, her face twisted with pain. There's a moment's silence. I hold my breath. Then we break into hysterical laughter.

"Fuck, sorry." I reach for her again as she straightens up. "Did I hurt you?"

"I'll live," she murmurs.

"Gently, Charles, if you please!" Mr. Acevedo calls, but I only have eyes for Tori. She's laughing, and she's gorgeous. "Juliet may be dead, but you don't have to fracture her skull too."

"Shit, I'm sorry . . . I'm so sorry." I clear my throat and look back at Eleanor.

"It's OK." She rubs the back of her head. "There's quite a bump, but the things we do for art . . ."

The others laugh.

"Nonetheless, that was very powerful, Charles. That's exactly how I would like to see this scene on the night. Just be a little more careful with Juliet's head." He looks around. "Any further comments?"

Tori nods. "Make sure you don't drop your voice too much. I could hear you from the front row, but I think even with microphones, it would be pretty tricky from further back."

I nod. "OK, true."

"But it was good. Both of you, you were very good."

"Thank you."

Tori smiles. I analyze it and come to the conclusion that it's not forced.

"So let's continue."

I try to pull myself together and get back into character. These might be the most important scenes in the whole play, and I get the feeling we're rocking them. We really are good.

I fight my last duel with County Paris, who was supposed to marry Juliet. He comes into the tomb, and I kill him before desperately kissing the remnants of poison from her lips. When that fails to work, I drink my own. I speak my last line, kiss the last kiss, and I'm not even thinking now as I die beside her. I'd never have expected that it would be so much harder to lie motionless on this stage and keep my eyes closed than to take an active role.

Suddenly, everything seems to be taking ages. Eleanor wakes up beside me, full of hope, until she sees me and the friar tells her what happened. It requires every bit of my self-control not to react in any way as I feel Eleanor's hands on my shoulders and face. She's so good that, even though I can't see her, I get goose bumps. Her sobs, her despair, they're all real. However much I deserve it, she doesn't drop my head. On the contrary. Her every touch is gentle. Her fingertips are as soft as Tori's. I'm only thinking about Tori—and I only realize too late what a mistake that is.

When Eleanor thrusts my dagger into her ribs and collapses on top of me with a hoarse cry, it's fatal. I was already turned on by my thoughts, and her heavy, warm body on top of me is not exactly helping.

Fuck . . .

I'm burning up, and I can only pray that the denim of my jeans is thick enough that Eleanor won't feel anything. This is so bloody awkward, and if it wouldn't wreck the scene, I'd roll onto my side slightly so that . . .

Eleanor tenses. She can feel it. Shit.

Breathe. Don't react. Don't think about Tori and maybe it'll stop.

Eleanor's silent breath is tickling my throat. Her hand is on my chest. Like Tori's hand. When we had less on.

Throbbing, heat, fuck, fuck, fuck.

I hear the others' footsteps, their words in the epilogue. It's nearly over. Thank God.

And . . . shit. If it's nearly over, that means Eleanor's about to roll off me and get up.

Applause rings out. I blink.

Eleanor lifts her head. "Want me to stay lying here a bit longer till you've calmed down?" She spoke so softly that only I can have heard, but the blood rushes to my cheeks.

"Shit, sorry," I whisper. "It's not you." I pause. Did I just insult her? It's not that Eleanor isn't attractive. Oh, *God*...

"I should hope not," she declares cheerfully, getting up. As she does, she glances over to the side and leans down again. "Tori really is looking super cute today."

Cute...

I suppress a groan as Eleanor rams a knee into my thigh as she stands.

"Don't mention it." Her lips form the words soundlessly. I take the hand she holds out to help me up. The pain does help me back to my senses. All the same, I kind of hide behind her as Mr. Acevedo showers us all with praise.

Tori's eyes are on me, gleaming. I want to kiss her. I want to replay the scene with her. I want her to be the one lying on me, and then I want to lie on top of *her*. There are so many things I want, for fuck's sake, and I want them now. But the thought also fills me with hot panic, as I'll have to tell her I've never done it before.

"What are you doing later?" Tori asks as Mr. Acevedo wraps up the rehearsal just before dinner and we pack up.

I'm about to say, "Nothing," when I remember that it's Wednesday and I promised to help Dad.

"Bakery." I sigh.

"Right away?" Tori asks.

"After dinner," I say.

"Hm." Tori doesn't look away. "I could..."

"Yeah," I say at once. "If you want to, that is. You don't have to. I mean . . ."

"Shut up, Charles," she whispers, laying her lips on mine.

More heat, more throbbing. I'm pathetic, and I wouldn't change it even if I could.

We meet the others in the dining room. I eat fast, and Tori keeps glancing at me.

"I'll come down later," she whispers as we kiss again outside.

TORI

It's a fresh April evening as I sneak out through the side gate and down to Ebrington. It's not quite wing time yet, but I'd still rather not be seen. It was hard enough not being spotted by Ms. Barnett after dinner as I went up to my room to change my school clothes for something more comfortable.

Charles hasn't locked the shop door. He emerges from the bake room as I close it behind me and the bell rings. He's wearing his dark-red apron, and he's got his sleeves rolled up. I want to be kissed by him. He obliges every time he moves from table to counter, weighs ingredients, scrapes out bowls, or drags new flour sacks from the cellar.

I was genuinely intending to help him with his work, but let's be honest here. I spend most of the time staring at his strong forearms and broad shoulders. His hands are covered with flour, and soon, so's my hair. My lips, my cheeks. We're kissing constantly. Brief kisses in passing, longer kisses where we stand still and slip hands under jumpers. His hands are cool on my belly; his tongue is hot in my mouth. And then my heart stops as he kisses his way across my throat and gently bites into my shoulder. And my body responds.

This is new. I don't know this side of my best friend yet, but I like it. I hold my breath as he pulls me to him again by the hips. I need more of it. I need his crotch against mine, and oh, I can feel him. Hard against my stomach.

For a moment, I forget to breathe, and Charles takes possession of my mouth. I always thought that was a silly phrase when I read it in books, but it really is true. I get it now. Charles's hands on my face, his thumbs on my temples, his thighs between mine as he pushes me back, against the large table in the center of the room. He kisses me more deeply, his leg presses against me, and I feel it in my whole body. Hot throbbing. It spreads. Between my legs, in my belly. Slow, fluid.

Kissing—this stupid apron, I can feel the knot behind him and the strap around his neck. Charles takes my hand. He holds it tight, and I understand.

"We're nearly done, OK?" he says with that divinely hoarse voice, and all I can do is nod. I quietly thank God as we leave the bakery behind us and Charles comes to the west wing without hesitation. He doesn't let go of my hand as we flit down the hallways. It's almost wing time, and we don't want to get caught.

We don't meet a soul, and we sigh with relief as we reach my room. Charles shuts the door, turns the key, and when he comes face-to-face with me again, I go weak at the knees. He doesn't take his eyes off me as he walks toward me, to carry on where we left off earlier.

His hot lips dot my face, my neck, and my cleavage with kisses as I slip off my jacket. I grab the hem of his hoodie, and Charles lowers his head so that I can strip it off him, and once I'm done, his face is between my breasts. My body stretches toward him, and I have to lean my head back. He wraps his hands around my bum and lifts me. Briefly, quickly, the way he sets me down on my bed is desperately attractive. Before he can pull back, I wrap my legs around his hips. I pull him to me; he presses himself against me. It's a new angle, one where I can feel everything. I want to sink back and close my eyes, but I want to press up against him too.

We don't speak, there's only our rapid breathing. It's like our hands had never known anything different, even when we were making ourselves keep our distance. Now I ask myself how that was ever possible.

I need him. I *need* him. Charles. I can't think of anything but the fact that it might happen. That I might have my first time, with him.

He pauses, almost as though he's thinking the same thing. I know what he wants to ask when he looks at me. Dark eyes, flushed lips. What are we doing here?

I look back at him.

I don't know, but I want it.

"Would you like . . ." His voice is hoarse; he clears his throat. Heat, more heat in my belly. He's aroused too, and somehow, that soothes me. "Do you want me to stop?"

"No," I say. "Don't stop."

"OK." He steps between my legs, but he's not moving. "I haven't got any . . . Well . . . You know."

"In the bathroom," I say.

He opens his mouth but doesn't speak. I feel myself blushing. He wasn't expecting that. I can see it on his face. A few weeks ago, I wouldn't have expected it either, but if the night of the New Year Ball and Valentine Ward taught me anything, it's that I don't want to be the one who has no condoms to hand, if it comes to it. It was a precaution I justified to myself on grounds of feminism, not fear. I wouldn't have done it with Val if I hadn't felt comfortable. At least I don't think so.

Charles kisses me on the lips, then moves back so that I can get up. My heart pounds as I slip into the bathroom and glance in the mirror before I take one of the plastic packets out of the drawer. My cheeks are pink. He's already messed up my hair.

When I get back to him, I wonder for the first time who there was before me. Only Eleanor? Or anyone else? The question pops briefly into my jealousy-poisoned brain, but I don't allow it to ruin this moment for me. I'll ask him about it sometime, but not now.

I force myself to breathe more slowly as he comes toward me. Charles takes my hand and wraps his around the condom. We kiss, slowly. He pauses in front of me.

"Do you really want to?" he asks.

I turn my head and run my lips over his cheekbones. Only very gently, but it makes him shiver.

"Yes," I whisper. "Do you?"

He kisses me on the lips. "Yes."

"OK."

My stomach is tingling with nerves and anticipation, but there's no fear. Only excitement, but excitement is good. This, with Charles. I want it to be good.

His belly is hard as I slip my hand under his T-shirt and down to the waistband of his jeans. His breath catches as I pause. Our eyes meet. Then he pushes me down onto the bed. I pull him with me; I have to close my eyes as he sinks down on top of me. We keep kissing, and then I feel brave enough to let my hand slip between us. Over his stomach and the stiff fabric of his jeans. Charles groans quietly. He presses himself against my palm and tilts his hips. Oh, my goodness. So this is what it's like. And I like it. I really do.

He takes the condom packet between his teeth so as to have both hands free to undo his fly. I lie beneath him as Charles unbuckles his belt, then tugs down the zip. I pull him closer to me, and this time, there's only my leggings and his boxers between us. Hardly anything. Way too much.

There's a more intense rubbing, with no kissing because he's still got that little packet between his teeth—at least, until I take it from him. Charles follows my lips with his, and then he's kneeling over me. His jeans are on the floor; he reaches for my hands and pushes me back onto the mattress again. He picks the condom up again and rips it open with his teeth as I reach for the elastic of his boxers. It's fast. Faster than I imagined it, but that's probably a good thing.

I hardly dare breathe, I stare at the ceiling as I push down my leggings and my knickers. He's looking into my face, so

I have the courage to spread my legs until I can wrap them around his thighs.

Charles leans over me. I pull him down until I can feel his pelvis against mine. And then he's right next to me.

I want to shut my eyes, and at the same time, I don't want to. We keep moving; he reaches between his legs. I dig my fingers into his shoulders, hear his heavy breathing and my thundering heart. And then he's suddenly deep inside me. It's true—it does hurt, quite a lot in fact, and not just for a moment. So much so that I have to remind myself to keep breathing.

"Are you OK?" Charles whispers, stopping.

"Yes."

Relax.

Exhale.

It's working. I can feel it getting easier, the pain easing. Charles waits until I nod, then he withdraws slightly and presses into me again. Deeper this time. Very deep. I didn't know there was so much room in there. His hands rub over my sides, and then it hits me.

We're having sex.

We're sleeping together.

I can feel him right into my belly. His trembling, his movements. I groan as he moves faster, and I have to cling to him. His hot breath on my collarbone, my fingers in his T-shirt. Firm muscles beneath my hands, my legs, his belly on my belly when he thrusts really deep into me. Yeah, *thrusts*. Charles is actually thrusting. Firmer, faster, as I whimper his name.

He's not being cautious anymore; he's rough, and I'd never

have thought I'd like that so much. I didn't know he could. That he can *be* like this. There's barely any strength in my legs, but I press against him, arch my back, closer, I need him closer.

"Tori." He shuts his eyes, his hand is close to my head, his arms are shaking. "I have to . . ."

He wants to pull back; I won't let him. His muscles are as hard as stone; his whole body is shaking. I grab his hair, I kiss him, I whisper his name, and then he groans. Throatily, deep, inside my mouth. I feel dizzy. He leans his head back, his mouth open. His eyes are closed, his eyebrows contracted. I don't know if I've ever seen anything more beautiful.

When it's over, he softens. First his face, then his whole body, the weight of which I only remember when he sinks onto me.

26

SINCLAIR

I always thought I'd have so much to think about once it finally happened. Do I look good, am I doing this right? Do I need to move more, less, faster? God knows, but now, in this moment, my head is surprisingly empty. Everything just happens. Yes, it's awkward and sometimes I don't know where to put my hands and legs, but apart from that, it's like a dream.

It's like a dream. Tori under me, her hot skin, her soft belly. She wraps her legs around me and lifts herself toward me. At first, we were still kissing, but I can't kiss now. Even breathing is hard. I can only move with Tori, and she's so hot and tight and . . . Fuck. I clench my fists beside her head but nothing helps. She moves, I move, she lifts her hips, I lift my hips. Pull back, slide into her, slowly, again, slowly, again, then faster, deeper. Until our hips are locked together and a muffled sound from her lips reaches into my mouth. She digs her fingers into my shoulders, she presses her thigh against mine, and God, the scent of her. Her sweat, her trembling.

"Tori, I have to . . ." I pant, and I want to pull back, but she's holding me tight. Her eyes are brown, her cheeks are red. She's perfect.

"Charles," she whispers, and she kisses me.

And I come. There's nothing I can compare it to. I'm inside her. I can feel everything, everything all at once. Her fingers on my neck as I arch my head back and have to shut my eyes before I collapse onto her. She's not moving. She's lying beneath me, quietly. I can feel her pounding heart.

"Fuck," I whisper.

Thirty seconds, it can't possibly have lasted any longer. *Fuck, how embarrassing.*

She strokes my hair but doesn't say anything. I have to sit up. Now. But my muscles don't want to.

"Shit, I'm sorry." It's still hard to breathe.

"That's OK," she says. "It was still nice."

Nice . . . *Nice.* Fucking shit.

I feel so hot, but now it's hot shame in my cheeks. I pull out of her and roll onto my side.

Tori lifts her head as her phone rings. At that moment, I realize what we've done.

We've *done it.* In her bed. My first time, and she didn't even come close to an orgasm because I'd finished before I could even ask her if she liked it.

Tori avoids my eyes. Her phone is still ringing. "Maybe I should . . ." she says, not looking at me.

"Yeah."

She reaches for her knickers and her leggings. Punch in the guts.

I sit up. "I'll be right back," I mumble, but my voice is so quiet that I don't know if she even heard me.

I throw the condom away in the bathroom and wish I could punch my own face in the mirror. My reflection is mocking me. My cheeks are flushed; it's clear what I've just been doing.

My blood is still boiling, but I feel like shit. *Rookie. Failure.* She bloody well had a condom ready. She wanted to have fun. I bet it lasted longer with that fucker Valentine Ward.

I lower my head and force myself to breathe deeply. OK, it was crap. But seeing that I've been single forever, she must know that it was my first time and that I . . . I didn't really have it all under control. If you ever even should, but fine. Maybe she'd like to try again. Today, or some other time. I just have to tell her the truth, it really isn't hard.

I reach for the door handle. Tori's got her back to me, and she's still on the phone.

"No, Will." She sounds so insistent that I stop. "Right now. Dr. Henderson has to have a look at it."

My blood runs cold. She turns to me, and I see the panic in her brown eyes.

"We're in my room. Give us five minutes."

TORI

Kit looks worse than Will had claimed on the phone. Worse than the last time his dad lost it. He's got a split lip and his nose is bleeding, but it's the color of his face that scares me. Kit's as white as a sheet, and he's clutching his belly as Charles and I walk toward them in the street in Ebrington under cover of darkness.

"Why didn't you call an ambulance?" Charles comes around to Kit's other side so that he can help Will support him.

"He doesn't want one," Will says, tight-lipped.

Kit gives a quiet groan, his hand still pressed to his stomach. He looks apathetic, and it makes my own belly ache as he lurches.

"Dr. Henderson's on his way," I say. Or so Olive said when I phoned her in a panic to ask her to tell her dad. It would take him at least twenty minutes to get to Dunbridge. "We only have to make it as far as the school."

The road from Ebrington to Dunbridge Academy has never seemed longer to me. Olive is standing under one of the archways in her joggers, glancing nervously in our direction.

"He should be here any moment," she keeps saying as Charles and Will take Kit to the sick bay.

"Good grief, lads . . ." Nurse Petra murmurs, waving the boys through. Kit groans as he sinks onto a couch, and trying to straighten his legs makes him whimper with pain.

"Dad, hurry!" Olive's voice is shaking. I turn and see Dr. Henderson, who is pulling off his hat and scarf as he walks. He seems to grasp the situation at once and doesn't waste time asking questions. Kit's belly looks as stiff as a plank, and when Dr. Henderson tries to feel it, he writhes under his hands.

"Would you call an ambulance please and then bring me all the Ringer's solution we've got?" he asks Nurse Petra.

Will is ghostly pale, and Charles pulls him slightly aside.

"What's wrong with him?" Will's voice trembles. "Dr. Henderson?"

"We'll look after him," he says in Olive's direction. "Please, all of you, wait outside."

Olive's face is hard. She looks as though everything within her is rebelling against pushing Will out of the room. He doesn't start to cry until the paramedics arrive and he's not allowed to go too. I've never seen my little brother in this state. It's heartbreaking.

We follow him out into the courtyard where the ambulance is casting blue light up onto the school walls. It's late, there are no sirens, but it's only seconds before all the dorm curtains start twitching.

My heart stumbles as Mrs. Sinclair's dark Range Rover pulls up. She immediately gets out and walks over to the ambulance. I can't hear what she's saying to Dr. Henderson and the paramedics before they shut the doors and the doctor gets into his own car, presumably to follow them. Will pulls away from my arms and tries to run to him, but Mrs. Sinclair holds him back.

She looks startled as she sees Olive, then me, and finally Charles.

"What on earth has been going on here?"

27

SINCLAIR

We're in Mum's office. Tori is standing behind the chair her brother's sitting on, soothingly stroking his shoulders while he explains what happened. I know most of it—Tori told me—but to hear from Will how Kit has been spending as few nights as possible at home because his dad might get angry at any time and his mum doesn't do anything to stop him, makes my throat tighten.

Mum feels similar. I can tell from the look of self-control on her face as she stands there, leaning on her desk and listening to Will.

"Why didn't you come to me at once?" she asks in the end. She looks from Will to Tori to me. I gulp and lower my head.

"Kit didn't want to," Will says eventually. "I could hardly convince him even to talk to Henry."

"Henry knew about this?" Mum's voice sounds a little higher pitched than normal, a sure sign she's annoyed.

"He wanted to tell you. But Kit . . . he was afraid of what would happen if people found out. Ebrington's a small place. People might stop going to the shop, and that would make his dad even angrier. He'd already threatened to take him away from school."

"William, Christopher just had to be taken to Accident and Emergency in an ambulance," Mum says.

I bite the inside of my cheek as his eyes fill with tears again.

"I'm going to have to inform social services."

"No, please. Can't you at least wait until you've spoken to Kit? He'll kill me when he knows that I—"

"William," she interrupts him. "It reflects well on you that you want to protect your boyfriend, but as head teacher, it is my responsibility to tell the authorities. Christopher is under eighteen, so I have no choice. And I assure you that he won't have to leave Dunbridge, whatever Mr. Irvine threatens." She waits for him to nod. "We will find a solution for him," she promises. "All that matters is that Kit is safe now."

"I have to see him," Will says. "Please."

"Dr. Henderson will give you a lift to Edinburgh tomorrow."

"But—"

"It's late, William, long past wing time." Mum's eyes fall on me. "I'll tell Charles as soon as I've heard from Dr. Henderson, and he can let you know."

I nod.

"Do you want me to talk to your parents?" Mum asks, but Will immediately shakes his head. Tori tenses. I can feel it, and I think I understand why. Kit's father drinks, as far as I understand it, and even though I don't think Tori's mum would ever hit her children, it's still the alcohol that breaks everything.

Tori, who never drinks. Tori, who spent the night of the New

Year Ball taking care of me because I was so hammered I can barely remember a thing. Just her face, blurrily, her in my bed.

Once I get back to my room, I lie there, staring at the wall. It's late, dark, quiet. But my mind is racing because too much has happened today. Rehearsing with Eleanor and getting a hard-on was embarrassing; having sex with Tori and not lasting even a minute was way more embarrassing.

What's wrong with me? What the fucking hell is wrong with me?

She had condoms. Either she knew before I did where everything was heading or . . . she's just always prepared, on principle. I feel so stupid when I think about the act I put on to everyone. Buying condoms at Irvine's with Henry and Gideon, then keeping them in my locker at the sports center, like I'm ever going to use them. Instead, I was just happy for Henry to use them before they went out of date and I'd have to face the fact that I'm a pathetic loser. It's all one huge joke. In my offstage life, I've only ever kissed one woman, and that's Tori. I wouldn't change that, or maybe I would, just so I wouldn't be that loser with no clue.

I don't know how often Tori and Val had sex, but I feel an urgent need to find out so that I can compare myself unfavorably with him. I'll bet he could keep his dick inside her longer than thirty seconds without coming. I've spent an unhealthy amount of time imagining everything that could go wrong the first time, but I didn't think of that.

It was still nice.

Nice.

I don't want Tori to find sex with me nice. Well, I do, of course.

I want her to feel safe. But I also want her to come so often and so hard that she doesn't know who she is anymore. Or does that kind of thing only happen in films? Why don't I have a big brother I could ask?

Henry... Shit. I'm going to have to ask Henry. Wow. But I've got no choice.

I want to get it right. Like Val presumably did. God, I don't want to think about Tori lying beneath him, arching her neck, arching her back. What did he say when she came? Her name? Some fucked-up stuff? Is she into dirty talk? Jeez, it feels like I should know this stuff about my best friend, but at the same time, I *have* to know. I have to find everything out so that it'll be good next time. Not nice. Good. Seriously good.

Why couldn't I manage it?

I shut my eyes.

Because I was nervous. And insecure. Because I'd never done it before and didn't want her to know that. As if there was anything wrong in that. I hope she sees it that way too, and I can't actually imagine Tori judging me. In her place, I'd probably have liked that. To be her first. Loved it, even.

Ha. In that case, I guess I should have found the guts to tell her sooner how I felt. This is what I get for it. Thirty seconds of sex and a head full of chaos.

28

SINCLAIR

Kit had an emergency operation at the Royal Infirmary in Edinburgh. His shit of a father had beaten him so badly that he'd ruptured his spleen. Will is surprisingly composed as he tells us this. The doctors say Kit would probably have died of internal bleeding if he hadn't got help last night. I think Mum knows too. She did tell children's services, and that means Kit won't be going home. I don't know the details, but if I understand correctly, she'll give him some kind of scholarship so that he can board at school.

It's been a wild few days, and I haven't seen much of Tori, because she's been spending a lot of time with her brother. The insecure part of my brain keeps trying to convince me there might be other reasons for that too. I try to ignore it, but I can't deny that things have been weird between us since we slept together.

Henry wouldn't be Henry if he hadn't instantly noticed that something was up. I ask him after dinner what he's doing for the rest of the evening, and he says he'll come around later. Soon after that, he knocks on my door; he's wearing joggers, his school hoodie, and his grim socks-and-Birkenstocks combo and carrying a packet of biscuits, plus tea in his favorite mug.

We talk about Will and Kit for a while, and I learn that Mum gave Henry a bit of a hard time for not telling her about their problems. Although in the end she had to agree that he couldn't really have done so, seeing as Kit had sworn him to secrecy.

Henry's gone back to calling me Sinclair, as is only right and proper. So now, when he eyes me and sips his tea, I know what's coming next.

"So, Charles, what's up?"

I decide to ignore the fact that he keeps using my first name when he wants to steer the conversation subtly around to Tori. Instead, I ask, "How's Emma?"

"Fine." Henry runs his thumb around the rim of his mug. "She saw her dad last weekend. I think it went well."

"That's nice."

"Yeah, it is," he says. I say nothing. "And how's Tori?"

"How should she be? The whole thing with Will and Kit is stressing her out." I shrug my shoulders.

"Understandable," Henry says. "What does your mum think about you two? Does she know?"

"That we're together?" He nods. "She was pleased," I say. Because she really was. "So's Dad." It would be more truthful to say that they looked at each other with a told-you-so expression on their faces and smiled gently.

"How about Tori's parents?" Henry asks.

"Yeah, them too. Or I think they are." I gulp. Tori hasn't told me they weren't, anyway. But I also get the impression that

Charlotte and George Belhaven-Wynford have other worries just now. Tori hasn't been home for ages, which is definitely to do with her mum and the drinking.

"Lovely, that's nice." Henry goes silent.

When I look over, he's eyeing me.

"What's up?" he asks.

"Nothing."

"So how's it going with your first girlfriend? Got any questions? Need any tips?"

I hate Henry, but I know he isn't being ironic. Hardly surprising—he's the baby of his family. I suppose he's been waiting his whole life for the chance to be the one with pearls of wisdom to dispense in relationship matters. And it's not like I wouldn't be grateful. He and Emma are endgame. And what he had before, with Grace, wasn't bad either. Henry knows how it works, let's be honest here. Meanwhile, I've got room for improvement, to put it mildly.

"Yeah, there is something." I squirm.

Henry puts down his mug. I wish he wasn't focusing his full attention on me because, given what I need to talk to him about, there's no way I can look him in the eye.

"What is it?"

I gulp.

Oh, shit, if only I'd never said anything...

But Henry won't let it go now, I know him well enough to be sure of that.

"Sinclair?"

I shut my eyes.

"Oh," Henry says as I open them again. "You've done it."

"What?" I blurt. "What makes you say that?"

"I don't know." He shrugs. "Some kind of intuition."

"You're kidding?"

"Haven't you then? Sorry if so—don't feel under any pressure. And about the other day, when I burst in on you, I've been meaning to say I'm sorry if that was annoying of me. There was no need for it."

"Henry," I say, and he goes quiet. "Shut up."

"No, I had to say that."

"OK, got you, but that's not it."

"What then?"

"Yes, of course you're right. You know, with your intuition." I pause. "We . . ." Shagged? Slept together? Made love? Hell, none of those things, considering how it went.

Henry tries to keep his face as neutral as possible, but he looks like he's bursting with pride. I'm certain he'll tell Emma all about it. They've probably been betting on it—I wouldn't put it past them.

"I'm happy for you both."

"You're happy?"

"Yeah. Shouldn't I say that? Sorry, but I really am. You two are totally made for each other." Henry really does look pleased. "But was it good? I want to know everything! Well, not everything, just as much as you want to say. You don't have to tell me anything if you don't want to."

"Henry, just shut the hell up."

"Yeah, sorry. Sorry." He claps both hands to his mouth, but the look of challenge in his eyes betrays him.

I wish the ground would swallow me.

Was it good?

He should be asking Tori that, not me. And according to her, it was nice. It's amazing how much damage that fucking word has done to my fragile male ego. But I guess I deserve it.

"Well, no." I stare at my knees, because I simply can't meet Henry's eyes while I'm embarrassing myself like this. I don't know what I'll do if he laughs. Laugh too, and later cry tears of fury because I'm a wuss. Not over the crying—I'm kind of glad that I'm someone who can cry reasonably often. It's kind of a release. But this whole sex thing is driving me mad. I get a horrible feeling that other people don't turn it into such a big deal. They just do it.

"No, you don't want to go into detail?" Henry asks carefully.

"No. No, it wasn't good . . . Or yes, it was. It was good. It was damn good. For me, at any rate. I hope it was at least a little bit good for Tori. I don't know. Fuck . . ." I force myself to take some deep breaths. Henry doesn't interrupt. He doesn't say anything, and that's driving me crazy.

"Didn't it work?" he asks eventually, when I can't say another word. "That wouldn't be a disaster. The first time with Grace, it didn't work. I was too nervous."

"God, stop it," I mumble.

"Ha, no, it's not a disaster. I didn't last long with Emma at first either, but fortunately, I usually managed to return the favor."

This is actually stuff you don't necessarily need to know about your best pal, but it's kind of comforting all the same.

"I don't know what to do," I groan and let myself drop

backward onto my bed. "I was in her, and well, then I was finished right away. I don't think she was anywhere near coming."

"Maybe she can't come that way."

Don't think about the fact that we're talking about Tori here. Just don't think it... "So what should I do?"

"Ask her what she likes. And tell her what you like." It sounds so simple when Henry puts it like that.

"Don't you dare tell me *communication is key*," I grumble, because I know Henry.

He laughs. "Hey, what can I say? Communication has certainly proved useful so far."

"Maybe I should have told her it was my first time."

"Didn't you?" Henry asks.

I shake my head.

"Got you."

"I didn't want to kill the mood."

"I promise you, that kind of thing never kills the mood."

"You can't know that."

"Sinclair, it's important. Talking to each other, I mean. Especially during sex. Or afterward, before the next time."

If there is a next time . . . But we'd better not think that either. There has to be a next time. Because, OK, maybe it was anything but optimal, but nobody can tell me there was nothing between us. The start was promising. There was a spark. It was genuine. I get goose bumps thinking about it, and Tori has to kiss me like that again, and pull me to her, and touch me, or I'll die.

"It's not fair, everything always works out for you," I mumble.

Henry laughs. "For Emma and me? *Everything* never works.

Sometimes nothing works. Sometimes some things do. You never know, and that's normal."

"If you say so . . ."

"Emma didn't come our first time. Only afterward, when I was totally focused on her. And like I said, it didn't work out right away with me and Grace either." Henry looks at me. "By the way, do you think there's been something funny about her lately?"

"Grace? What do you mean?"

"I don't know. Maybe I'm imagining it, but she doesn't seem happy. And . . . she's lost weight, hasn't she? Even more, I mean."

I try to remember the way Grace looked at our last rehearsal. "To be honest, I hadn't noticed. But I wasn't thinking about it."

Henry nods. "I'm a bit worried."

"She's spending a lot of time with Gideon," I say. "During rehearsals too. You could ask him."

"I don't want to interfere, you know?"

"I don't think it's interfering. If he thinks it's weird, say you're looking out for her as school captain."

Henry seems unconvinced. "I just hope she's all right."

"And if she isn't, that's not your fault."

He darts a glance at me. "Yeah, well . . ."

"She understood, Henry. Definitely."

"Yeah, and she's seen me with Emma every day since. But I'm scared it's not that. Or not just that. Anyway, never mind. We're talking about you here."

"We're not."

"Yes, we are. We have to come up with a strategy for next time."

"Henry, I really don't know if I want to be thinking about you and your strategy when we next . . ."

"OK, fine, you're right."

I laugh. "So what's the solution? What do I do now?"

"You've got ten fingers and a tongue, so just be a bit creative, OK?"

Creative . . . coming from Henry. My friend has many talents, but—sorry—creativity is not normally one of his strong points. Why that should be different in bed is a mystery to me, but the sounds I can sometimes hear through the thin wall to his room don't exactly suggest that Emma isn't getting the full benefit of it.

But maybe he's right. Maybe talking really isn't a bad idea. Asking what's good and what isn't. And until then, I'll just pray it's not too late.

TORI

Kit had to spend a week in hospital. He's doing OK; he was lucky, and instead of going home to his parents, he's moved into a vacant room on the fifth-form wing. Close to Will.

Mrs. Sinclair ensured that Kit gets a full scholarship. It won't solve his issues with his father, but at least he's safe now.

Of course, the story of what happened, and the news that Kit was rushed to hospital in an ambulance, soon got around. I haven't seen him at break times yet, but he and Will are at the midnight party in the old greenhouse this evening. He looks about as battered as Charles did after his punch-up with

Valentine. I try not to think about how lucky Charles was that Val didn't give him anything worse than a black eye and a fat lip.

I can feel Charles's eyes on me the whole time. The others are talking, laughing and drinking. Charles isn't drinking, but he's constantly looking in my direction. We haven't had a chance to talk in peace since last week. The conversation we need to have feels too important to be squeezed in at break or during a rehearsal. But it's inescapable. We had sex. It was my first time. And I think Charles needs to know that. If he doesn't already. And if I can't pluck up the courage to address the subject, all I can do is guess. Charles will understand it's important to me. He's not like Val, who would definitely have laughed and then said it didn't faze him that I hadn't done it before. Who would probably have been irritated with me for making things complicated again if I'd tried to talk to him about it.

It's not like Charles and I never argue, but it's different. I get him. I can generally predict it if something's going to rile him. He doesn't come up with totally unexpected accusations, and he doesn't insult other women. Dark-red flags—and my friends could all see them. But me? I defended Val to them. Because he was so deep in my head that I couldn't see it. Because I wanted to heal his broken soul. Whatever the cost—in this case, my self-worth.

I don't know what it is about Val, but it was like an evil spell that suspended all my common sense. I've read so many books, and I always thought nothing like that would happen to me. Because I've got my principles and a healthy awareness of myself. Because there are enough people in my life to remind me of that and to protect me. Ha, and they did too, but I wouldn't believe them. Val came between us. Right from the start, he bad-mouthed my friends, and that bothered me the whole time. It was the first, and maybe the most important, sign that he's dangerous. But I wouldn't see it—until Charles had to get into a fight with him.

I walked away from Valentine by my own strength that night, but who knows where it would have gone from there? Who knows if I'd eventually have given in so that he'd leave me in peace? I'm so glad I didn't. That this first time will always belong to me and Charles. The thing I secretly wished for. To lose my virginity with him, even if "lose" is such an inappropriate word. Because "lose" suggests you should keep it, as if it's some kind of honor. If I lose my virginity, it's because I've made a conscious decision. It shouldn't mean *Don't worry about it, you're so young. It's good for you to wait.* It should mean *Don't worry, you don't need some erect dick inside you to prove that someone found you sexy enough.* But nobody ever tells you that.

I jump as I feel a hand on my shoulder. Charles runs his fingers gently down my spine before resting both hands on the back of the armchair in the old greenhouse.

"Hi," he says.

As I turn toward him, he kisses me. Just like that, even though everyone can see.

"Hello," I whisper as our lips part again. "What's up?"

"Are you all right?" he asks. "You look sad."

"Sad," I repeat.

"Yes." He doesn't look away. "So I just wanted to make sure."

"I'm not sad," I say. And that's not even a lie, because the mere fact of him asking makes me the opposite of sad. And it reminds me that it doesn't matter what happened—or almost happened—with Valentine. That's in the past. A mistake, an experience, which I've learned from. This, Charles and me, this is the present. And it's perfect. No red flags, just Charles, who breaks off his conversation with his friends to come over and ask if I'm OK.

He suppresses a yawn, burying his face in my shoulder as he does so. I stroke his hair.

"Are you tired?" I ask.

Charles kisses my throat. "Are *you* tired?"

I shrug. I might have been just now, but he's creating a tingle in my stomach that's pushing all tiredness away.

"Want to go?" I ask all the same.

He freezes. Then he kisses the spot behind my ear and whispers, "Yes."

"Come on." He pulls me up.

Emma says something to Henry, and they wave us goodbye, grinning to each other. They're impossible.

Charles doesn't let go of my hand as we leave the greenhouse and step outside. *It really is spring*, I think, because the air is warmer than I expected. Suddenly, I can hardly wait. Summer nights with Charles, wing time while it's still light outside, creeping out to swim in the loch in the last of the daylight, never sleeping, never waking out of the dream.

I start to guess what Charles has in mind when he pulls me into the north wing and we walk down the dark corridor toward the theater. It's not locked. I giggle quietly as Charles pushes me into the dark auditorium. The middle of the night. Just the two of us. The heavy door falls shut, and the silence in here is different. It wraps itself around us like a heavy cloak as we walk down the steps. The faint light of the emergency exit signs is enough for me to know where to put my feet. Down below, in the front row, Charles switches on the little lamp that Mr. Acevedo uses to make notes when we're rehearsing in small groups.

"Ever been here at night before?"

I jump as Charles comes to stand behind me. Close behind me. His voice sounds clearer in the amazing acoustics, but that's not what's giving me goose bumps. It's the way it cracks slightly, which I find endlessly attractive.

"No, have you?" I turn so that the edge of the stage is at my back. And Charles's right in front of me. The light falls sideways onto his face.

He answers me with a kiss, and I thank my lucky stars. It's a different kiss. It's deep and thoughtful, slow, intense. It's a perfect kiss. And perfect hips are part of a perfect kiss, pressed together, and the suppressed trembling that's making my knees weak.

"Tori," he whispers as his lips glide over the corners of my lips. He pauses just a few centimeters from my face. I can hear him gulp. Another of those sounds that will now always drive me crazy. Charles, at night, swallowing, aroused, the two of us in the theater. "About last week . . ."

Last week. When I think about last week, I mainly think about our trembling bodies in my bed. Did he notice something?

"Yes?"

He moves away a little.

"Do you think it counts as a first time when it only lasted about thirty seconds?" he asks, and my blood runs cold.

OK, then. He knows.

My laugh sounds high-pitched, awkward, and I want to cry. On the spot.

"I wanted to tell you," he continues.

Hold on . . .

"What did you want to tell me?"

He looks at me, just for a moment. He's nervous, I can see it. I see him bite his lip gently before he answers. "I'd never done it before."

"What?" I blurt out.

He *what*?

Is he pulling my leg? Had he really not? What about Eleanor?

I open my mouth, but I don't speak.

"Say something," he begs.

"It was your first time."

His jaw muscles tense. "Yes."

"Why didn't you say?"

Yeah, why didn't he? We'd probably both have been more relaxed if we'd known it was a debut for both of us.

And he knows that. Doesn't he?

"I didn't want it to be weird." Charles looks down again. "It doesn't matter."

"It does matter," I say. "Of course it matters." And then, "It was my first time too."

He didn't know.

I'm sure of that as he jerks his head up and his eyes widen.

"Wait, what?"

I say nothing.

"But I thought..." He hesitates. "Val?"

I laugh out loud. "God, Charles. No."

"You were prepared; you even had condoms, I thought..."

"No." I don't know why my eyes are suddenly stinging. "That was just a precaution. I wanted to be ready just in case. But luckily, I never used them with him."

Charles stares at me, and I can practically see the cogs whirring in his brain, the puzzle pieces I've thrown him over the last few weeks fitting together. Random scraps of the past that I wish I could forget but never will.

"Tori, I didn't know..."

I shake my head. "Why would you?"

"We're so stupid," Charles whispers. He sounds genuinely shocked.

I have to laugh. "We really are."

"But... what made you think it wasn't my first time?"

I hesitate, then just say it. "Eleanor?"

He looks at me like I've gone mad.

"That's a no, then?"

"Tori, *no*. God, no."

"But anyone can see your chemistry on the stage," I justify myself.

"Yes, but does that mean you have to have sex?"

"I don't know—you're the actors."

"Tori." He swallows, hard. "You're the only person I've ever kissed off this stage." I flush. "And the only person I've ever wanted to kiss."

"But Eleanor, in the third form . . . Everyone knew you were into her."

"Yeah, because that's what I wanted them to think. So nobody would notice I was into *you*."

"But why? What would have been so bad about that?"

"I don't know. Because we were just friends and I was scared."

My heart is pounding, my blood churning. So much truth, my head just can't process it all quickly enough. But I take a step toward him. "We're not just friends," I say. "Look at us."

And he looks at me. I've never been as aware of myself as I am in this moment, and I pray he'll never stop. Never again.

His kiss is unexpected. I love that it makes my stomach lurch. I love that I can bury my fingers in his hair, and I love that Charles heaves me up onto the stage. I'm above him now, and I love that he has to put his head back so that he can keep kissing me.

"So we had our first time together?" I repeat, because I still can't believe it.

"Our first kiss and the first time."

"I love that it was so bad."

"It really was bad." Charles looks up. "And I'm embarrassed I only lasted—"

"Stop it," I whisper. Then I kiss him. He runs his hands over my knees and up my thighs. Slowly, firmly. "Just try to hold on longer this time."

He stops; he looks at me.

"What? Did you think it was going to stay a one-off?"

"I don't know."

"Sinclair . . ."

"Hey." He looks genuinely hurt.

"What?"

"Don't call me that."

"I've called you that for six and a half years."

"Exactly, and that's quite long enough."

"OK, if you say so."

"I do say so."

I budge back a little as he puts both hands on the edge and jumps up to me with such force that he throws me back onto the stage.

"So what do you want to do now?" he asks as he kneels over me.

I forget what I'd been going to say because his mouth is suddenly so close to mine. His perfect mouth with his perfect curved lips.

"I want to do what we were doing at mine," says the pathetic remnant of a brain inside me. "Only for longer. And more often."

"Longer and more often," he repeats. "I'll do my best."

I want to say something witty, but before anything comes to mind, Charles lowers his hips onto me. And oh . . . he's ready. There's no denying that.

I grip his shoulders and pull him closer to me. It's basically all very similar to last week, but after a while of kissing and undressing and rubbing on each other, Charles runs his tongue down my throat, over my collarbone, and then downward.

He hesitates for a moment as the back of his hand strokes my left breast, and I hear myself inhale. Sharply. "Not good?" Charles asks in that divinely hoarse voice.

"Good," I manage. "Do it again."

He smiles briefly, then his hoarse breath caresses my skin as do his fingers, and my nipples go hard. I'm finding it harder and harder not just to shut my eyes and let my head fall back. When Charles licks my belly and further down, I have no choice.

The sound that escapes me is a suppressed whimper. Normally, I'd feel awkward, but I know that I don't have to be embarrassed of anything with Charles. Least of all when I feel him shudder gently.

"Is that . . . good?" he asks as his fingers slip between my legs and I die.

I press my lips together and nod.

"Sure?" He stops. God. *Don't.*

"Please," I beg. "It's good. Very good."

I didn't know that anything could be as intense as Charles's hand moving against my pulsing core. He only lowers his head to kiss the insides of my thighs.

We don't say much. Only things like *here, harder, don't stop*, and it's already a hundred times better than last week. Now and then, he asks, but not often enough for it to get annoying.

My knickers are wet; I only realize I'm still wearing them when Charles hooks his finger inside the elastic and looks at me. I lift my hips so that he can undress me, and then I'm lying naked before him on the stage. My heart is racing with excitement.

He takes his time, running both hands over the outsides of my thighs and my hips. Over my belly and my breasts, back to my shoulders, which he presses into the floor. My breath catches as he hastily grabs my wrists. I forget where we are as he pushes them to the floor beside my head and pauses above me.

"Hi," he whispers, his face only centimeters from mine. His gorgeous mouth and the lust in his eyes.

"Hey." My voice shakes. His scent envelops me. "Everything OK?" I ask as the seconds pass and he doesn't move.

Charles nods. "I just wanted to look at you," he says, leaning down and kissing me. Deep, slow. Very, very deep. I groan in his mouth as he lowers his hips onto me. I can feel him through his boxers, and for a moment, I think I'm nearly there. Charles's fingers around my wrists, his lips on mine, his movements, faster and then slower—it's almost perfect.

I don't know how long we've been lying here, kissing and touching each other, when Charles leans back and gasps for breath.

"Tori," he says. "I . . ."

I grab his shoulders. He rolls onto his back and pulls me onto him. *Onto him.* Yes. I'm dizzy for a moment.

"We have to . . ."

"Yes," I gasp, my fingers already on his trousers. Seconds pass, then I shove my fingers under the waistband of his boxers.

Charles groans. My best friend, his eyes shut, his mouth slightly open, who's been exploring almost every inch of my body. The pulling at my core is growing stronger as I feel him freeze beneath me. And then I feel him in my hand. Throbbing, hot. Charles's head falls back.

"Tori." He gasps as I move my hand. "If you keep doing that . . ."

"Yes? What will happen?"

"Nothing good." He presses his lips together.

"Hm." I push my hand back a little and then forward again. Charles's hips are against my thighs. He presses himself into my hand: He likes it. And I like the fact that he can hardly control himself.

I pull him aside, he opens his eyes and rolls willingly with me until I'm under him. I reach for his waistband again, Charles straightens up to pull off the boxers, and then we're both naked. He kneels over me, his legs right and left of my hips. He reaches for his trousers and into one of the pockets.

I have to laugh as he proudly presents me with the condom.

"Very good," I joke, but all further remarks stick in my throat. He looks me in the eye.

"Will you sleep with me?" he asks quietly.

"Yes." I clear my throat. "How about you?"

"Also yes." I feel his warm breath on my throat as he leans over me once he's pulled on the condom.

I try not to hold my breath as he moves his erection between my legs. *It won't hurt. It won't hurt. It won't . . .*

Charles kisses me, so endlessly gently that I forget what's happening. Then I exhale as he penetrates me.

"Sorry," he whispers, resting his brow against mine. For a moment, neither of us moves. I force myself to breathe and to relax. Charles waits until I nod. Only then does he move deeper. I raise my hips toward him a little, and Charles begins to move. Slowly and carefully at first, then we speed up.

This time, it's better. Perhaps it's down to what he was doing with his fingers earlier, or just to the fact that we took our time, but I find it hard to keep lying still. And so does he. I can feel it. Our kisses are less precise, gasping for air, kissing, holding tight. My fingers glide over his back, sweaty skin, heavy breathing.

"Can you come like this?" he asks.

God, his voice.

"I don't know," I manage. "Maybe . . . Oh."

I don't know what he's suddenly doing differently, but it *is* different. A different angle, a bit faster, faster, God . . .

I feel the contractions, the throbbing, and the heat; I cling to him. "Don't stop," I beg. His back muscles are rock hard. *Don't stop . . . Please don't stop.*

"Fuck, Tori," he gasps, and his throaty voice tips me over the edge. I have to throw back my head, shut my eyes, and when a sound I've never heard from my lips before escapes me, I feel him stiffen above me.

I already know what it's like when he comes inside me, but this time it's different. More intense. I forget where we are, I just let myself be overwhelmed, and for a few seconds, nothing else matters. Nothing but Charles, above me, in me, everywhere, while a hot wave of arousal floods through my body.

I turn to him as he sinks onto his back once he's eventually pulled out of me. The stage is wet with our sweat, and I'm so warm. Charles's chest rises and falls heavily. He looks at me.

"Did you . . . ?"

"I did."

"Truly?" He looks so pleased, it makes me laugh.

"Yes, truly."

"Oh, yes."

"It was good. It was . . . whoa."

"Yeah, whoa. For me too."

I taste his salty sweat as I run my tongue over his top lip and kiss him.

My heartbeat is slow to settle. Like his, which I can feel as I lay my head on his chest.

"Do you know how hard it was not to lose control right away?" He tips his head back.

"I can kind of imagine, and I'm very proud of you."

"Henry was right," he mumbles.

I raise my head. "Henry?"

He blinks, startled.

"You talked to Henry about having sex with me?"

"Er, yeah?" He looks overwhelmed. "I was kind of desperate after last time, if you know what I mean."

I have to laugh. "And what was his advice?"

"To ask you what you like."

"Henry's so clever."

"Isn't he?"

"That's a fact." I kiss Charles again. I'm addicted to his scent and to feeling his skin on mine. For a while, I lie next to him, but in the end, the drowsiness surrounding us can no longer mask the fact that it's a bit chilly. When I shiver slightly, he raises his head.

"Shall we go to my room?"

I nod right away.

29

SINCLAIR

That dickhead Henry has sent me three sock emojis, with a question mark, to which I am sadly forced to reply with a middle finger. He sends me the smiling face with halo and then the hear-no-evil monkey.

I hate him.

In the end, we've already done the essentials in the theater. I'm not quite sure how, given tonight's events, I'm ever meant to stand on that stage without immediately getting hard, but I guess it was probably worth it.

Shit, yes, it was worth everything. Tori's face just before she came. I don't think I've ever seen anything as beautiful. The sounds she made. Her arousal, the pleasure I gave her. If I could spend the whole rest of my life doing just one thing, it would be that. Bringing Tori to climax. All day long. With my mouth, my tongue, my fingers, my dick. It really was kind of incredible. So much better than last time. And not only because she grew tight around me and started to throb, so that I didn't have a hope in hell of holding on even a second longer. But because it was clearly as good for her as it was for me. Because this time, it felt like sleeping together. Not in, out, wham, bam. I don't know what I'm going to do if it keeps getting a bit better every time. Because every time, we get to know something new, discover something about each other. Oh, God, I can't wait. All the things we can still do. If Tori wants to.

I think she does. She kisses me as we fall to my bed, almost before we've kicked our shoes off. I pull the duvet over us, and Tori lays her head on my chest.

"Will you sleep here?" I make no effort to hide the hope in my voice.

She nods. "Yeah, unless?"

"Yeah." I put both arms around her. Our bodies are touching. Everywhere. I'm only too aware of that, but I can feel that she's tired. Her muscles relax; I stroke her shoulders. She loves that, and I know it. Her hand is lying on my chest, and she's not moving. I think she's fallen asleep, but then she starts talking.

"Are you nervous?"

"What about?"

"The performance." She runs her finger up to my collarbone. "It's not long now."

"True," I say. Only a few weeks, and I don't feel anywhere near ready. We're still a long way off running through the whole play. The way things are going, we won't have many chances to do so before the opening night. If at all. Don't think about it . . . "Yes. I think I'm pretty nervous."

"Nerves are good," says Tori. "They mean it matters to you."

"I never expected to find it this much fun," I admit.

"Being on stage?" she asks. "The Aquarius in you." She says it so matter-of-factly that I have to smile.

"But I still wish you'd got a part too."

"Maybe it was meant to be this way. I don't have to be dying of nerves on the first night, and I'll be able to look after you."

"Also true."

"And we've got next year's play."

"True again." I hug her tighter. "Then you'll be Juliet."

"And you'll be Romeo."

I shrug. "I doubt that Mr. Acevedo would let anyone play the lead twice."

"What if nobody else is as good as you?"

"You're forgetting Henry," I say.

Tori laughs. "I'm sure Henry's the last person to have theatrical ambitions."

"That's what you thought about me."

"Yes, but only until I properly thought about it."

"I still don't understand why Valentine didn't snatch the main role for himself," I murmur.

I feel Tori tense and immediately regret mentioning him.

"I think Val has a very good idea of what he can and can't do. And if he doesn't see a thing as worth putting any effort into, he'd rather make fun of it."

He's so immature . . . I bite the thought back.

"He's so immature," says Tori. I suppress a laugh. "No, he really is. I'm still annoyed with how childishly he behaved at the auditions. And that I was sitting there with him and the others. I hope they don't come to the performance."

"That would be better. I doubt he even understands the play," I add. "Mr. Acevedo said the other day that every year there are kids in the audience who don't get it, so they laugh. But he also said every play is like a mirror held up to each member of the audience. What they end up saying about it tells us more about them than about us."

"That's one way of looking at it."

"Yeah, right?"

Tori nods. "I'm supernervous." She puts a hand on my shoulder, and I don't think she has any idea how wild that drives me. "I can't believe the school year's nearly over."

"Are you spending the summer in France?"

Tori shrugs. "We haven't discussed it. Probably, though." She turns her head and blinks up at me. "Will you come with us again?"

"If you'll have me."

"Of course we will."

I have to smile. I've missed spending the summer with Tori's family at their holiday home in the South of France.

"Or we can go traveling together," she says. "Interrailing. Just take a backpack and one train after another, through Europe. Unless you'd hate it?"

"I'd love it."

"Genuinely?"

"Genuinely. We could go to Verona. I need a photo of you on Juliet's balcony."

Tori laughs softly, and it's the loveliest sound in this whole damn world.

"Then where?" she asks, squirming to and fro until she's found a comfy position.

"Venice and Florence, obviously," I say. "Via Paris and Zurich."

"Zurich's not that pretty," Tori says. "Just expensive."

I shake my head. "With you, everywhere's pretty."

She smiles.

TORI

The days are growing warmer and the evenings are longer, so naturally, we have end-of-year exams to do. Each teacher suddenly finds something they need to cram into us. May and June would be stressful enough anyway, but now that the performance is getting closer, those of us without exams are spending almost every afternoon in the theater, and I can't get anything else done. I can't even remember when I last posted on Insta or TikTok, but there's more important stuff right now. My nights are reserved for Charles, and although I've never slept less in my whole life, I feel more awake than ever.

This afternoon, too, I'm heading to the north wing after study hour because there's a rehearsal any minute.

I meet Eleanor on the west-wing staircase, where she's coming down from the floor above us, a spring in her step.

"Hi, Tori," she says, in a tone that makes me prick my ears. And yes, once we've chatted about her final A-level exam, which was last week, she pauses.

She glances around as we walk along the hallway. "I don't

think I ever said how happy I am for you and Sinclair," she says. "And I hope you aren't giving a second thought to Val. He's not worth it."

That tells me he got into her head, the way he's in mine. And I hate him for that. "Thanks. Maybe you'll have to teach me. How not to waste time thinking about him, I mean."

"It takes a while. Maybe even longer."

"Great."

"I don't know exactly what he said to you, but if it wasn't nice, that's on him, not you. And you didn't deserve it, even if he tried to tell you that you did."

I force myself to nod. "I'm so pissed off," I say. "With him, but especially with myself. For letting it get that far."

"It's good that you're angry," Eleanor says. "But don't be angry with yourself. Honestly, Tori, be kind to yourself. Please. You have to stop thinking the way he taught you to."

And suddenly Eleanor's not a rival anymore; she's an ally. Maybe she was the whole time, but I was so paranoid that I couldn't see clearly.

"I'll try." I pause, but I have to say it. She deserves an apology. "And I'm sorry, Eleanor. I was jealous of you and Charles. I hope I didn't show it."

"Jealous?" She sounds surprised. "Because of the role?"

I chew my bottom lip. "A bit of everything, I think. I thought Charles and you . . . I thought there was something between you."

"Hold on, didn't he say anything?"

My blood runs cold. "Didn't he say anything about what?"

"About me . . . I mean . . . ?" Eleanor trails off. I can't move.

"Tori, there was nothing between us," she says. "We met up before we started rehearsing and talked about how far we wanted to go. I told Sinclair about Sophia. My girlfriend. I asked him not to tell anyone, but I assumed he'd have let you know anyway."

Girlfriend...

Girlfriend—as in *spoken for*, as in *She's with someone, so she didn't want anything from him*. The whole time, I've been hating her for nothing.

Why am I like this? Why couldn't I just have trusted Charles?

"So he didn't say anything?" Eleanor guesses when I still don't reply. I shake my head. "Well, now you know." She gives me a small smile. "It looks like Sinclair really can keep a secret. Not that I expected anything less."

"I'm sorry, I didn't mean to—"

"It's fine, Tori," she interrupts. "He only ever had eyes for you." She smiles. "I know he's no mysterious alpha-male rugby captain, but believe me, you'd rather be with someone who treats you the way you deserve. Which he does. Mrs. Sinclair brought him up right."

"She really did," I say.

"Maybe I should have told you sooner. It must have been really awful for you, seeing us on stage together."

"It wasn't great," I admit, "but the two of you are so good together."

"Thank you. He's really fun to work with. And so are you as assistant director. It beats me how you always keep on top of everything."

"Me too." I laugh. "Is Sophia coming to the opening night?"

"I didn't want her to at first, but I think she will, yes. The Leavers' Ball is the following weekend, so it's worth the trip up for her. She's a student in London." She lowers her voice as we come closer to the theater.

"That's nice. And thank you for keeping asking how I was while I was still seeing Val. It was reassuring to know you were around."

Eleanor smiles. "You're welcome, Tori," she says, slipping through the theater door ahead of me.

30

TORI

The upper sixth have finished their A levels now, and I've never been so aware that I've only got one more year at Dunbridge Academy before it's our turn to be nervously awaiting the results. I've never taken much interest in it before, but I've just come out of a geography exam and see Eleanor, Louis, and a few others from their year who I've got to know better doing the play. I hear a few scraps of conversation.

"Val looked really sick during the exams, did you hear?"

"Do you think he didn't get the grades?"

"What will he do if he hasn't?"

I'm irritated with myself that my first reaction is one of sympathy. It really would be crap to fail your A levels. Especially given his parents' expectations and his overachiever of a big sister. I wouldn't wish that on anyone, not even Val. Unless, of course, he didn't do any work until it was too late because he was relying on having his uncle at the school to coach him through. Then he'd deserve all he got.

But who am I to judge?

What is it to me whether Val passes his exams? Mind you, I do care, because what if he came back to do retakes next year? In our form. Oh, God, no . . .

The mere idea of that makes my throat constrict. I'd been banking on never having to see him again after a few more weeks. I'd be fine with that, especially since he's recently started dating Chloë in the fifth form, and I feel an urgent need to warn her. Like Eleanor felt about me.

"Sorry, I . . . Oh." I ram both feet into the ground as I turn the corner and almost collide with someone.

"Can't you look where you're going?"

I shiver as Val's eyes meet mine. They're icy.

"I could ask you the same question," I snap.

For a moment, Val looks as surprised as I feel. But just the sight of him makes me livid.

He huffs and eyes me up. "Are you here to apologize?"

At first, I think he's pulling my leg. But he's straight-faced. He means it. I laugh in disbelief. "Seriously? Apologize? What for, Val?"

He narrows his eyes to slits. "For being as underhanded and sly as Eleanor."

He says it, and he means it. I can see it on his face. Valentine Ward slithered into my mind, made himself at home there, like a virus, and feels no guilt. Not even a hint of it. And he'll never change, no matter how many ugly breakups he has. It'll always be the woman's fault, never his. Obviously, because we're all obsessive, sick, and pitiable.

But I'm done with being angry. I'm not wasting any more

energy on him. He's not remotely worth it. An almost eerie peace spreads through me as I slowly shake my head.

"The only thing I'm sorry for is having got involved with you in the first place. That, and that you'll never understand it."

"You're making a fool of yourself," he says. "Did you really think I was serious about you?"

Aha, we're going down that line now. "Val, I don't wish anything bad on you. Just for you to meet someone who treats you the way you treated me."

"Yeah, me too," he calls after me as I walk away. "That's the least I deserve."

That's the least you deserve.

My heart doesn't start racing until I've turned the corner and I'm going downstairs. I've got ten minutes till my next class, so I drop onto one of the benches out in the courtyard.

It's really weird. I wish I could claim that I truly believe all that. Believe I'm done with Valentine and be absolutely certain that what he did to me was out of order. But a horribly large part of my brain can't stop asking stupid what-if questions.

What if I'd given him fewer reasons to get angry? What if he's kind of right?

Because I did kind of want it. To be Valentine Ward's girlfriend. To go to the New Year Ball with him, to feel special. To feel those butterflies in my stomach that all those bloody romance novels talk about. The nervous fluttering I always felt around Val—I honestly thought that was it.

But now I don't think that feeling of butterflies in your stomach is necessarily a sign of love. It's my body's way of telling me that something isn't right. It's nerves. It's tiring. Excitement, anxiety. Will he notice me? Will we have fun? How can I please him? And oh, God, it's so wrong, yet I kept on doing it, ignoring all the little warning signs.

Everything Eleanor said about him a while back feels true. That the way he treated us wasn't OK. That maybe it was toxic. I always thought a toxic relationship was one where someone's partner manipulates them into losing trust in themselves. But apparently, there are subtler versions. Valentine and I were only mildly toxic, but that doesn't make it only mildly bad. And we weren't even in a relationship. We had a few date-like evenings and we kissed. But even so, I can't stop thinking about it. Should I have noticed sooner? Did I only put up with it so I didn't have to admit that everyone around me was right?

It's no basis for anything if you feel sick every time you see him. Because you never know which version of him you're going to get. Because his words and actions are always out of sync, and his voice changes more quickly than the Scottish weather.

Fall in love with the person you feel safe with. You feel calm with. That's the person you love. Because you're yourself around him, without even noticing.

I knew who that person was, I knew it the whole time, and that's probably the worst bit of this whole thing. Because there'd have been no need for any of that with Val if Charles and I had got our act together a bit sooner.

Charles. He's the person who feels like home. He was that person right from the start, and part of me knew it all along. Whenever I saw him. He's my best friend, my soul mate, my lover.

And he's gorgeous in uniform, the blazer setting off the breadth of his shoulders as he and the others come through the gate. I stand up as they approach.

"So?" he asks, taking my hand. "How was geography?" The mere fact that he knows which exam I had says more than a thousand words.

"Fine." I shrug. "How was Latin?"

"Don't ask . . . At least it's over with."

I have to smile. "Did Henry finish in half an hour again?"

"Of course he did. Twenty-five minutes, tops. Which gave him plenty of time to daydream about Emma, so we don't need to guess at what those two are up to now!"

"Yeah, they're out for a run, of course."

"Aye, right, what else?" He puts his arm around my shoulders and lowers his voice. "Oh, but it's today, isn't it?"

"Maeve's birthday?" I ask. Charles nods. "I think so."

"Did you get the chance to ask Emma what they're doing later?"

"They don't have any plans," I say. "She'll get him to come down to the bakery about eight."

"Excellent," says Charles. "We can bake the cake before that."

"I hope he'll be pleased. You don't reckon he'll think it's in bad taste, do you?"

Charles shakes his head. "I think Henry will be pleased and that Maeve would like it too."

"She really would."

"So shall we go down straight after dinner?"

I nod and stand on tiptoe to give Charles a kiss. He looks surprised for a moment, then kisses me back.

"What was that for?"

"Just because," I murmur, pulling him toward the door.

Olive appears suddenly. "Hey, have you heard?" she asks. "The uniform policy's not changing."

"What?" I pull away from Charles. "Why?"

"Mrs. Sinclair's going to announce it in assembly. I heard from Dad. Apparently the governors voted against it."

I laugh quietly. "Seriously? *They* get to wear whatever they want."

"They were of the opinion that dressing *appropriately* is one of the traditions of Dunbridge Academy." Olive shrugs.

I laugh again. "So what do we do now?"

Charles glances at me.

"What are you doing this evening?" I ask Olive.

"Nothing, why?"

"Good, meet you at the bakery after dinner then."

SINCLAIR

It's a long time since it's mattered to me so much for a cake to be good as it does with this birthday cake for Henry's sister, Maeve. He has no idea when Tori and Olive open the shop door to him and Emma just after eight. Then he spots Gideon and Grace and starts to look a little uncertain. I was surprised too, but I respect Grace for wanting to be here for Henry this evening, even though I can imagine how painful it is for her to see him with Emma.

I'd expected that my friend would cry, but I feel extra bad about it this time. Perhaps because Henry's trying his hardest to pull himself together as he stares at the cake. The candlelight flickers in his glittering eyes.

"Really?" he asks for the third time, bending over slightly as I nod.

Tori takes my hand as Henry hesitates.

"Happy birthday to you," he whispers, then blows out the candles. Emma wipes away his tears and gives him a hug as he steps back.

We don't talk about it so often anymore, but I can imagine that, at moments like this, it feels as unbearable as it did right after Maeve died.

I hold off on cutting the cake until Emma lets go of Henry. The others all give him a quick hug, and then it's my turn.

Henry and I don't often hug, but when we do, we do it properly. After almost seven years at school, he really is like a brother to me, and the idea that he might just not be here one day makes me want to boak. I'll never be able to comprehend how he must feel, but I know I'll always do everything in my power to make it a bit more bearable for him. Even if it's only a stupid cake—I'd bake him one every day if it would help.

Today it's helping. I'm sure of that as Henry watches—lips pressed together like always when he's trying not to cry—while I cut the cake. I give him the first slice and, because he's Henry, he passes it to Emma. Then I hand plates around to everybody else. Grace's smile is kind of strained as she looks at her piece. Her eyes go to Gideon. "Want to share?" she asks. Gideon hesitates, and I can't help noticing the way he looks at her, but he nods, if slightly unwillingly. And I don't think that's because he feels he's being shortchanged. I remember what Henry said that time. Looking at her now, even I can see that Grace has lost weight. Gideon takes a bite, then pushes the plate firmly back to her.

Henry glances sidelong at them, then turns his attention to his own plate. You can see he doesn't have any appetite, but it's Maeve's favorite, so he has to try it: the chocolate cake we supply to the Blue Room Café in Ebrington, and it's turned out incredibly well, though I say so myself.

"Another slice?" I ask Henry as he pushes his plate aside.

He shakes his head. "No, thanks. But it was perfect. Maeve would have given it ten out of ten."

"Excellent." I scrape my plate clean with my fork.

"You know this Farewell to the Upper Sixth at the end of the month," Emma says suddenly, "what will it be like?"

"Kind of like the Monday assemblies, only more of a celebration," Olive explains.

"Mrs. Sinclair gives a speech, there are photos, and drinks and nibbles afterward," Gideon adds.

"Oh, OK. I thought it was something like the Abi prank."

"The what?" Henry asks.

"The Abi prank. In Germany, when they've finished their Abitur, the leavers play some kind of practical joke. Don't you have anything like that?"

I look around the room and shrug.

"No, but it sounds fun," Tori says. "The Farewell is more of a formal thing."

"Uniform, then?"

Henry nods. Earlier, at dinner, everyone had been talking about the fact that Tori and the others hadn't been able to change anything.

"I've been thinking," Tori says slowly. "If we really want to get anywhere, we have to go public, make our voice heard. How better can we do that than on social media?"

"What were you thinking?" asks Grace.

"Set up Instagram and TikTok accounts," she explains. "Partly so that everyone else at school knows what we're planning, and partly to get attention, which in turn will get us coverage."

"So we keep going?" Emma asks.

"Well, the Farewell to the Upper Sixth would be the perfect opportunity," Olive says.

Henry sounds concerned: "It's kind of a major occasion."

"All the better," says Tori.

"Yes, we could start on Monday, when Mrs. Sinclair gives the news," says Olive. "As a little taster of what we'll be wearing for the Farewell."

Grace straightens. "I'm in this time. How about you, boys?"

"It's breaking the rules," says Henry.

"Maeve would love it," I say. "It was so important to her."

"She would love it," he agrees. "So does this mean we're wearing skirts?"

"We're wearing skirts," I confirm. "For Maeve and for equal rights."

Emma jumps up and measures Henry's hips, then her own. "I've got one that's too loose. I bet it would fit you."

"We'll take care of the Insta," Tori tells Grace and Olive. "Put up all the key information so everyone can join in."

"Yes." Henry sounds properly excited now—it's cute. "Maybe the others really will join in. That would be just what Maeve always wanted. Everyone can wear whatever they like."

Emma turns back to the cake. "Well, I'd say that's worth another slice, wouldn't you?"

31

TORI

The new Instagram profile I've set up with all the information about our campaign got almost a hundred followers just over the weekend. After the morning assembly—at which a surprising number of girls wore beige or dark-blue chinos, with the boys in pleated skirts—the photos I shared in the story were reposted so often that we passed the thousand mark in just a few days. People at other boarding schools say we've inspired them to protest against their dress codes too, and total strangers assure us of their virtual support.

And it's working. The teachers look stunned when they first see us, but it doesn't take them long to give us appreciative nods and whispers of off-the-record support.

Mr. Acevedo looks particularly proud as we pass him after the assembly in which Mrs. Sinclair informs us that she was unable to persuade the governors, and that this has to be the last time we break the rules. If only she knew that this was just the start.

Charles was coy at first when he tried on one of my skirts

yesterday evening. I can't blame him. It must feel weird to be unrestricted down below when you're used to wearing trousers all the time, but he didn't moan much, or make fun. Unlike Valentine and his pals, who—obviously—think the whole thing is ridiculous.

Val spends the whole of assembly, and later on at breakfast, laughing about us with his gang. I'm too excited by how many people have joined in the campaign to be annoyed. Girls in every form have left their skirts in their wardrobes and worn ordinary trousers with their blouses and blazers. The lads are a bit more reluctant, especially in the lower forms, but that's OK. There's another assembly next Monday when we can make our protest before the grand finale—the Farewell to the Upper Sixth.

But we might not even need to, as I notice when we meet Charles's mum later in the corridor. Her eyes run over Emma, Olive, and me, then come to rest on Henry and her son. It would be untrue to say that I'm not at all afraid of her reaction, seeing that none of us have changed like she told us to at assembly. But I'm not prepared to back down again.

"Mrs. Sinclair," Charles greets her, and I wonder how he can keep such a straight face.

"Good morning, all of you," she says. "You know that I have to issue another reminder of the official dress code, right?"

"I would like to speak to you about that," Henry says, "as school captain, on behalf of everyone at the school. Tori will back me up."

Mrs. Sinclair sighs. "Fine. You two come and see me in my office after study hour. Although I can tell you now that nothing about the situation is going to change."

"With all due respect," Henry gives her his politest school-captain smile, "we'll see about that, Mrs. Sinclair."

SINCLAIR

I suspect it's thanks to the media attention that, after a lot of back and forth, Mum psyches herself up to announce a gender-neutral uniform policy—against the will of the governors. It doesn't mean us boys are about to start wearing pleated skirts, but we could if we wanted to. And the girls are now allowed to wear trousers, even on formal occasions.

The Instagram profile that Tori set up for our campaign went sufficiently viral for Mum to be interviewed by the local press.

Something must have happened, though, which I notice at dinner at home on Saturday evening: She looks anything but happy.

"Is everything OK?" I ask as I sit down with her and Dad.

Mum sighs. "I'm afraid not." She looks at me. "The governors are still on at me about the uniform business. They won't change their minds."

"Meaning?"

"They're furious, and they're demanding an instant return to the traditional dress code. Some parents are even threatening to take their children out of the school."

"They're what?" I blurt. "Seriously? Over a stupid uniform policy?"

"You know that your fellow pupils come from a wide range of

cultures, Charlie. It's important to me that Dunbridge Academy is an inclusive and liberal place, where everyone feels comfortable, but I also understand that it can be hard to let go of old beliefs and be tolerant toward newer ones."

"How can it be a liberal place where everyone feels comfortable if it's going to give way over something so silly?"

"Charlie, this is about one day a week . . ."

"This is about the principle, Mum."

"I'm on your side, love," she says, which makes everything all the more frustrating. "And I really have tried to explain to the governors and the parents' council that even an elite boarding school, for all its traditions, has to move with the times."

The parents' council . . . a.k.a. Valentine Ward's mother, who's been gunning for Mum for years and won't miss an opportunity to kick up a fuss. Unfortunately, Veronica Ward is also one of the school's most influential backers, and regularly donates eye-watering sums of money, possibly in the hope that it will somehow help her waste-of-space son to scrape through his A levels.

"Unfortunately, some of them are very set in their ways."

"So what does that mean?"

"Charlie, it's breaking my heart, but if certain people stop donating money to the school, things will soon be looking grim. And they've made it very clear that they don't approve of their sons and daughters being taught at an institution that's undermining traditional values."

"But we can't let them do that!" I protest. "That's exactly how people like the Wards always end up winning, just because of their shitey money. Mum, you can't let this happen."

"I'm afraid there's no solution that will keep everyone happy here."

I want to reply, but I bite the words back.

Mum might believe it, but that makes it our job to find one.

TORI

"They said what?" I laugh. "God, how old-fashioned can you get? Just because we're standing up for equality? The governors get to wear whatever *they* like, don't they?"

Charles shrugs. He's sitting on a bench in the courtyard. "Mum thinks it's stupid too."

"But she still won't do anything?"

"As head teacher, she has to take everyone's interests into account," Henry says.

"I think freedom of choice is in everyone's interests, don't you?"

"Man, Tori, sometimes things just aren't that simple," Gideon puts in. "Obviously I'm in favor of everyone being able to wear what they like. But I'm also in favor of staying at this school, and just now, that's looking shaky. At least, if you ask my dad."

"Do your parents really have that much of a problem with it?" Olive asks.

"They're worried. And I'm not the only one. I've spoken to a few people in other years. Especially the younger ones—there are loads of kids from conservative families who want to send them somewhere else."

"So we're giving up?" I wonder. "I think our families would be better off worrying about their children being discriminated against at this school."

"I know, Tori," says Charles, but I look past him to Valentine, who's just walking by with a few of his guys. He gives me such a look of contempt that hot rage begins to boil in my belly. He definitely got his parents involved, because he can't stand the idea that we might succeed with our campaign. And it doesn't even matter to him—hopefully he'll never have to set foot in this school again after this term. He probably just about scraped through his A levels, and his parents will get him into university *somewhere*, I'm sure. It's hard to express how much you can despise a person, even before he started sabotaging our plans, which is making me mad with rage.

"Where's your pretty skirt, Sinclair?"

Charles whirls around, and I grab his wrist.

"Shut the fuck up, Ward." It's actually Henry who steps in and gives Valentine a withering glare. Henry, who takes his job as school captain dead seriously and never swears in public. But also Henry whose sister died—his sister who would be livid if she knew what was going on here.

"No problem. I brought you a little something, but there's no need for words." He slaps a round sticker on Henry's back. "Want some more? Here, they're on me." Val reaches into his trouser pockets and throws a handful at us. The stickers flutter to the ground as Val walks off. Charles catches one and turns it over. "BRING BACK MANLY MEN," I read.

I burst out laughing.

"God, how Neanderthal can you get?" murmurs Charles.

Emma peels the sticker off Henry's back and crumples it in her hand.

"I reckon he actually means it." Olive sighs.

"We can try again next year," Emma suggests. "He'll be gone by then, so his mum won't be on the parents' council anymore, right?"

There's an awkward silence. Henry's saying something now, but I'm not even listening: Suddenly I've got this idea.

"What's up?" Charles asks, looking at me. "Tori?"

Bring back manly men...

OK, Valentine Ward, we're on the same page.

You want trouble?

You've got it.

32

SINCLAIR

I never thought the upper sixth would join in. Not for their Farewell, which, apart from the official Leavers' Ball, is the most important celebration at the end of the school year. Tori's hashtag has been trending on Twitter, TikTok, and Instagram since last week, and I'm sure it's not entirely a coincidence that everyone is suddenly so enthusiastic about breaking gender norms and posting #bringbackmanlymen selfies. Valentine Ward looks like he'd rather go straight for his pals' throats, because he's one of the few lads who haven't forgone their trousers in solidarity. Almost the whole rugby team has joined in, wearing pink tulle skirts, dresses, or kilts. OK, so the last of those is traditional male attire in Scotland, but it's the symbolism that counts, right? Eleanor and the other final-year girls are rocking their jumpsuits and trouser suits.

"Oh, my God," Tori whispers—she's currently on her phone, probably to share new stories on the Insta account, which has almost forty thousand followers now.

"What?" Olive comes over.

Tori holds out her phone.

"What is it?" I repeat as I see the repost of her latest story.

"Whoa, is that real?" Olive breathes. She grabs the phone and stares at Tori.

"Yeah, I think so. It looks real."

"What *is* it?" I insist.

"Hayes Chamberlain reposted it," Tori explains.

"Who?" Emma and I ask simultaneously.

"Hayes?" Tori repeats, sounding so incredulous that I just shrug cluelessly.

"The singer? From London? Come on. Everyone knows him."

"Is he the one out of that band?" Emma asks, and Tori nods proudly.

"You know, I said the other day they're apparently making a film of one of Hope MacKenzie's books? There are rumors he's going to be in it. Which would make total sense because I think he's a friend of Scott's. You know, Hope's partner."

Emma's looking as baffled as me, but Tori just ignores us.

"Oh, God, that would be wild. I'll die if it's really true."

"If you haven't already died because he's reposted your Instagram story," I say.

Tori grabs my arm. "That's true. Oh, God. That means he's seen it."

"Or his social media people have seen it," Emma mumbles.

"Hey, no. Leave me to my illusions." Tori laughs, and Emma lifts her hands apologetically. "Either way, it'll get us way more attention."

"I saw a camera team talking to your mum earlier," says Olive.

I raise my eyebrows, although I shouldn't really be surprised. Over the last few days, loads of different media have been reporting on the minirevolution at our school. Most have interviewed Henry and Tori together, as school captain and the instigator of the campaign. You could say it's been a success, and as much as I'm pleased about the change we'll hopefully bring about, it's just as satisfying that this is the ultimate kick in the teeth for Valentine Ward. I really hope Mum can push the new uniform policy through, but I'm actually pretty sure that, if it happens, it won't be until the next academic year. After the initial backlash, she sent out an official letter to all parents, and apparently loads of them have got in touch to tell Mum they support us. Even Gideon's family are OK with our aims now.

The Maeve Revolution is a total success and helps me forget—at least in the short term—how nervous I am about my stage debut, which is just around the corner. The last few weeks have passed me by like a film. Once the exams and last pieces of homework were out of the way, Tori and I, and the rest of the cast, were free to spend all our time in rehearsals. Everyone else has been watching films in class or going on trips in the local area.

I don't think I've ever seen less daylight than at the moment; while the others are sunbathing in the grounds or down at the loch, we're almost permanently inside the dark theater.

Despite my protests, Tori forces me to spend the little free time we have left doing fun stuff to distract me from panicking. We go for a ride to celebrate Mum having finally bought Jubilee for the school. I've never seen Kendra as relieved as she was just now in the stables when Mrs. Smith told her she can, of course, still ride Jubilee like before. It's no secret that Kendra would rather do pretty much anything else.

It actually feels a bit like I'm out on my own horse when Tori and I set off. I've picked Stanley for Tori, one of the best-natured school horses. She loves him with a passion and gets on very well with him out in the grounds too.

We chat about the play as we ride down the wide forest path toward the sea. It was Tori's wish, so of course we have to go to the beach, like we always used to do. It's almost uncanny the way all the stress of the last few weeks drßops away from me the moment I get into the saddle.

Tori gives me a look of satisfaction, but whenever she thinks I'm not watching, the anxious expression creeps back into her face. I know why. Because however much we're all longing for the summer holidays, Tori's worried about such a long time with her parents.

"Are your folks coming to the opening night?" I ask casually.

"They want to, but I don't know."

"You don't know if you're OK with that?"

She nods slowly. "That makes me a really crap daughter, doesn't it?" she says in the end.

"No, Tori," I say. "It's perfectly understandable." After a short silence, I ask, "Do you know how your mum's doing?"

"She was devastated when Will told her and Dad that he probably won't come to France."

It's tricky, because I can kind of see all sides. Tori and her brother, who can't bear to spend the whole summer holidays watching their mother get worse. And Charlotte Belhaven-Wynford, who wants to go away with her children because she barely sees them during term time.

"We can go with them if you want," I say, but Tori shakes her head.

"I think it'll be better if we have our own plans."

Which we do. Four weeks' Interrailing, halfway across Europe. I don't know what we'll do the rest of the time. Mum and Dad would like me to go on holiday with them, and they'd be happy to take Tori. I'd rather not think about what that would mean for her parents.

"I'm sorry everything's so complicated," I say.

Tori smiles despondently, and I bring Jubilee to walk a little closer to Stanley so that I can lean down to her from the saddle. It's only a wee kiss, but afterward, she looks more cheerful.

I sense how hard it is for Tori to talk about this, so I change the subject. For a while, we discuss European capitals and which routes will help us get the most out of our trip, until the trees thin ahead of us and we reach the coast. Tori smiles, she's positively glowing, and I can't stop looking at her, even as we gallop along the beach. Eventually we have to turn back so that we'll be in time for study hour. We see each other later, in the theater, where my tension immediately dissolves into the air. It's been nothing but chaos for days. We're rehearsing in costume now, which doesn't ease my nerves, but does help me slip into character even more easily.

In the week before the performance, we manage our first complete run-through, which is a total disaster. I forget my lines in four places, Eleanor almost breaks her ankle stumbling on the steps in the baggy trousers, and our mics pack up in the middle. Tori's a bundle of nerves as she and Mr. Acevedo try to salvage what they can. These days, she seems to know Eleanor's and my lines better than we do. At any rate, she doesn't have to look it up any time we need to be prompted—mind you, she wrote a lot of the script.

The night before we open, I don't sleep. I toss and turn, asking myself why I ever thought it would be a good idea to take the lead role in a play that the whole school will see—parents and teachers too. I'm going to make a total tit of myself, but at the same time, I just want to get it over with.

Tickets for the first night sold out in days. Mum and Dad will be there, Tori's parents too. I can barely eat a bite of lunch.

As we begin on our makeup around five, I don't know whether I want to boak from fear or because my stomach is completely empty.

Marian, who's on the wardrobe team with Olive and Nathan, slaps a ton of makeup onto my face and even more cream into my hair to create the swashbuckling, nonchalant style that apparently Romeo has to have. I shut my eyes as she tugs at my hair and try to get into character.

What does it matter that I'm green with nerves and want to die? For the rest of this evening, I'm not Charles, I'm Romeo. Waiting for his Juliet. Where even is Eleanor? Is she feeling as crap as me, or has she got her nerves under better control?

I blink as voices outside grow louder. Is that her? Before I can turn around, the door flies open, and I see Louis in the mirror as he walks in. He's already wearing Mercutio's black shirt and dark trousers.

"Sinclair, we've got a problem," he says, not wasting any time.

"What?"

Marian moves away so that I can turn around.

"Where's Eleanor?"

"That's the thing." He sighs. "She's been clinging to the toilet for an hour, can't stop boaking."

"Oh, God!" I exclaim. "Poor Eleanor. I could pull a whitey with nerves myself..."

"No, you don't understand," he interrupts me. "Did you eat the spaghetti carbonara?"

"What?"

"For lunch."

"No, I had half a sandwich..."

"You dodged a bullet, man. Looks like it was off. The sick bay's full of people with food poisoning."

"You're kidding me?" I stare wide-eyed, but then I realize what this means. "But... Dr. Henderson must have some miracle cure so she can still act, right?"

"Sinclair, she can't even keep down a sip of water." There's panic in Louis's eyes. "We're so screwed."

"What about the others? Is it just Eleanor or...?"

"Imogen, Estelle, and Nick, but they're only musicians and servants. The others couldn't eat."

"Fuck, OK." I stare up at the ceiling. "So what now?"

Louis gives a helpless shrug as Mr. Acevedo bursts in.

"Is there anybody here?" He looks totally rattled, so I guess he's heard the joyful tidings. "Louis, Charles!" He stops. "Please tell me you didn't eat the spaghetti."

We shake our heads.

"OK." He points at Louis, then me. "Good? Good?" He ticks something off on his clipboard, then looks up. "Then it really is only our Juliet who can't go on."

"There you are." We turn around at the sound of Tori's voice. She appears in the doorway and stops when she sees us. "Have you heard that Eleanor's got food poisoning?"

TORI

I fall silent.

Charles, Louis, and Mr. Acevedo. They're standing in wardrobe with Marian, Olive, and Nathan. Charles's sitting on the chair by the huge mirror, and they're staring wordlessly at me.

"Victoria," Mr. Acevedo says, not taking his eyes off me. "What did you eat for lunch?"

"Nothing, I was too nervous," I say hurriedly. "You too, right?" Charles nods.

"Have we got an understudy for Juliet?" I ask. "I saw Grace. She didn't eat either. I think she could play Juliet if I sat in the front row to prompt her." None of them speaks. "Don't you think?"

"We need Grace as the Nurse. Nobody can replace her," Mr. Acevedo says.

I gulp. "OK, yes. Then . . . how about . . . ?"

"Victoria, you can play Juliet."

I laugh. "Yeah, right. What I was going to say was, how about

Jennifer? She probably doesn't know the script as well as Grace, but . . ."

"Victoria, you can play Juliet," Mr. Acevedo repeats, stressing every individual word. That's the moment I realize he means it.

"What?" My voice sounds two octaves too high. "No."

"Yes, Victoria. Nobody knows the play as well as you." Mr. Acevedo glances at his watch. "We've got two hours. Get into costume and makeup, and then you can both come up to me to go through the key scenes before—"

"No!" He doesn't get it. I start to shake. "Please, sir, I can't. I can't play Juliet and—"

"Yes, you can." Charles stands up.

I draw back as he comes toward me and lift both hands because my heart is suddenly hammering. The idea is so absurd that part of me still hasn't taken in what Mr. Acevedo just suggested. Another part of me is going up in flames.

"You know the whole script, seeing how often we've rehearsed together."

"No. Absolutely no way, Charles."

"Tori." He reaches for my hands, and I want to run because there's something so final in his face. Louis, behind him, is nodding. Olive too. She looks way too excited. Happy-excited. Mr. Acevedo, on the other hand, looks like he doesn't know whether to laugh or cry. I understand that feeling perfectly well, but just now, I mainly feel panic.

"Look at me." Charles's hands are cool, but I won't let him calm me down. My fear is justified. I can't play Juliet. So there won't be a play. I don't care. OK, I do care—we've put so much time and energy into this, it would be a disaster if it can't go on, but that would be better than me standing on that stage, making a fool not just of myself but of the whole drama club, Mr. Acevedo included. There's no way he can want that!

"No, I'm not looking at you, and I'm not playing Juliet either." My voice is trembling. That's proof positive there's no way I can speak in front of all those people.

"Yes, you are," Charles says. Why does he sound so calm? His thumb is stroking the back of my hand. "You can play Juliet, and I'll be Romeo. And we'll pretend we're in the bakery. Just the two of us, OK? We've rehearsed together, and it was always great."

I shake my head silently, and my eyes start to sting.

Shit.

I bite my bottom lip in the hope that the pain will distract me from bursting into tears.

"Tori," Charles repeats. He's smiling. He has to stop. I don't want to calm down, and I don't want to play Juliet. I don't want to be here at all. He kisses me. "'Your mouth has cleansed my lips from sin,'" he says in his Romeo voice. In my head, I'm answering him as Juliet. It's like a reflex action.

"'Then give it back to me,'" I whisper.

"Yes, I can see it—it's going to be brilliant." Mr. Acevedo claps his hands; Charles smiles and squeezes my fingers. I'm relatively certain he's dying of nerves, but he's trying not to show it. "Get into the costume and come back here for makeup. You'll be amazing, Victoria, I believe in you."

Wonderful. So nothing can possibly go wrong, then.

I'm on the verge of hysterical laughter as Mr. Acevedo scurries out of the room like an agitated hen. "I'll inform the others," he says over his shoulder as he goes.

My knees are like jelly as Charles looks at me again.

"I . . . I have to sit down," I mumble.

Louis immediately grabs a chair and pushes it over to me.

"Hey." Charles crouches in front of me as I let myself sink back into it. "You've been at every rehearsal. You know the script."

"You don't understand, it's not just about the script. It's about the acting. I'm no actor!"

"Want to know my trick?"

I say nothing. *No, because then I'd actually have to do this.*

"I'm no actor either. I'm just a guy who isn't afraid of making an eejit of himself anymore. And who thinks about you. The whole time, Tori. It's always worked."

My heart skips a beat. "But I *am* still afraid of making an eejit of myself."

"Then stop."

"No, Charles, I . . . I can't."

"Me either, but we'll get through it together." He puts his hands on my knee. "Nobody will be looking at us. It'll just be us two. Nothing else matters."

It's no use. I have no choice. Damn all those stupid daydreams where I imagined being Juliet. Me, not Eleanor. I've changed my mind. I don't want to play her. I'd never known how terrifying the idea of getting up there is until now.

Charles's still crouching there, looking at me. Eyes full of hope and anticipation. Yes, really. He's pleased. What's wrong with him?

"I swear to you, I'm going to boak in a minute," I whisper.

33

SINCLAIR

It's crazy. All this, this whole day, and I really wouldn't want to change places with Tori. I've had months to get psyched up for the whole school watching me lay bare my innermost being. Tori's had two hours. And she goes paler with every passing minute as the auditorium gradually fills.

I pull her away from the curtain so she can't see how many people are in the audience.

It's a miracle, but Eleanor's costume fits her almost perfectly. Her long, copper-colored hair tumbles in waves over the shoulders of her white blouse, with the dark-red trousers. She looks breathtaking. Strong, yet vulnerable. She looks like Juliet.

We're not talking anymore as the play begins and we sit in a little room behind the stage, waiting to make our entrances. My first scenes don't involve Tori, and I know she's going to freak when I leave, and we won't see each other again until we first meet on stage. In front of all those people. There are a lot of them. Bloody loads, but I don't let myself take that in until I've said my first few lines and got myself into the scene.

The audience is hushed, and I think they're coming with us. They laugh in the right places and hang on my lips. After a few minutes, I feel myself relax. I'm starting to have fun. Honestly, there's nothing I can compare it to. The adrenaline that's coursing through my body is making me wider awake than ever before. I think I'm good. I hardly make any mistakes, and if I do, I manage to cover it up elegantly enough that the audience doesn't even notice. I make out Mum and Dad in the front row; Emma and Henry are a little further back. Even Valentine Ward is there, but I don't care.

I hear for myself from backstage as the audience gasps in astonishment during Tori's first scenes. I wish I could be with her, but I can only stand behind the curtain, praying silently that everything will go smoothly. And she's doing an outstanding job. We barely have time to speak as she and Grace make their exit and I go on again.

A little later, when the music strikes up for the ballroom scene, and Romeo sees Juliet for the first time, the excitement is making my fingertips tingle. And then I see her.

I've got my back to the audience, but I still hear the quiet whispering as Tori and I are on stage together. And then I don't hear another thing. I can see only her. Juliet, beautiful and charming, with an elegance that takes my breath away. I don't have to act it—I can feel it, and all I have to do is let that show.

The first few minutes of our first scene together are entirely unspoken. Silently approaching, stolen glances. Like a secret dance that belongs only to the two of us.

I don't think Tori is acting either: She's feeling it, the same as me. She looks calm and composed, only her clammy fingers, which I take in mine, give away that she's dying of nerves. I meet her eyes and try to put everything I can't tell her just now into that look.

Breathe.

You are so beautiful.

Everything's going to be fine. We're going to smash this.

TORI

I don't know how I'm capable of standing on this stage, saying the lines I've always been reading along with from my seat or speaking in the bakery. My brain reels them off; my mouth speaks them. It happens without any control on my part. I hear what Charles says and forget it that same second. There's only him and me, and the next line and the next and the next.

I've never felt like this before. Like nothing's real, not even myself. My body is doing the things that need to be done. I'm Juliet. I'm her worries and her hopes, her yearnings and her fear.

I don't even take in the existence of the audience. Maybe this is how it feels to get high. I'm not even sure if there really are people here.

When we come offstage and wait behind the curtain for our next entrances, I can't speak to anyone. I just stand next to Charles, drink water, and don't let go of his hand. I don't think I've ever been as focused on anything in my whole life.

My first scene without him was bad, but not as bad as the one where not even Grace, the Nurse, is on stage with me. There's just me, on the balcony that's nothing more than a little gallery with a wooden ladder leaning up against it, because Mr. Acevedo prefers a minimalist set.

It's the attention of several hundred people fixed solely on me. I haven't the faintest idea how my body can be this calm.

I don't even try to copy Eleanor, because I know that can only fail. I speak the lines differently from her, in my own way. I'm thinking about Charles. I put all my despair, and all my fascination, into them.

It goes crazily fast. Our first kiss, a real kiss, Charles's lips on mine, warm, calming; his flight from Verona; the elixir I have to swallow so that I can be dead for a couple of days.

I'm almost more afraid of this moment, when I have to lie motionless on the stage, than all the scripted scenes put together.

Charles finding me, his hands shaking me by the shoulders, lifting me.

Don't move.

Just don't move.

I was afraid I'd want to laugh, but I hear his despair, and it's so real that laughing is the last thing on my mind. He's acting even better than he does with Eleanor. I don't have to look at him to be sure of that. I can hear that he's crying, just from his voice, quiet yet clear in this deathly silent space.

His hand movements are precise and gentle; his lips stroke over mine before he lays me down again.

Keep your breathing shallow so the audience can't see.

When Charles has taken the poison and slumped down beside me, I count the seconds until I can wake up.

The fact that there's only a little light on us while the rest of the stage is dark makes it easy to weep bitter tears when Juliet realizes that Romeo is dead.

I am aware that these are my last lines on stage, so I force myself to forget everything. Nothing else matters. Only Charles, who doesn't move as I take his face in my hands and kiss him because I love him, and then I find his dagger, kneel beside him, and raise it.

I've had one single rehearsal, earlier on, with Charles and Mr. Acevedo, but I don't think about that as I slip it between my ribs and sink to the floor with a cry. I don't think about anything. My mind is blank.

It's over.

I'm dying.

Charles's body tenses, barely perceptibly, as I collapse onto him. It's a relatively comfortable position, for which I'm secretly thanking my stars, because I'm going to have to hold it for the next ten minutes.

My heart is racing, but I only notice once I'm lying with my head on Charles's chest and feel his beating surprisingly calmly and slowly. Is he asleep? For a moment, I'm genuinely unsure, but then I feel his hand, on the side facing away from the audience, reaching for my body. His fingers stroke my leg, it's a tiny *we did it*, and he doesn't stop until the very end.

I force myself to breathe more slowly, and with every passing minute while Capulet and the Nurse find us and say their final lines, my pulse settles more. The adrenaline is draining from my body. Charles's here, everything is fine. We actually did it.

"Hey."

I jump as he moves beneath me. Why is everything so loud all of a sudden?

It takes me a while to twig that it must be thunderous applause. Then I see that the curtain is closed. I raise my head; the others are already hugging.

"Did you nod off?" Charles sounds amused and thrilled all at once as I clamber up from him.

"Only for a moment," I murmur. He kisses me, and I'm weak at the knees as I stand up. Charles holds out his hand. I see the delirium in his eyes, and the relief.

"We did it," I whisper, but it's drowned in the applause, which is still going strong.

"We did it," Charles repeats, wrapping his arms around me and lifting me. We kiss, and everything else just fades away.

Mr. Acevedo is shooing the others around the curtain so that they can make their bows to the delighted audience. Charles and I are to go last. After Louis, Gideon, and Grace, who receive enormously loud claps and cheers.

Charles lets go of my hand, slips through the curtain, and the crowd goes wild. It's the moment that the last remnant of panic drains from my body, making way for pure euphoria.

Charles is standing in center stage, holding his hand out to me. As I make my way forward, everyone stands up. They actually stand up.

I run to Charles and take his hand so that we can bow, but he takes a step to the side and begins to applaud himself. Because this is my moment. And I know I'll never forget it.

I bow. As I straighten, I see for the first time how many people there actually are, because the auditorium lights are on.

Emma and Henry are jumping up and down, cheering; Charles's parents are in the front row; Will and Kit are a little further back, next to Mum and Dad. I knew they'd come, but to see them now, from up here, after I've played Juliet and not screwed up, is indescribable.

My heart is racing again, but with joy this time.

We leave the stage to come on again with the whole cast. Charles and I take Mr. Acevedo by the hands. It's incredible, and it doesn't stop.

I want it never to stop.

34

TORI

We raised glasses to one another backstage, hugged, and constantly reminded each other of how great we'd been. I answered Eleanor's message, which she must have sent at some point shortly before the performance, telling me I'd rock and apologizing for it being such short notice.

I'm genuinely sorry for Eleanor, because she deserved to have everyone cheering her today. I can only start to feel moderately less guilty once she texts me that she's got a place to study acting at the Royal Academy of Dramatic Art in London—the most famous stage school in the country—and will be duly celebrating with Sophia as soon as she's well enough. She'll be the star of the RADA stage, I'm sure of that.

The foyer is rammed with parents and pupils, who all turn to look as Charles and I walk through the throng. His mother comes toward us and hugs first me, then him. So does his dad, who can't stop gushing.

I didn't see Will coming, and there's such force in his hug that it almost sweeps me off my feet. It takes ages for him and Kit, Emma, and Henry to finish congratulating us. Now I finally see Mum and Dad, who are standing a little to one side. Will and Kit have gone back to them, and I hesitate for a wee while. Charles slips his hand into mine and pulls me to see them. It's no secret that my parents love him, he knows that, and he's beaming as they greet us and shower first him and then me with praise. Dad looks like he might burst with pride at any minute and Mum's not much different. To my shame, though, as she hugs me, I look first to her eyes. She's sober, I'm pretty sure of that when she gives me a squeeze and I don't smell booze. I should be glad, but the night is still young. Who knows what'll happen later? But I can't think about that now. I want a bit longer of being happy and carefree—that's not too much to ask, is it?

In the end, Dad looks at Mum once Charles's gone back to talk to his own parents.

"We'd love to go out for a meal with you and William," he says.

"Kit and I wanted . . ." Will begins, and I talk over him.

"Charles and I thought . . ."

We laugh. "There's the summer festival in Ebrington," I explain. "We're planning to catch up with our friends there."

"I see." Dad nods. "We've booked a table in Edinburgh. I promise we'll keep it quick, but there's something we have to talk to you about."

"OK, I'll tell Kit," Will says, vanishing into the crowd.

"Can Charles come too?" I ask.

"I think it would be better just the four of us, darling," says Mum. My stomach cramps, but I say nothing.

Charles looks concerned when I tell him, promising I'll join him and the others in Ebrington later.

Mum and Dad try to fill the drive to Edinburgh with small talk, but it's never felt longer. Once we're sitting in the restaurant, I wish they'd just get to the point, and I think they can sense our impatience, because there's a tense silence at our table once the starters are out of the way. Mum asked for water, not wine.

I can suddenly hardly breathe because all I can think of is Olive crying in the costume store because her mum's cheating on her dad and she's afraid they'll split up.

Is that it? Do they want to tell us they're separating? Did they carefully choose to do so in public so that we won't show awkward emotions or make a scene?

My pulse calms a little as Dad lays his hand on Mum's fingers for a second. He wouldn't do that if they were about to tell us they're getting a divorce, would he?

"Your mother has something to tell you," Dad begins.

He sounds gentle but determined. Like he has to use his words to give her a little push in the right direction.

"You might have noticed that we haven't said any more about how we'll be spending the summer holidays this year," Mum says.

"France?" asks Will. "I thought it might be OK for Kit to come too, if you don't mind."

"He'd be very welcome, darling." Mum smiles, but it looks slightly forced. "But you'll have to go without me."

"What?" Will darts a look at Dad, then me. "Why?"

"There was a cancellation at a clinic in London. I'll be traveling down next week."

Silence.

Clinic...

"Really?"

I only realize that it's my voice asking the question when Mum nods.

"I'll probably be there for eight weeks, but it might be longer. I'm sorry you're only hearing about it now. I got the call this week. But you'll be able to visit me anytime, and we can talk on the phone." Mum's voice catches as I reach for her hand. It just happens.

"We'll visit," Will states.

"Course we will," I add.

Mum smiles, and there's a telltale glitter in her eyes. "That would make me very happy."

"So you're trying again?" I manage to ask. "You're talking about rehab, right?"

My voice dropped with every word, but Mum heard. "I can't go on like this," she says. "And I can't do it on my own. I want to be there for you both . . ." She pauses. "I want you to be happy to come home again."

Her voice breaks, and my throat clenches. "We'll always be happy to come home, Mum," I whisper. "Whatever happens. Always."

Will gulps hard.

Mum lowers her head. Dad's eyes meet mine. I see the relief on his face, and the hope. He didn't force her: This time, she wanted it herself, I'm sure of that. And that's the best starting point for things actually getting better.

"I'm so proud of you two," Mum says. "And I'm going to make sure you can be proud of me again too."

SINCLAIR

Tori joins us just as I'm starting to worry. It's already half past ten, but the Ebrington summer festival is just getting going. The whole town is full of tents and long tables, occupied by a mishmash of locals, tourists, and Dunbridge pupils. The sun's gone down, but there are still kids running around the streets.

"Hey." I jump as I feel hands on my shoulders. The others wave to Tori. As I turn around, she looks happy, but I think she's been crying. Or is that just exhaustion? After all, it's been a long and dramatic day. I can't be sure, so I stand up.

"Are you OK?" I ask, stepping a few feet aside with Tori. "How was dinner?"

"She's going into rehab again." Tori's voice sounds choked, and it takes me a moment to process.

"Your mum?"

She nods.

"That's good. That *is* good, right?"

"Yes, it's good. I think." She gives me an uncertain smile, and I pull her closer. Tori throws her arms around me and presses her face into my shoulder. "What kind of a crazy day has this been?" she murmurs.

"I don't know what you mean, Juliet."

"That really happened, didn't it?" She shifts away from me slightly. "We actually performed *Romeo and Juliet*?"

"And we rocked."

"So now you can never accuse me of being inflexible and nonspontaneous."

"Like I ever would." I kiss her. "But you're right. I love you, my spontaneous girlfriend."

There, I said it. Just like that. Because it's true.

Tori smiles. "And I love you too," she whispers, kissing me back. "Come on, we need to find the others. Might be our last time all together before everyone goes off for the summer."

I'd have nothing against standing here alone with her a bit longer, her lips on mine, but we've got the whole night. And the whole summer. A whole life.

Tori stops as Olive comes toward us.

"Are you leaving already?" she asks.

Olive nods. "It's the swimming gala tomorrow," she says. "I need to get my sleep."

"Oh, yeah," Tori lets go of me and goes to give Olive a hug. "You'll leave them all for dust!"

"I'll do my best," says Olive, but she sounds confident. She's clearly relieved at having got through this year. It's been a tough one for her, and I think she's really going to have to work hard next year too. Henry's already offered his help, so I'm not too worried.

"Message me when you get back—I want to know every detail."

Olive smiles. "Will do. You can do a bit more partying for me.

You two were amazing today." She waves and disappears into the darkness.

I love to see Tori looking so content and chilled. Not even Valentine Ward can affect how happy I'm feeling—he and a few of his pals came past just now, already steaming. Obviously, they're way too cool for the village festival. They're sure to be down in the Dungeon, getting absolutely wasted. Not long now, and he'll be gone. Forever. It's almost too good to be true.

I force myself not to waste any more thought on him as we head back to our friends. They give us a cheer and budge up so that Tori and I can sit down. Henry's got his arm around Emma—they can't keep their hands off each other, even though they've got a while before Henry flies out to visit his parents in Kenya and the two of them have to spend no less than three whole weeks apart. Doesn't bear thinking about. Mind you, I'm one to talk. I wouldn't like the idea of being without Tori for so long either. Fortunately, we get to spend the whole summer together. Our Interrail tickets are booked, and we've settled our route. It's our first big adventure together, yet it can't compare with what we've already been through. And that was just the beginning. I have to keep repeating it to myself, over and over again, as I look at Tori, hardly able to believe my bloody luck.

It's like every year just before the long holidays. A mixture of satisfaction and slight wistfulness that another year at Dunbridge Academy is behind us. But this time, it's different. Because we've only got one left. The upper sixth, after which we'll be scattered to the winds. I can't think about it. I just can't. And it doesn't matter yet, because we're all here. Gideon, Grace, Omar, Henry, Emma, Tori, and Olive, even if she's asleep. I can't imagine ever being such good friends with anyone as I am with these people.

The others are talking about the play; our successful uniform rebellion, which is still making waves on social media; their plans for the holidays and the next school year. I don't know what time it is, but the tables are gradually emptying, and the sky is pitch black. Tori fights a yawn; I'm about to ask her if we should head back when Emma suddenly jumps up.

"Em?" Henry reaches for her hand, but she doesn't even seem to notice. "What's wrong?"

Her eyes are fixed on something beyond us. "Can you see that?"

I turn but can't see anything alarming.

"What do you mean?" Tori asks.

"Shit," Henry mumbles. I'm standing up too now, and I can see what they mean. The dark clouds of smoke rising behind the houses of Ebrington, barely visible against the night. Beneath them, glowing flames are leaping into the sky. It's such a surreal sight that, for a moment, I just stare in fascination. But then I realize what it means.

Every sound fades into the background, yet I can hear raised voices around us.

"That's Dunbridge," says Gideon flatly. "The west wing, I think. Fuck . . ."

Tori's standing motionless beside me. She's pale.

"Oh, my God." Grace's voice trembles, and she grabs Gideon's wrist. There's blind panic on her face. "Olive." That's all she says.

Olive...

My blood runs cold. Fire, it's the west wing, Olive went back ages ago to get some sleep. I have to call Mum, no, the fire brigade—first the fire brigade.

I hear sirens in the distance.

My heart stops. Tori digs her fingers into my arm.

And then we run.

uncorrected proof

Glossary

A levels — Advanced exams taken at age seventeen or eighteen, similar to AP tests but required for college admission, graded from A* to U. The lowest passing grade is E, and U is ungraded.

A&E (Accident and Emergency) — Emergency room.

Abitur — Final exams in the most academic schools in Germany, required for college admission.

boak — Throw up (Scottish).

enrichment — Extracurricular activities period.

forms — Grade levels in some UK schools. First-formers would be called sixth graders in the US, and upper sixth is the equivalent of twelfth grade.

GCSE (General Certificate of Secondary Education) — Standardized exams taken at age sixteen and required to move on to A levels. Most students study around ten subjects.

GLOSSARY

half-term	Week-long break in the middle of each term/semester.
houseparents	Adult supervisors living in dormitories.
lessons	Classes/periods.
marks/markers	Grades/graders.
minging	Disgusting.
plait	Braid.
PSHE (Personal, Social, Health, and Economic Education)	A class on social and life skills, sex education, career advice, and so on.
revision/revise	Studying for exams.
rugby pitch	Rugby field.

Acknowledgments

It's a long time since I've enjoyed writing a story as much as Tori and Charles's. It just flowed out, almost writing itself. All the same, *Anyone* could never have appeared without the amazing behind-the-scenes work of so many fantastic people.

They include Michaela and Klaus Gröner from erzähl: perspective literary agency, who work so tirelessly on behalf of my stories and me. I'm eternally grateful to be with you.

I would like to thank all the wonderful people at LYX. Your dedication and love of stories make it an indescribable privilege to work with you. Especially you, Alexandra. Sometimes I don't know if I'll ever be able to write another book without you. It was, as always, a pleasure to tinker around with *Anyone* with you and to see the story grow. Many thanks to Susanne George for improving the text and making it shine. I owe many thanks to Stephanie Bubley, Ruza Kelava, and Simon Decot for your trust in me and my books—I really do appreciate it. Thanks to Simone Belack, Teresa Krull, and Sina Braunert for the world's best marketing; Andrea Berlauer for the fantastic launch party; Sandra Krings for the unique sprayed-edge editions; Jeannine Schmelzer for your gorgeous design for the series; Sarah Schneider for

ACKNOWLEDGMENTS

the audiobooks; and Barbara Fischer and Franziska Pürling for such amazing press relations.

A huge thank-you to Danielle Finnegan at LYX and everyone at Authors Equity for your enthusiasm and expertise.

My thanks to my wonderful colleagues Gaby, Rebekka, Lena, Anna, and Merit, because you very probably kept me from going insane long ago.

Thank you to my family for your unbounded support, without which I'd never be able to do all this.

Thank you to my amazing beta readers Anni, Greta, Annika, Jule, Julia, Leo, and Evi. Your comments and messages about Tori and Charles meant the world to me. Without you, the story wouldn't be what it is today.

My thanks to all (budding) booksellers for your amazing support.

I cannot thank my readers enough. You can't know how much it means to me that you read and recommend my books and describe Dunbridge Academy as a feel-good place. I thank you from the bottom of my heart for having already shown so much love to Tori and Charles in *Anywhere*. It is so motivating and fulfilling to write books for you. I hope we'll meet again in the next book, for the third and final time that we hear the words *Welcome to Dunbridge Academy!*

Translator's Note

It's been a lot of fun coming back to Dunbridge Academy and resurrecting my knowledge of *Romeo and Juliet* from GCSE English for this text while my patient husband, Dave, answered a lot of questions about school Shakespeare performances past.

Ciara Bowen and Chloe Mitchell were enthusiastic and helpful dialect coaches, while Emma Frith was a fount of knowledge on the subject of horses and riding.

Many thanks also go to Stef and the team at Quercus—and to Danielle at LYX and Authors Equity for your sensitivity in adapting the US editions. As noted after *Anywhere* came out, it truly does take a village to translate a novel. Thank you all so very much!

uncorrected proof

About the Author

Rachel Ward, MA, MITI, lives in Wymondham, near Norwich, UK, and has been working as a freelance literary and creative translator from German and French to English since gaining her MA in Literary Translation from the University of East Anglia in 2002. She specializes in translation for children and young adults, as well as in crime fiction and other contemporary literature. She can be found on social media as variations on @FwdTranslations and @racheltranslates.

Sarah Sprinz was born in 1996 in the south of Germany. After she finished her medical studies she moved back to her home region by the Bodensee. When she's not writing, she finds inspiration for new stories during long walks along the lakeshore and plans her next trips to Canada and Scotland. She loves writing afternoons in cafés, maple syrup, and connecting with her readers on Instagram (@sarahsprinz).

uncorrected proof

Keep reading for an excerpt from *Anytime*

uncorrected proof

1

OLIVE

"Take it slowly, pet."

I bite back the snappy answer that's on the tip of my tongue and force myself to take a deep breath. It's costing every last scrap of my self-control to ignore the sharp stabbing in my right shoulder. It brings the tears to my eyes—annoyingly, I only took my last painkillers a couple of minutes ago. They don't kick in right away and I had no way of knowing that Mum and Dad would get here so soon, be standing in my room ready to take me home from hospital. I've been here weeks, which seems like a lifetime, and now everything's going too fast.

"Let me take that," says Mum, reaching for my bag. There are a few clothes, some wash stuff, books and cushions, mostly brand new because I couldn't stand the smell of smoke ingrained in the things they were able to save from my room after the fire at Dunbridge Academy in early July. The flames didn't reach the girls' bedrooms on the third floor of the west wing, but the fire raged in the stairwell and almost completely destroyed the lower half of the building. Nobody could tell how bad the damage was for several days. Not till the police and insurance experts combed through the charred remains and collapsed beams—by which time I was in intensive care. It's not like I knew anything about it. Why would I? Almost two weeks intubated on a ventilator, because if I'd been awake, the pain from the burns would have driven me insane. It was still unbearable when they eventually brought me round. It still is, especially around my right shoulder where they had to do a graft, covering it with skin from my thigh so that the wounds could heal. Expressions like "autologous," "split-thickness" and "mesh graft" are part of my everyday vocabulary, because this is my life now. And I hate it.

"I'll help you, pet," says Dad, the moment we're outside and I'm reaching for the handle on the back door of his car. He opens it for me, like I hadn't spent weeks in physio, relearning every stupid movement, and continually failing at the easiest tasks. Standing up for a while. Putting on a T-shirt. Doing my hair in a ponytail, for fuck's sake, like I did every time I walked from the school to the pool, but I won't be doing that again any time soon, won't be training again in the near future. I'm not being pathetic or melodramatic. The doctors said so, repeatedly, when I couldn't take it in, and, yeah, they're just as insensitive as people say. Dad's the exception, maybe.

I can do it myself. I don't need your help. It's hard not to say the words. But it's more than I can manage to say "Thank you" to him instead, as I slip onto the back seat. I avoid his eyes, and after a moment, he shuts the door. Our gaze meets again in the rearview mirror as he glances at me once he's sat in the driver's seat, next to Mum.

My parents don't deserve my rage. What happened isn't their fault. It's nobody's fault. Except for the bastards who were smoking in the Dungeon on that July night. During their investigations, the police found a cigarette stub in what remained of the upper sixth's party cellar. Dozens of people were there but apparently nobody saw a thing. They've closed the case now. Accident, not arson. A tragedy, a misfortune. But the good luck amid the bad is that nobody died. Apart from my dreams but, hey, I'm supposed to be grateful.

You were seriously lucky. If that burning beam had fallen just a tiny bit differently, it wouldn't just have caught my shoulder: it would most probably have killed me. And maybe I'd have been better off if it had, but saying that out loud would just make Mum and Dad do a U-turn and deliver me straight back to the hospital. So I sit in silence in our car, with my silent parents, who are getting a divorce. It's just a matter of time: Mum with her guilty conscience over the affair I caught her out in months ago in Ebrington, Dad still with no clue. I want to cry but I can't. I'm here, I survived. I will keep on surviving. It's not even that hard if you just get a fucking grip.

Come on, Olive. Keep it cold, live up to your reputation. Be your old self. Except I'm not my old self. Everything's changed.

Don't forget your friends. Don't forget that you finally get to see them again tomorrow. At school, not in hospital, where they all came to visit as soon as I was well enough. They couldn't come so often once term started, though, and I get that. They're in the upper sixth now. Without me.

Damn tears. I blink.

"Are you OK, darling?"

"Yes." I gulp and lean back on the headrest. Dad's heading for Stockbridge, our part of Edinburgh. I feel it every single time he glances at me in the mirror. He doesn't believe me. Because he knows me.

Nothing is OK. I'm tired, knackered actually, I'm in pain, and there's so much rage inside me that I want to scream. The anger was there even before the summer, but for different reasons. It's been almost a year now. Since everything's been going downhill and I've been feeling like I've lost control of my life.

Why did it happen to me? Why did I have to be the one who headed back to school early on that shitty July night? Why didn't I say, "Fuck getting eight hours' sleep," ahead of the swimming meet the next day and spend the evening with my friends at the summer festival in Ebrington? All for a bloody competition I didn't even take part in because I was in a coma, hooked up to the machines in intensive care.

That was nine weeks ago, and at first nobody was certain that I'd ever wake up again. It wasn't just my lungs that were damaged by the heat of the fire and the toxic soot, a burning beam fell on me on the stairs, long after I'd blacked out. The biting smoke, my racing heart as I ran for my life down the west-wing stairs. I can't remember exactly where I lost consciousness. I only remember how incredibly loud the flames were. And how dark it was. Black, hot, panic, panic, panic. And then, what felt like just seconds later, white, beeping, pain. Hospital. Still panic, panic, panic. The same fucking panic even now, like my brain can't grasp that I'm safe. That it was bad but I'm apparently made to survive bad stuff. What choice do I have?

Lucky. I was lucky. I have to tell myself so again and again. What an incredible stroke of luck that I was the only person to get so seriously injured in the fire. Not that I'd wish it on anyone else. Not even my worst enemies. Not, incidentally, that I have any. Not even my mother and the man who decided to smash up our family with her. I wouldn't wish a thing like this even on them. Not on anybody. But I wouldn't wish it on myself either.

Unfortunately, what you wish for and what you get are two very different things. Everyone on my floor had gone down to the festival in Ebrington. It wasn't so far for the younger kids on the ground floor and the first floor to get out, away from the flames. The stairs were empty as I ran down toward the flames, through the smoke, which was already so thick I couldn't breathe, even holding my pajama sleeve over my mouth.

I jump as Dad brakes sharply, swearing under his breath. The seatbelt cuts into my shoulder. I grit my teeth with pain but don't make a sound. Dad has to believe I'm fine. Otherwise I can forget our deal. It took hours of arguing and tears of desperation before he and Mum finally agreed that I can do the rest of my physio as an outpatient and go back to school next week.

It's bad enough that Dad can hardly look at me. He's really trying to hide it behind his professionalism, but whenever he's with me, it's totally obvious. My own father, a doctor, can't bear to see me like this. Even though it's his vocation to help the sick. That clearly doesn't apply to his daughter, and I'm not naïve enough to think it's because I don't matter to him. Quite the contrary, and that's the whole problem. Mum and I are everything to him. My dad's a loving man and the fear of losing me almost destroyed him. I know that. Mum knows that.

Livy, sweetie, promise me. Her piercing eyes, her hands on my arms when she caught up with me in Ebrington that time, months before the fire, back when I didn't know what real problems were. Looking around frantically, low voice, still speaking. *Promise me that you won't tell your father. It would break his heart, Olive.*

We're approaching our house. Mum glances over her shoulder to me. I immediately look away. The sight of our drive and the façade of the three-story townhouse in dark stone doesn't exactly help. I've never spent less time here than in the last few months. And that's saying something, given that I'm at boarding school and only home for occasional weekends in term-time.

I feel like an intruder into the marriage of convenience that used to be my family. Dad's carrying my stuff; Mum's eyes are just as laden with expectation. *You won't say anything, will you, my darling?* I can see it on her face. Every single time I've looked at her since that evening over a year ago. But I can't worry about it now.

I step into the porch. It smells the same as ever. Coffee, old leather and the citrussy air fresheners Mum puts everywhere. I stand on the step to take my shoes off and feel like a failure because my body's telling me it's going to keel over in the next forty-five seconds if I don't sit down. I, Olive Mary Henderson, can't even manage to take off my shoes standing up. I didn't know it was possible to despise yourself this much, but it really is.

Later, eating dinner with Mum and Dad, I feel like I'm on the outside looking in. I still hardly have any appetite, but I've got just about enough sense to finish up my plate of rice and vegetables. I'll never regain my old fitness if I don't eat enough. I didn't have many reserves to start with and my time in intensive care has used them all up. The muscles built up from swimming and regular weight training—gone without a trace. My body's like jelly, and even the bloody bowl is cracked. Everything's so knackering.

"Is it OK to go straight up to my room?" I ask after dinner, because the fatigue is suddenly pulling at me. I long ago gave up being angry about going to bed when primary-school kids are still watching TV. I have to give myself time. Isn't that what everyone keeps telling me?

I stand up. Dad hesitates. I should have known earlier, when he glanced at Mum. I sit down again.

"We'd like to talk to you about something," he says slowly.

I don't move. I manage to say, "OK," but it sounds more like a question.

"We understand that you're longing to get back to school, Olive."

"Back to normal life," I correct him. Normality. Everyday life, far from cheerless hospital rooms and constantly stressed-out doctors, who look at my shoulder, ask if I've had a bowel movement, as if I wasn't a seventeen-year-old girl—i.e. someone embarrassed by their entire life at the best of times—then hurry on to the next room without even looking me in the face.

"We know that, love," says Mum, glancing briefly at Dad. "And we want to make that possible for you."

"We spoke to Mrs. Sinclair last week," he goes on. Hold on. Why didn't I know about this? "She's happy that you want to go back so soon, but she's also very concerned about you and your health. As we all are."

I nod, holding on to my self-control. "But you'll be there to keep an eye on me," I say. Two mornings a week, at least. And any time Dad isn't scheduled to be at Dunbridge as the school doctor, Nurse Petra will be there in the sick bay. It's virtually the same as the hospital. I don't need twenty-four/seven care: I need a glimmer of hope.

"Yes, I will," he agrees seriously. He folds his hands over his lips. "Olive, your mum and I agree with Mrs. Sinclair that it will be better for you to repeat the lower sixth."

"What?" I laugh. I really laugh. Then my face freezes. Mum and Dad are looking at me in silence. "That . . . You can't mean that."

"It's the only way you can—"

"The lower sixth?" I interrupt Mum. "But they can't just leave me behind! What about my friends?"

"We know you found last year a struggle, Olive. It's a big step up to A levels and you only just scraped through your exams."

We may be in Scotland, but at Dunbridge we do A levels, four or five courses in the lower sixth, dropping to three for our final year. So she's got a point. Not that I'm admitting to it. No way.

"Yes, but Mrs. Sinclair and all my teachers had faith that I could do it. She said so!" My heart is starting to race, I'm raising my voice, starting to shout as I realize that Mum and Dad aren't here for a discussion. They're informing me of a decision they've made for me, as if I'd asked them to.

"We know that, Olive," Dad says calmly. "And we're not making this decision lightly. But that was before the fire. The new term has already started, and you know you've got to switch from A-level PE to Spanish—there's a lot of catching up to do there. The upper sixth is stressful enough as it is, and you can't just cram in a whole year's worth of Spanish on top of that. It's just not feasible."

Not in the state you're in.

Not while you're still so weak, still having nightmares.

"You can't do this," I yell. "Mrs. Sinclair said—"

"Olive, we're your parents. Until you're eighteen, we have to take responsibility for you."

I jump up. My shoulder throbs, but I hardly notice the pain. It's nothing compared to the despair rising inside me.

"You can't do this," I repeat, because my mind's a blank. Mum and Dad just sit there. The tears well up. "But what about my friends?" My voice cracks. My friends in the upper sixth. Having this one last year with them before we're scattered to the winds was the only thing driving me on to make quick progress.

"They'll still be there, pet," says Dad.

Mum says nothing, won't meet my eyes.

I shake my head and turn away. I can't let them see me cry. Not again. I bite my bottom lip; I straighten and walk tall. I don't cry until I get to my room.

uncorrected proof

Content Warning

(and spoiler warning!)

This book contains potentially triggering content. This includes
*Toxic relationships
Eating disorders
Domestic violence
Substance abuse and addiction*

Ready for your next romance obsession?
Visit us at LYXBooks.com and follow us online @LYXBooks